W9-DFP-849

WITHDRAWN

The Hunt

This Large Print Book carries the
Seal of Approval of N.A.V.H.

The Hunt

Allison Brennan

Thorndike Press • Waterville, Maine

The Hunt is a work of fiction. Names, characters, places, and incidents are the products of the author's imagination or are used fictitiously. Any resemblance to actual events, locales, or persons, living or dead, is entirely coincidental.

Published in 2006 by arrangement with The Ballantine Publishing Group, a division of Random House, Inc.

Thorndike Press® Large Print Basic.

The tree indicium is a trademark of Thorndike Press.

The text of this Large Print edition is unabridged.
Other aspects of the book may vary from the original edition.

Set in 16 pt. Plantin.

Printed in the United States on permanent paper.

Library of Congress Cataloging-in-Publication Data

Brennan, Allison.
    The hunt / by Allison Brennan.
        p. cm.
        "Thorndike Press large print basic" — T.p. verso.
        ISBN 0-7862-8660-1 (lg. print : hc : alk. paper)
        1. Serial murders — Fiction.   2. Serial murderers —
    Fiction.   3. Young women — Crimes against — Fiction.
        4. United States. Federal Bureau of Investigation — Fiction.
        5. Large type books.   6. Psychological fiction.   I. Title.
    PS3602.R4495H86 2006
        813'.6—dc22   2006007804

To Dan

ACKNOWLEDGMENTS

Football coach Ara Parseghian said: "A good coach will make his players see what they can be rather than what they are." I would be remiss if I did not first thank my editor, Charlotte Herscher, who not only showed me the potential of this story but let me find my own path to *The End.*

Kevin Brennan, associate wildlife biologist for the California Department of Fish and Game, provided me with a wealth of information about and practical experience with peregrine falcons and the responsibilities of wildlife biologists. And he called his birds by their radio frequency, *not* by a nickname.

Once again, Wally Lind at Crime Scene Writers was instrumental in providing facts about forensic investigations, particularly firearms and how biological evidence becomes corrupted. If I got anything wrong, it is certainly not because of him.

7

In addition to being understanding about my bizarre working hours, my husband, Dan, also explained (multiple times) just how a car engine works and how to clog the fuel filter. If I misunderstood the process, it's due to my own mental block regarding anything mechanical.

A former student at MSU-Bozeman, Dan also helped bring Gallatin County alive for me, through his memories and pictures.

Thanks also to my first readers, Kathia, Michele, Jan, Amy, and Sharon; my speed readers, Karin and Edie, who went above and beyond to help me whip this book into shape; and of course my children, who are beginning to not like pizza as much as they used to.

PROLOGUE

I don't want to die.

Her breath came in shallow gasps, her mouth gaped open as she violently pulled air in and pushed it out. In. Out. Focus. Run, Miranda, run! But be quiet. Left foot. Right foot. Left foot. Wasn't that a Dr. Seuss book? A hysterical giggle threatened to escape but she swallowed the sound. Quiet. Above all, breathe quietly.

Miranda grimaced at the thrashing behind her. A sob escaped from her friend. *Sharon, shut up!* she wanted to scream. *He'll hear you! He'll kill us!*

She ran faster even though Sharon was falling farther and farther behind. Daylight was scarce. One, two hours left at the most.

If they didn't make it to the river, he would find them.

I don't want to die. I'm too young. Please

God, I'm only twenty-one. I won't die! Not here, not like this.

Miranda's sight blurred as sweat dripped into her eyes. She didn't dare wipe her face for fear of losing her balance on the rocky terrain. Her bare feet ached with each step, but they were so cold only the sharper rocks cut through the numbness. *Watch where you're going! One wrong step and you'll break your leg and he'll find you . . .*

A faint, familiar echo reached her ears. She wanted to stop and listen but didn't dare slow her pace. She scurried another hundred feet before putting a name to the sound.

Water! Running water.

It had to be the river. What she'd promised Sharon would lead to freedom. She silently thanked Professor Austin and his tedious geology class. Without it, she wouldn't have known where to run, wouldn't have recognized the signs indicating a river was close. After the miles she and Sharon had already covered, surely now they would make it.

From behind, a shriek.

Miranda stopped at Sharon's startled cry, then whipped around, her heart gripped with dread. Sprawled on the hard ground, Sharon lay half obscured by undergrowth, sobbing in pain.

"Get up!" Miranda urged, panic clawing her.

"I can't," Sharon sobbed, her face buried in decaying leaves.

"Please," Miranda begged, not wanting to backtrack. She glanced over her shoulder, toward freedom. The water so close.

She looked back at Sharon and bit her lip. *He* was still out there. If she stopped to help her friend, he'd kill them both.

She took a step toward the river. Guilt tickled Miranda's spine. She *knew* she could make it alone.

"Go," Sharon said.

Miranda almost missed the single word. Her eyes widened at the implication. "No, not without you. Get up!"

For a moment, Miranda thought Sharon hadn't heard her, whether by choice or distance. Then, slowly, the blonde pushed herself up on all fours. Sharon's terrified eyes locked with Miranda's. *Please, Sharon, please,* Miranda willed. *Time is running out.*

Sharon grabbed a small sapling and braced herself. "Okay," she said. "Okay."

Miranda sighed in relief as Sharon took a shaky step forward. She began to turn toward the river, toward freedom.

Whap-whap!

The shot echoed in the forest. The flutter

11

of wings and the squawking of startled birds broke the silence. As Miranda watched, Sharon's chest opened. Deep red, darkened by shadows of dusk, spread across the filthy white shirt. In the moment between life and death, Miranda watched Sharon's stunned expression turn to bliss. Relief.

Death was better than suffering.

"Sharon!" She covered her mouth with her hand, tasting and smelling rotting dirt. The coppery scent of blood hung in the air. Her chest heaved with mute sobs as she watched Sharon's body fall to the ground.

"Run."

That voice. Bloodcurdling in its dry, grave monotone. The same emotionless pulse he'd used when he fed them and whipped them; when he touched them or raped them.

She trembled even before she recognized his silhouette. In camouflage pants and a thick black coat, he stood among the trees, face obscured by a cap and the darkening sky. Three hundred feet away? Two hundred? Closer? She would never make it. She would die.

His shout echoed through the mountainside. He took one step forward, cradling a rifle. He brought the stock up to his shoulder.

Miranda ran.

CHAPTER
1

Twelve Years Later

Nick Thomas stared at the outline of the petite body under the blinding yellow tarp. He pinched the bridge of his nose, swallowing anger so bitter he could taste it. The foul stench of death surrounded him and he turned away.

He still pictured the dead, broken body of twenty-year-old Rebecca Douglas as he'd found her only an hour ago.

"Sheriff?"

Nick looked up as Deputy Lance Booker approached. He was clean-cut, a good cop, though a mite wet behind the ears. Much like Nick had been twelve years ago when he'd been called out to his first murder scene. "Deputy."

"Jim said there's a guy claiming to be an FBI agent at the road wanting to be let through. Quincy Peterson."

Quinn. Nick hadn't seen him in years, ten to be exact, but they'd shared an e-mail relationship since he was elected sheriff more than three years ago. After the Croft sisters had been found.

Now there were seven dead girls. Seven that they knew about.

"Let him through."

"Yes, sir." Booker frowned, but relayed the orders through his walkie-talkie. In matters that would as a rule fall under their local jurisdiction, no law officer welcomed outside interference, and usually Nick was no different. He didn't mention that it was his call to Quinn last week that precipitated this visit.

Nick turned and walked away from the deputy, away from the bright tarp, down the path to where Rebecca Douglas's last steps were evident. He squatted next to an unusable footprint, a mess in wet, hardening mud. It might have been Rebecca's last step. Or the killer's. It had rained nearly three inches in the last two days, a deluge that saturated a ground recently recovered from a cold, wet Montana winter. The clouds had broken this morning, the sky such a vivid blue and the air so refreshing that Nick would have enjoyed it if he hadn't been called to a crime scene.

He closed his eyes and breathed the clean, crisp air of his Gallatin Valley. He loved Montana, the vast beauty and sheer majesty of its mountains, its swift rivers, green valleys, big sky. The people were good, too, down-to-earth. They cared about their neighbors, took care of their own. When Rebecca Douglas was declared missing, hundreds of men and women — many from the university where she'd been a student — had scoured the wilderness between Bozeman and Yellowstone looking for her.

Nick's jaw tightened in restrained fury. Good people, but for one. One who had killed Rebecca and at least six other women in the past fifteen years. And other women were still missing. Would they ever find their bodies? Had the harsh Montana weather or four-legged animals obliterated their remains? He'd never forget finding Penny Thompson's remains — nothing but a skull and scattered bones. She was identified through her dental records.

Nick surveyed the area. Tall pines grew primarily downslope; as the mountain rose the trees thinned out. The ancient, heavily overgrown road he'd driven on was unmapped. Possibly an old logging trail, it appeared to end here, in this natural clearing roughly thirty feet square. On the edge of

15

this clearing, Rebecca's body lay.

They'd mark off the area in grids and search for anything that might possibly lead back to the killer. But if it was the same bastard, they'd find nothing. He was so damn perfect in his every crime that even their one surviving witness could tell them little. Defeat weighed heavily in Nick's heart, but he would not give up.

Sometimes, he hated his job.

He turned when he heard an SUV roll into the clearing, rocks and muddy clumps of leaves shooting out from the backs of all four tires. Sun reflected off the windshield and Nick shielded his eyes to watch Quinn approach.

The SUV jerked to a stop behind Nick's dark green police-issue truck. The driver's door opened and Quincy Peterson jumped out, slamming the door behind him and striding toward Nick. Quinn hadn't changed much since Nick had last seen him, still looked more like a damn cover model than a fifteen-year veteran of the FBI. Nick stood and absently brushed the dirt off his jeans.

"Rebecca Douglas?" Quinn nodded toward the covered body. His face was blank, but his dark eyes revealed the same anger and sadness that Nick felt.

"Yep. We'll need a positive ID, but—"

There was no doubt it was the missing woman. He glanced at Quinn and raised an eyebrow at the bandage over his left eye. "Bar fight?" he asked, half joking.

Quinn reached up and touched the bandage as if he'd forgotten it was there. "The last few days have been eventful," he said. "I'll tell you about it later." He glanced around. "When are you processing the scene?"

"I wanted you to check it out first, but I have my men waiting up on the main highway."

Nick didn't know why the Fed made him feel so inferior. Maybe it had something to do with Quinn's quiet confidence, his knack for seeing through bullshit, always getting to the heart of the matter. Or maybe it was because Nick had puked his guts out at his first murder scene and Quincy Peterson hadn't.

Or maybe it was because the woman Nick loved was in love with Quinn.

Despite all that, there was no one Nick trusted more than Special Agent Quincy Peterson.

Quinn bent down, pulled on latex gloves, and lifted the tarp. His square jaw clenched and a vein twitched in his neck at the sight.

Rebecca had been beautiful. Now, her long blonde hair was tangled, matted, and caked in mud. The happy face reproduced on thousands of flyers was gone. She was swollen, bruised, grotesque in death. The recent rains had cleaned some of the dirt from her naked body, leaving her pale and blue.

Her neck had been cut, slashed deep with a sharp knife, though there was very little blood to see. Most of it had been washed into the ground by the storm, along with any trace evidence. Her body showed signs of abuse. Torture. Bruises of all shapes and hues of purple covered her skin. Her breasts had been clamped into some sort of vise. The strange marks wouldn't have indicated that to most eyes, but both Nick and Quinn had read the coroner's reports for each of the six other women murdered in these woods, and had grown familiar with this killer's M.O.

Quinn removed the tarp to study the victim's legs and feet, much as Nick had done when he first arrived on scene. Her left leg was crooked, broken. Her feet were covered in raw blisters and deep cuts. From running.

She was thin, so pale, empty. Clinically, her gaunt skin told the cops that she'd bled out, her life drained from her. She'd died quickly; nobody could survive long with their carotid artery sliced open. Small consolation for the previous week of terror she'd lived through.

Quinn covered the body. "Coroner been called?"

Nick nodded. "He'll be out by noon. He was in the middle of an autopsy on that hiker we found up on the north ridge the other day."

"So who found the body?"

"Three boys — the McClain brothers and Ryan Parker. The Parkers have a spread three, four miles west of here. The boys took a couple horses for the day, were going to shoot their .22s at rabbits and whatnot." He shrugged and added, "It's Saturday."

"Where are they now?"

"A deputy took them home. Told them to sit tight at the Parkers' until I came by."

Quinn nodded, surveying the scene that Nick had marked with yellow and black crime scene tape. Observing the clearing, the old path, the trees.

"It looks like she came up through that brush over there," Nick gestured. "I checked it out, but didn't go down the trail yet."

"If you can call it a trail," Quinn said, frowning at the overgrowth. "I'll take a quick look while you call in your team. How many people do you have?"

"I have a dozen of my own men right now, more later, and a crime scene specialist. I'll

19

need volunteers if we're going to do this right."

"Agreed. The more eyes the better, but no hotshots. We can't have someone going off half-cocked."

Quinn put his hand on Nick's shoulder. "I know you were hoping the bastard dropped dead after Ellen and Elaine Croft were found. I'm sorry I couldn't come out personally then. But Agent Thorne is good. She would have found something."

Nick agreed, but he still felt so damn helpless. The Butcher was the only bastard who had ever gotten away with murder under his watch. "It's been three frickin' years! Three years since he killed. And we had nothing then — no clues, no leads, no suspects."

"And there are other girls missing." Quinn didn't need to remind him. The missing girls haunted Nick in his sleep.

"It's been slow, but we're gathering evidence," Quinn continued. "We have casings, bullets, a partial from Elaine Croft's locket. We'll get him." Quinn turned and Nick watched him walk down the path. He sounded so confident. Why couldn't Nick feel the same?

He glanced down at the outline of Rebecca Douglas. At least she would have a proper burial. Closure for her family. But not for him.

He thought of Miranda.

He started toward his truck. He'd already put in the call for all available law enforcement to head to this location. Then he heard the unique but familiar sound of a Jeep bouncing over the rough trail. He didn't need to see the vehicle to know who approached.

"Damn."

The red Jeep jerked to a stop behind Peterson's rental. Almost before the truck halted, Miranda Moore jumped out, the mud no match for her heavy boots and confident stride. Deputy Booker approached her, and she glared at him without stopping as she pulled a red down-filled vest over her black flannel shirt. In any other situation, Nick would have grinned at the way Booker backed off.

Then she focused her sharp blue eyes on him.

His heart quickened and his stomach lurched. If only he'd had more time to prepare for her inevitable arrival. If he'd been warned she was on her way, he could have steeled himself for the confrontation.

"Miranda," he said as she approached, "I—"

"Damn you, Nick!" She poked a finger at his chest. "Damn you!" Nothing intimidated Miranda. Though she was tall for a woman — at least five-foot-nine — he had six inches and a hundred pounds on her. You'd think he'd intimidate her, that any man would frighten her after what she'd gone through, but he guessed he shouldn't be surprised. She was a survivor. She didn't expose her fear.

"Miranda, I was going to call you. I didn't know for certain it was Rebecca. I didn't want you to have to go through it again."

Her darkening eyes told him she didn't believe him. "Screw that. Screw *you!* You *promised* you'd call." She brushed past him and strode over to the tarp, staring at the covered body. Her fists clenched, her shoulders reverberated in tension.

Nick wanted to stop her, to protect her from seeing another dead girl. Most of all, he wanted to protect her from herself.

And she'd always been perfectly clear that she didn't want Nick's protection.

Miranda worked to control her temper. She shouldn't have yelled at Nick, but dammit! He'd *promised.* For seven days she'd been searching for Rebecca, the nightmares destroying the few hours of sleep she allowed herself. He'd promised she'd be the first to know when they found her.

Neither she nor Nick had expected to find Rebecca alive.

She stared at the sunny tarp in the middle of the quiet earth tones of the land and inhaled sharply, her throat raw with hot anger and unwanted ice-cold fear. Her fists squeezed into tight balls, her nails digging into her palms. She knew it was Rebecca Douglas. But she had to see for herself, force herself to look at the Butcher's latest victim. For strength, for courage.

For vengeance.

She pulled latex gloves over her long fingers, knelt beside the still woman, and fingered the edge of the tarp. "Rebecca," she said, her voice a whisper, "you're not alone. I promise you I'll find him. He'll pay for what he did to you."

She swallowed, hesitated, then drew back the tarp to reveal the girl she'd been searching for, twenty hours a day for the last week.

At first, Miranda didn't see the swollen face, the slit throat, or the many cuts washed clean by the rain. The image of the twenty-year-old in Miranda's mind was beautiful, as she had been when she was alive.

Rebecca had a contagious laugh, according to her best friend, Candi. Rebecca cared about those less fortunate and volunteered one night a week reading to the infirm at Deaconess, according to her career counselor, Ron Owens. A straight-A student, Rebecca had wanted to be a veterinarian, according to her biology teacher, Greg Marsh.

Rebecca hadn't been perfect. But no one had shared the less attractive stories while she'd been missing.

No one would ever repeat them now that she was dead.

As Miranda watched, the image of Rebecca she'd held so close to her heart during the hours and hours of searching morphed into the broken body before her.

"You're free," she told her. "Free at last."

Sharon. I'm so sorry.

"No one can hurt you anymore."

She reached over and touched Rebecca's hair, brushed a matted piece to the side, cupped her cheek.

Stay in control.

She repeated her mantra. How many times would she have to go through this? How many dead girls would they bury? She'd thought it would get easier. But if she didn't keep her emotions tight and protected, she feared she'd collapse under the enormity of the Butcher's continued success — and her own failure to stop him.

She eased the tarp over Rebecca's face,

hating to do it. The act of covering the body reminded Miranda of the other dead girls they'd found. Of Sharon.

The morning Miranda led them to Sharon's body was so cold she shivered constantly under the half-dozen layers of clothing she wore. She'd wanted to return the day after she'd been rescued, but she hadn't been allowed to leave the hospital. When she tried walking on her own, her damaged feet had failed her.

She'd been too numb to cry, too tired to argue. She mapped out the location as best she could remember, but the search team couldn't find Sharon.

Miranda couldn't bear the thought of her friend's body exposed for yet another night. Leaving her to the grizzlies and cougars and vultures. So the following morning she withstood the pain in her legs and led the search team and law enforcement back to where Sharon lay. She had to see her one last time.

She might have been in shock; that's what the doctors said. But she walked with help. She knew where Sharon had fallen, would never forget it. She brought them to the spot, and there Sharon lay. Exactly how she'd fallen when the killer shot her.

Silence filled the air, birds and animals mourning with the humans. Even the spring wind held its breath; not one leaf rustled as everyone finally grasped exactly what had happened to Miranda and Sharon.

The sudden cry of a hawk split the stillness, and the wind gently blew.

The medic covered Sharon's body with a bright green plastic tarp while the sheriff's team started searching for evidence. Miranda couldn't stop staring at the tarp. Sharon was dead underneath it, reduced to a lump under a sheet of plastic. So wrong, so inhuman!

It was then that Miranda had first broken down and cried.

An FBI agent carried her the three miles back to the road. His name was Quincy Peterson.

CHAPTER
2

When he saw Miranda, Quinn stopped in his tracks. His breath hitched in his chest and he sidestepped behind a thicker shelter of trees so she wouldn't spot him.

Ten years had passed since he'd last seen her, but the impact was the same. First, a mixture of awe and respect — he had yet to meet a person with greater resolve than Miranda. Next came love and pride, followed quickly by anger and frustration. So entwined. He couldn't turn off his emotions like a faucet; how could she have shut him out so easily? How could she have walked away from their relationship without giving him a chance to explain?

He still had hope she would be able to put aside her blinding obsession with the Butcher and come back. But that hope had diminished with the passage of time. Now, he feared she would kill herself through neglect of her own needs.

Her back was to Nick; only Quinn could see the agony etched on her face.

As he watched, Miranda closed her eyes and shook her head, as if to rid herself of a nightmare. Or a memory. She pushed herself up from the ground, wiped her eyes with her forearm, and walked around to the dead woman's feet. She stared at Rebecca's covered body for a good minute before bending down and lifting the corner of the tarp.

Quinn didn't have to be standing at her side to know what Miranda was staring at. Rebecca's feet and legs, caked in mud from running. The broken leg. The evidence of her flight.

"How long?"

Even from his vantage point fifty feet away, Quinn heard the anger and pain in her voice. She whirled around and glared at Nick. Her jaw tightened as she struggled to control the pain.

Always, the control. It was a miracle she hadn't had a nervous breakdown with the weight of the world carried on her shoulders.

"Eight, ten hours?"

Quinn didn't hear Nick's response, but Miranda's guess was probably accurate.

"Dammit, Nick! He had her for eight days. She almost got free. We're only a few miles from the damn road. Four miles and she broke her leg. And, and he, he—" She stopped and turned away from Nick.

Watching Miranda wrestle with her control, Quinn felt uncomfortably like a voyeur. He yearned to go to her, take her in his arms as he'd done before, to just hold her. He hadn't told her everything would be all right. He'd never told her the pain would be bearable. Quinn was just *there*. And for two years, just being by her side helped her regain her life and her strength. He knew it had.

But it hadn't been enough.

"Doc Abrams is on his way," Nick said. "He'll be able to tell us more."

"You promised, Nick." She peeled off her latex gloves and shoved them into a pocket. Pinching the bridge of her nose, she approached the sheriff.

Quinn couldn't avoid Miranda any longer, but he dreaded the meeting.

"Don't try to protect me, Nick," she said as Quinn came up behind her.

"Don't blame Nick, Miranda. I told him not to call you."

Miranda heard the familiar voice: low, warm, as smooth as melting butter.

Miranda's heart doubled, tripled its beat. For a moment, for much too long a moment, she couldn't say a word. She had dreamt of that voice and the man who possessed it. She spun around.

Quinn Peterson.

For a second, a brief moment, she forgot everything that had happened between them ten years ago and felt the ghost of his arms wrapped around her, the soothing murmurings he'd whispered in her ear.

The only time she'd felt truly safe since the attack had been in Quinn's embrace.

He had changed — and yet he'd stayed the same. A few random strands of silver shot through his sandy hair. It fell just a little too long across the top, partly covering a bandage above his eye. His dark eyes still saw everything, but now faint lines fanned their edges. He was still physically fit, dressed too well for the Montana woods, and she could still taste his lips on hers, though they hadn't seen each other for a decade.

She hated the memories that rained down on her, hated even more that seeing Quinn Peterson reminded her of her worst failings at a time when she needed all her strength and courage.

"How dare you!" She berated herself for the quiver in her voice.

"I know you enjoy torturing yourself, Miranda, but I didn't want to witness it." Quinn came closer, standing a mere foot from her. She resisted the urge to step back. She would *not* back down. Not this time.

A tic pulsed in Quinn's jaw. She remembered it well from when he was angry. Or worried.

"What are you doing here?" Her voice was stronger, but she didn't trust herself to say more.

"I called him," Nick said.

She turned to face her best friend. "You?"

Nick straightened enough to show he was uncomfortable. "I've been keeping Quinn informed since I became sheriff," Nick said. "I need him and his resources."

"You've been working with *him* for—" She thought back to when Nick had first been elected sheriff and threw her hands up in the air. "*Three years!* And didn't let me know? How could you? I thought you of all people understood."

"Miranda, I want this bastard almost as much as you do."

Quinn interrupted. "I'm here to catch a killer. I shouldn't have to tell you the FBI's resources are greater than Nick's department's. If you have a problem with that, you can leave."

Quinn's intense dark eyes cut through her defenses with the precision of a laser. She grew uneasy from the scrutiny. Cataloging her fear, her insecurities. Waiting for her to crack, to break. She would *not* let him see her weak. Could not let him see her fall apart. Too many times in the past she'd gone to him for strength, support. She'd cried in his arms, told him everything she thought and felt and believed.

He'd used it all against her when he kicked her out of the Academy.

She had plenty of time to break down later. Tonight. When she was alone.

"I know this area better than every deputy in the department," Miranda said, her voice cracking as she fought to keep her temper and emotions in check. With one deep, probing look, Quinn had reduced her to raw nerves.

She turned her attention back to Nick, gathered her strength. "You're going to be searching for evidence and bringing in volunteers. You need me, and I need to be here. I need to look. I'll see things no one else will see. I'll—"

"Stop." Quinn closed the short distance between them, putting a hand on her shoulder. She stared at it, wanting both to slap it away and fall into his arms.

She glared at him and he dropped his hand.

"You need sleep," he continued, his voice

softer. "You've been searching for Rebecca all week. How many hours have you taken for yourself? You're living on coffee and junk food. Go home."

"No. No!" She turned from him, fearing the tears she'd been fighting all morning would escape.

Not now. Not in front of Quinn.

"Miranda, I'm calling in a team," Nick said. "We won't be ready for at least two hours. Doc Abrams needs to claim the body. Come back later."

"Nick, I don't think—" Quinn began.

Miranda interrupted him.

"I'm going to tell the volunteers. Two hours, I'll be here." She couldn't look at Quinn, not now when her feelings raw and exposed.

She walked past Nick, touched his arm. "I'm okay." She didn't know if she said it for his benefit, hers, or Quinn's, but saying the words out loud helped her swallow the fear that had crept to the surface. Quinn's presence had rattled her almost as much as the Butcher's latest kill.

Quinn watched Miranda drive off in her Jeep. He'd handled her wrong. It didn't used to be like that. Back before she decided becoming an FBI agent would somehow fix her problems, Quinn had known exactly what to say, when to touch her, when to give her space.

But once she landed at Quantico, her obsession with the Butcher took over her life. Or maybe it had been there from the beginning and Quinn just hadn't seen it.

Why couldn't *she* see it?

"Why'd you do that?" Quinn asked Nick. "She's in no condition to search for evidence. Did you see her when she was looking at the body? She's going to lose it."

His gut had twisted at the pain he'd seen on Miranda's beautiful, gaunt face. As if she were reliving Rebecca Douglas's final minutes.

"That's where you're wrong, Quinn. Miranda's stronger than you think."

"She's punishing herself for surviving."

"I don't know about that—" Nick began.

"I *do*. Miranda has a huge case of survivor's guilt and it's grown over time. Every time another girl is abducted, she takes on her death as if she were to blame."

"I know she's personally involved, but she's an asset to the team."

"Miranda doesn't know the meaning of the word 'team.'"

"You haven't worked with her for the past ten years. She won't break, she'd solid."

"You're letting your personal relationship

34

interfere with common sense." Quinn cringed. He sounded jealous. Dammit, he *was* jealous. When he'd first learned of Miranda and Nick's relationship, it hurt more than he wanted to admit. You'd think that after all the years they'd been apart Quinn would have gotten over her. Yet, since Miranda walked out of his life, the few relationships he'd developed had been superficial and short-term. In Quinn's heart, Miranda would always be the only woman.

Nick shot him a look. "You don't know what you're talking about." The sheriff started walking toward his truck.

"Don't play coy with me, Nick. You've been involved with Miranda too long not to know better. She's playing you. She's good at that."

Nick turned back to Quinn. "Miranda and I broke up two years ago."

Nick's face told Quinn he wasn't happy about the arrangement, and his voice sounded almost accusatory. Quinn was both surprised and pleased that Nick and Miranda were no longer a couple. Then he chastised himself for caring. After all, Miranda wouldn't have anything to do with him.

"You never told me."

"Why would I? I'd take her back in a

heartbeat. Not that I have a chance now." He looked down the path Miranda's Jeep had taken. "Not with you in town."

"She hates me." Hate might be too nice a word. Loathe, despise, or abhor might be more fitting.

"She should," Nick said glancing at him. "If you'd had me booted from the FBI Academy the day before graduation, I'd hate you. But she doesn't."

Quinn didn't know about that, but remained silent.

Nick added, "If she hated you, she'd already be my wife."

CHAPTER
3

Miranda broke every traffic law on the books driving back to Montana State University in Bozeman. She dreaded telling the search volunteers that Rebecca was dead.

Nick was right: they needed the resources of the FBI if they were going to catch the Butcher. But out of all the agents in the country, why Quinn Peterson?

She thought she'd gotten over his betrayal years ago. She loved her job, had a good home, family who loved her, and loyal friends.

Then she saw *him;* now she realized deep down, in the farthest recesses of her heart, in the corner she'd thought long hardened against love, she still ached for him.

Why couldn't she be as nonchalant and formal as he had been? Miranda very much wanted it to appear that she didn't care in the least that Quinn had both ruined her career and broken her heart.

Miranda pulled into one of the many parking lots on campus, gripping the steering wheel so hard her knuckles were white with the strain. She slammed the gear shift into park and shut off the engine. She tried to shove Quinn back into the mental compartment in which he'd been stuffed for years, but he didn't go willingly.

She took a deep breath and watched a group of girls walk toward search headquarters in the Student Union Building. Then a pair of girls. Then a group of professors.

No one walked alone. Not when they were reminded about the Butcher. But how long would it take before they grew complacent again? A month? Two? A year? Miranda never forgot. The Butcher lived with her every minute of every day, taunting and tormenting.

The dean of students had allowed search volunteers to take over one of the large rooms in the Student Union to coordinate activities. Although Miranda worked for the Sheriff's Department in the small Search and Rescue division, they didn't have the space to bring in people to phone, copy flyers, distribute maps. Like the other times girls disappeared, the University provided the space they needed — anything to help. In times of tragedy, students and teachers united.

Why did it take death for people to see the value of life?

It had been three years since the last murder. Last *known* murder.

Miranda couldn't forget the other girls who'd disappeared. This time last year it was Corinne Atwell. No one had seen her since her car was found in a ditch on Route 191 outside Gallatin Gateway. Was she a victim of the Butcher? Of another killer? Or had she run away? The very real possibility that Corinne had been the Butcher's victim, her body decomposing in the wilderness somewhere in the millions of acres between Bozeman and Yellowstone where the Butcher hunted, haunted Miranda.

Thoughts like these creeping across her brain gave her insomnia.

Whack! Whack!

The whip came down once, twice, stinging her raw flesh and she tried to scream, but her voice had long since deserted her. She was left to her silent tears, and the echo of Sharon's pleas.

Their pleas meant nothing to the faceless monster who tortured them. Their relief when he left soon turned to horror. They'd become dependent on him. He fed them, gave them water. If he left forever, they'd die, naked and chained to the floor in the middle of nowhere.

But he did return. To release them. So they could play the part of prey in his sick game. The hunter and the hunted.

Finding the Butcher meant more than justice. Only he could tell them who he had killed. That he had so much control over the grief of the living ate at Miranda constantly.

Rebecca had survived eight days in the hands of that madman, that murdering bastard. She had almost escaped. Almost.

As with Sharon, "almost" meant shit when you were dead.

Sitting in her car in the parking lot, Miranda took a deep breath. Closing her eyes, she buried her head in her arms, using the steering wheel as an armrest.

The tears came fast, anger and frustration boiling over in hot, salty rivulets down her cheeks. Her body, already sore from days of backbreaking searches, ached from the tension of facing Quinn again. She sobbed and shook, no sound escaping except the harsh intake of ragged breaths. It took her several minutes to control her grief. Even once she'd composed herself, it was hard to stay calm: when she looked at her face in the rearview mirror she saw death.

Seven times she had seen the dead girls.

But there were nine young women still missing, their remains nothing but bones scattered in the wilderness. Bears and mountain lions didn't care much for human dignity, didn't adhere to Judeo-Christian burial rites.

Why me?

Why had she survived when so many others hadn't? Why had he picked her in the first place? Why Rebecca Douglas or the Croft sisters? It made no sense. It hadn't then, and it still didn't now that she'd had twelve years to examine and reexamine everything leading up to her kidnapping, everything she'd endured in that godforsaken one-room torture shack, everything that had happened since she escaped.

She owed her father, that much she knew. If her father hadn't taken her on the hunting trips she loathed as a child, she would never have known how to cover her tracks, how to deceive the hunter. She was the prey, but unlike the deer or bear her father hunted, she was an intelligent human being. She could outthink her pursuer, hide and run, run and hide, until she dove into the river . . . even if she had died in the icy water, she still would have won.

He would not have killed her. She would have escaped, stealing from him his trophy, his prize.

She'd not only won, but lived.

If Rebecca hadn't fallen and broken her leg, would she have survived? Would she have made it to the road? Though not from Montana, Rebecca had been born and raised in the small, mountain community of Quincy, California. Similar terrain and — Miranda's thoughts detoured from Rebecca.

Quincy. Damn, she couldn't escape him.

Wiping the tears from her face, she glanced once more in the rearview mirror. No wonder Quinn thought she couldn't handle the search. She looked horrible. She'd lost weight she couldn't afford to lose. She hadn't bothered with makeup and her dark hair, though clean, was limp.

What was she thinking? Why should she care what Quinn Peterson thought? He'd destroyed their bond long ago when he made it clear he thought her sanity hung by a thread.

She'd told him he was wrong, but he hadn't listened. Well, she'd proven him wrong, hadn't she? She was a functioning human being, doing just fine without the likes of Quinn Peterson.

She had responsibilities, and right now her duty was to tell the volunteers to stop searching. She dreaded this particular task, but she needed to handle it herself.

With a deep breath, she left the security of

her Jeep and entered the makeshift search headquarters. Several students were on the phones, taking information or imparting details to aid in the search. A team had walked in just ahead of Miranda to pick up another section of the grid she'd mapped.

None of it mattered.

The tears she thought she'd buried sprang back into her eyes and she pinched the bridge of her nose. She swallowed them back. *Not now.*

The strangled cry of one of the girls snapped Miranda to attention.

"No. NO!"

Judy Payne, Rebecca's roommate, was the one who'd called the police when Rebecca didn't come home Friday night. She hadn't left the headquarters since it had opened, answering phones, sending e-mails, printing thousands of flyers. Now, she stopped folding letters and stared at Miranda with wide eyes.

"Judy." Miranda crossed the room to where the college girl sat, shaken.

"No, please." Judy searched her eyes for something other than the truth, tears streaming down her face.

Miranda squatted next to the young, pretty blonde and took her hands. She had thought with each passing year it would be easier. The searches were well planned and executed, volunteers trained and competent, cops diligent and resolute. But it only got harder. Each time it was so much harder. Each missing girl took one more piece of Miranda's soul with her to her grave.

"I'm sorry." What else could she say? Sorry seemed so inadequate, so *empty*.

Judy collapsed into Miranda's arms. Miranda held her, rocked her, murmured sounds into her ear, words that didn't mean anything but she hoped comforted.

There was no need to say anything to the other dozen people in the room. Judy's reaction told them what they needed to know. Tears rolled down the faces of the men and women who had believed, for a time, that they would find Rebecca alive.

Karl Keene, a young teaching assistant, approached them. Looking up, Miranda saw his eyes were also damp. She wanted to reassure him, and Judy, and everyone else, but there were no words. The weight of Judy's grief fell hard on Miranda's shoulders. What in the world could she reassure them about? That *this* time the police would find him? That *this* time he'd made a mistake?

She wanted to scream at the injustice that another girl was dead and they had nothing on her killer.

Instead, she reached out and squeezed Karl's arm.

"I'll take care of her," he said, and took hold of the sobbing girl.

Miranda blinked back her own tears as she watched Karl wrap his arms around Judy and lead her outside. For a split second, she wished someone would hold her. Comfort her. Tell her everything was going to be okay, even if it wasn't. Sometimes she needed to believe the lie.

But Quinn had given up on her, and she'd let Nick walk away. She had no one.

When they were gone, she noticed the other people in the room staring at her. She cleared her throat and spoke, her voice rough.

"Sheriff Thomas discovered Rebecca's body this morning about four miles west of Cherry Creek Road and ten miles south of Route 84. Deputies are searching the area for clues, but—"

"It's the Butcher?"

Miranda turned to the person who'd interrupted her, then looked down. It was Greg Marsh, Rebecca's biology teacher, a squat, round man with rimless glasses.

"I — I can't say. I—" she began.

"Yes you can. You were there." He pointed to her feet. She looked down and blinked.

She hadn't noticed the mud caked on her boots.

"Greg, you know I can't say anything."

"You don't have to." He turned and left the room.

The others continued staring at Miranda. She needed to be alone, but she had a duty to everyone in this room. Though alive, they too were victims of the Butcher. Guilt crept down her throat as she fervently wished at times like these that she felt no responsibility to the victims, living or dead. What could she say to console Greg, Judy, the others?

She knew what Rebecca had gone through. And thanks to the newspapers detailing the tragedies each and every time the Butcher killed, so did everyone else. There was no consolation. Everyone knew Rebecca had been tortured, raped, and hunted like an animal.

Everyone knew the exact same thing had happened to Miranda.

She swallowed the humiliation, the pain, the fear-tinged anger boiling within. Few people talked to her anymore about her own abduction and escape. She knew they whispered among themselves about her, but she ignored it. She had to. Thinking, knowing, what people thought about her made dealing with her nightmares more difficult.

Miranda sighed in relief as tear-filled people gathered in the corner, murmuring among themselves. They didn't expect her to talk, to placate them. To tell them everything was going to be all right when nothing would ever be all right until the Butcher was caught.

She walked over to the map she'd created of the area they'd been searching. She'd divided Gallatin County into four quadrants, uneven because of the mountainous terrain. Each quadrant was split into dozens of segments.

They hadn't covered even two quadrants since last Saturday.

Six red dots, almost invisible to the naked eye, identified where the bodies of six college girls had been found. Hand shaking, she pulled a fine-tipped red pen from her pocket and placed a dot where Rebecca had died. The seventh victim. The seventh *known* victim, Miranda reminded herself.

She didn't need the red dots to tell her where the bodies were found; she didn't need the blue dots to tell her where the women were last seen. She had the same map — with far more detail — on the wall of her home office. Too many nights, she sat on her bed staring at the topography, willing the dots and lines and grids she'd created to tell her something, anything, about this bastard who hunted women.

A sob caught in her throat and she covered her mouth with her hands. She turned her attention to the dot southeast of Rebecca's and touched it. Sharon's spot.

She had to get back up the mountain. Only, Quinn was there.

Twelve years ago Quinn had been her rock, her support. He'd saved her in ways she remembered when she allowed herself to. Alone, in bed, with only her quiet tears for company.

She'd never forget meeting him at the hospital the day after she took the sheriff's search team to where Sharon had been killed.

Though he'd carried her three miles the day before, she'd been too upset for a formal introduction. She hadn't even known his name. And she was grateful he didn't bring up her breakdown as he spoke to her while she lay in the hospital bed.

He didn't coddle her like the nurses; he didn't cry like her father; he didn't shuffle his feet nervously like Sheriff Donaldson had when he interviewed her the day before.

Quinn Peterson stood like granite, tall, strong, firm, never wavering, never letting her see pity in his eyes.

Her entire body ached. The cuts on her feet stung even with the antibiotics and painkillers. Many of the cuts on her body had to be stitched, leaving scars she'd have for the rest of her life. The doctors had saved her breasts, though the damage had been severe.

She was alive, Sharon was dead. The scars on her skin were nothing compared to the jagged pain of guilt splitting her heart.

"You don't have to do this," Special Agent Quincy Peterson told Miranda when she said she would take him back to where she and Sharon had been held captive.

"Yes I do, Agent Peterson," she'd said when they left the hospital. "I have to take you."

She couldn't think about her pain. Not now. She would do anything to find the man who murdered Sharon, because her best friend was dead and she was alive.

If it took going back to the rotting, moldy, rodent-infested hovel she'd been imprisoned in for seven hellish days, she would do it.

"I understand," he said, and she believed he did. Everyone else who'd spoken to her seemed to want to placate her, but not this man. "Do you think you could call me Quinn? Agent Peterson seems too formal."

"Okay."

She had pinpointed the general area on the map and they drove in as far as they could before having to get out on foot, but they were three miles away.

If only they'd run in the other direction! They'd have hit a narrow road, but a road nonetheless. Would that have changed their fate? Would Sharon still be alive?

"I told her we should split up," *Miranda whispered when it was just her and Agent Peterson — Quinn.*

"That was a good idea."

"Sharon refused. We were so scared, I didn't argue. And—" *She stopped.*

"Go on."

"We didn't understand why he was releasing us. Until we saw the gun. Then it was very clear — he wanted to hunt us down like animals. I don't think we even thought about it, we certainly didn't talk about it. We had no time. He told us to run."

Run. Run!

"And we both knew exactly what he was going to do. He was going to kill us. Injured game." *She laughed bitterly.*

During that walk, Quinn stayed at her side. Asked her quiet, firm questions. Never saying he was sorry. Never placating her. Never telling her she should have done something different, as she had the million times she'd questioned herself in the seventy-two hours since she'd been found on the bank of the Gallatin River.

She led them right to the decrepit shack in the middle of Nowhere, Montana, six miles west of the river where she'd jumped to her freedom. She stared at the rotting, worn planks that had been thrown up, seeming too weak to support the corrugated tin roof. She'd seen the outside of the shack for only a brief moment before she and Sharon started to run. But the inside of the cabin was burned into her mind.

Miranda couldn't go inside. She sat in the dirt and cried.

Quinn went in. The sheriff's people gathered evidence at his direction. Sheriff Donaldson was nearing retirement and wanted to catch Sharon's killer as his swan song, so he took all advice from the FBI agent he'd called in the day before.

Quinn then sat down on the ground next to her.

"You're going to get your nice pants dirty" was all she could think of saying. He certainly wasn't dressed for a mountain trek, but he didn't seem to care that his expensive shoes were scuffed and dirty.

"I will find this guy. I promise you, he will pay for what he did to you and Sharon."

She stared at him, searching his dark eyes for pity, revulsion, or distaste. All she saw was strength, compassion, and anger.

"I will do everything I can to help."

51

But in the end, for all the internal agony Miranda endured going back to the shack, searching the woods, finding the bones of a body they strongly suspected was the Butcher's first victim, they couldn't catch the killer. They didn't have any clues to direct them. Little evidence, fewer leads, no suspects.

Two months later Quinn was called back to the Seattle field office. She thought she'd never see him again, and it hurt because she really liked him.

She was wrong. Quinn returned a month later, just to see her.

That was when she really began to heal.

CHAPTER
4

When Miranda was eight, her mother died of ovarian cancer. Devastated by the sudden diagnosis, short illness, and death, Bill Moore quit his high-level marketing job in Spokane and relocated with Miranda to Montana's Gallatin Valley. He purchased a run-down lodge thirty minutes outside Bozeman on the road to West Yellowstone, near Big Sky, and lovingly, painstakingly renovated it. By the time Miranda was ten, she knew everything about stripping, sanding, and varnishing. Almost single-handedly, she had refinished the floors on the main level of the inn.

The deep canyons, breathtaking vistas, and endless sky eased the pain of a grieving family twenty-five years ago. The same environment saved Miranda after the Butcher, and again after Quantico. And now, with Rebecca's recent murder and Sharon's ghost weighing heavily on her mind, taking a quick detour to the Gallatin Lodge seemed necessary. She told herself she needed to stock up on provisions, but the truth was she just wanted to see her dad.

Bill Moore sat behind the registration desk filling out the ubiquitous paperwork he loathed. The enormous moose head — which Miranda named Bruce when she first saw it twenty-five years ago — was the Lodge's mascot. It stood sentry over the desk and her father, the sight of which rarely failed to bring a smile to her lips.

Except on days like this.

Glancing up when Miranda walked in, Bill's face fell. He looked every one of his fifty-seven years. His hair, though still abundant, was now salt-and-pepper. Wrinkles lined his ruddy complexion, and his once strong body was almost imperceptibly sunken. Miranda's gut twisted. She was the cause of the pain she saw every day in his pale eyes. His love for her was killing him, day by day. Knowing that — and not being able to stop the direction her life took her — heaped even more guilt onto her heart.

"Daddy." She didn't need to say anything else.

"Randy," he said, his voice gruff, "come here."

He left the desk and she walked into his

arms, welcoming the embrace. Her father had never been stingy with hugs. "It was him," she whispered.

Her father's arms held her close. She breathed in the unique combination of spicy aftershave, rich coffee beans, and pipe tobacco. He smelled like home and love and everything good in her life.

"You're going out again."

"I have to." She stepped back, took a deep breath, and gave him what she hoped was a reassuring smile.

"I'll pack some sandwiches. How many will be searching?"

"Maybe twenty, twenty-five. Nick's calling in volunteers to pair off with his people. Training them now. I don't have much time."

"Go get your things. I'll put together something for you all to eat."

"I love you, Daddy."

He touched her cheek, then turned toward the kitchen.

She would have given anything to turn back the clock and protect her father from what he'd endured since she came home twelve years ago broken and hollow. Sometimes, she thought her father still saw her half-drowned and naked on the riverbank. Beaten, damaged, past exhausted.

But alive.

Which was more than she could say for Rebecca. Or Sharon. Or Penny, Susan, Karen, Ellen, and Elaine. Or the nine other girls who'd disappeared without a trace during spring over the last fifteen years.

Under normal circumstances, Miranda enjoyed the peaceful walk down the winding gravel path to her private cabin. Her father had it built for her when she returned from the FBI Academy at Quantico ten years ago, announcing, "Randy, you need your own place. But I'd be mighty lonely if you moved to town."

Bill Moore would never be alone. He was well liked and admired by everyone in Gallatin County, and his lodge did well with both the summer tourist trade and winter skiers, as well as locals coming in for dinner or Sunday brunch throughout the year. The lodge had eight suites upstairs for guests; twice as many cabins dotted the eighty-some acres Bill owned. Longtime friends visited often; strangers were like family. That was Bill's way.

Miranda longed to sink into her private hot tub and watch the day go by through the picture window. Soak until she was red and raw from water almost too hot to tolerate. Cry until there were no tears left.

Instead she grabbed extra ammunition for the .45 auto she carried and retrieved her shotgun. Her dad would provide food, but she packed her survival kit. Three days of dry food and water pouches, knife, flare gun, and matches stacked into the bottom half of a backpack. She added the ammo, as well as a lined Gore-Tex jacket, change of clothes, and thermal blanket.

She would never be caught unprepared.

Fifteen minutes later she walked into the commercial-sized kitchen and watched as her father and Ben "Gray" Grayhawk — cook, general handyman, and friend — loaded an ice chest with water bottles and individually wrapped sandwiches. There were at least forty meals. Six thermoses were packed into a box, along with Styrofoam cups and a green garbage bag for trash.

She put her backpack down by the door and wrapped her arms around her father. "Thank you, Daddy." She smiled her appreciation at Gray.

"Your father won't say it but I will," Gray said. "You watch yourself, young lady. Don't be going traipsing off into the woods without backup. Don't be the hero. Be smart."

"I'll be careful." Miranda loved Gray, even though he worried constantly about her. A few years older than her father, his long, braided silver hair, high cheekbones, and flat face bespoke his Indian heritage, but his green eyes favored his European mother. Born in Bozeman, he'd moved away as a teenager, returning after serving three tours of duty in Vietnam.

It was Gray who had taught her about guns.

The three of them took the food and beverages to Miranda's Jeep. As she was about to get in, her father grabbed her arm. His blue eyes, a pale reflection of her own, shone with worry and concern. "Randy, be careful."

She nodded, unable to say anything for fear the tears she'd held at bay since her moment of weakness at the university would break free. She hopped in, waved, and drove away.

Bill watched the Jeep until it disappeared around the bend, just past the sign that announced: *You're always welcome at Gallatin Lodge.* He took out his bandanna, blew his nose.

Gray clamped his large hand on his friend's shoulder. "She'll be okay, Billy. She has a strong spirit."

"I know. I know." He breathed in deeply, eased the fresh mountain air from his lungs. "She deserves to be happy. I just love her so much, I hate seeing her go through this over and over again."

"It's what she's meant to do. You can't force her down your path, just like Nick couldn't force her down his."

Bill glanced at his friend. "Quinn Peterson called for a room."

"You give him one?"

"Yep."

"Miranda ain't gonna be too happy with that."

"Don't I know it." But he had amends to make. He only hoped that Miranda would forgive him when she learned the truth.

Elijah Banks thanked the God he no longer believed in that his luck was finally changing.

He tore out the back door of *Gazette* headquarters in Missoula and jumped into his rusting pickup truck. A quick glance at his watch told him he had just enough time to swing by his apartment and grab an overnight bag.

The Butcher had struck again. Rebecca Douglas's body had been discovered an hour ago, and while the sheriff was being all hush-hush about it, Eli's sixth sense told him it was the Butcher.

Co-ed missing about a week. Found dead. Butcher. Damn, he wished he'd been there from the beginning, but his editor wouldn't give him the time. Instead, he'd spent Monday and Tuesday in Helena writing about yet another political bribery trial, and the last three days interviewing old people who'd had their identity stolen.

Boring boring boring.

But now that he had a dead body to follow up, his editor had given him the assignment. His police contact had provided few details, only that the woman's body had been found and Sheriff Thomas ordered radio silence, called in the coroner, and was currently out at the ridge off Cherry Creek Road, south of the interstate.

If he played his cards right, he could catapult himself off of this mountain hellhole and land himself a real reporter slot in a real newspaper in a real city.

His apartment was only half a mile from the paper. He kept the truck running, and ran upstairs to throw clothes and his shaving kit into a backpack. He grabbed his tape recorder, extra pencils and pads, and his journal.

Twelve years ago Eli had started the journal to document everything about the Butcher investigation. Even when he moved up to Missoula, he'd kept informed every time another college girl was abducted, another body found.

The Bozeman Butcher. He'd named the killer in the first article after Moore's story got out. It wasn't his first choice. He wanted to name the killer The Woman Hunter, but his editor at the *Chronicle,* the stupid jerk Brian Collie, didn't want to piss off the hunting community and told him to come up with something else. "Butcher" didn't really fit because the guy didn't really butcher his victims. He hunted them, then either shot them or sliced their throat. But the moniker stuck.

Collie was still around, never having amounted to much of anything because he'd never aspired to be more than the editor of the two-bit paper in Bozeman. Unlike Eli. He'd beaten the town and gotten as far as Missoula. At the time, it seemed like the perfect step. First Missoula, next Seattle. Then New York.

The plan had stalled in Missoula. But now — now there was hope he wouldn't be stuck here for the rest of his miserable life.

Five minutes later, he was pulling onto the interstate headed south, toward the cow town of Bozeman. Normally he dreaded the drive, but today he fidgeted with excitement.

A hot story was just what he needed to land him a choice job at a major paper. Good-bye Missoula. Hello New York City.

CHAPTER
5

Quinn tapped his fingers on the dashboard of Nick's police-issue SUV. He hated being in the passenger seat. It seemed to take twice as long to get anywhere.

"You didn't give me a lot of details on the phone last week," he said to Nick. "The Douglas girl was abducted on Friday night?"

"Her roommate called it in about one Saturday morning. She hadn't come back to the dorm after her shift at the Pizza Shack, the one right off the interstate. The responding officer found her car in the lot, her keys on the passenger seat."

"Her purse?"

"Missing."

Few personal effects of the young women had ever been recovered, which made Quinn suspect the killer kept them as souvenirs. To remember his victims.

"We bypassed the standard missing persons wait time because I knew, in my gut, it was the Butcher."

"Was her car disabled?"

"No."

"That's a change." Quinn wondered why, when up to now every victim of the Butcher had been stranded by the side of the road. Evidence showed that each vehicle had been disabled with molasses in the gas tank. The molasses clogged the fuel filter, resulting in no gasoline reaching the engine. The car just died two or three miles after the victim's last stop.

When Penny Thompson disappeared fifteen years ago, her car had been recovered down a steep ravine. There was blood on the steering wheel, but no definite sign of foul play; the investigators at the time felt she'd wandered off and gotten lost due to a head injury, but the case had been left open.

Three years later, when Miranda's car was found by the side of the road halfway between Gallatin Gateway and her father's lodge near Big Sky, the Sheriff's Department quickly connected the dots and called in the FBI.

Quinn's life had irrevocably changed from that day forward.

"Some people insisted it wasn't the Butcher, but—"

"Your instincts were right on the money."

"Unfortunately."

"We have two distinct advantages," Quinn said. "First, a change in M.O. He didn't disable the car. Maybe he didn't have time. Maybe he acted spontaneously. Or maybe Rebecca Douglas knew him, wasn't scared of him when he came up to her."

"I thought of that angle, but all of the interviews so far have yielded squat."

"I'd like to go through your notes."

"Whatever you need." Nick paused. "What's the other advantage?"

"We found her body so quickly. It doesn't help that it rained last night, but maybe the coroner can find something to tie back to a suspect, a hair, a thread from his clothes, something." After viewing the body earlier, Quinn didn't hold out much hope there'd be any usable evidence found on the victim, but science constantly improved and if there was anything to be found, he was confident it would be.

"If we can find the shack where he kept her captive there's a much better chance any evidence would still be helpful," Nick said.

"Good point." Even when they'd found the dilapidated structures where the Butcher had restrained his victims before releasing the women in the wilderness, any evidence had been tainted or destroyed. The dampness, mold, and rot of the shacks destroyed most biological samples. They had no DNA, no fingerprints except for a partial that came up blank in the AFIS database, and no suspects.

The profile Quinn had prepared twelve years before had been updated to reflect the older assailant. Then, he'd reasoned that the Butcher was a white male between the ages of twenty-five and thirty-five, but tack on another ten years and the youngest he could be was thirty-five, more likely forty. Physically strong, methodical — in fact, he was an obsessive planner, with patience and fortitude. He didn't lack confidence, which was why he never doubted he could catch the women he released. Not that it was too difficult to track a naked, barefoot woman through the woods.

Quinn had been pulled off the investigation after two months because there were no leads and little evidence. When no other women disappeared, the powers that be didn't feel scarce resources could be expended in the futile search for Sharon's killer.

The Butcher had waited three years after that before abducting two other girls, but no bodies had ever been recovered. Few serial killers had the patience to wait so long between attacks, but there were no like crimes reported in the rest of the country.

The lack of continuity, the sporadic nature of the assailant, gave police next to nothing to go on.

Quinn pounded his fist against the dashboard. "I want to get this bastard."

Nick didn't say anything as he turned onto a gravel road under an arch that read *Parker Ranch*.

Quinn vaguely remembered Richard Parker from the time he spent on the Butcher case. Mover and shaker in the state, federal political connections, locally elected to some office. Supervisor, he thought.

Richard Parker had never been a suspect. Quinn remembered he'd been arrogant and something of a blowhard, but seemed sincere in wanting to find additional resources for the Sheriff's Department at a time when tax dollars were especially tight.

The Parker residence reminded Quinn of the Ponderosa. He almost expected Ben Cartwright to answer the door.

"Sheriff," Richard Parker said as he opened the large door. Parker had aged well, Quinn noted. About fifty, his blond hair hadn't yet begun to gray and the wrinkles around his dark eyes were minimal. Six feet tall and lean, he had the broad shoulders and defined muscles of a man comfortable working a ranch.

Parker turned to Quinn. "Special Agent Peterson, right?"

Quinn nodded. "Good memory, Mr. Parker."

Parker smiled weakly. "It's Judge Parker now, but don't mind the formalities. Call me Richard."

Judge. Quinn glanced at Nick, irritated that his friend hadn't clued him in to the politically sensitive situation. Quinn hated playing politics.

"Thank you."

They followed Parker through the wide, dark-paneled foyer into the large living room, bright from east- and south-facing windows and two long, narrow skylights.

Everything was immaculate and perfectly placed, as if the Parkers were expecting a camera crew from *House Beautiful.* Hunting trophies and framed prints of outdoor scenes decorated the light-colored walls; oversized, heavy pine furniture was simple and functional. A hint of femininity showed in the floral throw pillows complementing the dark fabric couches and chairs. A gun cabinet was prominently displayed along one wall, above it a huge fish with a plaque that read *White Sturgeon, 71 pounds, Kootenai*

River, June 10, 1991.

"I sent the boys to the barn to tend to the horses," Parker said. "Can I get you anything to drink? Coffee, soda? Probably too early for Scotch." He motioned for them to sit.

"We can't stay, Richard," Nick said. "I've called in all my deputies, and we have a group of volunteers to work the area. It's going to be a long day."

"I understand. The boys were pretty shaken up. You'll go easy on them?"

"Of course," Nick said.

"Do you need horses? I can have Jed bring over six or seven. And I'll give the hands the afternoon off if you need them."

"Much obliged, Richard," Nick said. "We'll need to search on foot to avoid contaminating possible evidence."

Parker nodded. "Yes, yes. Of course." He closed his eyes and shook his head. "I thought — I guess I thought that it was over."

I didn't, Quinn thought. "Serial killers only stop when they are incarcerated or die."

"But it's been three years."

Quinn shook his head. "There is every reason to believe Corinne Atwell was also a victim of the Butcher, and she went missing May first of last year. The wilderness is unforgiving. Animals, weather, terrain. We may never know how many girls he's killed."

"What's the FBI's interest this time?" Parker raised his eyebrow. "You weren't here when the twins were found."

"Actually," Nick corrected him, "Special Agent Thorne was here after the Croft sisters were abducted, and again when Corinne Atwell turned up missing. I called Agent Peterson in last week because of his familiarity with the case. I don't have to tell you that the resources of the federal government are far greater than our county's."

Quinn had no more time for small talk. Kids needed to be interviewed as soon as possible after witnessing a crime or finding evidence. If left too long to think about things, their minds tended to replace facts with fantasy, much of it from television. "Where are the boys, sir?"

"In the barn." Parker motioned for Quinn to sit. "I'll get them for you."

"No need. I think they'll be more comfortable if they're doing something with their hands. Grooming horses sounds like a good task."

"I'll take you," Parker said.

Nick held Quinn back several feet behind Parker to speak to him privately. "I want to see the horses' hooves," he said quietly. He couldn't imagine that the boys would have any reason to lie, but he liked to confirm statements with solid evidence.

The stable stood several hundred feet behind the house and Quinn heard the low murmur of the boys within the stalls.

"Ryan! Sheriff Thomas is here to talk to you."

Ryan Parker was almost eleven, the image of his father with blond hair and brown eyes. Unusually handsome for a young boy, he seemed older, almost worldly, compared to the McClain brothers.

"Ryan," Nick began, "this is Special Agent Quincy Peterson. He's with the FBI."

Ryan's eyes widened with excitement. "The FBI? Really? Can I see your badge?"

"Ryan," his father said sternly.

Quinn ignored Parker and squatted down so he looked up at the boy. "Sure," he said as he pulled his wallet out of his jacket pocket. He flipped it open and showed his badge and credentials to the wide-eyed kid.

Ryan didn't touch, but looked with interest. "Do you have to go to a special school to be a special agent?"

"After four years of college, I spent sixteen weeks at a special training camp called Quantico. I also took an extra year to get a master's degree in criminology."

"Is it hard?"

"Parts of it. You want to be a federal agent?"

Ryan glanced at his father, and Quinn noticed a touch of fear in the boy's eyes. Perhaps his father simply expected him to follow in his footsteps, Quinn thought. He could relate. The fact that he wasn't "Doctor Peterson" still weighed heavily in his parents' house. "Maybe," Ryan said, noncommittal.

"Can Sheriff Thomas and I ask you and your friends a few questions?"

"About the dead girl."

"Yeah."

Sean and Timmy McClain were brushing a horse, though they'd been listening with interest, evident from the fact that the smaller brother was brushing air.

"Guys, come over here," Quinn called.

They dropped the grooming tools in a bucket and rushed over, introducing themselves. Sean was the older brother, acting tough and important. Timmy, the smaller boy, couldn't stop moving, his eyes wide with interest. Quinn noted Ryan's leadership role in the trio as he stood and the boys gathered behind him, sitting on stacks of hay. Quinn didn't like the way Richard Parker stood formally at the side, looking every inch a judge, but considering this was an informal interview with minors, he couldn't very well ask the father to leave. Especially when the father was an attorney.

"Ryan, why don't you tell me what you boys were doing this morning, in your own words. Timmy, Sean, pipe up if you think of anything to add. There are no right or wrong answers. And no one remembers everything, so one of you might remember something another doesn't. Understand?"

They all nodded as Quinn and Nick took out their notepads. Ryan spoke. "We took the horses out at seven this morning. Sean and Timmy spent the night because we wanted to go early, and they live in town."

"Mom works weekends," Timmy said with a bob of his head. "We come here a lot."

"It's probably fun to hang out at a ranch with horses and cool stuff to do," Quinn said, smiling.

Timmy nodded. "Oh, yeah, and we get to—" His brother hit him hard in the arm.

"Shut up," Sean said. "They only want to know about the dead girl."

Timmy looked sheepish.

"That's okay," Quinn told the younger boy. "You never know what might be important in an investigation."

The boys had left the ranch early and ridden across the pasture to the east. They took an overgrown trail intending to find an Indian burial site on the north ridge.

"You know you aren't supposed to go that far," Parker admonished. "That's a treacherous path. You're damn lucky one of the horses didn't break a leg."

"I'm sorry, Pa," Ryan said, looking down.

"Go on," Quinn said. Just what he needed was a scared kid and belligerent dad. "Where's the Indian site you were looking for?"

"We don't know. That's why we were looking. Gray, you know, the caretaker at the Lodge down there," he motioned vaguely south, "says it's up on the north ridge, above Mossy Creek. Even he doesn't know exactly where it is, just that it's there and we'd know it if we saw it. We looked all last summer and couldn't find it. And since it's been raining all week, this was the first good day to look for it."

Quinn remembered Gray. How could he forget the time he spent at the Gallatin Lodge when he was investigating Sharon Lewis's murder? Or the weekends he came to visit Miranda on personal time?

Shaking his head, he pushed Miranda from his mind. It was harder now that she'd crept in, unbidden, but he had to focus on his job.

His job was to stop the Butcher.

Nick said, "You didn't get to Mossy Creek."

Ryan shook his head. "The horses started acting a little spooked, and then we heard a large animal. We steered them into a clearing and saw a brown bear sniffing at something. I fired my rifle to scare him away. Then we saw her."

Ryan and Timmy had stayed in the area while Sean — the oldest of the three at twelve — took the old logging trail back to the main road and rode his horse three miles to the nearest phone.

"Did you touch the body?"

They all shook their heads vigorously. "I went close," Ryan said. "A couple feet away. It didn't seem real, you know? Until, well, until I saw it was that girl who's missing. That's when Sean went to get help. But I didn't want to leave her there, you know? The bear could come back and, well, I just didn't want to leave." He looked down at his hands clasped tightly in front of him.

Quinn reached over and squeezed Ryan's shoulder until the boy looked him in the eye. "You did the right thing."

He stood and his joints popped from squatting so long, reminding him that he'd be forty this fall. "Thank you, Judge," Quinn said as he turned to face Richard Parker.

An impeccably dressed blonde with vivid green eyes stood next to Parker with a blank expression. Parker's wife? Quinn was surprised he hadn't heard her approach.

"Mrs. Parker?" he asked, hand extended.

She took his hand, her grip surprisingly strong for someone who looked so fragile. Her fingers were icy cold, though the day had warmed considerably since he'd viewed the victim earlier this morning. "Delilah Parker." Her voice was smooth and cool.

"Special Agent Peterson, ma'am."

"I've made lemonade and banana bread in the kitchen, if you would care for some."

Quinn was about to decline when Nick said, "Thank you, Mrs. Parker. We are much obliged at your hospitality."

She beamed at Nick. "Excuse me, I'll ready a tray." She hurried off.

Quinn dragged his heels as they followed Judge Parker to the house. "We need to get back to the ridge."

"Some things you don't do. Refusing food from Mrs. Parker is one of them."

"Playing politics," Quinn mumbled sarcastically.

"Ten minutes will save me months of headache. Believe me. I declined the first time, too." Nick rolled his eyes.

Quinn wasn't quite sure what to make of the Parker family. Though the judge joined them in the dining room, Quinn noticed he and his wife didn't speak much to each other.

Mrs. Parker's impromptu get-together was surprisingly elaborate. She served the lemonade in crystal and the banana bread with fresh whipped cream on white bone china. Quinn felt uncomfortable with the formality, but Nick seemed to accept it with ease. When Quinn complimented her on a beautiful home, she beamed. The Stepford Wife of Montana, he thought, hiding a grin.

Nick was true to his word. Ten minutes later they were on their way, headed back to the stable to collect samples from the horses' hooves before leaving.

"What's with Parker's wife?" Quinn asked as he shut the passenger door of Nick's truck. "A little formal for a morning snack, wouldn't you say?"

Nick shrugged as he started the ignition and drove down the long, winding road leading from the Parkers' ranch to the main highway. "She likes entertaining. I declined the first time I came out here years ago when a couple of their cattle had been stolen. After I was elected, Judge Parker explained that his wife takes hospitality seriously, and he'd appreciate it if I accepted in the future."

"You should have told me Parker was a judge. I didn't even remember he was an attorney."

"Nonpracticing at the time. He was on the Board of Supervisors. Now, he's a state Superior Court justice. Word is he's up for consideration to the Appellate Court."

"That's a big jump."

Nick shrugged. "He has friends in high places."

"Wonderful," Quinn said cynically.

Nick shot him a glance. "You're not thinking that Richard Parker has anything to do with what's been happening to these girls?"

Quinn didn't say anything for a minute. "I don't know," he said honestly. "We have no witnesses, and Miranda only had vague impressions of her attacker's shape and size."

The Butcher not only kept his victims bound in chains to the floor, but he blindfolded them. Miranda swore she would know him by smell, but a man's scent would be next to impossible to get a conviction on. They needed hard evidence.

Quinn hadn't realized how much he had missed Miranda until he saw her today. He'd wanted to touch her, make sure she was really there, in the flesh and not another dream.

"She led us to the shack she'd been held in," Nick continued. "She tracked down where the Croft sisters had been imprisoned. Miranda has led us to more evidence than anything you or I could have done on our own."

Quinn knew it, and he knew why. The very reasons why Miranda would have made a damn good FBI agent were the same reasons why she would likely have gotten herself killed.

Miranda was driven, steadfast, unwavering in her pursuit of a killer. But she was obsessed with the Butcher. The case ate at her until it consumed her existence. Quinn didn't blame her. Hell, who would? The bastard had destroyed her life. She'd had to rebuild it, brick by brick. And, amazingly, she had become an intensely strong woman. No longer a victim, but someone whom Quinn greatly admired for her ability to heal.

While she had dealt with being raped and tortured better than any victim he'd ever met, she hadn't handled the survivor's guilt. She blamed herself for Sharon's murder, and her decision to join the FBI was more to avenge Sharon than to become an agent. And, ultimately, it was her need for vengeance that showed up in the psychological tests. Quinn had gone to bat for her time and time again, but when faced with the results of repeated sessions with the shrink, he had to agree Miranda wasn't ready.

He ran a hand over his face and closed his eyes. Because he'd loved her, and because his recommendation as much as her qualifications led to her acceptance into the Academy in the first place, he'd insisted that he be the one to tell her.

It hadn't gone well.

He would never forget the look of betrayal in Miranda's deep blue eyes when he told her she was out of the Academy. Was it really ten years ago? Damn, he missed her.

"Shit," Nick muttered as he slammed on the brakes. Quinn jerked in the passenger seat, opened his eyes.

There were at least thirty Jeeps, trucks, and cars parked along Route 84. Quinn scanned the area. "Miranda finally gained some sense. Her Jeep isn't here."

Nick glanced at Quinn as he carefully turned onto the rough logging road. "You think she didn't just drive in?"

"You said no unauthorized personnel could use the old road," Quinn said. "I would—"

"Quinn, she *is* authorized. She's the director of Search and Rescue, a division of the Sheriff's Department." Nick paused.

"Miranda doesn't want to be protected, so give it up."

"It has nothing to do with protection, and everything to do with jeopardizing this case."

"Miranda knows these woods better than anyone, including me. I'd be surprised if she didn't have every hill and crevice memorized. She has a frickin' map on her bedroom wall! She sleeps and rises to six red pins staring at her, reminding her that she survived." Nick took a deep breath. "Seven. Seven pins now."

Quinn glanced at Nick's hard profile, but couldn't miss the emotion tightening his expression. He didn't know whether it was his naked emotions or the rawness in his voice, but Quinn knew with certainty that Nick was still in love with Miranda. He pictured Nick in Miranda's bedroom staring at the map that had become such a focal point in her life. Nick would be wanting to help Miranda find peace, but unable to tear her away from her nightmares. Quinn shifted uncomfortably.

He'd heard about their relationship from his partner, Colleen Thorne, when she returned from investigating the Croft sisters' murder. Years after Miranda stopped speaking to him, refused to see him, it still hurt to think about her with another man. Even one he liked and respected.

Damn, he'd loved her! Few women could compare to Miranda. Her intensity, her laugh, her strength, her strong sense of right and wrong. Everything about Miranda was passionate, from how she lived her life to her quest for justice.

That she'd turned to Nick when she was ready for another relationship irritated and hurt him. She'd forced him to give her space, and against his better judgment he did. But she never came back to Quantico, never returned his calls, never accepted that he'd made the only decision possible. Then, she started seeing Nick.

He didn't want to know about their relationship, but he couldn't stop himself from asking, "What happened?"

"What?"

"Why'd you two break up?"

Nick shrugged. "Lots of things. Mostly, I couldn't stand not being able to protect her."

"Hmm." Miranda didn't need protection, except from herself. What she needed was to get over the guilt. But she never recognized her obsession, let alone did anything to fix it.

"I think what did it was I wanted to take her away from Montana," Nick said. "I could be a cop anywhere. I'd always thought

Texas would be a good place to live. A helluva lot warmer than the Gallatin Valley."

"I can just picture you with a white ten-gallon hat," Quinn said with a half-smile.

"Miranda wouldn't leave. She's determined to do what she can to protect the women of Bozeman. She teaches a self-defense class every week at the University. She heads up the search and rescue — not just when another co-ed turns up missing, but when hikers are lost, skiers disappear in an avalanche, anything. Last year two little girls wandered off from their campsite just this side of the Wyoming border, in Yellowstone. Miranda tracked them, found them, and brought them to safety."

Quinn said nothing. What could he say? He had no claim to Miranda, no right to know anything about her. But dammit, he wanted to. He wanted to know everything that had happened in her life during the ten years since he'd last seen her.

"Thanks for coming, Quinn," Nick said several moments later. "I know it's not easy on you to work with her."

As Nick stopped the truck behind Miranda's red Jeep, Quinn said, "I have no problem working with Miranda, but if she crosses the line she has to be pulled."

"Agreed."

They got out of the SUV and the first thing Quinn noticed was Miranda standing up on a ledge, hands on her hips.

"Where have you been?" She bounded down the embankment and stood in front of them, jaw set. "You said two hours, it's been nearly three!"

Though pale and thin, her deep blue eyes rimmed with fatigue, Miranda was a beautiful woman. A bundle of barely contained energy and strength Quinn had always admired.

"We went to interview the boys who found the body," Nick said.

Quinn wanted to ask Miranda what business it was of hers, but bit his tongue. She was part of the investigation, at least for the time being. Nick had already established her role and Quinn wasn't going to step on his toes.

Not yet, anyway.

So the sheriff had brought in the Feds again.

It was easy to spot the city boy, all done up in new blue jeans, stiff boots, unused down jacket. All the times the hotshot government types came to town looking for clues, they'd found nothing.

Because he was smarter than all of them.

He recognized Agent Peterson. He'd been around before, a long time ago. He'd proven to be an able opponent then — he'd been so close, but couldn't see the forest for the trees.

He almost laughed at his pun. Fools. All of them.

Except *her*. The one who got away.

His entire body tensed and the horse beneath him shifted uneasily on the mountain path, high up from where the cops milled about. He forced himself to relax, patted the gelding gently until the horse calmed. Soothing the animal also helped him contain his anger.

He wanted to kill Miranda Moore so badly he could feel her body beneath his. He pictured himself inches from her face. Grabbing her hair and jerking her head back. Exposing that white throat. Feeling her entire body tremble as he unsheathed his knife and held it to her neck.

One swift slice and her warm blood would coat him and the earth.

But she'd got away. He'd lost. His failure ate at him, a reminder that he was flawed. He should never have gone after a local. It wasn't her he'd wanted, anyway. It was the blonde she had been with. He didn't have a choice; if he wanted the blonde, he had to take her friend.

He still wanted to kill her, but he couldn't. She'd won, after all.

Twelve years ago his greatest fear of being caught lay with Miranda Moore. Had she seen or heard anything that would lead the police to him? He'd been so careful, but he hadn't thought she'd live. He'd felt cheated watching her fall off the cliff into the Gallatin River, certain she wouldn't survive.

He'd been surprised and worried when he saw the news reports the next day that she was alive.

But as time passed, he relaxed. She didn't know anything, either didn't remember or never saw him.

No, he couldn't kill her now. But if she got too close, that would change.

He glanced at his watch and frowned. He hadn't planned on being here this late. Gently urging the gelding along the narrow mountain path, he headed South.

CHAPTER
6

"Do you all understand what you're supposed to do?" Nick asked after detailing the responsibilities of the search team. One sworn Gallatin County sheriff's deputy or Bozeman police officer was paired with one volunteer. Three out of four on-duty cops stood there, some worried, some excited, most sipping the hot coffee Miranda's father had had the foresight to send with her.

Miranda looked around at the men and women who made up the search team. They'd be searching for evidence. Bullet casings, footprints, torn clothing. Anything that might lead them to the killer.

She caught Assistant Sheriff Sam Harris staring at her and turned her head. She didn't like the man who'd lost the election to Nick when he ran for sheriff a little over three years ago, six months before the Croft sisters were killed. When Nick made the fifty-year-old deputy the undersheriff, Miranda told him he was making a mistake. Harris would undermine him every chance he got. Nick disagreed, and Miranda tried to keep her feelings to herself.

It was one-thirty P.M. They had less than five hours of daylight left.

Miranda intended to pair off with Cliff Sanderson, a Bozeman cop she respected who helped her teach the self-defense class at the University. She waved at him as she crossed the clearing and he smiled back, his boyish dimples taking ten years off his thirty.

"Nick," she said as she approached him for her assignment. "I want grid C-1 through 10. Sanderson and I can cover it, and I think—"

"You should stay here," Quinn told her, arms crossed.

She glared at him, his dark, intense eyes trying to command her to do his bidding. She couldn't help but remember the many times she'd appreciated his intensity, the way a mere gaze melted her like butter on a hot griddle.

She ignored him.

"C-1 through 10," she repeated as she hoisted her backpack over her shoulders and cinched the belt around her waist. She adjusted her .45 in her waistband for comfort.

"You have a gun," Quinn said through clenched teeth.

"So do you," she snapped back, instantly regretting showing that he'd gotten to her. "Do you have a problem?" Damn, she was being sarcastic, a sure sign of insecurity.

She glanced around. The cops and volunteers had grown quiet, showing interest in the brewing argument. However, she certainly didn't want to be the center of attention.

"Nick," she said quietly.

"You're with Peterson," he said just as quietly, refusing to look at her.

"What?" she exclaimed, forgetting the audience.

"You're with Peterson or you're not going. You can have the 'C' grid."

She got the area she wanted, just not the partner. She almost said she wasn't going.

But that was exactly what Quinn Peterson wanted. "Fine," she said through clenched teeth.

She turned on her boot heel and spotted *him*. Elijah Banks. Long dirty-blond hair tied in a leather band, wire-rim glasses, narrow face on a skinny frame. She'd never forget the so-called journalist who'd made her life a living hell after she thought she'd put hell behind her.

Jaw tight, she strode over to the edge of the clearing where Eli stood, camera around his neck, rapidly writing God-knew-what garbage on one of his ubiquitous notepads.

"Banks!" He looked up and grinned. Stopping right in front of him, her feet almost touching his, she grabbed the notepad from his hand. Without looking at what he'd written, she ripped the pages out and threw the pad on the muddy ground, then tore his notes into tiny pieces.

She saw red every time Banks crossed her mind. Every time she saw his pathetic name in the newspaper. Every time she remembered the secrets — her secrets — he'd written about for everyone to read and pity her.

Eli held his hands up and took a step back. "That's my property you just destroyed." The damn half-smirk never left his face.

"What fool let you into a secure crime scene?" She glanced around, hating the commotion she was making but unable to stop herself. "You just waltzed right in, didn't you?"

Nick tapped her elbow and urged her to step back, standing between her and the reporter. "Eli," he warned, "you need to leave."

"Sheriff," Eli said in that condescending mocking tone Miranda despised, "can you confirm that the body of Rebecca Douglas was found this morning by Judge Parker's son?"

"You know I can't confirm anything until the body has been identified." Nick tensed at Miranda's side. Damn, how did the press find out so quickly?

"So there was a body found?"

Miranda wanted to scream at Eli Banks, to tell him that Rebecca wasn't a *body* but a *person,* but that's what he wanted. A reaction. She swallowed her anger and spun around, walking right into Quinn. He put his hands on her elbows to steady her.

She glanced up at him, startled.

"He's not worth it," Quinn whispered.

She didn't, couldn't, say anything. Being this close to Quinn unnerved Miranda. When he looked at her, stared at her with the familiarity of a lover, she couldn't help but remember she had loved him once, and he'd loved her.

At least, that's what he'd told her.

"Let's go," she finally said, and stepped around him. She breathed easier.

Nick watched Miranda and Quinn leave, then turned back to Eli. "This is my investigation, Eli," he said. "You're trespassing on a crime scene. I'll make a statement tonight."

"Right. After the paper goes to bed. Good

plan." He pulled another notepad from his shoulder bag and flipped it open. "Why don't you save me the trouble of writing how uncooperative you were and give me the information you know you're going to have to share with me later?"

Nick bit the inside of his cheeks to refrain from saying something he most definitely didn't want to see in print.

"I cannot confirm that the young adult female body found this morning is in fact Rebecca Douglas. The body has not been identified and is currently awaiting the coroner's examination and family identification."

"But it was the Butcher, correct?"

"The coroner's report should be helpful in that determination."

"Come on, Nick. Let's get real here. You know the Butcher had Rebecca Douglas for the past week."

"Don't push me, Eli. I remember that the parents of the Croft sisters read about their daughters in the damn newspaper before they even knew they were dead."

Eli had the good sense to look sheepish. "Okay, off the record. I promise I won't print anything until the coroner confirms it."

"You're getting nothing, Eli. You know that old saying, 'Fool me once.'" Nick had given him one tidbit three years ago when the Croft sisters had been found; he'd never trust the asshole again after seeing his off-record statement in print.

"Aw, come on, Nicky," Eli said. "One quote. One quote for the paper and I'll wait like a good little boy for your statement tonight."

"Deputy." He motioned to Booker. "Get this man off my crime scene."

Elijah Banks had rubbed salt in every one of her wounds, starting by printing a picture of her being loaded into a Lifeline helicopter twelve years ago after she barely survived her jump into the icy Gallatin River. What had been a terrifying, humiliating, soul-shattering experience for her had won him some award in some stupid journalism contest. Worse, the photograph had been reprinted in major newspapers across the country.

She couldn't stand him. But sometimes she suspected she didn't despise him because he was doing his job in the most obnoxious way possible, but because seeing him reminded her of the worst day of her life, which he'd immortalized in a photograph.

The sun slipped behind Gallatin Peak.

Miranda was numb, but the sudden dip in temperature reminded her she was cold. So cold.

Sharon was dead. He'd shot her in the back. He was coming for her.

Run, Miranda, run!

She stumbled down the steep slope, grabbing a sapling to slow herself. The river was closer; the rush of the rapids a steady hum echoing against the mountainside.

Where was he? Was he close? Did he see her? Did he have her in the sights of his rifle?

She didn't dare look back. If she saw him, she feared she'd freeze like a deer caught in head-lights. And he wouldn't care that she'd stopped. He'd kill her and leave her body to be eaten by scavengers, picked apart by vultures, her flesh a meal for the cougars . . .

No! Stop it!

Sharon.

She hadn't wanted to leave Sharon, but Sharon was dead and he would have killed her too if she'd stayed.

When he'd first unlocked the chains that pinned her to the floor she thought for sure he would kill her. She was so weak. He brought water and stale bread for them to eat, feeding them after he raped them. First Sharon.

Then her.

Stop it!

But she couldn't. The flood of images hit her as she half ran, half stumbled down the moun-tain, the river calling to her.

If she survived, she would go back for Sharon. She had to. She couldn't leave her exposed in the woods. Sharon deserved more.

She was her best friend.

Suddenly, the land dropped sharply. Miranda tried to stop her descent, but the momentum propelled her forward. She fell to her knees, then started to roll. The river — she felt the dampness, heard the roar — and then she was falling, falling . . .

Sheer luck plunged her into the water and not atop a rock. She thought she'd been cold as she ran down the mountain; nothing prepared her for the freezing river. She hit the rocks and silt on the bottom.

She was going to drown.

After all she'd been through, she was going to drown in the river, the river she'd told Sharon would save them.

Calling upon her remaining strength, she pushed off the bottom as the current propelled her violently forward, tossing her like a rag doll.

She sputtered to the surface and gasped for air. She spread her body out, allowed the water to transport her downstream, fighting the violent rapids from dragging her under.

Get to the bank. Just get to the other side, away from him, and grab something. Anything.

A bend in the river gave her an opportunity. She grabbed at tree roots that whipped her face.

Her hands slipped, and they were gone.

She was so weak. Maybe dying here would be better. She didn't want to remember. How long had he kept them captive? At least six days. Seven? Eight? She'd lost track of time, of the days and nights.

Who would take them to Sharon?

Her body slammed against a boulder and she cried out, but realized immediately that she'd stopped moving. The current kept fighting with her, to send her farther downstream. But she held on to the rock and finally saw where she was.

Three feet to her left was a dead cottonwood lying partially in the water, its branches a trap for debris, turning the bank into a natural dam.

Three feet.

She'd run miles over the mountain, down the slope, and had been dragged along in the river. She could make it three more feet.

She had to. For Sharon.

Miranda breathed deep, gathered her strength, and angled herself toward the dam. One. Two.

Three.

She kicked out, stifled the scream that rose in her throat as she thought she'd missed the branches.

She made it. Her body slammed against the dam, and she held on. Slowly, she pulled herself out of the river. So slowly she thought she'd die of hypothermia. In the diminishing light her body looked blue. Maybe it was blue.

How long it took her to drag herself from the river, she didn't know.

But she made it. And collapsed on the bank.

Two hours later the search team found her.

Miranda swiped at her tear-stained face, hating herself for letting the callous reporter get to her, for making her remember the day she lived and Sharon died.

"Miranda, do you want to talk?" Quinn said.

She'd almost forgot he was behind her.

"No."

For Rebecca, Miranda could tolerate being within ten feet of Quinn; the dead deserved justice and she begrudgingly admitted that Quinn was damn good at his job.

"You okay?" he asked, sounding concerned.

"I'm fine." He didn't care, she reminded herself.

Once upon a time he'd cared. Or she thought he had.

She didn't remember when her respect and appreciation for his determination turned to love. It hadn't happened right away.

He'd listened to her without placating her. He'd encouraged her, and even when the days slipped away and they didn't catch Sharon's murderer, she felt that she'd accomplished something.

It wasn't until a month after Quinn was pulled from the investigation, when there were no leads and nothing more he could do, that Miranda suspected she had romantic feelings toward the FBI agent. In fact, she hadn't known she'd missed him until he showed up at the Lodge one Saturday morning, three months after the attack.

"Hi."

She couldn't have been more surprised when Quinn Peterson walked into the dining room where she sat, alone, staring out the plate glass window at the vast canyon below.

"Agent Peterson — I mean, Quinn. I didn't know you were coming." Her heart beat rapidly. "Do you have information? Did you find him?"

He shook his head. "No news. We didn't have a lot to go on."

"I know. I just hoped—" She sighed. "Then why are you here?"

He fidgeted as he stood in front of her, looking slightly less confident than usual. "I — I wanted to see you."

Her heart beat rapidly. Thump-thump. Thump-thump. It pounded in her ears and she thought for sure she'd misunderstood him. "Me?"

"I haven't stopped thinking about you."

"Oh." That sounded stupid.

"I know it's inappropriate. Just tell me to leave, and I won't bother you again."

"I don't want you to leave."

She didn't know what she was doing, but at that moment she knew that if Quinn Peterson walked out of her life, she would regret it forever.

"I'm not going to rush you, Miranda." He sat down across from her and reached for her hand, but didn't take it.

"I'm not scared of you," she said, staring at his hand. Maybe she was scared. Just a little.

Then she looked into his eyes and saw empathy, concern, and affection, but not pity.

Never pity.

She took his hand and squeezed it.

"One day at a time," he told her.

"Okay."

For the first time since the attack she believed she'd be okay. In time, she would make it.

And she had made it, in spite of Quinn Peterson.

She focused now on what was important: tracking Rebecca Douglas's last steps. Her past with Quinn Peterson was just that, in the past.

The job demanded that she focus on the environment around her, look for freshly broken plants, torn clothing, anything that would help re-create Rebecca's escape. Anything that could lead to the man who had hunted her like an animal and slit her throat.

Though last night's rain and the rough terrain almost guaranteed they would fail today, hope was one thing that never deserted her. Hope kept her moving forward, each day, each year, after every abduction and every murder. Hope that they would find the Butcher and justice would win in the end.

If she lost hope, she would also lose her mind. Quinn would then shake his head smugly and say, "I was right."

"I'll take the left," she told him, breaking free of her introspection. "You go that way." She motioned to the far side of the narrow trail.

"Stop," he commanded.

She turned to face him. They were far enough across the ridge that they could see no other teams, voices fading behind them.

Damn, he was handsome with his windswept dark blond hair and solid, square jaw. Even the slightly uneven angle of his nose was sexy. But she would not let his good looks shake her resolve.

"What?" she asked through clenched teeth.

"You're not calling the shots, Miranda.

I'm here — officially — to help the sheriff with his investigation. I can't allow you to start giving orders."

"Let's get one thing straight, *Agent* Peterson," she said, keeping her face blank. "You may be the hotshot federal agent in to rescue the bumbling country idiots, but don't make the mistake of thinking you have any real power here. I've lived here, worked here, made a *home* here. These people will listen to me. They trust me. Don't pull rank or I'll make your life hell."

Anger flashed across his face and the familiar tic pulsated in his jaw. But she saw the realization in his eyes that she was right. Good. She started to turn back to the task at hand when he reached out and spun her around.

Her arm swung up and broke his hold on her. "Don't touch me," she said, her voice low. Her heart beat too fast. She remembered Quinn's touch. His probing caresses, his lingering kisses. She burned with the memory of how combustible they were together. How much she had loved him. How he had shattered her confidence, her hope, her heart.

It had taken her a long time to learn to be touched by anyone. She'd become comfortable with physical contact again. Still, twelve years after the attack, if someone touched her when she didn't expect it, her fear was almost palpable.

She hated the Butcher. He'd stolen so much from her.

Quinn looked momentarily surprised and took a step back. "Don't make threats you have no intention of acting on," he said, his voice matching her tone. "You won't interfere with me because you want justice as much as I do. Maybe even more."

They stared at each other. Miranda detested how he scrutinized her with his intelligent eyes, as if he could read her mind, see clear down to her damaged soul. She straightened her back and didn't waver from his gaze.

"Since you have professional experience in search and rescue, you're an asset," he continued, "for now. But if I think for one minute that you are behaving in any way that is unprofessional or could jeopardize this investigation, I will have you pulled."

Her jaw worked, itching to respond, but instead she turned away to control her unsettled feelings. It wasn't his threat that bothered her — it hurt to realize he still believed that she would fall apart. For years, she'd harbored that same, almost crippling fear every waking moment. She pictured herself falling apart each night when she closed her eyes.

But she persevered. She'd made it ten years without collapsing under the weight of her fears; she couldn't let his doubts weaken her resolve.

She wanted to share her struggles, but feared he would use her confidences against her as an excuse to take her off the investigation. Everything she'd told him before Quantico had been used against her, all her fears and insecurities and overwhelming need to right wrongs had forced him to expel her from the Academy. She had learned her lesson. She wouldn't give him any ammunition now that might be used against her later.

She kept her mouth shut. She hadn't broken twelve years ago, and she damn well wasn't going to break today.

"Very well, Agent Peterson," she said formally. She started down the path, focusing on the ground and the shrubs, concentrating on Rebecca. She heard Quinn fall into step with her, taking the right. He muttered something, but she couldn't make out the words.

She hoped she'd pissed him off.

They proceeded carefully. Miranda kept the map. They spoke only to point out potential evidence, and Quinn photographed and tagged anything even remotely relevant.

About a mile from the ridge where Rebecca had been found, Quinn pointed to four deep impressions in the mud. "She fell here," he said as he photographed the spot.

Miranda stared at the holes, seeing Rebecca's naked body shaking with cold and panic. And hope. Because without hope, she wouldn't have run.

Miranda closed her eyes. If she were alone, she would have gone back in time and remembered the many times she had fallen. Each time she questioned her ability to get up. Each time, she rose because she hoped she could make it.

"Miranda," Quinn said quietly.

She quickly opened her eyes. Quinn of all people couldn't witness her reliving the past. He knew too much about her, what she'd gone through; ultimately, she felt that had been the reason he'd kicked her out of the FBI Academy. He feared she'd lose it when on a case and jeopardize the team, endangering herself and others, if she found herself stuck in her own waking nightmares.

She had to keep her fear to herself.

"It was raining," she said, coughing to cover up any emotion that might creep into her voice. The overgrown path was even denser here, though it was obvious someone had run through. The moist branches didn't break easily, but there were a few hanging at a forty-five-degree angle, and several small plants and saplings had been trampled.

"Because it was raining," she continued before Quinn could interrupt her contemplation, "he had to follow her from behind. The noise of the storm would have made listening for her difficult, so he wouldn't have strayed far from her path." Unlike his pursuit of her and Sharon, she thought. He'd run parallel to them most of the time.

"You're probably right," Quinn said, looking at her with an odd expression.

She didn't want to read anything into it, good or bad, so she turned to her map. She made a very small red mark where Rebecca had fallen. "Look at this terrain," she said, her voice becoming excited in spite of the company.

Quinn looked over her shoulder and she tried not to breathe in his still-familiar, all-too-masculine scent. "This spot? This is a mountain."

"Yes, but here," she pointed, "is a clearing. This area was logged years ago, but they planted new growth. Maybe eight, ten years. These trees will still be relatively small. Because this trail goes to this clearing, I think she came from there. But she twisted around and around, not running straight. Too scared. Not thinking rationally." She shook her head, tried to rid her mind of Rebecca's fear. "But we can cut through here and get to the clearing in less than thirty minutes."

"No," Quinn said, shaking his head. "We stay on the path Rebecca took. We're looking for evidence."

She clenched her hands in frustration and turned to face him. "We can return along the path she took, but I just *know* she ran through the clearing. That's how he kept her in sight. With the rain and poor visibility, he couldn't risk giving her too much lead time. And the ground would have hampered Rebecca more than him because she was weak, barefoot."

Miranda's excitement grew as everything suddenly became clear to her. "She didn't run long. She couldn't have. He wouldn't have risked it, not when it was getting dark and the rain was heavy. Which means the cabin is nearby. It has to be!"

Quinn stared at her for a long moment. Would he disagree with her? She couldn't believe it. She knew this land like the back of her hand, understood how the Butcher thought. How he lived for the hunt more than the rape. Yet he'd never given any of them a lot of lead time. Two minutes. He'd told her and Sharon *two minutes* and then they were fair game.

She was about to demand that Quinn come up with a better plan, relying on her experience and training to argue her point, when he said, "All right."

Before he could change his mind, she smiled and said, "Follow me." She stepped off the narrow trail and cut through thicker trees and growth.

Quinn's training told him Miranda was probably right. It was a good call and confirmed that — as least as far as the search was concerned — Miranda would be more help than hindrance.

The air was cooler, more humid, and darker in the middle of the forest. The dank smell from the recent storm made Quinn think of life and death, as if the forest had been reborn in the wash of the rain.

If they found the cabin Rebecca was kept in, they might find evidence to lead them to the Butcher. He'd been too elusive for years, no pattern to the abductions, except that he hit during spring. April. May. June.

Twelve years ago they hadn't recognized a pattern. When Miranda and Sharon were abducted, the time of year didn't seem to hold any significance. But when Quinn's partner

Colleen Thorne investigated the Denver sisters' abduction three years ago, the spring pattern seemed obvious. Every known Butcher victim had disappeared in the spring.

They'd consulted with Hans Vigo, the FBI's key profiler, who said either the season held special significance to the killer or something in his job or personal life prevented him from killing the rest of the year.

Or, it could simply be convenience. Montana's hunting season was predominantly during the fall months. Accidental discovery would be less likely in the spring, when legitimate hunters weren't out searching for game.

But the key to the psychology of this particular serial killer, Vigo said, was that he needed total control. When Quinn questioned why he gave up the control to give the women lead time to escape, Vigo reminded him that the women had no control. They were naked, injured, weak from minimal food and water, and the two-minute lead time was a ruse. He could easily catch up to them, staying back just far enough so they thought they could get away, and when he tired of the hunt, he'd move in for the kill.

"This is the only aspect of his life that he has control of," Vigo said. "Remember that.

When you find him, you'll learn he has no control over his life or his job."

For example, Vigo said, as a child the killer would have been subject to a domineering, abusive parent. The abuse was likely both physical and mental, and if he fought back, the punishment for his disobedience would have been severe. He likely was restrained in some manner as a child, either locked in a small room or tied up.

He'd have a job that didn't necessitate a lot of contact with the public. On the surface he would be able to function normally and there wouldn't be any indication of the evil that lurks in his soul, but he wouldn't do well in situations where he had constant communication with people.

The Butcher wouldn't have a lot of control over his career, but that was largely of his own making. He would be relegated to low-level employment because of his inability to associate with people on a day-to-day basis. He might have a rote position, such as in a factory where he repeats the same tasks, leading to frustration because he has above-average intelligence. He could very well work outdoors — in construction for example, moving from job site to job site and not developing any close relationships with fellow workers.

They'd never had a suspect. Every time an MSU woman disappeared, her boyfriends, ex-boyfriends, and college professors were interviewed and dismissed as viable suspects. The killer was someone of above-average physical strength, great patience, and superior knowledge of the wilderness between Bozeman and the northern boundary of Yellowstone National Park. He knew where every hunting shack was located, every abandoned cabin, all the places he could imprison one or two women for a week to torture and rape them at his leisure.

No one they'd interviewed fit that profile.

Quinn admired Miranda's thought process. But of course, he'd never doubted her intelligence. She used a combination of common sense, knowledge, and instinct that guided her in the right direction most of the time.

He bit his tongue, loath to admit he still had feelings for Miranda. Hell, he thought about her all the time. In his weakest hours, the time between midnight and dawn, when his resolve to put her aside wavered and he remembered how she looked, how she tasted, how she smiled at him when he held her.

He didn't know when he'd fallen in love with her. When he'd visited that first Saturday after the Butcher investigation fell apart for lack of evidence, he knew he'd be coming back to Montana every free moment. At least once a month he spent a weekend with her. He didn't rush her, couldn't rush her, but together they formed a bond he'd never thought he'd wanted to find.

Even now, ten years later, he realized he'd never severed what united them. He was still drawn to Miranda. Why had he recommended her to the Academy in the first place? If he'd only encouraged her to wait, to give her career choices more time to develop, to think about what she truly wanted, everything that came after would have been avoided. He wouldn't have had to hurt her.

And maybe they would still be together.

He'd believed for the longest time that she would come back to him. Their love, he thought, was unbreakable.

He was wrong. She'd never sought him out, never tried to listen to his reasons, and instead she'd turned to Nick.

Quinn shook off his frustrations. No sense thinking about the if-onlys and what-might-have-beens. He made the most difficult decision in his life ten years ago; he now had to live with the consequences.

He allowed Miranda to lead, not admitting he felt a little out of sorts unable to see the sky. Shadows surrounded them, making it difficult to know in which direction they were headed. He was almost certain they were still moving northeast. But "almost" could get them lost.

He had to trust that Miranda knew how to get them out of here.

Forty minutes passed and Quinn was ready to turn back when suddenly they stepped into a clearing, the sun a welcome sight.

Ponderosa pines, thirty to forty feet tall, grew evenly spaced as far as he could see. Miranda's excitement was palpable.

"Follow me," she said, gesturing impatiently. "We'll find the entrance to the path and backtrack."

They skirted the edge of the clearing, and about two hundred feet away they found it.

Quinn bent to examine the deep impression in the soil. The long gouge in the earth testified that Rebecca had fallen to her knees. A small sapling was bent. Had she pulled herself up?

Now he knew the killer had come this way. The growth was too thick to effectively track his victim unless he had used the same path she did. He photographed the evidence, then glanced up.

Miranda was gone.

CHAPTER
7

The hair rose on the back of Quinn's neck. Where was Miranda?

He called out her name. He stood, looking for her, pulling his Sig Sauer from his holster, braced for anything that might happen.

Had the killer returned? To watch the investigation? His heart beat double time. If that bastard touched her — He clamped down on his emotions, focused his energy on finding Miranda. He prepared to call in reinforcements.

"Miranda!" he called again, louder. A command to respond.

"Over here." Her voice was faint. He spotted her nearly a football-field length away, down the slope, in the middle of the clearing.

He sighed, frustrated and relieved. Keeping her reined in seemed an impossible task. He hoped Nick knew what he was doing.

She waited for him to catch up to her. "Don't wander off," he snapped.

Without acknowledging him, she pointed. "Look."

He stared at the ground. Buried in the mud, barely discernible from the storm-disturbed earth, was a long gold rifle casing.

He photographed the shell, bent down, and with his gloved hands placed it in an evidence bag.

The find was incredible. They'd only recovered two other casings they could for sure say belonged to the Butcher. Either he picked them up after firing or the search parties simply couldn't locate them in the dense wilderness. The casings had been wiped clean of fingerprints — he'd likely worn gloves while loading his rifle, but there was always hope the killer would make a mistake.

The killer used a .270-caliber rifle. Unfortunately, it was a very common gun used to shoot virtually every game animal on earth, so it would only help once they had a suspect and could inspect his guns. A firearms expert would be able to determine from the recovered casings and bullets if a specific gun was used; finding that gun was the proverbial needle in a haystack. Virtually every male over the age of fourteen in rural Montana owned the same type of firearm.

Little good any of the evidence they had would do them until they brought in a suspect, but anything was better than nothing.

"She almost got away," Miranda said, her voice cracking.

Quinn expected to see tears or hurt in Miranda's eyes. Instead, he saw anger. Raw and on the surface, her deep midnight-blue eyes staring beyond him to where Rebecca had died.

He slowly rose and looked over to the narrow opening of the path that Rebecca had ultimately stumbled upon. "He shot at her from here," he said, though it was unnecessary.

"Because she was going to disappear into the undergrowth," Miranda nodded. "He knew the road was only a few miles away. He took the shot, though it wasn't ideal."

She looked around slowly, absorbing the scene.

Quinn said, "We need to call in a team. He shot at her before she had cover, but missed. The bullet is somewhere in there." He gestured toward the area from which they'd just emerged. "We may never find it, but with the right equipment at least we have a chance."

She finally looked at him, a strange combination of relief and fear on her face. She swallowed and it was gone, her control firmly back in place. "You're right," she said sharply.

He called Nick to fill him in on what they'd discovered.

"It's nearly five, Quinn," Nick said over the walkie-talkie. "By the time a team gets to your location, it'll be near dark. We can't get bright enough lights into that area. Mark it. First thing in the morning we'll be back."

"Dammit!" Miranda pulled on her pony-tail in frustration.

"He's right," Quinn told her.

"I know that," she snapped, leaning against a tree. She sighed and her voice soft-ened. "It doesn't make the delay any less frustrating."

They had several bullets, all extracted from the bodies of the Butcher's victims. Quinn didn't expect any stray bullet here to tell them much of anything — except to tie Rebecca's murderer to the other girls.

"We have an hour before we need to head back," Quinn said. "Let's look around."

In silence, broken only by the call of birds and scurrying of small animals or the occa-sional scamper of deer disturbed from their feeding, they tracked the killer's trail. The clearing went on for miles, and it was nearly five thirty when Quinn said, "We have to get back."

"Ten more minutes," Miranda said without stopping, her eyes scanning the ground.

"Miranda, tomorrow."

"But—"

"No." He reached out but stopped short of contact, remembering the quickly concealed fear in her eyes when he'd surprised her before.

Miranda obviously wanted no part of him. No use even trying to rekindle their flame.

She faced him, an inner battle over whether to argue or comply evident in her expression. Quinn concealed a smile. He appreciated the passion she brought to her work.

Before she could argue, he reached for her shoulder and squeezed. She didn't back off. The connection felt good.

"Miranda, I'm just as frustrated as you are. There is evidence out here, evidence that very well may lead us to Rebecca's killer. But we can't do her any good searching in the dark when we can't see the clues. Tomorrow morning we'll come back and start right here. We'll have the forensics team searching for the bullet, more people fanning out."

"We're close," she whispered. "I can feel it."

Quinn didn't say anything, and Miranda wondered if he thought she was crazy. Sometimes, when she was alone and feeling help-less, she questioned her own sanity. Every day she focused on the missing girls. And *him*.

The Butcher.

She may have lived, but he'd stolen her life just the same.

"You're right," she reluctantly agreed. "Let's go."

Quinn dropped his hand and she felt colder, like she'd lost some important con-nection. She frowned. She'd been alone for a long time. *Any* physical human contact — even a gesture as innocuous as a pat on the back — would disturb her.

Especially from Quinn.

She led the way back to the ridge, grateful she didn't have to look at Quinn any longer. Seeing him again brought up too many con-flicted feelings, too many thoughts she had buried for the ten years since he had be-trayed her and took from her what mattered most.

Not her career, but her trust.

Miranda lay awake after midnight, alone, physically drained and weary. She'd stag-gered into her cabin after eating a sparse dinner — to please her father, not because she was hungry — and turned the heat and bubbles on high in her indoor hot tub. She stepped in cautiously, the hot water almost burning her skin. As one foot grew accustomed to the temperature, she submerged the other one. Five minutes later, she eased back on the sloped seat of the tub and took a sip of wine.

She couldn't get Quinn out of her mind.

"Go away," she whispered to no one.

There was a time when she had counted the days until his next visit. When the sound of his voice over the phone made butterflies flutter in her stomach and brought a smile to her face.

When he started visiting her regularly after the Butcher investigation was put on hold for lack of evidence, she didn't know what to think or feel or how to react. She had liked him, liked him a lot, but in the back of her mind she worried she'd never be able to care about a man, never be able to let a man touch her intimately. She was scarred, her body so permanently damaged that even surgery could do only so much. She would never be a normal woman, inside or out.

With Quinn, she felt like a princess.

They'd taken long walks and he'd held her hand.

They'd talked for hours about everything — his family, his career, his dreams. Her family, her past, what she wanted in the future. And they talked about the Butcher.

She found herself wanting him to kiss her, but he never made a move. She worried how she might react if he did kiss her.

One evening they had been sitting on her porch swing at sunset. "Quinn?" she said, looking at their entwined fingers.

"Hmm?"

She glanced at his handsome, almost chiseled profile. His eyes were closed and he seemed at peace, a half-smile on his face. The setting sun made his skin more ruddy than normal, and she realized she cared far more for Quinn than she'd admitted to herself.

It had been a year since the attack. Her life had been on hold. She'd gone back to the University, but it wasn't the same. She found no interest in her major, business administration, or even in her minor, English lit.

She was tired of treading water. She wanted, needed, to move forward.

And she wanted Quinn with her every step of the way.

"Do you want to kiss me?"

She felt his body tense. Had she overstepped her bounds?

"I'm sorry," she whispered and looked away.

He lifted her chin with his finger and turned her to face him again. His brown eyes seemed black, his expression serious, and her breath almost stopped at the sheer *beauty* of his face. "I've wanted to kiss you since last September when I came back to see you. I've wanted to kiss you every day we've spent together, and every day we've been apart."

Warmth, deep, satisfying affection, spread through her body as the sincerity of his words stroked her soul. She leaned forward a bit and whispered, "Kiss me."

The light touch of his lips on hers made her shiver. Slowly, she put her arms around his neck. He kissed her with more urgency and she leaned into him. His arms wrapped around her and he pulled her close, his hands fisting in her hair at the base of her head, holding her tight but not too tight. To every shift she made, he yielded, every tentative touch on his face, his arms, his chest, he accepted.

She wanted more than a kiss.

"Stay with me tonight," she whispered in his ear.

He moved so she could see his eyes. "Miranda, I want to. I want to make love to you. But not tonight. Don't rush it."

She blinked, coldness washing over her.

For two minutes, she'd forgotten about

the Butcher. For two glorious minutes he'd been erased from her mind.

"It's been a year," she said, her voice flat. She turned away from him. "I haven't rushed into anything."

"I know. Honey, don't be angry. I want to make sure you want the same thing I do."

She bit her lip to stop herself from crying. Not because of Quinn, but because her life was so different from what she'd planned. She'd wanted to open her own business, something outdoorsy and recreational. She'd wanted to give river rafting tours in the summer and teach kids how to ski in the winter and help her dad run the Lodge.

"Nothing's ever going to be the same," she whispered.

He caressed her cheek until she faced him. The emotion in his eyes mimicked her internal turmoil. "No, nothing is going to be the same. But you're the strongest woman I've ever met. Your will to survive, not just what happened a year ago, but also reclaiming your life, humbles me."

She shook her head. "I'm nothing special."

He almost laughed. "Miranda, you're incredible." He lightly kissed her.

"I know that having Sharon's killer still out there is like a festering sore. It just doesn't go away. I wish I could have done more." He ran a hand through his hair, his voice rough with frustration.

"You did everything you could." She'd been impressed with the FBI and the police during the investigation. But now her case was cold. Unless the Butcher attacked another woman, he'd never be caught. It wasn't fair that another woman would have to be hurt — and possibly die — to find Sharon's killer.

She wished there was something more she could do. Not only to stop the Butcher, but to help find other killers. Men who preyed on women, who hurt them for their own sick, twisted reasons.

Why couldn't she? Why couldn't she be proactive? She'd been sitting around the Lodge for a year — doing what? Going to college? Helping her dad with the guests? But really, what she was doing was feeling sorry for herself and doing nothing productive with her life.

That had to change if she were truly going to learn to live with what had happened to her.

"What would you think if I wanted to go into law enforcement? I could join the Sheriff's Department." She continued on before Quinn said anything, becoming more excited as the ideas came to her. "Or maybe I could become an FBI agent! I'm smart, I'm almost done with my degree, I'm back in shape, and don't mind working hard. I can finally do something proactive for a change, not just sitting around here doing nothing. I'm tired of being a victim."

He didn't say anything.

"You don't think it's a good idea."

"I didn't say that."

"You didn't have to." She wanted his approval. She *needed* his support.

"Miranda, I want you to do what you want to do. But I had no idea you were interested in law enforcement. You never said anything."

"It was always just a thought in the back of my mind, but it developed fully as I sat here realizing that nothing is going to be the same and I need to take charge of my life."

"You have to be twenty-three to be accepted into the Academy," Quinn said.

"That's only a year."

"You have to finish your degree. A lot of agents get a master's in another field, like criminology or psychology."

"I'm a good student. I don't mind another year of school."

"The Academy isn't easy. It's physically and mentally grueling."

"I can handle it. Don't you agree?"

He paused. "Yes, I think you'd do well under pressure."

"Quinn, I feel like I have to help people. I can't explain it any better." She frowned. She could barely explain it to herself, all these new ideas and thoughts swimming around. But one thing was clear: she now had a direction and she wasn't going to lose her focus. Having a goal strengthened her resolve.

The Butcher was getting away with murder. She had to do something to stop another madman from doing the same.

"I'll help you if I can," Quinn said. "If it's what you want."

"It is," she said, more confident now that she had his support.

He wrapped his arms around her and they stayed like that for some time. As the sun finished settling on the other side of the mountains, as the night turned cool, as the nocturnal creatures began to scurry, she and Quinn rocked on the swing, content in each other's arms.

On that night, Miranda never would have believed Quinn could betray her.

An hour of hot water and jet action relieved most of the tension in her muscles, and when she stepped out her skin tingled, red and overheated and a little painful.

Rebecca was dead. Sharon was dead. But she was alive.

Guilt and confusion ate at her and she almost wished she believed in God like her father. Somehow, faith comforted her dad as it never had her. When she cursed whatever god had created the monster who had hunted her, who tortured women, she couldn't imagine he was the kind and benevolent God her father praised. It was the kind God who had led her home, Daddy said. Who gave her the strength to survive, the will to live, the river to dive into.

But, Miranda countered, by that reasoning, He was the same God who'd created a man who took sick pleasure in killing women for sport. Of tormenting and raping and hurting them. Miranda couldn't reconcile the two gods. It was much easier to believe in the devil.

Yes, evil was real. Alive. Burning.

She lay awake, body exhausted, mind too active to shut down. She pictured Rebecca running through the clearing, the rain beating down on her naked body, a madman chasing her. The loud report of his rifle firing, her body tensing, expecting to be hit. But the shot went wide and she was whole.

And she ran.

Ran down the path, stumbling, her feet

aching. Trying not to cry out when a sharp rock pierced her foot. Getting up fast every time she fell, knowing he was coming. Knowing he would kill her. With deep pleasure, without remorse.

Running, running — and then she tripped and landed wrong, breaking her leg.

She crawled, tried to hide, but already it was too late.

He came upon her. Instead of shooting the wounded animal, he slit her throat.

And her blood drained into the earth.

Miranda's hand flitted to her throat. She could feel the cold steel of the blade piercing the sensitive skin under her chin. Swallowing hard, she imagined Rebecca's terrifying last moments of life.

She'd been so close. Now she was dead.

Miranda closed her eyes and rolled over, burying her head in soft down pillows. The tension she'd so recently purged in the hot water now flooded back into her body.

Would he ever stop? Would they ever catch him and make the bastard pay for the lives he stole?

It just wasn't fair that this unknown, murderous predator was walking free while Rebecca Douglas lay in a cold box in the morgue.

It just wasn't fair.

CHAPTER
8

The birds stopped singing.

A sudden stillness settled in the crevices and trees of the canyon, the silence heightening his instincts. He counted. One. Two. Three.

There, southwest of his camp, the peregrine falcon soared into view like a fighter jet, sleek and elegant, a solitary trace of life across the vivid blue sky.

He drew in a silent breath, and with it the tangible, pungent aroma of pinion and junipers. Home. He wished he could remain here forever, in this canyon, with his raptors.

Theron rode the air current, deep wing beats interspersed with glides. He curved around and landed on the ledge of the sheer cliff where his nest was hidden in a natural recess of the red sedimentary rock.

Seeing Theron three weeks ago had been a welcome homecoming, and he stayed longer than he should have to watch his bird.

Male peregrines defend their territory and engage in breathtaking aerial acrobatics to entice a female to mate. Lay a trap, so to speak. Once a male convinced the female that he was the finest peregrine she'd ever meet, she would remain on the cliff ledge, day in, day out, leaving only once a day to hunt for food.

Theron had a mate. They would be together until she died. A beautiful specimen, he had named her Aglaia. *Splendor.* There was nothing as magnificent as a female falcon sitting high on the cliff, chest out. She wanted to be there, embraced her prison. Theron defended the cliff; Aglaia came willingly, to be protected.

Peregrines were the fastest birds in the world. He never tired of watching them soar, had sat from dawn to dusk waiting to observe one of the majestic birds hunting. Head straight, the raptor watched its prey with one eye, then folded in its wings and dove. Just before he reached his prey, the peregrine would pull out of the dive and hit it with sharp claws. *Wham!* Dead on impact.

They could also pluck a bird from the sky, on a level flight path. All birds were fair game. No one could outmaneuver the raptor.

Kaaaaaak-kak-kak. Kaaaaaak-kak-kak.

Theron was truly free. Something he, himself, would never be. Trapped and alone, his need to possess the unattainable, to hunt the imposters, was far greater than his quest for liberty.

Still, he had a lot in common with the peregrine falcon. When he first began studying the peregrine sixteen years ago, they were all but extinct. Defeated, but not destroyed. Then they came back in their glory, and he was there every step of the way to chronicle their victory.

It always bothered him that few of his colleagues wanted to document the falcons' lives. They put in their time, one required semester, so they could run off and work for some big corporation, or nonprofit environmental organization, or government agency. So they could *say* they tracked falcons, that they cared, but they really didn't.

Words were cheap.

He shook his head, his anger building. *Focus.*

He trained his binoculars on the ledge where Theron and Aglaia had made their home. When he'd left them ten days ago, they had finished the mating game, but he didn't know if there were eggs.

So he watched. For hours. The sun spread

its rays across the landscape, turning the dark morning woods into a glorious array of color. It became warm, and he removed his coat and ate his tasteless sandwich out of habit more than hunger.

As the sun dipped on the other side of noon, Aglaia peeked her head out. Theron followed and they stood on the edge of the cliff, the king and his queen, surveying their kingdom.

Kaaaaak-kak-kak. Caw caw.
Kaaaaak-kak-kak. Kaaaaaa-kak-kak.

His heart swelled as he listened to the raptors communicating. If Aglaia left, there were eggs. He waited and watched, patient, perfectly still among the trees and brush.

With her mighty wings, Aglaia burst from the ledge and swooped down, down into the river rock canyon below, before curving up and around and over the cliff. Silence fell again. The hunt was on.

Theron watched his mate disappear, then went back into the crevice. Incubation exchange. Theron was protecting the eggs while his bride hunted.

Nothing could have pleased him more. He longed to scale the cliff and see Theron up close. He'd done it many times before — the physically demanding job of tracking, documenting, and logging peregrines culminated when he took their eggs for captive breeding.

But he hadn't spent all night trekking through the cold river bottom, fighting overgrowth, stomping through the red clay that coated northwest Colorado, in order to bring eggs back to the University for incubation. He'd come back to watch and log and resist the urge to hunt again.

Fifteen years ago he had only wanted to find his own mate, find the perfect woman for him.

But there were no perfect women.

They all lied, they all manipulated. Even sweet, sweet Penny . . . Why had she told him she wasn't seeing the jock? Why had she told him she didn't even like the guy?

He *knew*. When he saw her lip-locked with him . . .

Penny was a liar like all the other women in the world. They said one thing and did something completely different. They told you they loved you, promised they wouldn't hurt you, but they didn't love anyone and always hurt.

Like his mother.

His mother, with words of honey that stung like a wasp. The way she touched him, made him do things to her.

Touch me there. No, no, no, there. *Yes. Don't stop.*

If he didn't do what she wanted, the punishment was far worse.

Sweetheart, it's for your own good. You have to learn.

She'd clamp his penis until he cried. He'd beg to be let free; he would do anything she wanted, just to stop the hurt.

Then his sister, constantly riding him, telling him she would help. And she did, for a while. She helped him until he trusted her, then the hurting started all over again . . .

It started when he was six. When his father left without a word. He used to think his mother had killed him, but the truth was even worse.

His own father hadn't wanted him.

Didn't his father know how his mother hurt him? Didn't he see the truth? Didn't he care?

His fists clenched around his falcon journal, a sob of bitter anger escaped his throat. What did it matter?

He leaned against the pinion closest to his post and closed his eyes, breathing in the rich pine fragrance, the sticky bittersweet sap, the undercurrent of moist earth, rotting leaves, decaying plants.

He relived the hunt.

His prey was good, but he was better. She ran, but he never lost sight of her.

He watched her fall, heard the snap of her leg through the pounding rain, and decided at the last minute to use the knife.

It was no fun to shoot fallen prey. What was the sport in that?

It had been dark, near midnight, but her blue-white skin stood out against the blackness.

He pulled back her wet hair with his left hand and brought the knife down without hesitation across her white throat. The warmth of her blood surprised him; he tasted it on his lips.

He dropped her where she'd fallen and stood.

The hunt was over, but the urge to find other prey clawed at him. His heart pounded in his chest, blood rushing throughout his body, as he remembered. The intoxicating power when he had her to himself. The feeling of victory that unfortunately diminished with each passing day until there was no choice but to hunt again. The thrill of the hunt was a brief high, and already he missed it. Longed for the power in his hands.

But he had an important job to do. Here, with Theron and Aglaia and their eggs. Watching, waiting, writing.

His birds needed him.

Resist the urge.

CHAPTER
9

Long before the sun rose over the mountains, Quinn woke, restless, his thoughts still trapped in dreams of Miranda.

The pundits repeat the mantra: *Time heals all wounds.*

It was a lie. Some wounds could never be fixed, especially when the wounded continued to peel the scabs.

Miranda lived and breathed for the Butcher. For justice. She'd spent the last ten years in limbo, between heaven and hell, waiting. Waiting for the Butcher to make a mistake. Searching the woods for remains of his victims. As penance or punishment for surviving.

Quinn had seen too many of his colleagues become so absorbed in a particularly difficult, agonizing case that everything else in their life suffered: their marriages often ended in divorce; they often neglected and lost friends. Seeking justice for the living and the dead could consume even the most emotionally stable professionals; with Miranda being a victim as well as an advocate, no one could be closer to the Butcher investigation.

She was a time bomb ready to implode. How she'd survived this long without a nervous breakdown, he didn't know.

That wasn't completely true, he thought as he dragged himself from bed. Miranda was indisputably the strongest woman he'd ever met. She'd withstood torture that would break most anyone, man or woman. She'd watched her best friend fall dead, shot in the back, and had the wherewithal to continue running. She'd taken investigators back to the body, led them to the shack where it all began.

Quinn loved and admired Miranda for her inner core, a spine that was hard as steel.

But what about Miranda's needs? Who was watching out for her, making sure she didn't push herself too far? Taking the time to pull her away from the depressing environment so she could regroup and regain her focus? He feared that unchecked, Miranda had become all-consumed by the investigation, sacrificing her personal happiness and inner peace for justice.

Looking at his own career, he couldn't

completely fault her. He'd been an FBI agent for nearly seventeen years. The only time he took a vacation was when his boss insisted. Except for the two years he and Miranda were involved. Only then had he voluntarily taken time off.

He stripped and stepped into the shower, turning on the faucet. The icy spray hit him hard before it warmed, but he needed the cold. When he had first learned what Miranda had gone through, he'd stood under ice-cold water as long as he could tolerate it. He'd wanted to experience a small part of her pain.

Nineteen minutes was his record. But the river was colder than the shower, and she'd survived.

He left Gallatin Lodge before anyone was up. He didn't want to run into Miranda here, not yet. She hadn't known yesterday he was staying here, and he wondered if her father had since told her.

He thought not.

Nick met him at McKay's, a diner around the corner from the police station. The restaurant hadn't changed much since he'd been away. Vinyl blue-and-white checked tablecloths, condiments centered in the middle, gray walls, and red plastic flowers sagging in sconces between marginally clean windows. Country music interspersed with a pair of wannabe comedians from the morning radio show filtered through the speakers bolted high in each corner of the room.

He asked Fran, the waitress, to refill his travel mug but didn't feel much like eating before the autopsy. He ordered toast, more to soak up the caffeine than because he was hungry.

Nick didn't look like he'd slept any more than Quinn had. He'd aged as well — twelve years ago, when Quinn first came to Bozeman, Nick had been a twenty-three-year-old rookie as shiny as a new penny. Now, lines crossed his face and knowledge burned in his eyes.

Murder aged you.

"What's the plan?" Quinn asked.

"I have a ranger coming out to take down any trees we need for evidence, and twenty-six law enforcement personnel, two who double as crime scene technicians." Nick glanced at his watch. "We have two hours before we need to be there."

"If we find the shack?"

"We'll process the scene and send the evidence to the State Crime Lab in Helena."

"You mentioned on the phone last week that Rebecca had been abducted outside her place of business. Any witnesses?"

Nick shook his head. "No one saw anything."

"Rebecca Douglas was in a public parking lot, not stranded by the side of a road. No one saw or heard anything?"

"I interviewed everyone who was at the Pizza Shack that night, even if they'd left long before Rebecca was abducted. If anyone saw anything, it didn't look suspicious."

"I wonder if she knew him," Quinn speculated out loud.

"It's always been a possibility that the Butcher is someone familiar to the college girls."

"Have you run all University staff and students who have been there for at least fifteen years?"

"We've run all staff who meet the profile through the criminal database, but no one pops. The worst we have is a sociology professor who was arrested in the 1970s for civil disobedience, and a janitor who was arrested for a felony DUI eight years ago."

"Do it again," Quinn said. Nick's brow furrowed, and Quinn backtracked. He didn't want Nick to think he was taking over. "What I mean is, we should focus on all single white males who were at the University either as a student, staff member, or professor under the age of thirty-five at the time

Penny went missing."

"Thirty-five?"

Quinn nodded. "The original profile suggested that the Butcher was a single white male between twenty-five and thirty-five, and that he knew at least one of his victims.

"We'd thought at first that he knew Miranda or Sharon, either from campus, the Lodge, or where Sharon worked," he continued. "But when we determined that Penny Thompson had been the Butcher's first victim, the odds are that Penny knew her attacker and Miranda and Sharon were strangers."

"But there were hundreds of potential suspects," Nick said. "I remember going on dozens of interviews and getting nowhere."

Quinn remembered. Far too many people had had contact with Penny, and when they'd narrowed it to those who knew her well — the boyfriend, her professors, her teaching assistants — no one fit the profile. It didn't help that her disappearance was three years before Miranda's and Sharon's kidnapping.

Quinn refrained from comment as the waitress approached with their toast. Bozeman was a small town, even with a university of twelve thousand students knocking on the city limits. Ears were big;

mouths were bigger.

"Sheriff Donaldson was convinced Penny was killed by her boyfriend," Nick said. "But that never panned out. There was no evidence to connect him to her disappearance. Once we suspected she was the Butcher's first victim, her father had already gotten rid of the car."

Nick finished his coffee and slammed the ceramic mug on the table. "We're floundering, Quinn. The bastard has racked up another victim and we have no evidence, no witnesses, no suspects. The press is going to have a field day."

"We found her quickly. That's always good news. When's the autopsy?"

Nick glanced at his watch. "Ten minutes. We should head over there." He drained his coffee.

Quinn dreaded the autopsy. He didn't know what he feared more: looking at the body of Rebecca Douglas on the table, or picturing Miranda under the same knife.

Fran approached the table with a carafe of fresh coffee and a newspaper. "Just delivered," she said as she slapped the paper in front of Nick. "If you don't mind me saying, Elijah Banks is an asshole and everybody knows it. His mother must be rolling over in her grave, poor woman."

BODY FOUND IN WOODS
No confirmation on identity
from Sheriff's Department

By Elijah Banks
Special to the Chronicle

BOZEMAN, MONTANA — Gallatin County Sheriff Nick Thomas would neither confirm nor deny that the female body found yesterday morning was missing Bozeman student Rebecca Douglas.

"Everything points to the Butcher," a source in the Sheriff's Department said on condition of anonymity.

Sheriff Thomas reluctantly confirmed that he is receiving outside assistance from an FBI Special Agent, Quincy Peterson, of the FBI field office in Seattle. The more experienced Peterson was part of the search for missing co-eds Sharon Lewis and Miranda Moore twelve years ago. Lewis was found murdered and Moore escaped, but was unable to identify her attacker.

The unidentified female was discovered early Saturday morning by Ryan Parker, 11, the son of Superior Court Judge Richard Parker, and two friends. By noon, more than forty sheriff deputies and volunteers were searching the woods four miles west of Cherry Creek Road, ten miles south of Route 84. No one was able to confirm what specific evidence they were searching for.

"When we found her, we thought she might be the missing girl," Parker said. "She didn't have any clothes on."

A source in the Mayor's office said, "It's about time," when told that the FBI was again part of the Butcher investigation. "We need a competent team of professionals to finally catch this killer. The young women of Bozeman are rightfully scared."

Last Friday night, Ms. Douglas left MSU's Hannon Hall in her own car for her job at the Pizza Shack off Interstate 191. She never returned to campus. Her roommate notified campus security that she was missing, and then called the Gallatin County Sheriff's office. Her car was soon discovered in her employer's parking lot.

The Bozeman Butcher's first known victim . . .

Nick slammed the paper back down on the table, coffee sloshing over the rim of his mug.

Quinn agreed that Eli's interviewing Ryan Parker was beyond the pale. Where was

Judge Parker during all this? Why hadn't he stopped him?

It wasn't just Ryan's interview. Quinn didn't like the way Eli jabbed at the Sheriff's Department. The last thing he needed was a turf war mucking up the investigation. Nick's people already thought he was an outsider; if they suspected he was trying to undermine Nick, Quinn wouldn't get any support.

He had to earn their trust.

"I'll make an official statement," Quinn said as he stood and tossed a few dollars on the table.

Nick glanced at Quinn as they left the coffee shop and stopped next to his truck. "Don't know what good that'll do."

"It's your investigation, Nick. I wouldn't be here without your invitation. You know that."

"Am I doing things right? Am I missing something? Did I —"

Quinn put up his hand. "Stop. Don't second-guess yourself. You've dotted your i's and crossed your t's, and don't think I wouldn't be the first one to say something if you hadn't. But I wouldn't go to the press, I'd go to you. I hope you know that."

Nick closed his eyes. "I know. I know. Eli just gets to me, you know?"

"Yeah. He's a dick."

They walked the block to the government center, where the medical examiner also had an office and laboratory.

"How'd Miranda take to you staying at the lodge?" Nick asked.

Quinn winced. "She doesn't know. Yet."

"Shit'll hit the fan."

"She'll deal with it."

Nick wondered. Miranda was already upset that he'd called Quinn in without consulting her. Not that he needed to, but he'd often asked her opinion about various factors in the Butcher investigation, particularly when dealing with the initial search. Over the years, they'd grown comfortable in their working relationship. It had been an easy step to turn their friendship into an intimate partnership.

The fact that he'd walked away two years ago because Miranda didn't return his feelings didn't minimize his dislike of Quinn practically sharing a roof with her. He knew, in the back of his heart, that Miranda wouldn't return to him. If she did, he would be second choice, after Quinn.

He didn't like that position one bit.

He liked Quinn. But he loved Miranda. And the thought of the two of them . . .

No. It wasn't going to happen. Miranda

had been devastated when Quinn pulled her from the Academy. She'd nursed that hurt and anger for years. She wouldn't get over it during the few weeks Quinn would be in town.

So there was still a chance, Nick thought as they turned into the medical examiner's outer office. In fact, perhaps Miranda would turn to him *because* Quinn was in town. He'd offer understanding. Sympathy. A shoulder.

No. He wouldn't settle for second place. Miranda had to *want* him, not be driven into his arms because of another man.

Ryan Parker sat high up on the ridge, confident no one could see him, and watched the people gather below. But his eyes weren't focused on the sheriff's deputies.

The bright crime scene tape drew him in. Reminding him who had lain there. He'd never forget the blue, naked body. The deep, dark red — almost black — gash in her throat. The cuts and bruises covering her skin.

But it was her eyes that haunted him now.

He hadn't slept much the night before. Every time he tried to sleep, Rebecca Douglas stared at him, her wide, frozen blue eyes fuzzy with death.

Ryan had seen dozens of dead animals in

his eleven years. When he'd shot a buck with his .22, a clean shot in the back of the head, his dad had been proud of him. He hadn't been all that proud of himself.

Hunting was okay. He didn't particularly like it, not like his dad and his uncle, but it was okay.

Fishing, on the other hand, was heaven. He'd fish every day if his parents let him. He felt independent, free, when he was out on the lake, or sitting on the eddy near the bend in the river south of his house, or just on the pier at the lake. It made him happier than anything else in his life. More than the horses. Certainly more than hunting.

And, too often, he was happier alone, without his parents.

Something about the quiet, maybe. Or the waiting. Sean and Timmy didn't have the patience for fishing. Timmy could keep quiet, but he fidgeted. Sean didn't even go anymore because Ryan refused to pull in the rod after twenty minutes of no bites. Sometimes his dad would sit with him for a couple of hours, and that was good.

But his dad was too busy now for long excursions to the lake.

Sometimes it took all day to catch a decent-sized trout or bass. Sometimes you didn't catch anything, but that was okay. Because it was the fishing, the waiting, the freedom that made all the difference in the world. Not the catching.

But Sean and Timmy didn't understand that.

Neither did his father, though he tried.

Ryan watched the people below, so small they looked like ants. He squinted and held up his fingers. So big. Less than a quarter-inch.

They didn't even know he was here.

He just wanted to see what they found. For some reason, he thought if they found the guy who killed that girl, he could sleep easier. It was as if the girl were a doe, her neck sliced, her eyes wide and unfocused and staring.

Ryan didn't like that. People were people and animals were animals, but someone had treated that girl like an animal. It wasn't right.

When most of the sheriff's people started down the old logging path, Ryan stood and brushed the dirt from his worn jeans. He had to be getting back, anyway. Because he'd left Ranger in the stable, it'd take him an hour to get home and he didn't want his mom to worry. She didn't ask a lot of questions, but she always knew if he was lying.

Ryan didn't lie, really. But sometimes, he didn't want to tell the truth. Avoiding conversations was the best way to handle his mom.

He followed the narrow springtime creek down the ridge, toward the wider path that led to the boundary of their ranch. He spotted hoofprints and frowned. They looked fresh, but he hadn't noticed any of the searchers coming this high up the ridge. Whoever it was, though, needed to reshoe his poor horse. The right hind hoof had lost a couple of nails, and the loose rocks and dirt would be getting under the shoe and embedding in the horse's hooves.

Lost in thought, he almost missed it.

The sun reflected off something in his path and he stopped to bend down and examine it.

At first he thought two snake eyes were glaring at him, ready to strike, and he teetered back onto his heels. He regained his balance and looked more carefully at the object.

It wasn't a snake, of course. The two eyes were small, dark gems. Deep green, like the pine trees at dusk. The gems were embedded in a simple silver belt buckle carved to look like a bird. Like an eagle. The gems were its eyes.

He reached out and picked it up, surprised when a piece of leather came with it, still attached to the buckle. Examining the end, it was obviously frayed and probably broke off when a hunter or hiker stopped on this high ledge to take a pee.

Ryan hesitated as he stared at the buckle. Should he take it to that FBI agent? Maybe it would be important to the investigation. His heart beat with excitement. *The Untouchables* was his favorite movie, and he never missed *Without a Trace,* the show about finding missing people.

But his excitement turned to worry. His father had told him specifically not to bother the sheriff. And he'd lied to his mother about where he was going. She would flip. She wouldn't yell or spank him or anything, but she had this *look,* and the look was scarier than any punishment.

He shivered and pulled his jacket closer, though the day was warming nicely. Stuffing the buckle into his pocket, he continued down the narrow trail toward home. If he saw Sheriff Thomas again, he'd show him the buckle.

It was probably nothing, anyway. Just some guy pissing in the woods.

CHAPTER
10

Every muscle in her body tense, Miranda followed Quinn, Nick, and the others down the path to the clearing they'd discovered the day before.

Nick had called in Pete Knudson, a ranger she'd often worked with on searches. If they found a bullet lodged in a tree, he would either cut out a segment or fell the whole tree in order to collect the bullet for evidence.

The tension gave her a mind-numbing headache she attempted to tame by swallowing three aspirin with a swig of water from her canteen. She could easily blame her pain on lack of sleep, a sparse appetite, or the stress of the Butcher claiming another victim. But she held Quinn responsible for the bulk of her discomfort. His presence unnerved her in ways she hadn't imagined.

For years, she'd lied to herself that his betrayal at the Academy hadn't mattered.

Though hurt at the time, she reasoned, she'd come back to Bozeman and made a good life for herself. After four years on the Search and Rescue team, she accepted the lead position when her boss, Manny Rodriguez, took a job down in Colorado. Her team, the two paid staff members and the more than two dozen volunteers she could call upon, trusted her.

"Miranda?" Nick said, falling into step with her, his ruggedly handsome face tight with concern.

"I'm fine," she answered the unspoken question.

"Yeah." He glanced at Quinn, who led the group.

"What happened at the autopsy?" She tried to sound professional but was unable to keep her voice from cracking.

"I left before Doc Abrams was done, but it's the same guy."

"We knew that."

"I'm sorry I didn't tell you about Quinn," Nick said, his voice low so no one could overhear.

"I'm sorry I yelled at you yesterday. You didn't deserve it after seeing Rebecca like that."

Nick still tried to shield her from reliving her seven days in hell. He didn't understand that while she couldn't escape the past, help-ing to find these girls gave her a measure of peace. She was doing everything she could to find the Butcher. And someday, he would be stopped.

She hoped to be there when he was cap-tured. She had to be, as if helping to catch him would release her from daily remem-brance and nightly terrors.

Nick let out a long breath. "Truce?"

"I can never stay mad at you for long." She smiled at him. She loved Nick. Just not the way he wanted.

She had tried. For three years she strug-gled to give him her heart. She *wanted* to fully love him. But the more she tried, the harder it became. Friendship, loyalty, strength — these were things she freely gave and received from her ex-lover. But her heart was still broken, and Nick couldn't put to-gether the pieces.

She glanced up at the only man who could.

Quinn felt like he was being watched. He paused at the edge of the clearing to collect his bearings, looked behind him, and caught Miranda's eye. For a split second, he thought he saw something other than anger on her long, narrow face. For a moment he saw a flicker of desire in her dark eyes, a physical need and emotional longing he vividly remembered from their past. A bolt of lightning would have jolted him less. He blinked.

Whatever he thought he saw was gone. Miranda's lips were locked in a rigid line, her face blank, her eyes narrowed and filled with suspicion and caution.

He turned back to the crew, eased his backpack off his shoulders, and removed his jacket. He took a long swig of cold water from his canteen to quench the heat that had risen inside him at the thought that Miranda still had feelings for him.

While the temperature had been in the midforties this morning, the sun now spread a pleasant blanket of warmth on the new growth field. Under normal circumstances, the hike they'd just made would have been invigorating and enjoyable.

Nick's deputies looked at him with a mixture of arrogance and wariness. Taking directions from a Fed was not in their rule book, but damn if he was going to let inter-agency hostility interfere with this investigation.

Quinn cleared his throat and said, "You'll see the orange flags where Ms. Moore and I discovered evidence yesterday. I want to find the bullets fired, if possible." He turned to address Deputy Booker. "Sheriff Thomas says you're the best shot in the department."

The deputy stood straighter. "I won the county competition, sir, but—"

Nick cut him off. "Deputy, go down to that flag over there," he gestured to the spot a hundred feet down-slope, "and position yourself as if you were shooting a high-caliber rifle at a moving target the size of a five-foot-two-inch woman entering the path there." He pointed to another flag about twenty feet away.

Booker swallowed, adjusted his hat, and glanced uneasily at Miranda. "Uh, yes, Sheriff," he said.

"Then you tell Ranger Knudson the trajectory and find the damn bullets." Nick turned to the rest of his men. "Fan out. You know what you're looking for. And if you find anything at all, call out for Agent Peterson or myself. No chatter on the com, just be thorough. The rain really hurt our chances at preserving evidence, but we might get lucky."

God knows we could use a little luck right now. Quinn glanced at the clear sky.

He walked to where Nick and Miranda stood at the opening of the path. ". . . the cabin," Miranda was saying as he approached.

"What?"

She barely acknowledged him. "I'm going over there to find the cabin." She gestured down the slope, past the flags where Deputy Booker worked with the ranger.

"Not without me," Quinn said. What was she thinking?

"Nick and I can handle it just fine."

"I'm staying here," Nick said. "I need to be accessible."

Quinn watched Miranda struggle with the prospect of being partnered with him again. Tough shit. She wasn't going out there by herself. And if she was right about the cabin being near the clearing, he had to go with her. For safety, as well as to gather evidence.

"Fine." Her voice was clipped and weary. She probably hadn't gotten much more sleep last night than any other night since Rebecca went missing.

Quinn sure as hell hadn't slept worth a damn, thinking about what Miranda had been doing for the past ten years. How her life had changed — and not changed. Wondering if he had done the right thing at the Academy. No, he had been right. But he'd done it all wrong.

He couldn't figure out how to fix it then, and now the divide between them seemed so much deeper. He'd given her time and space; he'd attempted to contact her, tried to talk to her, to explain. Hoped she'd come to realize leaving the Academy was the right thing to do at that time. But she never returned his calls and marked his one letter *return to sender,* unopened.

That hurt.

He pushed the memories aside and pulled out his canteen again. He took a long drink, then said, "Let's go."

They walked in silence, searching the ground for evidence. The occasional freshly broken branch or unusually deep impression proved they were on the right path. At one spot Rebecca had obviously fallen; a clump of long blonde hair was snagged on a bush, torn from her scalp. Quinn silently placed a bright orange flag at the spot, photographed it, and cut the branch, putting it with the hair into an evidence bag.

When he stood after completing his task, he noticed that Miranda had stopped as well and was staring at him. No, not at him. Beyond him. Seeing something that wasn't there.

His heart beat faster. It tore him up inside watching Miranda put herself in these situations where she relived what had happened to her; her anguish was tangible. He remembered Miranda finding Sharon's body, her grief, her pain undeniable. She was strong, but not indestructible.

He wanted to reach out, touch her and hold her.

"Miranda," he said softly. "Are you okay?"

She snapped her attention to him. "I'm thinking," she said. "She fell here. Why? No limbs to trip over. She's in the clear. He shot at her."

"You don't know—" he stopped. Could be. He followed her line of sight as she turned in a slow circle. "Maybe," he continued, "but where's the evidence?"

"She changed direction here," she mumbled, as if talking to herself.

"What?"

"She wouldn't have gone in a straight line after he shot at her, she would have detoured, turned, done *something* different to throw him off her trail." Miranda started walking in an arc, back and forth, until she stopped, fifty feet away and downslope, at a forty-degree angle from the path they had been traveling.

"Here!" Her voice was tinged with excitement.

Quinn met her down the slope. Two more casings. He flagged the spot. "We need to go down," she said, pointing down a precipitous slope.

"It's steep," Quinn said.

"Yeah, but this is the way they came."

She was right. A sapling had been stepped on and broken twenty feet in the direction Miranda led him. The edge of the clearing ended abruptly another fifty feet away. He stopped Miranda when they reached the perimeter.

Twelve years ago they had walked a similar slope together to the shack where Miranda and Sharon had been imprisoned. Quinn would never forget Miranda's courage that day.

"Are you ready for what we might find?" he asked quietly.

"Of course," she said. But when he caught her eye it wasn't anger brightening her dark eyes, it was memories.

Was she thinking of that day, too?

He reached out, wanting to connect with her, but she shook her head almost imperceptibly. He dropped his arm, angry with himself for trying, but wishing Miranda didn't insist on carrying the weight of Rebecca's pain solely on her shoulders.

They walked along the edge of the clearing, then stopped a moment later when something out of place caught his eye.

"Here," he said. He squatted to examine trampled undergrowth.

"Let's go."

He pulled out his firearm and nodded when Miranda did the same, holding a smaller nine-millimeter Beretta. He'd never forget her coming in third in the Academy shoot-off. Third was damn good in a class of one hundred.

But she'd been upset with herself that she hadn't come in first. Competition was tough at the Academy, but no one put more pressure on Miranda than she did.

Miranda breathed deeply, gathering every ounce of strength as she inched deeper into the descending woods. The forest became thicker when they left the sun-dotted clearing, the air cool and damp. The chill kept her adrenaline high, her eyes discreetly scanning for any sign of movement.

For the Butcher.

Scurrying animals, the call of birds, and their boots squishing the soft, wet, leaf-covered ground were the only sounds as they tracked farther into the woods. The air was fresh, clean from the rain, renewing the earth. But at the same time, an underlying, unpleasant scent of rotting mulch assaulted her. Reminding her of falling, of being filthy and cold and in pain.

Quinn paused to examine the path. This mountainside had a gentle slope, far from the higher, rocky terrain on which Miranda had escaped. Rebecca had been kept relatively close to civilization, only five miles as the crow flies.

Miranda closed her eyes and took a deep, calming breath. When she opened them a minute later, everything appeared brighter, more vibrant. The greens were greener, the browns browner. Shimmering sunbeams cut through the trees, flooding the ground with streaks of light. Miranda loved days like this best, after a cleansing spring rain, when everything was fresh and new, and her guilt at being alive faded.

A sparkle caught her eye.

A slight reflection off a rusting tin roof. She stared, so focused on her discovery that the sounds of the forest faded and she heard nothing but her own beating heart. The worn, sagging wood that held up the flimsy roof didn't look like it could have withstood the recent storm, but looks were deceptive. The cabin had survived harsh Montana winters, pounded by hard rain, half buried in cold snow.

"Miranda."

Her attention snapped to Quinn and she pointed. "There."

He looked, his expression unreadable. Pulling his walkie-talkie out of his belt, he depressed the mic. "Sheriff, we found a shack. About —" he glanced up the steep slope "— six hundred yards from the edge of the clearing. An orange flag marks where we left the field."

Static crackled. "Roger that," Nick's distorted voice broke the quiet. "I'll send a team."

"Roger. Out." Quinn pocketed the com and glanced at Miranda.

She tilted her chin up. She could do this. "Let's go."

Miranda stayed behind Quinn, close enough that she wouldn't miss anything. They both pulled on latex gloves to preserve what was most likely a crime scene.

Where Rebecca had been raped and tortured.

Miranda briefly squeezed her eyes shut, then blinked, surprised to feel tears forming. *Not now*, she admonished, her inner voice severe.

Quinn motioned for Miranda to stand back as he walked the perimeter of the shack. She didn't argue.

The small cabin had probably been here for decades. The wood was rough, worn, almost black. It should have been lying in a heap, rotting under layers of decaying leaves, covered in moss. Though it didn't look sturdy, the tiny building had been well constructed. An old, abandoned cabin, like so many others.

Until the Butcher found it.

With one hand Miranda took out her topographical map and viewed their approximate location and the path Rebecca had forged.

Her gut clenched at the visual representation of the co-ed's journey. Not because her escape ended in death, but because if she had walked four miles in the opposite direction, she would have made it to a dirt road that led to a small reservoir. She still might have died, but the open road would have given her a better chance.

Run. You have two minutes. Run!

The voice came out of nowhere and Miranda's grip tightened on her gun as she looked around, tamping down her panic while adrenaline pumped through her system.

No one. No one was there. His damn voice, low, gravelly, evil, plagued her. Damn him.

Rebecca hadn't had any chance in choosing her initial path, any more than she and Sharon had. They ran *away*. Away from their captor. If he stood there, right outside the narrow door, pointing a rifle at her heart, Rebecca would have run up the slope. *Away.*

"Miranda?"

Quinn's voice was soft but firm, and she was once again reminded that he had been her rock during her darkest days after the attack. She remembered the young, up-and-coming FBI agent she'd fallen in love with, a man excited about his life, his job, fighting the bad guys. And through it all, he'd steadied her, given her the strength she sorely needed.

She forced a blank expression on her face — she had a lot of experience perfecting bland interest — and turned to him.

Quinn had grown up. He was nearly forty. He no longer fidgeted, as if he'd forced himself to develop control of his one admittedly bad habit. He stood tall and erect, still confident, intelligent, but wiser. More seasoned.

He wasn't the man she'd fallen in love with any more than she was the same woman he'd claimed to love. He'd grown into the man she'd imagined he could be.

But he was still the man who'd betrayed her.

"I'm ready," she said quietly.

He opened his mouth to speak, but nothing came out. Instead, he nodded and closed the distance to the shack. Relieved, she swallowed a sigh and followed.

Fresh scratches on the weathered wood indicated a metal lock had been recently attached. Quinn had his gun poised. So did she.

She would never be caught off guard again.

Quinn tried the door and it opened. Unlocked. Cautious, he swung it slowly in, standing to the side in case the perpetrator was inside.

It was empty. Miranda relaxed marginally. While she wanted to catch this guy in the worst way, she feared seeing his face. Was it someone she knew? Someone she'd gone to school with? A regular at the Lodge? A local? A stranger?

Would she recognize him? Was he someone she saw every day?

That thought haunted her. The Butcher could be someone she considered a friend.

"Miranda?"

"What?" she snapped, regretting her tone. She didn't need to take her trepidation out on Quinn. It was her personal demons she fought.

Whatever he was going to say, he didn't. He began a careful search of the premises.

The one-room cabin, eight by twelve feet, housed only a bare, filthy, stained mattress in the middle of the rough wood floor. Dried blood mixed with dirt. The ceiling was tin on wood, pitched to keep the snow from destroying the building. Rebecca's clothes were in the corner. The jeans, yellow sweater, and blue windbreaker she'd last been seen wearing.

Her bra and panties were missing.

The smell hit Miranda. The scent of fear clung to the walls, as if Rebecca's terror was imprinted forever in the dark, moldy wood.

Not fear. No, fear had no smell. It was the dried sweat, the faint, metallic hint of blood as she breathed in, coating her sinuses, drifting down to her tongue where she tasted the coppery terror, before filling her lungs and heart with heavy memories.

The sex. The brutal, painful sex.

I'm so cold, Randy.

Miranda glanced around the hovel, certain she had heard Sharon speaking to her.

Not Sharon. Sharon's ghost.

The windowless room shrunk. The walls seemed to pulse, to breathe. As if they were creeping closer . . . and fear did have a scent. The cloying aroma of her own terror, her mortality, weighed her down, choking her.

Randy, I'm cold. We're going to die.

We're not going to die. Don't give up. We'll find a way out.

He's going to kill us.

Stop it! Don't talk that way.

Rebecca had been alone. No one to support her. No one to talk to, to cry with, to make promises to. All alone. Never knowing when he was going to return, when he was going to climb on top of her. When he was going to take the ice-cold clamp and squeeze her nipples until she cried out . . .

Aghhhh!

Sharon's screams rang in her ears, pounded at her head.

She would be next.

The walls breathed and sagged. Coming closer, closer . . .

She shook uncontrollably as Sharon screamed and sobbed. He was silent. Sickly silent. But Miranda knew he was raping Sharon again, the sick pounding of his flesh on hers, the slap, slap, slap of skin on skin. The scream as he twisted her nipples in the clamp . . .

She would be next.

The walls reached for her, wanting to suck the life out of her. Hand to mouth, Miranda ran from the shack, stumbled over roots, until she reached out and found a tree. Holding on to the trunk, she tried to swallow the horror that threatened her sanity.

Quinn was right. You're going to break.

No. No. *No!*

Deep breaths. Cleansing breaths. The smell of sweat and violent rape and blood faded away, replaced by the cool pine scent of the forest. Musty dirt and rotting leaves. Sticky sap.

Breathe in. Breathe out.

Her heart slowed, the pulse in her neck lost its frantic beat. She opened her eyes and stared at the rough tree trunk that she clung to.

Tree-hugger, she thought, and found herself suppressing a smile.

She pushed off the tree, rubbed her hands on her jeans, and gathered her courage, carefully sewing the threads of her sanity back together.

Breathe, Miranda. Breathe.

She stood and turned back to the shack, ready to try it one more time. She'd fight the claustrophobia that had been her damn albatross ever since the week she lived in hell twelve years ago.

Quinn stared at her and she held her breath.

CHAPTER
11

Quinn watched Miranda from the doorway.

She was falling apart, her face ghostly and pained. If the press got wind that one of the sheriff's own people was unstable, the entire investigation could be endangered.

Miranda held on to the tree as if it were a lifeline. He took a step forward, preparing what needed to be said. *Miranda, go home. Take care of yourself. You can't help us if you have a nervous breakdown.*

As he watched, she gathered herself together. She stopped shaking and stepped back from the tree. The quiet sobs that racked her body subsided. She bent over, took deep breaths, then stood.

And looked right at him.

Fear. Fear washed her face, but it wasn't the terror she'd run from in the shack. It was fear of him.

Anger and empathy battled inside. That

she would be afraid of *him* was upsetting, but he understood. After he'd told her flat out she was on the verge of a breakdown, it's no wonder she feared he'd remove her from the investigation.

Almost as quickly as he identified her apprehension, she masked it behind a stone face.

He was surprised that she'd pulled herself together so completely, so fast. He'd seen seasoned veterans walk into particularly brutal crime scenes and take longer than five minutes to regroup. Some took days.

But, he reminded himself, Miranda had had twelve years to mask her fears.

"Claustrophobia?" he heard himself say.

She nodded, her entire body visibly relaxing. Cocking her head with a shrug, she said, "I still get it sometimes." She paused, then added so quietly he almost missed it: "No windows."

Though she stood at ease, her eyes were watchful. Waiting for more. Waiting for him to jump down her throat. Is that how little she thought of him? That he would do something so cruel when she was down?

"Miranda," he said, approaching her. What could he say to reassure her? "I—"

The clamor of men descending the slope stopped his next words. He and Miranda watched Nick lead five deputies down to the shack. "We found three bullets in two trees," Nick said, glancing from Quinn to Miranda and back again. If he noticed their tension, it didn't show on his face.

"The ranger is working with my men to cut the segments out of the trunks and we'll send them to the lab in Helena." Nick turned to his men. "Fan out from the cabin downslope and see if you can figure out how he brought her here. Be mindful of where you step, stay on the lookout for anything foreign. Tire tracks, sled, garbage."

"Yessir." The men departed.

"We'll need a team down here to collect evidence," Quinn said.

"So this is it." Nick frowned at the cabin, a cloud passing over his face.

"No doubt, though we'll need to take blood and other samples." In the other shacks they had found, they were able to collect some forensic evidence, but the DNA samples were corrupt from exposure. The killer left no semen traces on the victims, no hair or blood. He'd used a condom, but he hadn't always used his penis to rape the victims.

Quinn glanced at Miranda and wanted to strangle the bastard who'd hurt her. This urge was different from his usual angry reaction to violent criminals. Stronger. More powerful.

Personal.

She caught his eye and held it. Her pale face was blank, but her eyes were full of questions.

"I think we're ready to go in. Miranda?" Quinn asked, wanting to give her the option of refusing, though doubting she would.

To his surprise, she said, "Go ahead. I'm going to head back."

Nick seemed as surprised as he was. "Let me call one of my men to escort you," he said.

"Dammit, Nick, I'm not going to get lost."

"Miranda," Nick said, "no one on my team is out of sight while on a search. You should know that better than anyone, since it's your rule too."

She sighed. "You're right. I'm sorry. I — I'm just tired."

Nick touched her shoulder and nodded. "Get some rest, Randy. We have plenty to do tomorrow, and we'll have to call it quits here in less than two hours."

"I'll do that." She waited while Nick called over for Deputy Booker to take her back. She glanced at Quinn.

"Thanks." She touched him lightly on the arm. A feather of a touch that conveyed more real emotion — other than anger — than anything they'd shared since his return to Montana. Their eyes locked, just for a moment, a mutual truce. And something more. Something deeper. Forgiveness?

He wasn't that lucky. Was he?

He watched her leave with the deputy. Wondered.

The sun settled well after the dinner hour to close the day as Miranda drove southwest to the Gallatin Lodge.

She couldn't stop thinking about Quinn's reaction.

She'd been so certain he was going to make a big deal about it, an "I told you so" kind of thing. Damn, she hoped he didn't feel sorry for her. That would almost be worse. She didn't need or want a pity party. All she wanted was a little room to breathe, just some understanding without sympathy.

And he'd given it to her. That put everything in a whole new perspective.

She didn't want to think about Quinn Peterson or his motives. Not now. Throwing her out of the Academy had shown her exactly what she was to him. A burden, a problem, expendable. Doing something unexpected and kind now didn't change the fact that he thought she couldn't handle the pressure of the Butcher investigation.

Despite her resolve to forget the past, it flooded her memories.

It had been the day before graduation and Quinn came by her dorm room. She'd just received the scores of her final exam and couldn't contain her enthusiasm. Throwing her arms around Quinn, she kissed him.

God, how she loved this man!

He entwined his hands in her hair and held her face close to his. His lips warm, firm, confident.

Hers.

They hadn't talked marriage, not in so many words. The one conversation that danced around the issue, Quinn had initiated. It was before she left Montana, right after she'd been accepted to the Academy, right after their affair of the heart turned physical. They agreed to postpone the discussion until after she graduated from Quantico.

She'd never had any doubt she'd pass. Her test scores proved her right.

She had a career she knew she would thrive in. A man she loved with her whole heart. Someone who understood her, cared for her, loved her without condition. Without seeing her as damaged goods. Someone who held her close when the nightmares came, who soothed away her anxiety with warm hands and gentle kisses. Who made love to her without holding back.

Now she was graduating. Her life was her own again. A new life. Whole. Complete. She felt reborn.

He held her tight, kissed her hair. His scent was so Quinn — plain soap under a hint of expensive aftershave. Slightly spicy, but it didn't overwhelm her senses. He was handsome, sexy, smart, understanding.

And all hers.

"Look!" she said, grinning madly, holding up the near-perfect score from her written final.

His dark chocolate eyes deepened. "Wow. That's a point higher than my final."

She kissed him again and almost giggled. *Almost.* She still hadn't learned to laugh the way she used to, and giggling seemed so — immature. But she hadn't been happier in years — since before the attack.

Nothing could stop her now.

Quinn took her hand and they walked through the courtyard outside the dorm rooms. Other soon-to-be agents walked in various states of pride, chattering amongst themselves. It was a beautiful autumn afternoon in Virginia. Tomorrow promised to be clear and in the seventies. Perfect for graduation.

But even if rain poured from the heavens, Miranda would be in bliss when she received her diploma from Quantico — and her first assignment.

She had beaten the Butcher and it felt amazing.

"I talked to Agent Clark," Quinn said once they were beyond the courtyard and walking leisurely through the paths that wound around the buildings.

"I told you — no special treatment on assignments. If they give me my first choice, great. If not, I'll work up to it." She had asked for serial killers and for admittance into the profiling program. Her master's in criminology and minor in psychology was a plus, but nothing was certain.

And she wanted to earn her assignment. She didn't want her relationship with Quinn to impact the decision.

"I know." He paused a long time and Miranda felt a prickle under her scalp. Something wasn't right. Quinn wasn't a talker, but neither was he reticent. He said what he meant and meant what he said — it had made all the difference in their relationship since Miranda had difficulty talking about how she felt, finding the right words.

"What's wrong? Don't tell me Rowan or Liv didn't pass." Not possible. Both of them were as focused and dedicated as she was. They were her first real friends since Sharon. And after the first week, they'd become more like sisters than roommates.

Quinn shook his head. "We talked about you."

"Oh, you and Agent Clark talked about me?" She tried to make her voice sound light and carefree, casual, but tension crept up her spine and butterflies fought in her belly. Something was very wrong.

"Doctor Garrett met with Clark yesterday morning. He was — um — a little concerned about your second psych test."

"Garrett's an arrogant ass," Miranda said, tucking her hair behind her ears. Her hand was shaking and she willed it to stop.

"Yeah, well, Clark listened to him. They're concerned about you. That you need a little more time."

They both knew what he was referring to. *Time.* Time had become an enemy. "It's been over two years, Quinn. What exactly did the fucking profile say?"

She stopped walking and looked at him. When he avoided her eyes she knew, *knew* she was screwed.

"That you have an obsessive personality,

and it might cloud your judgment and jeopardize the lives of your fellow agents."

"That's *bullshit!* And you know it. They can't — what?"

The worried look on his face ripped hope from her heart and she *knew.* Her life was over. Again. "What happened? Dammit, Quinn, what happened!"

His voice was flat. "Clark asked me what I thought. I told him you needed another year."

She hated the tears that sprung to her eyes. She could do nothing to stop them from spilling down her cheeks. A lead weight pressed on her chest and her breathing faltered. "Wh-what?"

He tried to take her hands but she stepped away. "Randy—"

"Don't call me that!" Angry at her weakness, she rubbed the tears away with the back of her hand, but more came in their place.

Quinn stepped back. "You have guaranteed admittance to Quantico next year. And you'll pass with flying colors, you know that—"

"I *did* pass with flying colors!" She stared at him through her tears. "You — he asked you. Why didn't you stand up for me?"

"You need more time." His voice was

quiet and he looked at her straight on. "Miranda, you rushed through college, your master's, you didn't do anything for yourself. You need to deal with the past so you can have a future. I don't know if you want to be an FBI agent for the right reasons."

"Spare me the fucking psychobabble. It's you — you th-think I'm g-going to fall apart. Th-That I can't do the job. Fuck you. I th-thought you of all people understood —"

She ran away.

Miranda shook her head and rubbed her left temple, forcing the memory back where it belonged. Buried. She hadn't realized how close to the surface those feelings were until she felt the moisture behind her eyes, but how could she be surprised? As soon as she saw Quinn yesterday, the years had melted away.

For a year she fought herself about returning to Quantico. She ignored Quinn, certain he'd give her useless platitudes and explain ad nauseam why she needed time off. She didn't want to listen to his reasons. He hadn't stood up for her when it really mattered; he'd called into question her motives, then tried to tell her it wasn't personal.

How could it be anything but personal?

She wanted to return to Quantico, but one thing held her back.

Fear. Deep, bone-numbing fear that the government shrink was right, that she was not only obsessed with the Butcher, but that if she ever found him, she really would have a nervous breakdown.

She never wanted Quinn to see her reduced to nothing.

The hunt for the Butcher kept her focused, sane. But when the hunt ended, where would she be? When the killer was caught and punished, what would she do? She had nothing else.

The emptiness of her life sucker-punched her.

She blinked, barely remembering the drive to the Lodge. Her Jeep was parked, but the engine was still running. She turned it off and drew in a deep breath, shaken.

She'd forgotten how much she once loved Quinn. She'd spent so much time dwelling on his betrayal that she'd forgotten she'd wanted — planned — to spend the rest of her life with him.

CHAPTER
12

Using Nick's computer, Quinn e-mailed his report to his boss as Nick approached with a paper cup from the coffeehouse up the street.

"Black, with a shot."

Quinn raised his eyebrow. "Shot?"

Nick cracked a smile. "Espresso. Added caffeine."

He laughed and accepted the coffee, feeling some of the tension roll off his shoulders.

Nick sat in the visitor seat across from his desk, waving Quinn back into his chair. "I finished logging the evidence," Nick said, "and Deputy Booker is going to take it to Helena first thing in the morning."

"Good." Quinn sipped the coffee. He noticed his index finger drumming the side of the cup and consciously had to stop the fidgeting. This case was difficult, but his frustration had more to do with Miranda than with the investigation.

He asked, "Did Doc Abrams confirm the blood was Rebecca's?"

"Same blood type; he's sending a sample to the lab to confirm DNA, but you and I both know it's hers." Nick paused. "Dammit, Quinn. The mildew and mold in that place is going to destroy any trace evidence."

"Perhaps, or maybe we found it quickly enough." The flat, filthy mattress flung on the cabin floor probably had nothing they could use, but the crime tech had vacuumed everything in the shack and each grain of dirt would be inspected by the lab. Quinn would see to it.

"I'm calling in a friend of mine to help," Quinn continued.

"Another FBI superagent?" Nick said, trying to be lighthearted, but Quinn detected a hint of something else, a tad bitter. He hoped Nick wasn't still angry about Eli Banks's *Chronicle* article this morning. Banks had slighted Nick because he was mad that Nick hadn't given him the quote he wanted, end of story. But the allusion that the FBI was coming in to clean up the investigation must have hit a sore spot.

Of course, knowing Eli Banks, this was the first of many negative articles.

"Not exactly. A lab tech, one of the best,

and a personal friend. Olivia St. Martin."

"That name's familiar. Isn't she a friend of Miranda's?"

Quinn nodded. "They were roommates at Quantico."

"Do you think it'll help?"

"Olivia would do anything to help Miranda. She'll come; I just have to ask. It was too late to call last night when I thought of the idea. There are few lab techs as dedicated as Olivia, and she specializes in trace evidence."

"Whatever you think will help catch this bastard."

"If there's anything in the evidence, Olivia will find it. Then we just need a suspect." It sounded so easy. But they had no suspects. Not even a hint of one.

Nine girls missing, seven dead. The missing girls were presumed to be victims of the Butcher because their cars had been found disabled two to four miles from their last stop.

After Miranda and Sharon's disappearance, the joint FBI–Sheriff's investigation yielded a bare-bones M.O.: the assailant disabled the victims' car by pouring molasses into the gas tank when they stopped for food, gas, or to use the rest room. He followed them until they broke down, and probably offered to help fix their car or give them a lift.

Quinn suspected that the assailant looked nonthreatening, was known to the victims, or caught them unaware when they got out of the car to flag down a motorist.

Even though Miranda was their only witness, Quinn didn't think her story was typical of the other abductions. In fact, he suspected either the Butcher had thought Sharon was alone or didn't think Miranda would return so quickly after trying to get help.

After Miranda led investigators to the shack, she told Quinn what had happened that night.

It still gave him chills thinking about it.

"Sharon and I went to Missoula to shop. A day trip. We decided to catch a movie."

Miranda paused, and her father reached over with water. She sipped through a straw. "Dad, would you mind finding a soda for me? I'd love a Coke."

"Of course." Bill Moore touched his daughter on the cheek, then left the room.

When the door closed, Miranda looked at Quinn and said, "He's hurting so much, I didn't want him to hear this."

Quinn kept his surprise to himself, but Miranda never ceased to impress him. After what she'd been through, that she'd think first of sparing her father's feelings showed her solid character as much as, if not more than, her will to survive.

She lay on the hospital bed, her black hair limp but clean against the stark white sheets. Her face pale, bruised — a bandage circled her head, her eyes were swollen and purple. Across her entire body, small and large cuts were covered with bandages.

He knew from the doctor's report that she'd been raped multiple times; that she'd needed dozens of stitches on her legs and stomach and breasts from cuts made by a sharp object; that she'd been tortured with a metal vise.

That she'd survived and escaped when everything was stacked against her amazed him.

That she was willing to discuss what had happened and help them find the bastard who did this to her and killed her best friend showed more character and spine than most of the agents Quinn had worked with possessed.

"The movie let out after nine," she said, "and by the time we were on the road it was ten. We were in Sharon's car, one of those Volkswagen bugs. I used to give her such a hard time about it." Tears welled up in Miranda's eyes, but she continued. *"I mean, it was stuck for months in the winter because she couldn't drive it in the snow or ice, the battery would be deader than a*

doornail when the snow melted . . ." Her voice trailed off and she swallowed. "But Sharon loved Herbie. You know, named after the Love Bug."

Quinn didn't push her, even when she closed her eyes. The trail of tears sliding down her face tore at him. He'd worked with many victims, in all states of hysteria, but something about Miranda's grief hit him hard. He found himself wanting to console her with more than words.

She continued on her own and he focused on taking notes.

"We stopped in Three Forks because Herbie was running out of gas, and I didn't think we'd make it to the Lodge, even though we were less than thirty miles away. Sharon was always doing that, running the car on fumes. Three times since I've known her she called me to bring her gas." She smiled at the bittersweet memory.

"We were hungry, and there was a fast-food place there, so we popped in for fries and a Coke and ate inside, because Sharon didn't like anyone eating in Herbie."

Again, she paused, but her eyes were open, staring at the ceiling. What was she looking at? Remembering? Trying to forget?

"Then we left. About five minutes later, Herbie started jerking, and a mile out of Manhattan he just stopped. Sputtered and died." She paused. "I should never have told her to stop. We might have had enough gas to get home. If only I'd—"

"Stop, Miranda," Quinn said, then cleared his throat. "Excuse me, Ms. Moore."

"That's okay. My name is Miranda."

"You can't think about what you might have done differently. None of this was your fault. It was all his fault. You have to know that."

"The press is calling him the Bozeman Butcher."

Quinn grimaced. "I hate the press."

"I'm beginning to," she said quietly. He wondered if she'd seen the picture of her being lifelined out of the valley. He'd hoped the hospital staff would have kept her from seeing the papers or watching the news. He'd already yelled at the sheriff for some of the details that had been released, not only about Miranda's condition but the investigation itself.

But now was not the time to think about that. He asked, "What happened after the car broke down?"

"I teased her. I teased her about Herbie and how she loved him too much."

She took a deep breath and continued. "I know the area and remembered that there's a pay phone at this little gas station that closes at dark. I was going to call my dad and have him pick us up."

"Why didn't you?"

"I was headed there. I was just around the bend, two, three hundred yards away, when a car came up behind me. It was two old people and they offered to give me a lift. I told them what happened, and they had a car phone. I mean, I don't know anyone who has a phone in their car, except the mayor. They let me use it to call my dad. He said he'd pick us up in twenty minutes."

She looked at him with such agony. "Why didn't I take the ride? Maybe they would have scared him off and Sharon would still be alive." She stopped, her voice catching. "I told them my dad was coming, to go ahead and I'd wait with Sharon."

"Miranda, you had every reason to feel safe."

"Nothing bad happens here. I never thought—" She stopped, stifled a sob, then continued. "I went back and Sharon wasn't there. I mean, she wasn't in the car. I called for her and she screamed for help."

"Where was she?"

"In the gully by the side of the road. I thought animal, bear, something — I didn't have a gun, I mean I have one, but I don't carry it around, you know? I yelled, tried to scare away whatever animal had terrified Sharon, and, and . . ." She stopped.

"And?"

"Nothing. I heard a sound behind me, I

turned, and . . ." She paused, thinking. "I smelled something sweet. Sickly sweet. My head hurt, then nothing."

She looked at him again, her eyes bright with emotional pain.

"Nothing until I woke up chained to a floor. I didn't know why I was so cold until I realized I had no clothes on."

Nick's office doubled as the task force room for the Butcher investigation. A map of the region south of the interstate all the way to West Yellowstone filled a good part of one wall. Colored pins marked where women had disappeared, where their bodies were found, and where they were held captive. A fine line traced the most likely route of their escape based on the evidence.

Except for Sharon, none of the seven known victims had made it more than two miles. Sharon had been killed four miles from the shack; Miranda had fallen into the river another half-mile away.

The remainder of the wall displayed a timeline with photographs and bullet-point information in Nick's small, neat block letters.

Quinn walked over to the board and reviewed the information he knew by heart, pleading for something to jump out at him.

Penny Thompson. Missing: 5/14/91.

Car abandoned in gully off Interstate 191, 2.7 miles from Super Joe's Stop-n-Go.

Penny filled her car at the Stop-n-Go at 10:46 p.m. Used rest room. Purchased a large Diet Pepsi and pretzels. Left approximately 10:55 p.m.

There had been no security camera on the pumps where Penny had left her vehicle.

At the time, the police treated Penny's case as a Missing Person with possible foul play. Because there was a small amount of blood on the steering wheel and it appeared her car crashed into the gulley, they never ruled out an accidental death. They didn't know they had a serial killer; Sheriff Donaldson felt her ex-boyfriend had killed her and dumped her car as a ruse, but couldn't find any proof to support his accusation. It wasn't until three years later that she was recognized as the likely first victim of the Butcher.

Two years later, Dora Feliciano disappeared. She didn't own a vehicle, but was walking home from work in downtown Bozeman. There was still a question as to whether the Butcher was responsible for her disappearance. The Sheriff's Department looked heavily at her live-in boyfriend, who had no alibi for the time, but no solid evidence connected him with her disappearance.

It wasn't until Colleen Thorne, Quinn's partner, came to Montana three years ago, after the Croft sisters disappeared, that Dora was even put on the board. Colleen's reasoning was that the Butcher was still developing his strategy. Dora had been an easy target — walking alone late at night. Bozeman was a low-crime town; most women used to feel safe.

Miranda Moore and Sharon Lewis. Disappeared 5/27/94. Sharon killed 6/2. Miranda found by Sheriff's search team.

Quinn's entire body shuddered remembering how close Miranda had been to dying. What she'd endured at the hands of the Butcher, her will to live, her escape.

The information on Miranda's sheet was longer, more detailed. That was when they'd realized they had a premeditated abduction on their hands. That they had a serial killer. They went back to Penny Thompson's case, but her father had long since gotten rid of her car and when the police tracked it down, the new owner said the carburetor had been so gummed up that he'd picked up a rebuilt carb and replaced it. The original had been junked.

In June of 1997, Susan Kramer and her roommate Jenny Williams disappeared. They immediately were considered victims of the Butcher because their abandoned car had molasses in the gas tank. Four months later, deer hunters came across Susan's body. It wasn't in good condition, but was identifiable through the autopsy. She'd been shot in the leg and chest.

Jenny's body was never found.

Nineteen ninety-nine was a banner year for the Butcher, Quinn thought with disgust. Three missing women from the University, all abducted separately, three weeks apart, starting on April twenty-eighth. None of their bodies was ever recovered. And in 2001 another woman, a freshman biology major from Florida, disappeared, leaving behind her disabled car three miles from her last stop.

Karen Papadopoulis's case was different only in that her body was discovered before her vehicle, which had been concealed off a little-used road west of Old Norris in neighboring Madison County. She'd been shot in the thigh by a high-velocity rifle, but that wasn't what killed her.

Her throat had been slit.

Quinn turned from the board with the familiar uneasy anger that the Butcher was smart and cunning and would keep on killing until he made a mistake. But he hadn't made a mistake yet.

"So we know the unsub has a vehicle," Quinn said as he paced. "But he can't drive all the way to the shack. All the women were slight, under 130 pounds. A man in shape could carry them."

"Or drag them on a makeshift sled."

"True, but we haven't seen evidence of that type of tracks, have we?"

Nick shook his head and pinched the bridge of his nose. "Okay, so he carried the girls up there. Sometimes two."

"Separately?"

"Most likely."

The Butcher was patient. Methodical. A planner. He had to have laid out his route before the abductions; the shack would have been prepared with chains and a lock on the door. He was strong enough to transport a slender woman over steep terrain, probably driving a four-wheel-drive as close as he could get before hoofing it.

They'd never found evidence that he used a horse, but Quinn couldn't rule it out. Since the Butcher was methodical, he could have painstakingly covered up horse tracks.

Quinn focused again on the map, his chin resting on his hand.

"The cabins are all fairly close, three to five miles, to some sort of road, or an unused, overgrown trail," he said. It wasn't a new revelation; he was simply trying to think of the investigation from another angle. "We've already determined that he's strong, but in addition to muscles, he has to be accustomed to long, arduous manual labor.

"Nothing came of the property search," Quinn continued. They'd run ownership records in the areas the other women were held in and came back with as many owners as cabins. "What about where Rebecca was found?"

"It's private property, a thousand-acre spread owned by a Hollywood type. He comes up once, twice a year. He probably doesn't even know the shack is on his land. His spread is on the other end."

"Have you checked him out?"

Nick paused. "No."

Quinn frowned. "What about his house?"

"He has a caretaker."

"I'll go check it out."

Nick's jaw tightened, and Quinn suspected Nick felt he'd neglected something. While it was an important avenue in the investigation, Quinn also worried Nick would feel threatened, especially after the negative spotlight the press was shining on the Sheriff's Department.

"It's a long shot," he told Nick. Nick didn't look placated.

"I'll go pull the records on the property. Be back in a minute." Nick left.

Quinn watched him close the door and frowned. Nick was letting the press get to him, and that wasn't a good sign. Colleen had given him a rundown, and labeled the Sheriff's Department under Nick's command as "very competent," but noted that the previous sheriff had been more lax in his reports and investigation, particularly with the missing girls. Quinn made a mental note to call Colleen in the morning and see if she had any further insight.

He turned back to the board. The key profile points of the Butcher were listed on the far right.

White male age 35–45.

Born or raised in Montana; superior knowledge of area.

Familiar with MSU; former student, professor or staff.

Molasses in the gas tank to disable the car; is there a reason for this trademark, or just convenience and effectiveness?

During World War II, American troops had disabled German tanks with sugar. It was a well-known tactic, displayed prominently on revenge-oriented websites. The FBI profiler Vigo considered that the Butcher might have once been in the military, but dismissed it. "He wouldn't have volunteered, and he's too young to have been drafted," he'd told Quinn twelve years ago.

They had a list of all the students, professors, and staff that fit the profile at the time Miranda was abducted. There were hundreds of them.

When they learned Penny was probably the first victim, it was three years too late. They still ran the records, ending up with hundreds of white males under thirty-five who had had contact with Penny on at least a casual basis.

Nick stepped back into the room and handed Quinn a note. "Here's the information about the spread, the caretaker, and the owner."

"Thanks." Quinn pocketed the slip of paper. "Where are the files from the Penny Thompson investigation?"

"In archives."

"Including the University records?"

"Hers? Or the suspects'?"

"All the men who had known her."

"Those totaled in the hundreds."

"I know."

"They were returned to the University."

Shit. He'd have to get a warrant because of the Privacy Act.

Quinn ran a hand through his hair. "We need to get them back. We've already determined that Penny was likely the first victim. After fifteen years, we can rule out most of those men on the list, but we have to go through them one by one. Cross off those who are married, dead, or moved far from the area. It at least gives us a place to start."

"It sounds like a long shot."

"I don't know that anything will come of it," Quinn said, his voice surprisingly bitter. "I really hate serial killers. They're smarter, shrewder, harder to pin down. Their mistakes are usually small. But this is all we've got."

Quinn didn't want to jump down Nick's throat again. He'd already made it clear this morning that following up on Penny's abduction was crucial.

Instead, he asked, "Did you ever wonder why the killer didn't come after Miranda after she escaped?"

Nick looked surprised. "Actually, no."

"I have. I've thought about it a lot. All my training says that the killer would hate her for getting away, a mistake, his screwup. He considers himself superior to women, or feels a driving need to prove his superiority because he felt inferior as a boy. He hates women. It's about control. Domination. But he couldn't control Miranda.

"The fact that Miranda got away should enrage him," Quinn continued. "But he's never gone after her. Which leaves me with the conclusion that he's proud of her in some fashion. Or, that he keeps her alive to remind him of something. The hunt, or that he lost his prize."

"That she beat him in the hunt?"

Quinn rubbed his forehead. "It just doesn't make sense. He should want revenge. He should have gone after her. Instead, it's as if he respects her enough to stay away.

"And that, Nick, goes against the grain and makes me think we could be looking in all the wrong places."

CHAPTER
13

By the time Quinn pulled up next to Miranda's Jeep at the Lodge, it was nearly midnight and he was physically exhausted. His mind, however, had different plans and moved in all directions.

The lights were on in the restaurant and he saw Miranda's father and his jack-of-all-trades partner Ben Grayhawk sitting at the bar. Bill motioned him over, and Quinn slid onto the stool next to him.

"Bill. Gray. Good to see you again."

Gray held up his glass of amber liquid and arched his brow in question. "It's the good stuff."

"Thanks," Quinn said. A double Scotch might slow down his mind enough so that he could sleep a couple of hours.

Bill reached above the bar and picked a glass off the rack, then poured Quinn a hefty shot from a half-empty bottle of Glenlivet.

"*Salut*," Bill said.

Quinn raised his glass and took a long sip. The Scotch slid down his throat like liquid glass and he sighed approvingly.

They sat in silence for several minutes. "You didn't tell Miranda I was here," Quinn said.

Bill shook his head. "I didn't want an argument. Randy can be mighty stubborn."

"I don't want to interfere with your relationship," Quinn said.

"You won't."

"I appreciate the hospitality."

Bill finished his Scotch and poured a short shot. "Randy says you found the shack where poor Rebecca Douglas was held."

"Yeah. She's a good tracker." Better than good, Quinn thought.

"Damn straight. She's a smart girl," Gray said.

Quinn remembered his interview with Ryan Parker and his friends. "Gray, I meant to ask you. Did you talk to Ryan Parker about an old Indian burial ground up north of the ridge? Few miles east of the river?"

Gray cracked a smile, revealing crooked white teeth. "Yeah, I did. The boys come down here on their horses on occasion; we have some good trails for exploring. They'd heard about it, of course. Kids at school say it's haunted, and you can only find it at night on a full moon." He croaked out a laugh, then coughed.

"You been there?"

Gray shook his head. "Naw. Don't even know if it really exists. Suspect it does; I've heard of the place since I was a boy. But my ma never knew where it was. We were always looking for it, though. Kept us out of trouble." He paused. "Does this have to do something with the murder?"

Quinn shook his head. "Doubt it. Just checking the kids' story."

"Ryan's a good boy," Gray said.

"You close to the Parkers?"

"Not really. But I teach a gun safety class. Had Ryan last year with the older McClain boy. And like I said, they ride our trails around here, I want to make sure they know the rules."

Bill stood. "You're welcome to sit down here as long as you like, or take the bottle to your room. I need to be up early, so I'd best be hitting the sack."

Quinn drained his glass and shook his head. "Thanks for the conversation." He bid them farewell and went up to his room.

An hour later, he was still awake. His mind couldn't stop thinking about why the Butcher never went after Miranda again. Somehow, he thought it was important, but for the life of him, he didn't know why.

He turned on the lights and sat at the desk. He jotted cryptic notes to himself that only he could understand.

Vigo. Hans Vigo was a top profiler with the department, as well as a friend. Maybe he had some new insights.

Old cases. He needed to review the case files of the victims again. Maybe there was a common thread — other than their gender and age — that tied them all together. Or maybe Miranda was unique. Why? Why was she spared? Yes, she escaped, but she'd have been considered a liability.

Wouldn't she?

Penny Thompson.

First thing in the morning, Quinn planned to head over to the University and pull every string he knew to get those old records.

Olivia.

It was two in the morning in Virginia, far too late to call Olivia, though he knew she wouldn't mind. He'd call her in the morning and ask if she had some time to help with trace evidence at the state laboratory in Helena. It would take diplomacy to bring a federal crime tech into the state lab, but Quinn was confident in both his ability to maneuver it and Olivia's ability to keep the relationship cordial.

Finally, he realized why he couldn't sleep. Hunger. He and Nick had grabbed a quick burger that he'd left half-eaten at the station.

Knowing Bill wouldn't mind if he raided the kitchen, Quinn went downstairs to make himself a sandwich.

Sharon slept and Miranda planned.

There had to be a way out. Some way. Any way.

Though blindfolded, she knew it was daytime. Not because of the light, but because of the lack of cold.

She didn't think she'd ever be warm again. At night she feared she'd freeze to death. But it never got that cold. Just cold enough that she couldn't stop shivering. Just cold enough that she couldn't feel her fingers and toes.

She'd gotten past wishing for her down comforter or hot coffee. At this point, warmth was a luxury. Survival was the only thing on her mind.

Two things clawed at her.

Would he keep them here forever? Feeding them bread and water and making them lie in their own filth?

Or would he kill them when he tired of hurting them?

Freedom wasn't an option. She sensed without him saying anything that he'd never release them. For the first three days she'd pleaded with him. But she knew. His lack of response told her he had no intention of ever letting them go.

She must have dozed off, because the sound of metal on metal startled her.

Click click.

He was unlocking the door of the room they lay in. She squirmed, her instincts demanding that she flee, but she was trapped on the floor, chained to the rough, cold wood.

Not again. Not again.

The rattle of chains woke Sharon. "No!" she screamed through her raw throat. "No, no! Please!" She started sobbing, but Miranda remained silent.

She had no more tears, no more pleas. He was coming to rape them or kill them. She was going to die.

Daddy, I love you. I love you and I'm so sorry. I hope you never know what happened to me. It would tear you apart.

She missed her father, longed to see him and have him hold her and stroke her hair, like he did when she was a little girl after her mother died.

"She's in Heaven, darling," he'd tell her, then murmur pretty words about what a wonderful, beautiful, painless place Heaven was.

Miranda didn't know what awaited her. Would she see the mother she barely remembered? Was it a paradise like her father had told her?

Or was there nothing?

Nothing would be better than what she'd endured these last five days. Five? Six days? She'd tried to keep track, but she didn't know. It may have been longer.

It was a small room. One step. Two steps. Sharon screamed.

"Don't touch me! Don't touch me!"

At the rattle of chains, Miranda swallowed her own terror. Hearing Sharon being hurt heightened her fear. Because what happened to Sharon happened to her next.

"What?" Sharon sounded confused.

Then Miranda felt her arms being lifted. The clank of metal on metal and suddenly she was untied.

A faint sliver of hope swelled in her chest.

He'd had them blindfolded, right? They couldn't identify him. Would he let them go?

Were they free?

Her legs were next.

"Stand."

A one-word command. She tried to stand, but stumbled and collapsed. "I — can't." She'd tried to keep her muscles strong through exercises, but she'd been flat on her back for so long her limbs no longer felt connected to her body. Sores ran up and down her back. Cuts had bled and dried.

"One hour. Use it well."

One step, and the door shut. Locked. Five words, the most he'd ever said to them at one time. But the voice remained unfamiliar, a dry monotone. Hollow and empty.

"He's going to let us go!" Sharon cried.

Miranda smelled something over the foul stench of her own body odor. She crawled over to the door, felt around.

Bread. Water.

"Sharon," she said. "Food."

Sharon bumped against her and they ate on the ground, huddled over their solitary slice of bread, drinking a small cup of water.

Miranda reached up and touched her blindfold. She'd almost forgotten it was there, it had become such a part of her.

The knot was tight and she was weak, but she took it off. Sharon did the same thing.

She was blind.

No, it was dark.

It took several minutes for Miranda to make out faint streams of light coming through knots in the wood of the windowless shack they'd been tied in for days. Sharon grabbed a shirt in the corner. It wasn't hers; it wasn't Miranda's.

Dear God, had there been someone before them?

Sharon put it on. "I'm sorry, Randy, I'm sorry. I'm so cold."

"It's okay," she said.

Miranda stretched her limbs as best she could, and like a baby learning to walk, pulled herself up using the wall in front of her.

Slowly, the feeling in her body returned. First tingles, then sharp pain.

"Work your muscles out, Sharon."

"But he's going to let us go."

"We don't know that. We need to be prepared."

"But I can't."

Sharon huddled in the corner, her arms around her legs, rocking.

"Do it!" Miranda commanded. She didn't want to yell at her friend, but she realized quickly that she had to be the strong one and take control of the situation. This was their chance to escape. She didn't know why their captor had untied them, but she would fight to the death before being chained to the floor again.

Sharon looked mad, but slowly she, too, pulled herself up and walked around the room, which wasn't more than ten feet by ten feet. Miranda tried the door, shook it with what little strength she had.

Locked. From the outside.

They used the hour well, stretching. Walking. And slowly, surprisingly, gathering back some strength.

Clink clink.

The door opened and light poured in.

"Come here."

206

They obeyed, scrambled outside, and Miranda stumbled to the ground.

Freedom.

She heard the distinct sound of a round being chambered into a rifle.

"Run."

Miranda looked over her shoulder. The man stood in the shadows, a mask over his face, late-afternoon light reflecting off the barrel of his gun.

The realization sucker-punched Miranda. He wanted to hunt them.

"Run. You have two minutes." He paused. "Run!"

She ran.

Miranda awoke with a start.

Run.

She'd heard his voice.

Sweat poured from her body. She sat up and blinked, swallowing a scream, surprised to find her gun in her hand. When had she grabbed it? In her sleep?

His voice.

No, it was her nightmare. The damn nightmare. He was in her head, taunting her. She had escaped. She had lived. But Sharon was dead. Shot in the back. And Rebecca, hunted down and killed, her neck sliced open like game.

Miranda blinked again, her hands shaking as she forced herself to put down the gun. Moonlight cascaded through the skylights, casting blue-gray shadows across her room.

Her bed was in shambles, the sheets twisted and damp, blankets on the floor. Her flannel pajamas were drenched in her perspiration, the tangible scent of her memories on her skin.

It wasn't even two in the morning. Four hours of sleep — she was surprised she'd collapsed so quickly after coming home. But she doubted she'd sleep another minute tonight.

She showered the sweat of fear off her skin, dressed in jeans, a turtleneck, and her heavy parka since the May nights were still cool, then left for the Lodge, Gray's famous pecan pie beckoning her.

She walked in through the side door, which was illuminated by a spotlight. The door was locked, but she had a master key. She crossed the dining hall and was about to enter the kitchen when she heard something.

She paused, her heart beating almost as fast as it had after her nightmare.

Scrape. Scrape. Creak. Then silence.

Tap tap tap.

Silence.

Someone was in the kitchen. Though the

moonlight illuminated the Lodge through picture windows, no lights were on. If it were a guest, her father, or an employee, they'd have switched on the lights.

An intruder.

She reached for the gun she'd stuffed in her fanny pack. She hadn't left home without a gun for twelve years. Cautious but determined, she approached the main kitchen door.

Tap tap scrape.

Bracing herself just inside the door, she reached for the light switch with her left hand while holding her right arm — the one with the gun — steady in front of her.

She mentally counted to three, then hit the switch and cocked her revolver.

A tall, half-naked man spun around, a fork toppling off his plate onto the floor.

"Shit, Miranda! Put the gun down."

She did, as her mouth fell open. No words came out.

The last person she expected to see creeping around the kitchen was Quinn Peterson.

CHAPTER
14

Miranda stuffed the gun back into the waistband of her jeans and stared at Quinn. "What are you doing here?"

"I called your dad from the road and he had a room. I didn't think we'd run into each other. I figured I'd maybe be here four, five hours sleeping." He put his plate down on the table. Pecan pie. *Her* pecan pie.

"That had better not be the last piece of pie," Miranda mumbled. Why had she said that? She'd meant to tell him to get the hell off her property.

He smiled, and Miranda blinked. She kept forgetting how good-looking Quinn really was. When she'd seen him the other day, she was so filled with rage and sadness and conflicting emotions she didn't dwell on his appearance. But seeing him now, his lean, tanned chest bare, his muscles clearly defined even though he was at ease, the scar on his upper right shoulder from a gunshot wound early in his career — it brought back memories. Good memories. Of waking up with Quinn and kissing that hard chest. And his hands — he had the most incredible hands. Large hands, callused palms, with surprisingly elegant fingers. Very talented fingers . . .

She glanced down to where a narrow trail of dark blond hair disappeared beneath the waistband of his gray sweats. She quickly averted her gaze, already feeling flushed from the adrenaline released when she'd thought he was an intruder.

Having Quinn here, in her kitchen, without the security of work, jerked the rug out from under her. He'd invaded her town, her investigation, and now her home. She hadn't thought about that day at Quantico — consciously — in years, and wham! The dam broke and she could think of nothing but.

She had no idea what he'd done in the last ten years. He could be married for all she knew. That thought disturbed her and she frowned. Brushing past him, she went to the cupboard where Gray kept his pies.

Sure enough, there was half a pecan pie sitting there, calling her name. She couldn't help but smile.

She took her time cutting a slice, feeling

Quinn's eyes burrowing into her back. She really didn't want to sit down and talk to him. Outside of the Lodge, in the woods, with Nick and the others around — that was one thing. But here, alone? No. It reminded her of their former intimacy. Reminded her how she once loved him. Reminded her of what could have been.

But she couldn't keep her back to him forever. She put her pie on the table, then crossed over to the large, walk-in refrigerator and retrieved a gallon of milk. She set it on the table, along with two glasses. She poured one for herself and one for Quinn, then sat across from him.

"Thanks," he said. His dark eyes were unreadable. What was he thinking? About her? About them?

She drank her milk, then dug into her pie. If her mouth was full she wouldn't talk, wouldn't say something stupid.

He continued to watch her.

She resisted the urge to squirm. During the past several years she'd regained control over her life, built a sense of relative peace. She had a job she loved, a job that did some good, even if she hadn't been able to find Rebecca before she was killed.

She had a few good friends. Nick. She still kept in touch with Rowan and Olivia, though she hadn't actually seen them in years. They e-mailed and talked on the phone, but for Miranda it was hard to get away. Impossible. She couldn't just up and leave Montana when *he* was still out there.

She loved Rowan and Liv like sisters, but how could she abandon those who needed her? Particularly the dead. Rowan and Liv understood that — they might be the only people who did.

"I should have told you I was staying here," Quinn said, breaking the silence.

She looked up from her pie. She noted he'd taken the bandage off his forehead. A thin, dark red scab remained, a reminder of his last assignment. She wanted to ask him about it, but didn't. She didn't want to care.

His firm, set jaw reminded her of his strength. He had been steadfast when she first met him. Resolved to find Sharon's killer. She'd helped him because she needed to do something to find the bastard who hurt her and killed Sharon. And then she'd fallen in love.

It didn't happen overnight. Time to heal, time to get beyond the pain — Quinn gave her everything she needed and more.

Then he ripped it all away.

"The techs preserved everything they could at the shack, and it's headed out to

Helena tomorrow. I decided to call Olivia and ask her to oversee the laboratory tests."

"Liv? She's coming here?"

"To Helena, if she can get away." He grinned. "Sometimes, threatening to take over an investigation will light some fires. They'd much rather take care of the tests themselves, even with a Fed looking over their shoulder, than have everything shipped to Virginia."

"Whatever it takes," Miranda said, with little hope. Even Olivia, who loved her job and excelled at it, couldn't find a clue where none existed. The climate and conditions destroyed any usable evidence.

"He'll make a mistake," Quinn said with confidence.

"Right." She didn't believe it.

"He might have already."

Her heart beat faster. "Why do you think that?"

"Penny Thompson."

"Why bring her up? Her murder was three years old when we found her body." What remained of it.

"I'm pulling all the University files again. Remember Vigo, the FBI profiler? He insists the killer knew his first victim personally. We spent so much time twelve years ago investigating the associations of you and Sharon

214

that by the time we learned Penny was the first victim, going back to her associations — then three years old — yielded us nothing. Her boyfriend, the guy the sheriff thought responsible for Penny's disappearance, had an airtight alibi during Sharon's murder."

Quinn added, "We're going to focus on the parts of Vigo's profile that would help narrow the list even more after so many years have passed — that the killer would remain single, would now be over thirty-five, that he has a flexible job, is physically fit, and has family in the area, or still lives here. It's worth a shot."

"It's a long shot," she said, she became a little excited. There would be hundreds of records to pore through and investigate, hundreds of men who on the surface fit the profile. But time would have weeded out many potential suspects, those who'd married, who'd moved out of the country, whose jobs were high-profile and inflexible. If they could narrow the list they would be able to dig deeper into those potential suspects and, with any luck, come up with a handful to interview. Maybe even get a warrant to search a car or house, especially if one of the suspects didn't have an alibi for the time of Rebecca's murder.

Maybe there was hope that justice would

win. Just a little. But she would hold tight to it.

"Right now, it's all we have." Quinn paused, then said in a low voice, "Miranda?"

She looked into his eyes, eyes that could melt her or anger her, eyes that reflected love or frustration.

It had been so long, she no longer knew how to read Quinn. He had changed. So had she.

His eyes were warm. The lids lowered almost imperceptibly. His face softened and he leaned forward just an inch. "You've lost weight," he said, his voice low.

"I know." She simply didn't think about eating when she was out on a search.

"You're still beautiful."

Her breath caught. Was that her heart fluttering? How could he still affect her so profoundly? After all these years, he remained part of her. An important part. He'd helped make her who she was today, both the good and the bad. Without him, she didn't know if she'd have been able to survive the darkest days, weeks, months after the attack. He'd been her rock, her salvation. Steady and sure, she'd fallen in love with him as much as for who he was as for what he did for her.

That he had such little faith in her after knowing her so intimately tore her up inside.

As if he'd read her mind, he asked softly, "Why didn't you come back to Quantico?"

What could she say to that? She didn't completely understand it herself. Except that his lack of faith and trust in her hurt more than the psychology test that said she had a problem with obsession.

"If I'm obsessive, a year wouldn't change it," she finally said.

"A year can make all the difference in the world."

"It had been two years, Quinn." Two years since her life was irrevocably linked with a killer.

He nodded, leaned back in his chair and fiddled with his fork. "I know."

They stared at each other. Quinn looked as lost and confused as she felt.

"I'm sorry I hurt you," he said suddenly.

She swallowed back tears. How could such a simple apology hit her so hard?

Because she knew it wasn't just Quinn. She *was* obsessive. There was her intense focus on the search — she'd put everything in her life on hold while looking for Rebecca. Her friends and family took second place to her job, whether it was finding a missing woman abducted by the Butcher or a lost child who'd wandered away from his campground. Nothing mattered to her except the search.

She wanted to *rescue* someone. While she'd had success finding lost campers, any woman the Butcher got was as good as dead. She desperately longed for a happy ending, but everywhere she looked there was sorrow and pain. Maybe that was simply a reflection of her own guilt.

If her reaction at the cabin was any indication, she'd never fully recovered from the attack twelve years ago. She would always be claustrophobic in small rooms. Windowless rooms. That's why she had skylights throughout her house and directly above her bed. She had to see the sky no matter which direction she looked.

But even the big sky couldn't stop Sharon's cries and the low, cruel monotone of the faceless killer every time Miranda closed her eyes.

"I should have returned to Quantico." She had never said that out loud before. It surprised her. She licked her lips. "I was just so damn hu—" She was going to say hurt. No. She wasn't ready to tell Quinn that. She couldn't tell him. "Angry," she corrected. "Blinded by anger, I suppose. And by the time the year was up, I was on Search and Rescue and I really liked it. I fit in. It's — I suppose it's what I'm cut out to do."

"You would have made a damn good

agent," he said, his voice gravelly.

Her heart skipped a beat. She wondered what he would do if she kissed him.

The stray thought startled her and she leaned back, her hands clammy. A good agent? Yeah, she knew it. A *damn* good agent.

One year. A year! She'd waited more than *two years* after the Butcher killed Sharon, restless, taking extra classes, working at the Lodge, learning self-defense. Anything and everything so she'd never feel vulnerable again.

When she walked out of Quantico ten years ago, she'd never felt more lost. She knew then she would never go back.

"Thanks." Her voice cracked. She wanted to yell at him, rage at the injustice of what he'd done — regardless of the reasons. Maybe there was a hint of truth in what he'd said, something she had done that indicated she might not be able to handle the job.

She focused on her pie and milk. Quinn did the same. The silence was both comfortable and awkward — she wanted to know what he was really thinking, but didn't have the guts to ask. She wanted to tell him she'd never forgive him, yet she wanted to extend an olive branch at the same time. The conflicting emotions weighed heavily on her heart and mind.

She and Quinn rose from the table at the same time and brought their plates to the sink. She ran water over them, waiting for it to get hot. He stood behind her, so close his warm, pecan-scented breath caressed her neck. She swallowed, not trusting herself to turn around. Not trusting herself not to touch him, kiss him, ask him to share her bed.

She wanted him to hold her so she could sleep. To love him so she could remember what had been the most wonderful time of her life.

His hands rested on her shoulders, so lightly she didn't flinch. She closed her eyes. He brushed her hair away from her neck, his long finger drawing a sizzling path from her ear to her throat. With his other hand, he turned her to face him.

When she opened her eyes, her mouth parted. He was so close, his naked chest inches from her. She felt the heat between them, as if he had his own thermostat. She swallowed, wanted to tell him to step back, but couldn't find her voice.

She was glad she didn't.

His lips touched hers so tenderly, if she hadn't felt the jolt of desire flood her body, she'd have doubted he'd kissed her at all.

Then he kissed her again, more firmly, his

hand moving from her shoulder to the back of her neck, kneading her muscles, holding her head to him. Deeper, his tongue gently parted her lips until their tongues lightly dueled, back and forth. She leaned into him, tentative at first, then found her arms wrapped around his neck, holding him close.

His kisses moved from her lips, down her jaw, to her neck. She shivered from the heat, from wanting him. A deep yearning that bespoke ten years without him. Without the man who knew exactly where to kiss, where to touch.

He softly kissed her behind her ear.

"I've missed you, Miranda."

She drew in her breath. Had he really missed her? For ten years she'd had to consciously keep Quinn in the far corners of her heart and mind because she didn't want to think about him, didn't want to miss him.

But now the dam had broken, and her repressed feelings rushed through the floodgates. For ten years it had been so much easier to pretend Quinn hadn't been such an important part of her life the short time she'd known him; now, it was like the time between hadn't existed. She still loved him, still wanted him, but the raw ache that had festered since his declaration at Quantico stabbed at her heart.

She stepped back and bumped into the kitchen counter. "Quinn — I don't know what I'm supposed to say to that."

"Why did you avoid me back then?" He squeezed her shoulders, his eyes shining with the same heat and desire she felt.

She shook her head. She couldn't have this conversation now, not when her emotions were so close to the surface. His affection confused her; it was much easier to remember his hardened stance against her graduation, his emphatic statements about her abilities when they first saw each other where Rebecca had died.

"I need to go."

"Miranda, don't walk away again. We need to talk."

Shaking her head, she pulled away from his hold. She had to think, impossible to do around Quinn. Her blood seemed to boil and bubble beneath her skin, her stomach churned with confusion and heartache and love all mixed up. Nothing made sense to her. It had been so much easier to exist, to control her emotions, before Quinn walked back into her life.

She glanced at him, saw frustration cross his expression. She turned and ran back to her cabin, feeling like a coward but not knowing what else to do.

Quinn stared after Miranda's retreating frame, his chest tight. He turned to the sink and noticed the running water. Had it been on the entire time? He slapped off the faucet.

What had just happened?

He thought at least she was opening up to him. She had softened her feelings toward him. That there was hope —

And that kiss. Time or distance made her taste even sweeter. He wanted more.

What was he thinking? That they could pick up where they'd left off? That he could tell her he still loved her and they could start talking marriage?

Quinn had never stopped loving Miranda. She irritated him, annoyed him, angered him, but he'd loved her almost from the beginning. He was proud of her, admired her intelligence, her strength, her perseverance. She was so beautiful. Seeing her sitting across from him eating pecan pie reminded him of ten years ago when he'd spent a two-week vacation here, at the Lodge. In her cabin. When they snuck into the kitchen to eat pecan pie and barely made it back to her cabin to make love.

He didn't have time for long-term relationships; he'd been involved with a few women over the years, but only briefly. None of them could compare to Miranda. Some were prettier, some were smarter, but none were *Miranda*. Her spark. Her strength. *Her.*

What had she been thinking? Why couldn't she just answer his question? He'd half expected her to jump down his throat, to yell at him about his decision at Quantico. He hadn't expected to see so much raw, needy emotion in her fathomless eyes.

Damn, damn, damn! He wanted to follow her, to explain his reasons again about why he'd pulled her from the Academy. She'd focused on the psychiatrist's opinion about her obsession with the Butcher, but that was only part of his reasoning. If it was only the shrink, Quinn would never have agreed to remove her from the program.

What Miranda had never understood, and he'd obviously failed to make her understand, was that her reasons for wanting to become an agent were all wrong. Working for the FBI wouldn't give her what she thought it would, and he feared she would have been miserable.

Maybe he should have let her be miserable. But he loved her too much, and she was too loyal a person to quit when she realized she'd romanticized the role of an FBI agent.

Plain and simple, she'd wanted to be an

FBI agent so she would have the authority to track down the Butcher. She'd never have been satisfied working in, say, Florida or Maine or California — unless the Butcher started hunting in one of those states. And she very well might have been assigned to the cyber squad, robberies, or political corruption — none of which would bring her any closer to facing down her demons.

He'd hoped that after a year off she'd come to realize that either she didn't want to be an agent at all or that she could put the Butcher far enough behind her to work on whatever the Bureau assigned to her.

He'd wanted her to return. She would have been a top agent if only she could truly put the past behind her. But Miranda's deep involvement with the Butcher investigation, from the moment she returned from Quantico, told him she'd made her decision long ago.

He closed his eyes, uncertain how to work through Miranda's pain and anger toward him. For a few minutes, they'd almost reached that comfort level where he could have said anything, and she would have opened up. But they hadn't gotten there, and he didn't know if they ever would. As soon as he stepped too close, she put up an invisible barrier.

Sometimes, Quinn wanted to shake Miranda until she listened to what he said, to stop her from continually questioning his motives. But tonight he'd just wanted to take her to bed and hold her close.

Until she opened up and talked to him, as well as listened to what he had to say, there was no hope of mending his broken relationship with the only woman he'd ever loved.

CHAPTER
15

In the way it is with some dreams, he kept pressing the mental rewind button to watch Theron soar through the sky, flying two hundred miles an hour, his wings beating deep and sure as he homed in on the swift and knocked the prey out of the sky with his sharp talons.

Over and over, he repeated this dream, at will. In the back of his semiconscious mind he worried about where he was, whom he was expecting, but for now he wanted to replay his raptor hunting.

He didn't wake up until the cold metal handcuff snapped across his wrist.

She was back.

He struggled in the sweat-soaked sheets and she laughed. The low rumble he knew all too well.

"What?" he asked, his voice thick from sleep. Theron disappeared, and he remembered where he was.

Back in Montana.

"I want you."

"No. I'm tired."

Silence. He came fully awake.

Never say no to me.

The waxing moon, three-quarters full, shone bright through the large windows, casting gray shadows across his loft. Highlighting his bed, his solitary dresser, his hunting rifle.

And *her.*

She wore black, her blonde hair pulled back into a tight braid. Her delicate jaw and pale skin lied — there was nothing soft about this woman.

She frowned at his automatic refusal. "I come out here in the middle of the night to give you pleasure and you say no?"

Pleasure? Maybe for *her.* Always for *her.* He hated that he reacted. He tried and tried to keep his body from betraying him. But she knew what to do.

Why had he returned? Because the urge was so great, he couldn't resist. The punishment for giving in to the urge to hunt was having to see The Bitch.

She stripped off his sheet and her frown deepened. "You're dressed."

She rolled him onto his stomach and

pulled down his boxers. She slapped his buttocks hard. *Whack!*

Whack! Whack!

"I'm sorry," she said in a voice that sounded sincere. "You know I hate doing that." She kissed the hot spot, where she'd hit him.

She loves it. He grimaced as she reached between his legs and grasped his dick. He was already semi-hard. Damn his body. Damn it to hell. Why did it react to her? Always. He should cut it off to spite her. Mail it to her in a pretty package. She liked it so much? She could have it.

Growing in her capable hands, he moaned, trying to bury the sound in his pillow. But she heard, and he felt her cold smile on his back.

"There, there, sweetheart," she murmured, releasing him and crawling up his back. She turned his body slightly so she could kiss him. "It's been a long time."

Not long enough.

"Yes," he said.

"Did you miss me?"

Hell no.

"Of course I did."

"I thought so. It's just been hard for me to get away."

Yeah, I bet.

For years, her husband suspected she was having an affair. But the stupid fool never imagined it was with *him.*

"I have a special treat for you."

No. No.

He turned his head and watched her retrieve a long dildo from her jacket pocket. One end was fat, the other slender. He hadn't seen it in a long time.

No.

She rolled him over onto his back, then stripped. She had a disciplined body. Though forty was closing in, her figure was trim, firm, and graceful. The body of a dancer, the face of an angel, the soul of a demon.

She straddled him. Not his penis. His face. She ground her damn cunt into him. "Make me come, sweetheart."

He couldn't refuse. He remembered what happened when he protested. So he ate her the way she liked. Maybe if she was satisfied she wouldn't use that damn thing on him.

She pushed so hard into his face he couldn't breathe. She damn well knew he couldn't. But if he pushed her away she would really hurt him.

She eased up enough so he could catch his breath, then rode his face hard as she orgasmed, clutching the headboard, moaning out loud.

"Oh, yes," she said as she slid down his body and licked her juices off his face. "That was nice. You deserve a reward."

No.

She spread his legs and smiled at his quivering erection, the moonlight casting blue shadows across her body, making her pleasure look sinister. Evil.

She was pure evil.

She caressed his penis almost lovingly. She picked up the dildo from the nightstand and slid the thick end into her wet cunt, moaning in pleasure. It had a strap and she buckled it onto herself.

"No," he croaked. He hated this and she knew it.

"Did you say no?"

Shit, he hadn't meant to. It just slipped out.

"I didn't."

"Don't lie." She slapped his face and he bit his tongue.

Damn bitch.

There was nothing he could do. If he protested — she knew his secrets. Every dark secret he had. She knew about the girls. Knew and mocked him. Enjoyed his rage, his anger.

Fueled it.

She gently touched his face, panting her pleasure. The pleasure she got from hurting him.

"I'm sorry, sweetheart. But you should know better than to say no to me."

She'd had him under her thumb for fifteen years and if he didn't do exactly what she wanted, when she wanted, she'd take the one thing from him that he valued most.

His freedom.

I hate you.

Did he? Yes! But there was a time . . . he remembered a time when he could reach out and touch her and she would console him. Lick his wounds. Hold him and murmur sweet words in his ear. Touch him kindly.

That time was long gone, but the past held him in an iron grip, unbreakable. Like *her.*

So he laid back and did nothing. He was her bitch and there was not a damn thing he could do about it. It hurt, but his dick was rock hard. Pleasure and pain, so entwined. Can't have one without the other.

She moaned and gyrated, on the verge of orgasm. If she came she'd stop, and he'd get no relief. She never cared about him. It was all about *her.* Always about her.

He imagined throwing The Bitch onto the

floor and sticking the damn dildo up her ass. He imagined slapping her silly until she begged him to stop. He could easily picture tight clamps around her tits, the tits she never let him touch.

The image set him off and he moaned in release.

She reached down and jerked him so hard his moan of pleasure turned to a scream of pain. As she hurt him, she came, her body hot and slick. She collapsed onto him and kissed his tears away. "That, dearest, was for saying *no.*"

I hate you.

She pulled out abruptly and took off the dildo. She dressed, then kissed him — almost tenderly — and released the handcuff. "I'll be back," she said with a sweet smile.

Under that fake sweetness she was an evil bitch. He watched her leave.

He hated her. But he was trapped for life. If he tried to kill her, he would fail. He wanted desperately to hunt her down and slice her throat. Watch her lying smile turn grotesque in pain. Watch her realize that her creation was her demise.

If he left, she'd find him. If she couldn't find him, she'd spill his secrets. He knew what would happen if she ever went to the sheriff. All tears and sweet softness. All a lie.

"I didn't know, Sheriff, until I found their driver's licenses . . ."

A lie, always lies. But they'd believe The Bitch. Crocodile tears and big eyes.

No one would believe him. They always believed *her.*

It was too soon, but his rage was building. His fear angered him even more.

Too soon, but what could he do? The Bitch had started it. She always had that air as if she were in charge. As if he had to listen to her and do whatever she said. When she released Penny from their love nest, she'd forced him to hunt. To kill.

He'd never wanted to kill Penny. He only kept her in the cabin to make her understand that he loved her, that the jock she was dating would betray her. He wanted to find out why she'd lied to him.

He'd never wanted to kill her. But sometimes the only way to get the truth was to hurt it out of people. That's how his mother did it, and he always told the truth.

Penny had almost come around. Everything he'd learned worked. She said what he wanted her to say. Let him touch her without screaming. They would have been happy together forever, if only he had a little more time to work on her.

But The Bitch didn't want him to be

happy. She followed him one night and took away the only woman he'd loved. She let Penny go.

Penny ran. Ran away from him when he begged her to stay. He hadn't wanted to kill Penny. He just wanted her to stay with him.

When he'd caught up with her, he realized everything she'd said to him was a lie. She didn't love him, didn't want to stay with him. Lies, lies, lies!

She died as painlessly as possible. He'd never wanted to hurt her. He just couldn't help himself. And she'd lied. It was just punishment. But he didn't want her to suffer.

The Bitch made him kill that first time. But when he looked down at Penny's lifeless body, he felt emboldened. Powerful. He had a touch of God in him, the ability to take life, or give it.

With the little black-haired woman — he didn't know her name was Dora until he'd read the newspapers — he developed a taste for it. He fucked her when *he* wanted, not when *she* wanted. He fed her when he wanted, not when she was hungry. He released her when he wanted, and she ran.

The thrill of the hunt was secondary to having power over life.

He always won. Except the one who got away . . .

He rose from bed, taking the sheet and wrapping it around himself. He crossed over to his desk and pulled open the drawer so violently that the contents spilled across the floor. Angry at himself, but mostly at The Bitch, he switched on the desk lamp and knelt on the floor to gather his treasures.

He stacked the driver's licenses he'd collected — twenty-one in all — and put them aside, Rebecca on top. He fingered her photograph, reflected not on the kill, but the life — the life she gave him when she ran. The life she gave him when she begged *him* for mercy. For anything. He called the shots. He made all the decisions and she had no say.

He rarely spoke to the women. They were nothing.

He picked up the worn leather notebook that held his life. He breathed in the old leather cover, feeling oddly at peace. Planning did that for him. Planning took time, focus, intelligence.

He had all three. And it was time to plan for the next hunt. The sooner the better.

Theron's eggs would be hatching soon. He certainly didn't want to miss it.

CHAPTER
16

BUTCHER'S LAIR FOUND
Dead girl identified as missing MSU co-ed

Special Report by Elijah Banks

Miranda's hands grasped the newspaper so tightly she couldn't read the words, but the photographs were unmistakable.

Reproduced beneath the headline was a photograph of the shack where Rebecca had been held captive; next to it, Rebecca's school picture, the same one that had been reproduced on flyers and distributed all over town.

"Goddamn him!"

She was about to toss the paper aside when something familiar below the fold caught her eye.

Her meager breakfast rose in her throat.

She swallowed and whispered, "The bastard."

Under the fold was another picture. Of her. Leaning against the tree outside the shack, her face stark white even against the grainy gray of newsprint. The caption: *Miranda Moore, Director of Gallatin County Search and Rescue and the only survivor of the Bozeman Butcher, assists the FBI in locating the dilapidated cabin.*

"I'm sorry."

She jumped at the voice. "Quinn."

He'd come down the path from the Lodge, but she'd been so focused on the newspaper she hadn't heard him.

"I would have spared you if I could."

She shook her head, tilted her chin up. "I'm fine," she insisted, though seeing the photograph had unnerved her.

"You give Elijah Banks power when you get upset at his theatrics."

"I'm not upset." She was lying. By the look on Quinn's face, he knew it.

"All right, I am upset, but I'll get over it." She paused, looked at him closely. "Why are you here?"

"I talked to Olivia this morning."

"And?"

"She'll be in Helena tonight."

"Really? Maybe she can come down here.

It's not a long drive. I'd love to see her."

"You have her cell number, call her."

"I will." She made a mental note to call Olivia tomorrow morning.

"I'm heading to the University," Quinn said, "but I wanted to tell you about Olivia. If there's anything in the evidence . . ."

"She'll find it," Miranda finished his thought.

"Right." He walked up the steps to the edge of the porch where Miranda stood. Her heart skipped a beat as he stood as close to her as possible without touching.

"Miranda, we need to talk. About last night, about Quantico."

She swallowed, wanting so much to forgive and forget, but unable to put aside the lump of betrayal in her soul. "There's nothing to talk about."

He stared into her eyes so long she glanced down.

"Miranda," he whispered. Then he kissed her.

Long, hard, and fast, then he stepped back. The kiss left her breathless. She couldn't speak.

"We will talk," he said firmly. "Be careful today."

He didn't wait for her answer, but left the same way he'd come.

Having a federal badge opened some doors and closed others. The new Privacy Act required that Quinn get a warrant before the University would give him the information he wanted. It took him all morning to have one drawn up.

By the time he got back to the college, it was after lunch. Fortunately, MSU's dean had already asked his secretary to pull the necessary records. They were boxed up and ready for him to take.

Four boxes. One hundred eighty-nine men.

By the time he arrived back at the Sheriff's Department, he had some ideas how to narrow the list. He just needed people.

Nick gave him deputies Booker and Janssen. The selected files reflected students who'd listed Montana or nearby Idaho or Wyoming as their residence prior to attending the University. The killer had an intimate knowledge of the area, so it reasoned that he would have lived in or near Gallatin County.

Quinn assigned the deputies the task of going through the names and removing anyone who was married, had moved out of the country, or was deceased.

He stared at the murder board in Nick's office and tried to think like the killer.

Why did he rape? Control. Anger.

Why did he need control? Because he didn't have control over his own life, especially as a juvenile. Had he been in foster care? Orphaned? Sexually abused? Were both parents in the picture? Had one of them physically abused him as a child?

Overwhelmingly, serial killers were sexually and physically abused as prepubescent children. That common trait had been used by defense attorneys to thwart the death penalty or cast blame on someone other than the killer for their horrible crimes.

The sad truth was that many children were abused — sexually, physically, emotionally. But most didn't grow up to become serial killers. While Quinn felt compassion for the abused children the killers had been, he held no such feelings for them as adults.

The Butcher took sick pleasure in torturing his victims before killing them. But there were two distinct trademarks that made him different from most other sadistic killers. If only Quinn could understand the Butcher's reasoning, he could get deeper into his mind and maybe closer to a suspect. It was a difficult task: serial killers were logical in their own calculation, but understanding that logic was virtually impossible if you didn't have all the pieces.

Several crucial pieces were still missing.

The Butcher's first distinctive trademark was his victims' imprisonment. That was about control. He both hurt them and cared for them — if you could call feeding them bread and water "caring." He said only a few words to them, and those were delivered with disinterest. The women were possessions, objects to do with whatever he pleased. Their screams neither excited him nor bothered him; they were irrelevant. Just holding them captive excited him.

The second — and perhaps unique — trademark was releasing the women for the hunt. There was always the chance they would escape. He seemed to revel in the game, giving them time to run before pursuing them. Not a lot of time, though. And the women were injured and demoralized in the process.

Not only did Quinn wonder why the Butcher hadn't gone after Miranda, he was surprised the Butcher continued to release and hunt his other victims after her escape.

Maybe he didn't give them as much time before starting the hunt. Maybe he kept them weaker. Or maybe he thought Miranda was an anomaly, and he had to repeatedly prove to himself he could still hunt successfully, that he was capable of complete dominance and control. Maybe he kept Miranda alive as a reminder of his one failure.

Quinn shook his head. He was starting to think in circles. He had no idea why the killer hadn't gone after Miranda. If *he* were a sadistic rapist who got off on hunting women for sport, he sure wouldn't let one get away. It seemed out of character somehow, and that bothered Quinn.

At five he headed out to meet with Olivia at the airport, leaving the two deputies to weed out suspects from the University list. By the time he returned in the morning, he expected to have a short list.

His instincts told him the Butcher would be on it.

Miranda found herself looking for Quinn that evening as she sat in the Lodge dining hall picking at a late supper her dad had prepared for her. She didn't want him to worry, but she wasn't hungry.

However, she had a strange craving for pecan pie.

She told her dad to go ahead and relax in his rooms, she'd take care of her dishes and close down the kitchen. She needed something to do to keep her mind off the Butcher.

Even if staying up was simply an excuse to see Quinn when he came in.

As she finished wiping down the counters, she heard voices in the lobby. Quinn. She rushed out, surprised to see Nick talking to Gray.

"Nick. Is something wrong?"

"No," he said. "I was in the area and decided to stop by."

"I'll make some coffee," she said.

"You don't have to. Frankly, I've had enough caffeine. Share a drink with me?"

Drinking with Nick was the last thing she wanted to do. Not because she didn't like his company — she did — but because it felt strange to sit alone with one ex-boyfriend while the other — Quinn — could walk in at any moment. She hadn't really thought about her intimate relationships with the two men until now, and it unnerved her.

But Nick was a friend first, so she smiled. "Sure. Gray? You want to join us?"

He shook his head. "I'm beat. I need to be up early to greet some seniors coming in from Los Angeles. They'll be here a few days."

Gray bid them good night and left.

Miranda led Nick into the bar, motioning toward a bar stool while she used the pass-through to grab his favorite beer. She opened one for herself.

"Thanks."

"Cheers." She tipped her bottle at him,

then took a long swallow.

She'd always enjoyed hanging out with Nick. They'd been friends before they were lovers. She hoped they still were, even though their friendship seemed a bit strained. She'd been satisfied with their relationship when Nick had asked her to move in with him. She'd said no. He'd walked away.

She'd been satisfied being friends and lovers. Nick wanted more.

Like what she'd had with Quinn.

Still, she'd had a warm friendship, a good working relationship, with Nick. Why had she been so adamant against moving in with him?

Simply put, she didn't love him. When he suggested it would be better if they kept their relationship out of the bedroom, Miranda had agreed. In hindsight, she wondered if he'd been expecting a protest.

The breakup had been a relief in the end.

"How are you getting along with Quinn?"

Miranda was surprised at his question. "Fine," she said automatically.

He raised an eyebrow.

She felt uncomfortable under his scrutiny. She almost felt as if she had to explain. "Seriously, he's doing his job and I'm doing mine and there's nothing more to it."

She was rambling. Why did she have to defend her working relationship with Quinn? Maybe it was because for years she'd complained to Nick about how Quinn had stolen her career, how he'd foiled her plans.

She never told him how much it hurt.

"He's got a couple of my men going through University records," Nick said. "They were still in my office when I called in thirty minutes ago."

"He told me he was reviewing the records from Penny's years at Bozeman. But there were hundreds of potential suspects then. I don't know how they can be whittled down if we don't have something more to go on."

"Quinn feels certain this guy is still single and leads a solitary life."

"By the way, where is Quinn?" She tried to sound disinterested, but didn't think she pulled it off.

"Helena. Picking up your friend from the airport, the lab technician."

"Olivia?" She'd almost forgotten Quinn had asked her to help.

Nick nodded and sipped his beer. "He'll be back late tonight or in the morning." He paused. "I wish you and Quinn the best of luck."

"I don't know what you mean."

"Don't you?"

"No."

Nick sighed, started peeling the label off his beer bottle. "You're obviously still in love with him. You've always been in love with him."

"That's not true." Was she protesting too much? She tried to explain. "You know how it was back then. But with everything that happened, I just — well, it's over. It's been over a very long time."

"Love just doesn't turn on and off like a faucet, Miranda." He sounded angry.

"I didn't say that, I—" She stopped. "Nick, I'm sorry." What else could she say? She knew Nick had feelings for her, feelings she didn't or couldn't return. The last thing she wanted to do was hurt her best friend.

He waved off her apology and stood. "I just wanted to check in on you since I'm off duty, so to speak." The sheriff was never really "off duty." It had been a running joke with them when he'd first been elected.

"There's nothing going on between me and Quinn," she said, then bit her tongue. Why was it so important that she convince Nick of that?

Or were her protests more about convincing herself?

He gave her a wry smile. "Believe what you want, Miranda, but the truth is your

247

heart has always been with Quinn. I never had a chance. But I only just realized it."

"I care about you. You're my best friend."

He nodded, and she knew she'd said the wrong thing. Nick was in love with her and she'd called him a friend.

Why did she always put her foot in her mouth?

"I know you care, Randy. You've always been a good friend. But a lousy girlfriend. 'Night."

She stared after him, wondering why in the world he'd stopped by. To see if she and Quinn were together? To convince himself of something? She shook her head as she finished her beer and tossed the empty bottles in the bin under the counter.

She'd never understand men.

CHAPTER
17

"You're a fool."

The Bitch was furious, but right now he didn't care. She'd make him pay for breaking the rules later. After the hunt. But now, she couldn't do anything.

He saw the gleam of excitement in her eyes.

He still hated her, but he hated her less on the nights they hunted together.

Her lack of patience irritated him, though.

"Why not that one?" she whined, gesturing at the brunette who had pulled into the gas station.

"No."

"Why not?"

"I want a blonde this time."

"You just had a blonde."

"I don't care, I want another one."

She sighed and tapped her fingers on the steering wheel. "I don't want to be here all night."

"It's never taken more than a couple of hours. Dammit, have a little patience!" She never had patience. She thought he was a freak because he sat in the middle of the woods for days on end logging data about his birds.

He didn't care what she thought about him. Right now, she was a help. Although most of the time he wanted to strangle her.

He didn't dare touch her neck.

The brunette drove off after filling her tank. It was nearly eleven in the evening. They'd been here two hours. Traffic had slowed considerably after ten.

He placed his binoculars in his lap and waited for the next car to turn into the highway strip mall. They had a great vantage point, well concealed, up the road from the gas station, on a private drive. He knew the owner of the house at the end of the drive. An old woman, deaf as a post, who went to bed with the sun.

He'd selected this place because it was a regular stop for college students. Between the gas station, the pizza place, and the small bar, he knew he'd find someone that suited him.

He wasn't picky. He just wanted a blonde again.

He'd hunted from this place once before.

As a rule, he didn't use the same place twice. Just in case. But enough time had passed. It was in this place that he'd found another blonde, twelve years ago.

If only she hadn't had a friend with her.

The Bitch never let him go after Miranda Moore. It ate at him constantly. But The Bitch thought Moore deserved to live since she got away. Always, she taunted him. Always, she rubbed his nose in his failings. He hated her. Hated both of them.

Someday he'd make them pay. They were two peas in a pod, teasing him, ridiculing him.

But for now he couldn't touch Miranda Moore. The Bitch said she'd turn him in. And he believed her.

"We'll kill Miranda Moore if she becomes a threat, but she's not," The Bitch said over and over again. "She beat you, sweetheart. I want you to always remember that."

As if he could forget with her constant reminders.

A Honda Civic pulled onto the frontage road. Bypassed the gas station and went straight to the pizza place. He raised his binoculars.

A blonde stepped out from the driver's side. His heart swelled, pounded in his chest.

The One.

Instantly he knew, just like every other time he'd hunted for women. She was The One, and he would have her.

"I'm going," he said.

"Wait."

"What now?"

"Look."

Grudgingly, he looked. The passenger door opened. A redhead emerged. Together the blonde and the redhead walked into the pizza parlor.

"Wait," The Bitch told him.

"No."

"I said no more pairs. It's too risky."

"All right."

She relaxed, and he opened the passenger door.

"Where are you going?" she demanded, almost leaping across the seat to grab him.

He stepped back, pocketing the bottle of molasses in his windbreaker. "I'm taking care of the car."

"You said you agreed!"

"No pairs. Trust me. I'll only take care of one."

She didn't believe him, but he didn't care. He had no use for the redhead. This time, he only wanted the blonde.

He'd have to kill the redhead first.

CHAPTER

18

The lights of Nick's truck illuminated the blue Honda Civic as he pulled up behind it, staying back thirty feet from the probable crime scene. He jumped out, leaving his lights on, and approached the responding officer, Brad Jessup.

"How's the girl?"

"The EMT said critical. They've already taken her to the hospital." Jessup checked his notes. "According to her driver's license, she's JoBeth Anderson. She had an MSU identification in her wallet and twenty-three dollars."

"What happened? Hit and run?"

"Doesn't appear to be any damage to the vehicle, sir."

"Who called it in?"

"Red Tucker, sir."

Everyone knew old Red. He owned the saloon fifteen minutes down the road at the

191/85 junction and was rumored to be the oldest man in Gallatin County.

"Where's he now?"

"I had him sit in my cruiser, sir."

Red sat at an angle in the passenger seat of Jessup's patrol car, feet outside the car. His thick shock of white hair was in need of a trim, and his weathered face had so many wrinkles it could pass for a map of Yellowstone trails.

"How're you doing, Red?" Nick asked as he approached.

"Been better. How's the girl?"

"Critical. If she makes it, it's because of you." Nick squatted next to him and took out his notepad. "Mind telling me what happened?"

"I leave the tavern at eleven or so nowadays. Need a bit more sleep than I used to. Saw the car by the side of the road and slowed, thinking someone might be in trouble, run out of gas or something. I didn't see anyone and thought they'd broken down and hoofed it back to the Junction, or up the road a couple miles. So, I started to speed back up when my lights hit on something in front of the car. I thought it might have been an animal, maybe the driver hit a small bear or something. So I pulled over."

Red shook his head. "I couldn't believe it was a young lady. Just lying there, half in the road. It's amazing that one of the big rigs didn't run over her legs."

"Did you see anything else? Anyone else?"

"No. It was dead quiet. I don't have a cell phone, but I didn't want to leave her there, so I waited for someone to drive by. Then I saw a phone near her, like she'd been holding it before she was hit. I used it. You think it was okay I did that?"

"You did the right thing. Did you touch anything in the car? The ignition? The hood? Anything?"

"Umm, maybe the roof when I leaned in. I was checking to see if someone else was in the car. You don't think — it was an accident, right? Hit and run? You don't think it's that killer again?"

Nick's stomach fell. Though he'd wanted to believe JoBeth Anderson's injuries were the result of something less nefarious than a serial killer, as soon as his lights swept over the car he was transported back twelve years.

Sharon Lewis's little Volkswagen Beetle had been found less than two miles from here. On this same road.

"I'll find out." Nick stood, knees cracking. "Can you hang out here a couple more minutes?"

Red nodded. "I couldn't sleep if I wanted to."

Nick pulled his jacket close as a wind picked up. Near midnight and the temperature had dropped considerably. It'd be below fifty tonight.

He prayed it wasn't the Butcher. Rebecca had been found only three days ago — Nick couldn't remember the killer attacking again so soon.

There was an easy way to find out.

His feet felt filled with lead, his heart twisted, as he approached the car. "Jessup!" he called.

"Yes, sir?"

"Did you run the tags and registration?"

"The car belongs to Ashley van Auden, twenty-one. Her residence is listed as San Diego, California, and her mail goes to a dorm at the University."

Where was Ashley?

Nick walked around the back of the car to the gas tank. He took out his flashlight and trained it on the small door. The Honda Civic had a release lever on the floor next to the driver's seat to unlock the gas tank. But most people in Montana didn't lock their cars when they stopped for gas or a meal, or even when they parked in front of their house.

And even if they did, the cars were easy to break into if you knew what you were doing.

He leaned closer, his Maglite illuminating a small trail of something thick next to the fuel door. He took in a breath, the sweetness of the molasses turning foul in the realization that the Butcher had struck again.

Nick wanted to kick something. "Jessup!" he shouted. "Call in the crime techs. I want everyone out here, full gear, no excuses."

"Sir?"

Ignoring Jessup's implied question, Nick pulled out his cell phone and pounded the key pad.

"Peterson here."

"Quinn, the Butcher has another woman. When will you be back?"

"I'm already on my way. Where are you? I'll be there in less than an hour."

Ashley van Auden felt hungover, like the time she'd drunk way too much champagne at her aunt Sherry's wedding. Her head thick, heavy, pounding.

She shivered and realized that it was the cold that had woken her. She'd never grown used to the cold weather in Montana. Coming from sunny San Diego, she was accustomed to fun and warmth and sandy beaches. She hated Montana, but MSU had a great wildlife biology program and she ultimately wanted to work with the endangered Bighorn Sheep in Southern California.

But this cold was worse than cold. She was chilled to the bone; her skin felt raw and exposed. No blanket covered her, no heater blew warm air over her body. And the room stank. Rotten, moldy. It smelled like a dead animal, as if a family of rodents had holed up in the corner and died a week ago.

This wasn't her dorm room.

Fear hit her as soon as she fully wakened. Not a steady increase of heart rate or growing worry, but an instant and deep terror. Panicked, she tried to sit up and realized she was restrained. Her wrists burned with the struggle of trying to get free. What had happened? Where was she? Where was JoBeth?

The last thing she remembered was the car stopped running. Just like that. It sputtered a couple of times and died. She was lucky to get it to the side of the road.

Jo said she'd call roadside service and got out of the car because her cell phone was all static. Another thing Ashley hated about the mountains. She never had trouble with her cell phone in San Diego.

She leaned over to check the CD changer and see if there was enough juice in the car for music. When she looked up, Jo was gone.

She stepped out of the car and saw the figure of a woman walking toward the trees on the other side of the road. Why had Jo crossed the road? "Jo? What are you doing over there?"

Then nothing. She remembered nothing else. Why couldn't she remember anything? What had happened?

She was naked. Restrained. Something bound her eyes, tight. Too tight. She heard nothing except her panic pounding in her ears. Her lips quivered, a sob escaped. She swallowed, trying to force her fear back.

Crack.

What was that? Was someone coming? Dear God, what was he going to do to her?

Rebecca Douglas.

Total fear embraced her and squeezed tight, draining every ounce of hope from her soul. They'd found that girl from the University, Rebecca. The newspaper said it was the Bozeman Butcher. The man who tortured women in the woods and hunted them like animals. The Butcher.

No. *NO! NO! NO!*

Dear God, please! Don't let him hurt me!

Her throat constricted, her chest heaved as she fought her restraints. Kicking and pulling and pushing. She wasn't going to die. She couldn't die! She had a full life ahead of her. Her friends. Her family. Her daddy had told her to be careful. To watch. To be cautious. That she was too friendly, too naïve.

She thought she'd been careful. What had she done wrong?

More than anything, she wanted to spare her father from the pain. She was his princess. What would he do when he found out she was missing? When she turned up dead? Tortured and — and — *raped*.

No. No. NO! This wasn't happening.

Where was JoBeth?

"Jo?" she whispered into the blackness. She listened, trying to force her racing heart to slow.

Nothing.

Then she heard it again. Something. Outside. Voices, whispering in the dark. She listened harder and began to make out words.

"I told you it was too soon!" The voice was low, but sounded like a woman's.

"Go away. Come back next week." A man. Gruff.

Slap.

"I have to get home. It's late. I'll come back tomorrow."

Mumble, something she couldn't hear. *Crack.* Nothing.

The silence heightened her fear, sounds as black as the blindfolded night. Then rustling. The call of an owl. Sounds of the night had been there all along, but until this moment she'd been too terrified to listen. A thrashing, a squeak, then quiet. A scurrying on the roof — tin. The sound of tin. She was in a shack of some sort and it was so damn cold.

Ashley knew the door opened not from a sound, but from an icy breeze.

Then a quiet snap, two pieces of wood brushing against each other. Breathing. He was here. He was here and so was she, only she couldn't do anything.

"Please, please, please don't hurt me," she cried out, her voice raw and cracking.

A loud crack resounded in the room, then a piercing pain on her inner thigh made her scream out. A whip.

Then he was on top of her. Intense, sharp pain between her legs shattered what little composure she had left and she screamed until her throat burned.

She thought she heard distant laughter. Then it was gone.

CHAPTER
19

Miranda paced the waiting room for two hours before finally sitting in one of the green plastic chairs that lined the wall of the emergency room. She'd learned next to nothing about JoBeth Anderson's condition. The hospital couldn't reach her next of kin in Minnesota, so they'd contacted the University. An administrator was tracking down her parents, but because it was life or death, they took JoBeth in for surgery.

When Miranda's phone rang earlier at two in the morning, she'd been pulled from a nightmare, grateful for the interruption.

It had been Nick. The Butcher had another victim.

At the time, Miranda hadn't questioned JoBeth being left behind by her attacker. Now, she couldn't stop thinking about it.

Why hadn't she been taken with Ashley?

Why had the Butcher attempted to kill

her, leaving her by the side of the road?

And why had he acted so soon on the heels of Rebecca Douglas's murder? His shortest interim period had been two weeks. Ashley had been abducted after just three days.

She needed to talk to Quinn and figure out what this meant. Were they any closer to catching the Butcher? Had something in this investigation tipped his hand? Or might this be the work of a copycat criminal? But Quinn and Nick weren't around to answer questions. They were interviewing possible witnesses at the Junction, where JoBeth and Ashley had stopped to eat.

From the floor nurse, Miranda learned that JoBeth had a life-threatening contusion on the back of her head. She had been hit three times with enough force to crack her skull. The doctors were focusing on saving her life, but even then she could have a broken spinal cord. Her injuries were serious; the blows had been meant to kill.

She is a survivor, Miranda thought. *Just like me.*

JoBeth didn't deserve this, lying in surgery as the doctors tried to stop her brain from bleeding.

Trapped in her brain could be something to lead them to the killer: maybe she had seen the Butcher, maybe she knew him, something to help! They needed a break. They needed the killer to make a mistake.

Miranda willed JoBeth to survive. To regain consciousness. To say, "Yes, I saw him, he is—"

Please make it, JoBeth.

Miranda sat in a hospital chair. As dawn peeked over the horizon, she closed her eyes. Just to rest for a minute.

JoBeth was still in surgery when Quinn walked in an hour later.

He wasn't surprised Miranda was in the waiting room outside the surgery wing. But he was taken aback when he saw her lying on a couch, asleep, her backpack a pillow. A wool blanket covered her thin body; her arms were crossed over her chest, holding the blanket close. Like a child. Innocent.

Her pale skin was relaxed in sleep, belying her body's simmering tension. He quietly approached; the sight tugged at his heart. Beautiful, strong, vibrant. Smart.

Passionate. Intelligent. Such a pain in the ass sometimes, she was so stubborn.

He licked his lips. He'd never be able to eat pecan pie again without picturing Miranda. Tasting her sweet, sugary lips as they melted into his. Feeling her body mold against his, a perfect fit.

He couldn't resist bending over and tucking a loose curl behind her ear.

Her eyes opened and she sat up abruptly, blanket dropping to the floor, a look of fear crossing her face before she recognized him. He felt bad that he'd startled her. He sat next to her and touched her cheek. Her skin was so soft.

She didn't pull back, but neither did she lean into his caress. He'd take what little he could get at this point. He certainly didn't want to jeopardize the tentative progress he'd made in getting her to trust him again.

As if he hadn't already made a mistake by kissing her. Even though at the time it sure didn't feel like a mistake.

"I'm sorry, Miranda. I didn't mean to wake you."

"I felt someone watching me," she said, her voice hoarse from sleep — or lack of it. She cleared her throat, the fear in her eyes now hidden behind her thick lashes. She took a deep breath and looked up at him. "What happened? JoBeth?" She jumped up and wobbled a bit. He took her elbow to steady her, and she didn't push his hand away.

Another small step.

"I just got here," he said.

She glanced toward the nurses' station.

"They promised to wake me if there was a change." She turned to the lone nurse behind the counter.

"Any word?" she asked. "JoBeth Anderson, she was in—"

The nurse nodded. "I know. She's out of surgery and was moved to the ICU thirty minutes ago."

"How is she?"

"I'm sorry, Ms. Moore, I can't tell you. You're not her next of kin."

Miranda tensed next to Quinn and bit her lip. He empathized with her — she was already grieving for Ashley, and worried about JoBeth.

Quinn pulled out his wallet and flashed his badge. "Special Agent Quincy Peterson, Federal Bureau of Investigation. If you would be so kind as to find Ms. Anderson's doctor, I need to speak with him."

"Yes, sir." The nurse picked up the phone and Quinn guided Miranda by the elbow back to the waiting room.

She sighed and put a hand to her head, shielding her bloodshot eyes. "Dammit, Quinn," she muttered. "Why?"

He didn't have to ask what she was talking about.

"We've taken the car to the Sheriff's Department and they're going over it with a fine-toothed comb. Scouring for finger-prints, hair, anything. The crime techs are still at the scene taking a sample of every rock, piece of dirt, and leaf in the immediate area. If there's trash by the side of the road, it's being sent immediately to Helena.

"If he made one small mistake, we'll find him, Miranda."

He tipped her chin up, forcing her to look at him. His heart twisted seeing the pain in her large blue eyes.

"I promise, I'm not leaving until we get answers."

She nodded, almost imperceptibly, then sank into a plastic chair and rested her head in her hands. He sat next to her, touched her shoulder. It felt so good to be able to touch Miranda again without her flinching. He rubbed her muscles.

"Do we even have a chance of finding him before Ashley van Auden dies?"

What could he say to that? "There's always a chance."

She looked at him, tension radiating from her in unseen waves, the tendons in her neck taut. She must have a splitting headache, and knowing Miranda, she'd just suffer with it. She'd told him once that pain reminded her she was alive. He thought it was more personal punishment stemming from her guilt that she'd survived and Sharon hadn't.

"I can see her, Quinn," Miranda whispered, her voice quivering. "Ashley. In the dark. Cold. Naked and scared. Terrified. Worse than I was."

"Miranda, don't do this—"

She shook her head, leaned into him as if imploring him to understand. He wrapped his arm around her shoulders and squeezed.

"No, no," she said. "I have to focus on her. I have to remember. Don't you see that it's worse for her? She knows. She knows he's the Butcher. Rebecca was killed only days ago; Ashley must be thinking she's next." Her voice caught, as if in a sob, but no tears came.

He gently pulled her all the way into his arms and enveloped her. Her body shook as she tried to contain her emotions. That she let him console her was a huge step, one that gave him hope.

And knowing there was hope opened his heart even more.

She took a deep breath and said into his chest, "I called Charlie with my search team," she continued. "We're starting out at oh-eight-hundred."

"You need to sleep," he murmured, rubbing her back.

She pulled back and shook her head. "I

can't sleep. Not knowing Ashley is out there. But — dammit, I don't know what to do! We search acres and acres and never find the women alive. But I don't know what else to do. I can't do anything."

Miranda had never been one to sit around and let other people do the job. She jumped in with both feet, from the beginning.

Before he could speak, to try and offer her some inadequate platitude, a tall, skinny doctor with a full head of dark, graying hair approached. "Agent Peterson?" he said, hand extended, dark eyes glancing at Miranda, then back at him. "Doctor Sean O'Neal."

Quinn shook it. "Thanks for coming out. What's the status of Ms. Anderson?"

"Is she going to make it?" Miranda asked.

Dr. O'Neal sighed, took off his glasses, and rubbed his eyes. He put his lenses back on and said, "I don't know. The odds were against her going in, but she held strong. Fifty-fifty, now that she survived the surgery. Sheriff Thomas contacted her parents out of state and I just got off the phone with them. The blows to her head were severe. Fortunately, her spine wasn't damaged. I feared the nerve had been severed, but it's good. Unfortunately, even if she wakes up, I have no idea what short- or long-term brain damage there will be.

"In short," the doctor continued, "she's in a coma."

Coma. Their best witness — their only witness — was in a coma. Fate sucked.

Ryan Parker awoke with a start. His heart pounded in the grayness of his room. He felt damp, and for a moment thought he'd wet himself, then realized he'd sweat in his sleep, enough to chill him.

But he was chilled even more from the nightmare.

He glanced at his digital clock: 5:46 A.M.

He swallowed several times and gagged because his mouth was so dry. He'd had nightmares before, but nothing was as real, as scary, as this one. Because this nightmare had happened. That girl really had been killed, and he'd seen her hollow stare in the middle of the woods, accusing him. He'd almost closed her eyes because of that *look,* but didn't want to touch the body.

But his nightmare combined reality with fiction. She hadn't reached out for him in the woods, he told himself over and over again. That was a dream, something his mind made up. It took several minutes for Ryan to separate what he'd really seen last week with what he'd imagined in his dream.

But Rebecca Douglas's blank eyes

haunted him whether he slept or not.

He slid silently out of bed and crossed over to his dresser, carefully sliding open the bottom drawer. Inside were his special things, in one of the few places his mother didn't search in his room. Cool rocks, a fish fossil he'd found at Yellowstone, a piece of petrified wood, baseball cards, wrappers from Double Bubble gum that had funny cartoons.

And the belt buckle.

He didn't remember the entire nightmare, but right before he woke himself, he'd pictured the belt buckle, the bird with the glowing green eyes.

He didn't turn on any lights, but felt around in the far corner of the drawer until his hand touched the cold steel. He froze, sensing something was wrong, but not knowing what.

He should have gone down to that FBI guy and showed it to him. But it was too late now.

It was probably nothing, just some guy pissing in the woods.

No, it wasn't.

His fingers wrapped around the metal bird almost as if they had a mind of their own. And at that moment, he knew what he had to do, whom he needed to show the buckle to.

His father wasn't the easiest person to talk to, but he was the smartest person Ryan knew. He was a judge. He'd know exactly what to do with the buckle, who should have it.

He started toward his parents' bedroom, then smelled coffee downstairs. He detoured into the kitchen, hoping his father was there.

He was. "Hi, Dad."

"You're up early."

He shrugged, fingered the belt buckle. "I was wondering . . . well, I found something and don't really know what it is. I thought you might . . ." That sounded stupid. He knew it was a belt buckle, he just didn't want to tell his dad where he'd found it.

"Sure, what is it?"

"There you are."

Ryan jumped. His mother walked in wearing her robe, and frowned.

"Delilah," his dad said, "I thought you were still sleeping."

"I woke up and you weren't there. I went to check on Ryan, and he wasn't there, either."

"I went to check on the horses, they seemed kind of spooked, and couldn't get back to sleep so I made a pot of coffee. Can I get you a cup?"

"I can get it myself," his mother said.

Ryan didn't want to talk to his dad with his mother there. He was sure to be punished for going back near where that dead girl was found. His father's punishments were usually lighter than his mother's. He'd catch his dad tonight.

"I'm going to get ready for school," he said.

"Didn't you want to show me something?" his dad asked.

"It's not important. I'll show you tonight."

"Okay."

His mother leaned over for a kiss, and he brushed his lips against her cheek, then his father's, before scrambling up the stairs.

I'll ask Dad about the buckle tonight.

CHAPTER
20

Before Miranda could leave the hospital, she had to see JoBeth Anderson. She had no trouble talking her way past the guard. Sometimes being Nick's ex-girlfriend had its advantages.

JoBeth was a survivor. She wasn't Rebecca or any of the dead girls. She was alive. More than anything, Miranda wanted her to know that she was strong and had to fight. Fight to take down the bastard who'd kidnapped her friend.

There could be clues to the Butcher's identity locked in her head. Her unconscious head.

JoBeth lay on a gently reclined hospital bed with a white blanket pulled almost to her neck. Machines beeped softly as her heart beat in her chest. Other devices monitored her breathing. Her brain activity. Her life.

She was alive and breathing on her own, an IV in her arm hydrating her. Miranda remembered too well spending a week in the same hospital. She couldn't wait to leave then; she didn't want to be here now.

"Wake up," she whispered. If they were to have a real chance of saving Ashley, JoBeth had to regain consciousness soon.

A large section of her head was covered with a thick white bandage, stark against her limp red hair. Her pale skin seemed almost translucent and Miranda wondered how much of it was from the attack and how much was her natural pallor.

"JoBeth," Miranda said, her voice thick with unshed tears. She sat in the chair next to the girl and swallowed. She didn't want JoBeth to perceive, through the coma, her own fear and worry. She wanted the girl to take her strength.

"Jo," she said, her voice stronger. "My name is Miranda Moore. I don't think we've met before."

What to say? She'd never faced a living victim before. Well, that wasn't completely true. She'd counseled rape victims, eased the fear of those lost then found, dealt with hysterical parents and worried children.

But never a victim of the Butcher. Except when she looked into the mirror.

She could do this. She had to. If anything in JoBeth's mind could lead them to the man who'd hurt her, Miranda had to find some way to get it out. To save Ashley.

"You survived, JoBeth. You are alive. I've heard that people in comas can hear what's going on around them. Focus on me, Jo-Beth. Focus. If you want to save Ashley's life, focus on my words."

Was that the right approach? Should she even tell her Ashley was in danger? What if that made things worse? What if the guilt killed her?

I survived. Sharon died.

Miranda squeezed her eyes shut and took a deep breath.

"I don't know why he didn't take you, too," Miranda said, looking at the unconscious girl. "But you're the lucky one. You're the survivor. You made it this far, and you're going to make it back to us. You have to. For Ashley. Because somewhere in that sleeping mind of yours is the key to the identity of the man who kidnapped her."

She hadn't forgiven herself for not remembering more about her days in captivity. For not being able to identify her attacker. The man who killed Sharon. She could hear his voice, the few times he actually spoke.

Bitch.

How do you like this?

Stay.

Run. You have two minutes.

She'd repeated those words to the investigators. To the FBI profiler. To the shrink she was forced to see. The cruel words spoken in a dull, even monotone didn't mean anything to her. Oh, the profiler made noise that her attacker had been sexually abused by a woman as a child and was "punishing" his tormentor, but what good did that do in the investigation? Miranda didn't know. Certainly if they *had* a suspect it might help. But the police had nothing. The FBI had nothing.

She'd been no help.

But maybe JoBeth would be.

Miranda sucked in a ragged breath. "Jo-Beth, I was the one who got away," she whispered. "The Bozeman Butcher. I escaped. But my best friend died. Her name was Sharon and I loved her. Like a sister. I shared everything with her. I never thought — well, I never thought anything bad would happen to us. But the Butcher took us."

Why had the Butcher not taken JoBeth? Miranda didn't know, and Quinn and Nick could only speculate. Perhaps he didn't have time to get her into the truck. Maybe she'd seen his face. Maybe she knew him.

Speculation that could be confirmed only by JoBeth Anderson.

"Jo, you need to come out of this daze you're in. I know you're in pain. I know it'll hurt. But if you don't wake up soon, the Butcher will kill Ashley." Miranda swallowed. "None of this is your fault. Know that. But you need to wake up and help us. Help the police find whoever took Ashley. Before he hurts her. Before he hunts her."

Nothing. No movement, nothing to tell Miranda that JoBeth had heard a word she'd said. Miranda squeezed her hand, rested her forehead on the bed, and took a deep breath.

She had a job to do. A woman to find. Before it was too late.

After a moment, she stood, stronger and with purpose. She touched JoBeth's shoulder and said, "You get better, Jo. Promise me, get well. I'll be back to talk to you. Maybe tonight, but definitely tomorrow morning, okay?"

She didn't expect an answer. She didn't get one.

Quinn couldn't park in front of the Sheriff's Department because of the dozens of media vehicles taking every available space. He frowned, parked around the corner, and approached on foot just in time to hear

Nick, who stood at the top of the steps, say, "That's all the questions I have time for. I have an investigation to run."

Nick turned and went back into the building while the reporters hurled questions at his retreating back.

Quinn ducked down the alley to avoid the reporters and flashed his badge at the deputy guarding the back entrance. He walked straight to Nick's office.

"What happened?" he asked as he poured himself a cup of coffee from the pot on Nick's sideboard.

Nick grunted. "Hell if I know, but there's someone from CNN calling up the public relations officer wanting an interview, and that guy from *America's Most Wanted* wants to come out this weekend to film a segment on the Butcher."

"It couldn't hurt. Those shows get a lot of attention." Though by the time the show aired in seven to ten days, Ashley would be dead.

Nick stared at him. "Have you seen the paper this morning?"

"No."

Nick tossed him the front section.

The headline screamed: *Butcher Strikes Again.*

"How'd he get it in?"

"Stopped the presses? I don't know. Most of the story could have been written before Ashley van Auden disappeared, though. Only the first and last paragraphs are related to her." Nick paused, drummed his fingers on his desk. "Did you talk to Banks?"

Quinn skimmed the article. "No. Not really. I ran into him yesterday at MSU, where he was snooping around."

"What did you tell him?"

"Nothing important." Quinn glanced up. "Why?"

"Read on."

Quinn continued reading. A recounting of Rebecca's abduction and death . . . Ryan Parker finding the body . . . rehash rehash rehash . . . Banks also wrote about a specialist being called in from the FBI crime lab, and added the fact that Quinn had retrieved 189 files of male students from the MSU Dean. He noted: *The files of suspects from Penny Thompson's disappearance had been returned to MSU, an example of the incompetence and disorganization evident in the investigation.*

Banks also blasted the Sheriff's Department and Nick in particular: *One anonymous source close to the investigation said, "The Sheriff's Department has mishandled this case from the beginning. It's about time someone competent steps up to the plate. We are living in a state of fear and it has to stop."*

It implied that Quinn had said Nick was incompetent without actually quoting him.

What a jerk!

"I didn't tell him anything, about Olivia or the files," Quinn said, tossing the paper back at Nick. "He's just trying to rile you up. It's an anonymous quote, Nick. Don't take it personally."

Nick's expression told Quinn his friend had taken the criticism to heart.

"We're doing everything we can," Quinn said. "We have the best of the best looking at evidence. We're searching all known shacks and cabins. We're taking Ashley's car apart and Rebecca's as well. And I have the list of men who could have known Penny whittled down to a few dozen. Much more manageable than the hundreds we had twelve years ago, and the nearly two hundred from yesterday. Let's get on it."

Nick stood. "I have some things to do."

"What?"

"Nothing important. Just some ideas."

"I'm here if you want to brainstorm. Bounce ideas around." Nick looked defeated, something Quinn had never expected from his friend.

"Seriously, it's nothing. But if something

comes of it, I'll call you. Keep following Penny's associates. I'm probably chasing shadows."

He left before Quinn could question him further.

Quinn frowned. Something was disturbing Nick, but maybe it was just the article. Still, maybe he should go with him and help with whatever he was looking into.

He looked down at the huge stack of files he'd picked up from MSU yesterday. They had culled out the men who no longer fit the profile. Fifty-two possible suspects remained. He needed to narrow it down further.

Quinn picked up the phone and started making calls.

She felt detached, as if she weren't in her body, just watching the scene unfold like a movie on the filthy floor in front of her. She'd seen the same performance many times and it never failed to both arouse and repel her.

He panted over her, fucking her like a doll. The girl was only there because she was tied to a stake in the floor. He never had been able to keep the interest of a girl. It was as if after one date, his potential girlfriend sensed he harbored dark fantasies she wanted no part of. He hadn't even dated since that first girl, in Portland. When she'd said no, he'd lost his mind. Broke into her house and raped her. The fool.

She alone understood his needs. An insatiable appetite for power boiled under her skin, searing her from the inside out, needing release. Watching him satisfy his craving gave her some measure of relief. But he was such a fool. When he raped these girls, they still had the power. Because he wanted them, needed them, they controlled him.

The girl had cried herself out.

It usually happened over time. An hour. A day. Sometimes longer. But eventually, the girl accepted her fate and lay still, not fighting, not screaming. Silent tears running down her face.

She almost laughed at the absurdity of the whole thing. He was like a bitch in heat, needing the women to satiate his growing appetite. But it was becoming harder and harder to get the same satisfaction; she could tell by the viciousness of his abuse. The last girl, before Rebecca Douglas, he'd beaten to death so she'd never even had a chance to run.

He slapped the girl, trying to get her to respond to him. The sound of flesh on flesh normally excited her, but today it didn't have the usual effect.

For the first time in her adult life, a sliver of fear ran down her spine. She stepped out of the shack and breathed in the cold, fresh morning air.

She didn't fear for herself as much as she did for him. He was her responsibility, and his rash decision to take another girl so soon on the heels of the last was stupid. She'd tried to talk him out of it, tried to manipulate him out of it, but he'd been adamant: He'd take the girl with or without her.

She couldn't allow him to do it alone. He needed her. To watch. To cover his tracks. To protect him.

The other reasons she stayed with him this time were a little more complicated to discern, even for her. She felt compelled to watch, hating the thought of him on another woman without her involvement. If he ever thought his satisfaction was better, more complete, without her around, he would go after more women by himself. Every time he kidnapped another one, the threat of discovery increased. If he took more of them, he'd be found out. It was only a matter of time.

So she was protecting him. It had nothing to do with what these women had that she didn't, right? All she was doing was watching out for him like she'd always done.

He could have these women, but only if

she was part of it.

He was led around by an invisible leash by all the women in his life. Her. The girls he raped and killed. And especially by the one who got away.

She hadn't let him kill Miranda Moore because her existence kept him more under her thumb than anything else. Fool. He was a fool. But he needed her.

Everything seemed to be running away from them. They were going to have to leave and find somewhere else to hunt. To protect him.

As soon as they were done with Ashley van Auden.

CHAPTER
21

Nick sat in the far corner of the Clerk and Recorder's Office above the courthouse and pored over damn near a thousand parcel maps from the region of the county where the Butcher hunted.

While he had told Quinn he had an idea, he really had nothing more than a little hunch that the Butcher had a specific reason for choosing this section of Montana to hunt in. Maybe an idea would come from reviewing every land transaction for the past fifteen years.

He could have assigned a deputy to this tedious task, but after Eli Banks's article questioning his competence and the fiasco of a press conference, he needed to step away.

He didn't believe Quinn had called the Sheriff's Department "incompetent." But Nick's ego was bruised knowing everyone in town was reading about the failure of the

Gallatin County sheriff to catch the Butcher. His term was up next year, and at this point, he didn't want to run again. Sam Harris was breathing down his neck, second-guessing each decision he made, and with Eli Banks back in town dogging his every step, the pressure was getting to him.

Nick had been second-guessing every decision he'd made over the last three years. It was completely unproductive. But last night, unable to sleep, Nick had made a list of every major turn in the Butcher investigation since he'd been sheriff. He wouldn't have done anything differently; every avenue they'd explored was logical and followed the little evidence they had. But every path led to a dead end, and he didn't see it changing now.

He was glad he'd called in Quinn. Though some of his deputies grumbled over bringing the Feds into their jurisdiction, Nick would use every possible resource to catch the Butcher. And with Quinn came a quiet confidence, natural leadership, and the presence of authority.

Nick couldn't help but feel a little like a bumbling country cop when standing next to the sleek city investigator.

And then there was Miranda.

He'd gone to the Lodge last night just to

confirm what he'd already suspected. That Quinn had reclaimed Miranda's heart. That there was no hope that he could find a place back in her life. Regardless of her words, Nick knew Miranda. Her heart had always belonged to Quinn, and the time she spent with Nick was secondary.

It hurt because he loved her, but he'd get over it. All he really wanted was her happiness and peace. If Quinn could give that to her, then he'd accept it.

He had to focus on something productive, something that might make a difference in the investigation. He was tired of looking like a fool in the press. Of questioning every decision he'd ever made, not only since he'd been elected sheriff, but since becoming a cop.

He knew he was a good cop. But the extraordinary crimes of the Butcher pushed the limits of his experience.

He'd looked into land records in the past, but only current ownership. The seven victims, including Rebecca, had been found on land owned by different people. Three were on government land. What about ten years ago? Twenty years ago? Was there some commonality to the Butcher's hunting ground?

Nick had his personal map at his side and began plotting ownership records. He pulled the history on every parcel himself because he didn't trust the staff at the Recorder's office to keep his interest in the property records secret.

And if nothing came from it, he certainly didn't want to see another failure highlighted under Eli Banks's byline.

Quinn wanted to know what Miranda was thinking.

They'd met up at search headquarters well after the dinner hour. Neither had eaten, and Quinn suggested they go out for a meal. She'd almost said yes. He could see it in her eyes.

Instead, she told him her father would have something waiting for her. Since they both planned on coming back to the University first thing in the morning, Quinn asked if she wanted to ride back to the Lodge with him. Surprisingly, she agreed and climbed into his passenger seat.

He tried to ring Nick, but he didn't answer his cell phone or pager. Not a surprise; when Quinn talked to him earlier in the afternoon, Nick had sounded short and testy. The pressure from the news media was intense, but Quinn hoped Nick would ignore it. That was usually the best recourse in these situations.

The priority was finding Ashley van Auden.

Quinn had further narrowed the list of men from Penny's time at MSU to forty-three. He still had the two deputies Booker and Janssen working on preliminary background checks for each and every one of them. In the morning he hoped to be able to whittle the list down even more, to under thirty; but either way, he'd split the list with Nick and his senior investigators to start the laborious process of interviewing each man.

It could lead nowhere. But at this juncture, unless Olivia found something in the evidence to point them in a different direction, he was out of ideas.

He couldn't count on JoBeth Anderson regaining consciousness. Or, if she did, that she would be able to name or describe her attacker. He hoped it would happen, but witnesses popping out of a coma at just the right time to finger the killer only happened in B-movies.

Still, he prayed she would fully recover and have information leading them to a suspect. Before Ashley van Auden died.

He glanced over at Miranda as he turned down the long paved drive that led to the Lodge.

"You okay?"

"Twenty-four hours since he took Ashley. I feel like I'm counting down. Time is against us. We can't possibly cover every grid on the map."

He hated the defeat in her voice. "Don't do this to yourself. Don't start imagining the worst."

"It's hard not to, Quinn," she whispered. "I keep up the front with the search team, with Nick — with you — but every time I close my eyes, I picture Ashley chained and cold."

Quinn pulled into the employee parking behind the Lodge and cut the engine. A security light outside the kitchen entrance illuminated the immediate area, but they still had privacy.

He reached for her; her body was rigid. "Miranda, I wish I could take the images and feelings for you. I would do anything to erase the pain in your heart. You know that, don't you?"

She looked at him. The artificial light reflected off her eyes, making them appear bottomless. He wanted to kiss her, to hold her and tell her everything was going to be all right, to take her to bed and keep her nightmares at bay.

He reached out and touched her cheek.

"I never stopped loving you."

Miranda's heart rate quickened as she stared into Quinn's eyes. He looked sincere.

She didn't know what to believe. Her head told her to forgive him, that in many ways he was right to have done what he did. However, in her heart, she felt he'd never truly trusted her, that his faith in her was fragile.

"Quinn, I don't know how we can ever go back."

He blinked, a wave of hurt crossing his face. She didn't want to hurt him. She didn't know what to do.

Quinn tucked a lock of hair behind her ear. The gesture was so intimate she had to glance down. He used to do the exact same thing all the time when they were together before. One simple touch and memories of how much she had loved him flooded back, filling her first with warmth, then apprehension.

They couldn't go back. She was a different person today than ten years ago when she was a naïve wannabe FBI agent.

His light caress gave her an electric connection she hadn't had in a long, long time. It was as if he could read her mind, as if he knew that she ached inside and couldn't say the words. That she longed to be held by him again, to just be held without talking or explanations or awkwardness.

She stared at him, wanting so much to share her feelings, to be held, to make love.

Slowly, tenderly, the way he'd made love to her the first time.

She turned her lips to his hand and kissed his palm. It was all she could do not to fall into his arms.

But she had to think about these feelings. Think about the repercussions. Could she trust him? Did he trust her?

It hurt that she didn't have an answer to these questions.

"Good night," she whispered, and jumped out of the car before she changed her mind.

She heard Quinn's door open and close.

"I'll walk you to your cabin," he said.

She shook her head. "Dad waited up for me." She nodded toward the lights in the Lodge.

She walked through the brisk evening air the few feet to the rear door. She felt Quinn's gaze at her back and wondered what would happen if she turned back and asked him to come with her. She wanted to. God, she wanted to.

But what if he used her emotional vulnerability against her? Took her off the search, took her away from the case? Even as she thought it, she realized he'd been nothing but supportive after the first day. If he had any doubts about her, he was keeping them to himself.

But *she* had doubts. For ten years she'd been certain that Quinn had taken what she'd shared in confidence about her feelings, her fears, her damaged psyche, and used them against her to have her kicked out of Quantico. Yet it had as much to do with her own insecurities and fear as it did with anything Quinn may or may not have done.

It was better to put a little distance between herself and Quinn. Better to forget their past. Forget the kiss in the kitchen. Forget how he touched her with fingers that seared her skin and made her feel like a woman again.

She still felt his touch on her cheek, and she longed for so much more.

She closed the cabin door, shutting Quinn behind her. Her emotions were too raw, too close to the surface. She had to keep her distance. Because he could so easily break her heart all over again.

Quinn dialed Olivia as soon as he stepped into his room at the Lodge. Still, he couldn't get his mind off Miranda.

She was driving him crazy. He couldn't stop thinking about her, didn't want to stop. He wanted to sit her down in a chair and talk it out. But Miranda wasn't the type of woman to have a reasoned conversation. She acted on instinct, reacted on emotion.

He'd explained his actions at Quantico in painstaking detail in a letter she'd returned unopened. He'd tried to talk to her then; he had to find a way to make her listen now. If he could just find the right words, he knew she'd understand and forgive him. But both his decision and her subsequent actions had snowballed into a huge web of complex feelings he didn't know how to untangle.

He was so proud of what she'd accomplished this last decade, both professionally and personally. But the Butcher still haunted her and she wouldn't let anyone in to help.

He ran a hand through his hair as he paced the large bedroom.

Damn the woman. Didn't he just tell her he'd never stopped loving her? Yet she still walked away.

Hadn't she believed him? He'd never lied to her, but given their past, maybe she questioned his sincerity. How could he convince her?

He'd made a huge mistake ten years ago when he gave her space. He had given her too much. He should have visited in person, explained his reasons clearly, and told her he loved her. As many times as it took for her to believe him. When she hadn't returned his phone calls, he thought the letter was the best approach.

He was wrong. The only way to deal with Miranda was face-to-face.

"Hello? Quinn, is that you?" The voice on the other end of the phone startled him.

He shook his head to clear it. "Sorry, Liv. I was daydreaming."

"Day? It's eleven o'clock at night."

"Did I wake you?"

"No. What can I do for you?"

Olivia was always serious, by the book. He admired her steadfast devotion to her job as a lab technician. No forensic detail escaped her.

"Did you learn anything?"

"I've only been here one day. Laboratory tests take time." She said this like he should know it, which he did. But, dammit, he wanted all the information *now*. What was the use of being in a position to pull strings if those strings didn't yield immediate results?

"Sorry," he mumbled.

"Right."

"Sarcasm from you?" he teased.

"I'm tired. It's one in the morning in Virginia."

"I forgot. I'll let you go."

"There is one thing."

He stopped pacing. "What?"

"There's some dirt that seems — I don't know, different."

"Dirt? From where?"

"Hold on . . ." In the background, Quinn could hear Olivia ruffling through papers. "Okay. There were ten soil samples taken from the shack where Rebecca was held, each from a different area of the shack and immediate surrounding area. Two of the inside samples were different than the soil collected from outside the shack."

"Different? How?"

"Distinctive. First of all, it's red. I don't recall from my studies the soil in Montana being red. And the fact that it doesn't match the outdoor soil set off my internal alarms. But this isn't my area of expertise. I overnighted a sample to Quantico for analysis."

"Red? As in, blood? Fire-engine red?"

"No, more like brick red."

"Brick?"

"But lighter than soil."

"You've lost me, Liv."

She laughed and Quinn smiled. Olivia didn't laugh much, but when she did it warmed anyone within earshot. "The color of brick, but with a texture more like clay than soil. Clay is very fine, but when it gets wet, the particles bind together."

"Like pottery?" He frowned, trying to picture what Olivia was explaining.

"Same principle, but this is a different type of clay."

"When will you know? Can you pinpoint where it might have come from?" He was about to ask a dozen other questions when Olivia cut him off.

"I'm rushing the analysis, Quinn, but the sample is still with Federal Express and my people can't do anything until they receive it."

"I'm sorry. But this sounds like the best lead we have."

"I know, I've been reading the case files you left with me." She paused. "How is Miranda?"

"Okay."

"And?"

"You know Miranda. She's working too hard, not eating enough. But she's good at what she does. I just wish it didn't hurt her so much." He sank onto the bed, staring at his own feet, but seeing only Miranda's dark blue eyes fill with the pain of the world.

"Quinn?"

"Yeah."

"You still love her."

"I know."

"Have you told her?"

"Yes."

"And?"

"She doesn't care. I hurt her, Liv. I didn't want to, but I had to."

"Can you explain that to her?"

"I tried." He sounded defensive.

"Yes, I remember you tried back then, when she was raw and emotional. What about now?"

"Nothing's changed, Liv. I've tried twice to talk to her, but she walks away. She doesn't want to listen."

"Make her listen."

"Dammit, I've *tried.*"

"Try harder."

Even though he'd meticulously plotted out his map, Nick almost missed the turnoff to Judge Parker's cabin in Big Sky.

Thick trees dipped low and scratched the roof of his SUV as he started up the steep slope. His headlights brightened the area directly in front of him, but the narrow gravel road was lined with a tangle of thick bushes and vines, brushing against his truck on both sides.

An hour ago, he'd been sitting at his kitchen table eating takeout and staring at the maps and property records he'd copied from the Recorder's Office when he plotted the deed to this particular cabin on the map. It jumped out at him: This property stood in the center of a fifteen-mile circle like a bull's-eye. This cabin was the only building accessible on foot from every crime scene they had discovered. While some of the terrain was treacherous and could take hours, a skilled hiker could handle it.

The Butcher was physically fit enough to make it.

Nick was treading on dangerous ground: the cabin was owned by Judge Richard Parker.

Even if his gut instincts were correct and the cabin was a stopping point for the Butcher, that didn't mean Judge Parker knew anything about it. The man owned ten thousand acres. He couldn't possibly police all of them.

Nick couldn't afford to have one of the most powerful men in Montana turn against him or the Sheriff's Department. It was best to investigate the cabin under wraps, then call it in if he learned anything.

It wasn't like he was going to confront anyone. All he wanted to do was confirm its existence and look around. If there was evidence of a break-in or recent inhabitation, Nick would bring in a team of investigators and talk to Parker about the place.

Parker hadn't claimed the property as rental income, but that didn't mean much. He could have leased it to friends for a weekend, or just used it himself. The judge had inherited it from his father, according to estate records. This particular dwelling was in the middle of nowhere, like many vacation homes in southwest Montana.

If Nick hadn't spent five hours at the Clerk and Recorder's Office reviewing every property record within a ten-mile radius of each known victim, he'd never have noticed this cabin.

He'd called Quinn as he neared the turnoff to Gallatin Lodge to see if he wanted to join him. But his voice mail picked up and Nick didn't leave a message. Driving down to Big Sky was a whim; his hunch would probably lead nowhere. After spending the last few days being beaten up in the press, he'd rather keep this theory low-key until he had some proof.

Pushing all doubt from his mind, Nick drove the two winding miles up the narrow, overgrown gravel driveway.

A sharp turn led right to the cabin's carport, and even though he was expecting the building it seemed to jump out at him. He slammed on his brakes, cutting his lights at the same time.

He turned off the ignition and got out of the truck. He shivered and zipped up his jacket. Now that the sun had disappeared, it was hovering around fifty degrees. The weather predicted a low of forty-two. He cringed thinking about Ashley van Auden.

When he'd dated Miranda, he noticed she had a thing for heat. Her showers were scalding. She bundled up in temperate weather. She had blankets and hot coffee in her car at all times. He'd thought it peculiar for the longest time. He never connected it to the Butcher's attack until one night, shortly before they broke up.

"Hey, Randy, let's head out to Meyer's Lake."

It was summer and still eighty degrees even though the sun was low. The night promised to be beautiful.

"I don't feel like it."

Nick frowned. He was used to Miranda's mood swings, but she was usually spontaneous. She loved to ski, loved to river raft, was the only woman he knew who relished being in the outdoors. It was one of the reasons he'd fallen in love with her.

Meyer's Lake was the place for couples to hang out and skinny dip.

Oh shit, he'd put his foot in it.

"I'm sorry. I should have thought—"

She cut him off. "I don't care who sees my body, Nick."

He frowned. "I wasn't thinking."

"It's going to be sixty degrees tonight."

He didn't get it. "I promise, we'll come home before it gets that cold."

She looked at him, disillusion in her eyes. "I'm not going swimming anywhere at night."

They'd ended up staying at Nick's place and watching a movie. Nick thought Miranda simply didn't want her scarred body to be seen naked, and he felt bad for suggesting it.

Now, he knew. It wasn't only being naked, it was being naked in cold water.

He found himself gripping the ten-millimeter police issue he carried. He almost reholstered it.

Instead, he decided caution was in order.

There were no lights on in the cabin. It appeared deserted. He marginally relaxed.

He circled the cabin. It was the standard A-frame — a large room or rooms on the main floor supported by pillars; a loft of sorts in the V of the roof.

He walked up the rickety staircase that led to the wraparound deck. It was obvious no one was here. Dark. No vehicle. Empty. Still, his entire body tensed, his instincts on alert.

He looked through a window, the half moon allowing him to make out shadows. Sparse furnishings — a couch, a chair, a table. No luggage. No food on the table. No gun or knife or woman strapped to the floor.

Yes, it had been a waste of time coming down here.

He holstered his gun, looked around the deck. Two lounge chairs were pushed flush with the house. He crossed the deck and stared at a lake a hundred yards away, the moonlight reflecting off the still surface.

What am I going to do now?

Well, no one knew he'd ventured out this way. Go home, sleep a couple of hours, tell Quinn he'd gone through the property records on a hunch that didn't pan out. Brush it off and focus on Quinn's fifty-some-odd men from the University.

It's what he should have done today rather than pursuing a long shot.

Nick turned away from the railing and saw a pair of boots sitting outside the side door.

Odd.

He reached for his gun.

Before he could draw his weapon, he was unconscious.

CHAPTER
22

Miranda glanced at her watch. It was already seven thirty in the morning; where was Quinn?

Because she'd left her truck at the University, she was dependent on Quinn for transportation back to town. Why had she agreed to ride with him last night?

You were exhausted. Yes, she had feared she would fall asleep at the wheel. Nearly two weeks of virtually sleepless nights had taken their toll.

She'd slept surprisingly well last night. No nightmares, no interruptions. But when she woke up in the morning, she remembered a conversation she'd had with Quinn a year before she was accepted into Quantico. Thinking about it now, she realized he had always had doubts, but not about her ability.

"I'm leaving tomorrow morning," Quinn said as he tucked Miranda's hair behind her ear.

305

"Tomorrow? I thought you had a week off."

"I did, but something's come up."

His tone clued her to the truth. "A murder."

"You don't want to hear about it."

"Yes I do."

"Miranda, why do you do this to yourself?"

They were sitting on the front porch of the Lodge. It was late evening and most of the guests had retired, or were having a final drink before the bar closed at eleven.

"I'm going to be an FBI agent, Quinn. I can handle the details." She'd signed up for psychology and criminology courses; she'd already received her bachelor's degree by doubling up on her studies last year. She would have entered Quantico this year, except she wouldn't be twenty-three for ten more months.

"You keep talking about it."

"I told you my plans."

"You did. I just thought you'd change your mind."

"Why?" Had she given him the impression she was flaky? She hoped not.

He looked at her, his dark eyes holding so much emotion she felt wonderfully, completely drowned in him. "I've been amazed by you for a year, Miranda. You've inspired me when I was becoming jaded with the job. Not catching the bastard who hurt you—" He swallowed and glanced away, but not before she caught a glimmer of moisture in his eyes.

"That's not your fault. He will be stopped. Someday we will find him."

Quinn slowly turned back to her, holding her hands tight. She leaned into him, content and confident in herself and her own sexuality for the first time since last spring. "You're so close to this. I — I think you're smart enough and driven enough to make a damn good FBI agent. But I think the Butcher investigation is driving you more than wanting to be an agent." He sighed and stroked her hair. "I don't know if I'm making any sense."

"I'll prove to you I'm capable." Did she sound panicked? No, just emphatic. "You said you'd give me a letter of recommendation. But if you don't want to, I can get others."

"I promised you a letter, and you'll get it."

"Besides, I won't be entering the Academy for nearly a year." She paused. "You didn't tell me about your case."

He held her close to his side and they watched the shadows. She'd bundled in four layers of clothing and had a blanket around her legs. Here, with Quinn at her side, she felt secure.

"The victim is a child," he said softly. "They're the worst cases."

"Miranda?"

She jumped, startled. Quinn stood at the base of the stairs looking at her quizzically.

307

"Ready?" he asked.

"Let's go."

She should have read between the lines back then. Thinking back on that night, she realized that Quinn had reservations about her career choice from the beginning. He gave her the letter of recommendation because he had promised, but he'd never expected her to follow through. She didn't know if she was more upset with him for his concerns or with herself for not picking up on them at the time.

She'd been so certain she'd wanted to be in the FBI. Listening to Quinn talk about the cases he'd worked and the murderers he'd put behind bars — it inspired her and gave her hope that she, too, could fight the bad guys and win.

But there was only one bad guy she really wanted — needed — to defeat. Not for the first time, she feared the shrink might have been right. Her determination to capture the Butcher drove her, had led her to the FBI. She wouldn't have called it obsession, but she focused on little else. How could she give up when *he* still hunted women?

In the car, Quinn said, "Miranda?"

"What?"

"Is something wrong?"

"No." Was it that obvious? She shot Quinn

a smile. "I actually slept pretty well last night."

"Glad to hear it. You needed it." He turned onto the main highway. She glanced at the dashboard clock: 7:50. She started planning the search, mentally reviewing the grids they'd worked on yesterday and wondering if there was someplace else she should send her team. Anyplace she picked was a shot in the dark.

"Does it even help?" she said.

"Excuse me?"

She hadn't realized she'd spoken out loud. "I was just thinking about the searches. Every time another woman is abducted, I pull out all the stops and scour thousands of acres. But does it help? We've never found one in time. We couldn't save Rebecca. Why did I ever think we could?"

"Don't second-guess yourself, Miranda. Nick was doing that yesterday because the press jumped all over him. You are an expert in search and rescue. I looked over your methods and routes and I would have done the exact same thing with the people and re-sources you had."

"You would have?"

"Absolutely. And if it weren't for your me-thodical searches, we'd never have found some of the bodies."

"But it was too late." They'd found the Croft sisters four weeks after they'd been killed. Rebecca less than a day. But it would have been weeks if Judge Parker's son hadn't stumbled across her body.

"I talked to Olivia last night."

"And? Did she find out something? She wouldn't have called if she didn't have news. What is it?"

"I called her," Quinn explained. "And she doesn't have anything definitive. But she sent some unusual soil samples to the FBI lab in Virginia. Do you know of anyplace around here that has red clay or red soil?"

"Red?" She thought back to her geology classes. "I don't think so. Not around here." She bit her lip. "Red clay? I could talk to someone in the geology department, they might have an idea."

"Why don't you ask — discreetly — when I drop you off at MSU? I'd come with you, but I need to meet with Nick about the University's records. We're going to split up the remaining stack. It'll be about three dozen men to check out, but right now it's the only thing we've got until Olivia comes up with something definitive."

Miranda glanced at Quinn. He wanted her to follow up on this? She hadn't expected him to include her in anything, in light of their past. Knowing that he trusted her to find answers, even if it was a small component of the investigation, meant everything.

"Thank you," she said.

"For what?"

"Trusting me."

He paused. "Just be careful."

The Bitch was going to skin him alive.

But what was he supposed to do? The damn cop was snooping around. What if he'd decided to break all those search and seizure laws and go into the cabin?

Well, he couldn't really say anything to The Bitch about that. She didn't know about everything he'd kept. She wouldn't understand. He *needed* a connection to the women he'd cared for. He touched their photographs and remembered everything about them. Their hair — how soft it was. How beautiful their throats were. And their breasts . . . he loved their breasts most of all. Beautiful, round, full.

No, The Bitch wouldn't understand.

But he had to get rid of the cop's damn truck. Run it off the side of the road maybe. Or ditch it where it could be easily found. Better to hide it or have it discovered?

He didn't know. That's why he'd called her in the first place.

She drove up the narrow driveway faster than she should, her wheels spinning, and almost slammed into the back of the sheriff's truck. She jumped out, her blonde hair bouncing off her back.

"You fucking *idiot!*"

"He was snooping."

"We gotta go." She stomped up the stairs and strode over to the door. "Where is he? What did you do with the body? Bury him?"

"He's with the girl."

She blinked, then her eyes widened. "Why the fuck would you drag his body miles away? Why not just bury him here?"

"I don't think he's dead."

"Why the hell not?"

He shrugged. He hadn't planned on killing him. He just knocked him out. There was some blood, but he didn't think he was dead. Once the sheriff was just lying there on the deck, there was no urge to kill him. What was the fun in killing someone who couldn't see it coming?

Oh, well. He'd never planned on letting the sheriff go. Eventually he'd die of starvation.

"You are an idiot. You're stupid, stupid! We have to go, leave Montana. You've ruined my life. Damn, damn, damn!"

The Bitch stomped and paced, pulling at her hair. He shrank against the wall of the house. There was no telling what she'd do in this mood.

She muttered and swore for ten minutes before turning around and pointing her long, bony finger at him. "Pack up. We're going. Leave the girl, leave Nick Thomas. They'll be dead before anyone finds them. I have some money put aside. We'll get new identities, maybe in California. Yeah, California is good. Los Angeles is a big city, and we'll lay low."

"No."

She stopped talking and stared at him. "What?"

"I'm not going. Theron and Aglaia have eggs. I can't go until they've hatched."

"You're going to jeopardize everything because of some stupid fucking *birds*?"

He tensed. "They're not stupid."

"They're *birds*. And didn't you tell me once that they're everywhere, even breeding on the ledges of skyscrapers in Los Angeles? If you need to go see the stupid things, you can just walk down the street rather than traipsing through muck in the middle of nowhere. Dammit, this is serious! You kidnapped the sheriff; we can't stay here. We have to go. And you will come with me."

Her disdain for Theron and Aglaia ate at him as The Bitch went on and on, making plans about what she would tell her husband, how they were going to buy new driver's licenses, when they would leave.

He wasn't leaving.

She lied, just like everyone else. She'd always told him she was proud of his work, how she admired his patience and how well he cared for the peregrines. But now she called them *stupid.* How could she? How could she think that way about an animal as sleek and fast and free and beautiful as Theron?

The familiar anger built, but this time it was different. The fury grew more powerful. More real. His own needs weren't essential anymore; this rage swelled into something more important than him.

If he didn't return to Theron, who would look out for them? Some bureaucrat from the state who identified the birds by their radio frequencies? Never. Theron had a distinct personality. Unique. He'd never allow him to be relegated to a mere number, one of many, nothing. Now that the peregrines were no longer considered an endangered species, no one cared about them like he did.

If he left, what would happen to them? Who would watch them? Track them? Protect them?

No. He wasn't leaving. And she couldn't make him.

Besides, he hadn't finished with the blonde he had hidden away. He couldn't leave until he was done with her.

Slap!

He raised his hand to his cheek, the heat from her assault spreading from his head to the rest of his body. He stared at her — he'd almost forgotten she was standing in front of him, talking.

"You haven't listened to a word I said! I swear, you're nothing more than a fool. Get your stuff together. *Now!*"

"No."

He sounded calm. In fact, he felt free. He savored his defiance.

"What?" She sounded shocked. Good.

"I'm not leaving. Not yet." He took a step toward her. He was seven inches taller than The Bitch, but he'd never felt bigger until now. He straightened his spine and stared her down.

She glanced away first, taking a step back. Was that fear on her face? Yes, it was. He knew that look well. He just never had thought he'd see it on her.

For years she'd coddled and neglected him; loved and hated him; protected and hurt him.

She no longer had any power over him. The years washed away.

Her eyes darted right and left, but she smiled. A shaky smile.

She knew.

"Sweetheart," she said in that cooing voice of hers. "Be reasonable."

"I'm not leaving until the eggs are hatched."

"But—"

His hand came down across her face and she staggered backward.

He didn't know who was more startled — her or him. He'd never raised a hand to her. Never seriously considered it.

But she'd never attacked his birds before.

He grew under the power of her fear. The tables had turned.

"You can do whatever you damn well please," he told her. "I'm not leaving."

CHAPTER
23

Nick remembered the first time he got drunk. Not simple intoxication. Mind-numbing, porcelain-god-bowing, ground-worshipping drunk.

He would gladly trade the pain in his head now for a three-day hangover.

A moan escaped his parched lips, the faint sound making his headache worse. His eyelids felt crusted with sand and shut tight by weights. Just the thought of moving intensified the pain.

But he was alive. That, he knew. Surely there wasn't pain when you were dead? Unless hell existed and he'd done something bad enough to merit eternal damnation. The way he felt now, he might prefer hell.

Cold seeped through the pain in his head. He shivered, then moaned from the pain of moving. Though deeply chilled, he wasn't outside. He was lying on his side, something harder than the ground beneath him. A wood floor. The smells. Mold. Urine. Dead animals. The musty stench of layer upon layer of damp dirt.

He tried to move his arm. His hands were numb, but not from the cold. They were bound behind him. He breathed deeply, riding the tide of pain as he exhaled. His breath came right back at him; his face was up against a wall.

What had happened? He'd been driving . . . where? That's right, to the small A-frame on the far southern boundary of Judge Parker's vast land holdings.

He hadn't seen anything suspicious and was about to head home. A complete waste of time, and he remembered thinking he was glad he hadn't bothered Quinn. He'd turned, seen a pair of boots, and thought it odd that they sat by the side door of an unused cabin.

He'd reached for his gun, but someone hit him from behind. He hadn't heard a thing, only felt a sharp pain . . . then nothing.

Until now.

Had his attacker been sitting in the dark in Parker's cabin the entire time Nick had been walking the perimeter? Why? Had someone broken in? Were people using it illegally? Or did Parker know them?

Was his far-reaching theory true about the Butcher using it as home base?

Nick knew with certainty that he wasn't in Parker's cabin. The foul odors and deep cold suggested a makeshift cabin or small shack.

Deep cold. Miranda hated the cold because of what the Butcher had done. Now, Nick was in the same position. Bound, on a cold wood floor.

Could Richard Parker be the Butcher?

Nick couldn't imagine the judge he'd known his entire adult life torturing women. But he partly fit the profile, didn't he? Maybe a little older. And he was married and certainly not a loner. But Parker was physically fit and had been raised hunting and fishing in southwest Montana. Of course, the most damning evidence was that Nick had been attacked at Parker's cabin.

FBI profiles could be wrong. The thought that Parker could be the Butcher sickened Nick. He remembered all the times he'd gone to the judge for help getting additional resources. The strings Parker had pulled to get the county to allocate more resources for searches that always ended with bad news. Could Parker have been laughing from the sidelines, knowing how wrong the police were in their analysis? Did he get some sort of sick pleasure watching Miranda search for women he held captive?

There was no concrete proof the Butcher was Parker. The killer could have staked out the cabin, seen that it was rarely used, and stayed there without incident. Or Parker could have rented it or loaned it to a friend.

Shit. He should have left the damn message on Quinn's voice mail. They could have surveilled Parker, put an undercover team on the house, dug deeper into Parker's past.

He'd spent so much time second-guessing himself this week that he hadn't listened to his instincts. Now he was paying the price.

A slight noise, a rustling, made him jump. Rodents? A bear?

No. The sound hadn't come from outside. He wasn't alone.

Nick didn't know how he knew it, but all at once he sensed someone else breathing the same air he was. Then he heard it. A faint whisper.

The pounding beneath his skull was so loud it took him a minute to understand the words.

"Who's there? Who's there?"

He tried to speak, but it came out a moan.

"Who's there?" Whispered. Hoarse. Female.

He licked his dry lips. "Sheriff." The effort to speak hurt.

"Who?"

Dammit, he could barely think, let alone talk.

He forced himself to swallow. "Sheriff. Thomas." He spoke each word carefully.

"Sheriff?"

Nick realized then that the person wasn't whispering. The voice was hoarse. Like when his brother Steve had laryngitis back in high school.

Or a throat raw from repeated screaming.

"Ashley?" Even speaking single words pained him, but he had to get over it. He was certain he had a concussion. And there was something wrong with his legs. Maybe they were bound as well, but he couldn't feel anything below his waist. Nick's entire body was cold and numb.

But he was alive. He planned on staying alive. And keeping Ashley van Auden alive, too. How he would do this was another story. He didn't know where he was, what time it was, or how the hell to get out of here.

"Yes." Her voice squeaked out, then ended in a sob. She was so close that if he wasn't bound he could reach out and touch her. "He's going to kill us. He's going to kill us.

It's him. The Butcher. He's going to kill us like all those others—"

"Shhh."

Ashley repeated her mantra over and over, making Nick's head throb. He tried to shush her, but couldn't, so he tried to ignore her. That failed, too.

"Ashley. Ashley." He repeated her name until she finally stopped sobbing.

She whimpered. "What?"

"We need to plan. Think." Think? Hell, he could barely calculate two plus two.

"I don't want to die," she sobbed.

Neither did he. "At some point he'll release you."

"And then he'll kill me! I know what he did to Rebecca Douglas. H-h-he slit her throat. He k-k-killed her!"

"Ashley. Stop." Nausea rose in his throat and his mind swam, dizzy. He took in as big a breath as he could; eased it out. In. Out. He couldn't lose consciousness again. It was too dangerous for both of them.

"Sheriff?"

From the concern in her whisper, he must have dozed off or passed out for a minute. "I'm here."

"You didn't answer me."

"Sorry." He exhaled. "Do you know where you are?"

"No. I'm blindfolded. I can't see anything."

"Did you see anyone when you were kidnapped?"

"No," she sobbed. "No one. Ohmygod, Jo! She's not here, she hasn't answered me. She's dead, isn't she? She's dead." Ashley started sobbing hysterically. It took Nick several minutes to calm her down. It wouldn't do any good for Ashley to know her friend was in a coma, so he lied.

"JoBeth is going to be fine. She's in the hospital, but she's going to be fine."

"Thank God, thank God."

Did the Butcher think Nick knew his identity? He must have felt threatened somehow to have attacked him at the cabin.

If that was the case, there was no way the Butcher would give Nick a chance to escape. Unless he found a way out, he was as good as dead.

"No matter what, when you get out of here, run. Don't do the expected. Try to cover your tracks. Avoid screaming or even breathing too loud. Stay in the trees. If it's night and you can't go on, bury yourself under leaves and hide. But as much as you can, run." He pictured a map of the places the Butcher chased the women. Everything was south of the interstate, west of Gallatin

Gateway. "Head northeast as much as possible. Eventually, in a day, maybe two or three, you'll hit the main road."

"How do you know?"

"I know his hunting ground."

"What about you?"

"I'll stay with you if I can."

She didn't say anything. Maybe she knew how injured he was. Or maybe she thought he wouldn't be released.

Several moments passed, and Nick thought Ashley had gone to sleep. "He hurt me."

Her voice was faint. Pleading. Almost childlike.

"I know, honey. I'm sorry." He was so sorry. Her abduction was partly his failure. He hadn't been able to protect the women in his town from the madman who stalked them.

That hurt as much as the pain in his head.

Lying here, on the cold, hard floor, Nick knew they were in a dire situation. The Butcher would be back before anyone could find them. No matter how many people were out searching, they'd never be able to cover enough ground.

He had to think, come up with a plan to save Ashley and himself.

But he feared it was already too late.

CHAPTER
24

Miranda knocked on the door of Professor Austin's basement office in Traphagen Hall. It hadn't changed in the fifteen years since she'd taken his class. Rocks were the prominent decorative item in the overstuffed office. Topographical maps of the western United States filled the walls along with faded charts of rock and soil comparisons. The entire room smelled like dirt and paper.

Professor Austin had already been old when Miranda was in his class; he hadn't changed. His white hair stood straight up, and his beard needed a trim. But his emerald eyes sparkled with recognition when Miranda cleared her throat to catch his attention.

"If it isn't Miranda Moore!" He stood, not noticing or caring when a stack of papers hit the floor, some sliding under his desk. No wonder he'd lost their midterm essays fifteen years ago.

"Hi, Professor," she said as he gave her a hard slap on the back and a wide grin.

"It hasn't been so long that you forgot to call me Glen?"

"Sorry." On the first day of class, Professor Austin insisted everyone call him by his first name. The problem was, he *looked* like a professor, and Miranda always felt uncomfortable calling him something as informal as "Glen." Maybe if his name were Archibald . . .

"What brings you here so early?"

"The Rebecca Douglas murder."

The professor's face clouded. "Poor girl."

"The investigators found something unusual and I thought you might be able to help."

"Me?" He sat on the corner of his desk and more papers toppled to the floor. He motioned for Miranda to sit in the single chair.

She removed a large box of books from the seat before sitting. "There's an unusual soil sample that's been sent to the FBI lab at Quantico for testing. It's red. Like brick. The lab technician says it's clay. I couldn't think of any place around here that had red clay or soil. I thought maybe you would know of some place."

"Hmmm." He looked beyond Miranda, over her shoulder at the wall behind her, lost in thought. "There's an area over by Three Forks along the Missouri, but I wouldn't call it brick-colored. Red dirt. Hmmm." He thought again, then jumped up suddenly, startling Miranda.

He crossed to the crammed bookshelf, pulled out a thick tome, and turned to the back. Nodding and muttering to himself, he flipped through the book and stopped. "Red soil, particularly clay, is an erosional product that is very common in the Middle Paleozoic sandstone formations."

Miranda felt like she was in school again. "What are the Middle Paleozoic formations?"

He glanced at her and frowned. "You passed my class, didn't you?"

"Yes, sir." But the information had promptly left her memory.

He shook his head and sighed. "The Paleozoic formations were created by shallow seas that covered much of the western U.S. from 500 to 250 million years ago, particularly the Four Corners states — Colorado, Utah, Arizona, and New Mexico — as well as a large slice of Nevada."

"But what about southwest Montana?"

"Well, like I said, there are fine clays and

soils all along the Missouri River. They come in varying colors and textures, but nothing that I would call red. Still." He frowned. "If I can see it, I might be able to tell you more."

"Thanks, Professor. Glen." She stood. "I'll see if I can have someone bring you a sample, but it's evidence and I don't know how much the lab retained."

"I hope you and Sheriff Thomas catch this guy. He's been terrifying the women of Bozeman far too long."

"Thanks." She left, her heart beating frantically. She pulled out her cell phone and called Quinn.

"Peterson."

"Quinn, it's Miranda. I just spoke to Professor Austin about the soil. He said there's a small area in western Montana that might have it. It's also found in New Mexico, Arizona, Utah, and Colorado. Can he take a look? He might be able to give us more information."

"I'll call Olivia and see if she can have someone drive it down to the University."

"Thanks."

"Is Nick over there?"

"With me? No. I haven't seen him this morning."

"We were supposed to meet thirty minutes ago at his office, and he's not here. I tried his house and cell phone and he's not picking up."

Miranda frowned. "That's unlike Nick."

"Hold on." Miranda heard Quinn mumbling in the background, then he came back on. "Deputy Booker has been trying to track him down, but no one has heard from him since yesterday evening when he called for his messages."

"I'll drive by his house. Maybe he's sick," Miranda said. Her stomach did flips. Something was wrong.

"Be careful," Quinn said. "Booker and I are going to call around and see who talked to him late yesterday. Check in as soon as you get to Nick's, okay?"

"I will." She shut her cell phone and crossed the campus to her Jeep.

Fifteen minutes later, Miranda stopped in front of Nick's small Victorian on a quiet street in downtown Bozeman. His SUV wasn't in the driveway.

The hairs on the back of her neck prickled. The house *felt* empty.

Miranda slid out of the car and cautiously approached the house. She didn't know why she felt so apprehensive: it was the middle of the morning in downtown Bozeman. Down the street, an old man was watering his lawn. Around the corner, she heard young kids playing a game of tag, their shrieks of laughter slicing the air.

But Quinn had sounded concerned. Nick hadn't checked in this morning.

She walked up the wide front steps and paused on the porch, staring at the bench she and Nick had often sat on, talking, during their years of friendship. It reminded her of what she'd lost after they split up — before they'd been involved, Miranda never thought twice about stopping over for pizza and beer, or just sitting around talking. But after they stopped seeing each other romantically, she'd never felt comfortable just visiting.

She'd always considered Nick her best friend. But during the last year or so they'd had only a working relationship. It saddened her.

She rang the bell, then knocked. "Nick! It's Miranda."

No answer.

She knocked again and looked through the narrow side window. Nothing moved within sight.

Leaving the porch, she walked down the carport toward the rear of the house. Everything seemed in place. No broken windows, no open doors.

She circled the house and noticed nothing

unusual. Nick kept a spare key in the shed in the rear of the property, so she retrieved it and unlocked the back door. The house was too cold — as if the heat hadn't been on the night before.

Nervous, she pulled out her gun. Foolish, she thought, but better a fool than dead.

The kitchen was immaculate except for a large plastic cup from a local fast-food restaurant. It sat on the edge of the counter and she picked it up carefully. It was half full. Nick kept his trash under the kitchen sink; she walked over and opened the cabinet door. On top was a bag from the same restaurant. She extracted it and looked at the receipt. Time stamped 8:04 the night before.

She put the trash back, looked around, but didn't see anything else out of place. She went upstairs and paused in the bathroom. Nick was a tidy person by nature. He had a place for everything. On his organized counter was a pill box with seven compartments, one for each day of the week. Nick believed daily vitamins kept him healthy, and Miranda couldn't remember a day he had been out ill. He always took them first thing in the morning, right when he got up, so he didn't forget.

She opened the compartment for *Friday.* Today's pills were still there.

She opened all the other compartments — maybe he wasn't as regimented as he used to be.

Sunday through Thursday were empty. Nick hadn't changed.

Going back to her Jeep, she called Quinn. "Nick's not at home."

"Shit."

"He came home last night after eight, but I think he left sometime later." She explained about the fast-food receipt.

"Do you know what he was doing yesterday?"

"No. I assumed you did."

"No idea."

"Where are you?"

"Nick's office."

"I'll be right over. I have a bad feeling about this."

"So do I." Quinn sounded as worried as Miranda felt.

Quinn was going through Nick's desk trying to find out where he'd gone off to when the undersheriff, Sam Harris, came in without knocking.

Harris was a short man who stood rigid in an attempt to make himself appear taller. Quinn had met many men in law enforcement like Harris, cops who enjoyed the power they had just because they wore a uniform.

"Agent Peterson," Harris said with a nod. "What can I do for you?"

"More, what can I do for you? It seems the sheriff has disappeared, and that puts me in charge. Of course, I'm pleased to have the FBI assisting our small department."

"We need an APB put out on Nick if it hasn't already been done. I asked two deputies to put together a timeline of Nick's entire day yesterday. We know he ate dinner at home between eight and nine. He called in to dispatch for messages at eight thirty from his home phone. But at some point he left and didn't return."

"It's done," Harris said.

"Thanks."

Quinn was about to ask if Nick's truck had Global Positioning — many police departments had installed the systems in their vehicles — when Harris spoke up.

"I need to brief the mayor on the investigation. She didn't hear from Nick after the press conference yesterday, and the mayor has asked for daily reports."

"Nick and I agreed that the mayor — and media — are on a need-to-know basis. I don't have to tell you that this is a very sensitive investigation."

"I completely agree," Harris said in a tone that conveyed the exact opposite, "but the mayor has been upset with the media coverage. She's being put under intense scrutiny not only by the local paper, but national news stations."

"Everyone's under the microscope," Quinn said. "It's the nature of the business."

Harris smiled thinly. "True, true. But you know which way shit flows. The mayor is under pressure, we're all under pressure."

Even under the most heated circumstances, Quinn usually handled local politics well. But this case was personal. First Miranda's involvement, now Nick's disappearance.

"I understand," Quinn said with forced restraint. "I will trust you to relay the appropriate information to the mayor."

Harris stared at him. "Let me ask you something, Agent Peterson. Put your friendship with Sheriff Thomas aside. Can you honestly say everything that could be done has been done?"

"I'm not going to stand here and play Monday-morning quarterback when we have two missing people," Quinn said. "I can assure you, I have found no fault with the Gallatin County Sheriff's Department."

"We're not a big department. We don't

334

have the resources for two major missing person's cases. Maybe the sheriff just needed a little time. He's been under intense pressure." Harris attempted to sound understanding, but an undercurrent of disdain was evident in his tone.

Quinn was about to respond when Harris cut him off.

"Perhaps now's the time to bring in some more of your people," he said, standing with his hands behind his back. "Since the sheriff is unable to request the assistance at this time, I would be more than happy to do it."

It was subtle to be sure, but coupled with Harris's tone, Quinn didn't miss the insinuation that Nick should have requested additional FBI assistance.

He took a deep breath before answering. "Thank you," he said diplomatically, "but a pair of agents are already on their way to assist with the interviews. They'll be here tonight. In fact, I need to get on it right now."

Miranda burst through the door while asking breathlessly, "Quinn, have they found Nick yet?"

She almost ran into Sam Harris. A look of distaste swam over her face, then she hid it. "Sam," she acknowledged.

"Miranda," he said in the same formal tone. He looked back at Quinn. "I'll be happy to talk to the mayor for you, Agent Peterson," Harris said with another curt nod.

"What was that about?" Miranda asked as she closed the door behind the undersheriff.

"Hell if I know. Power game?" He ran a hand through his hair. "Last thing we need are egos getting in the way of the job."

"No word?"

"Nothing."

"Was Sam acting his usual asshole self?" She rolled her eyes.

"More or less. Harris was right about one thing."

"What?"

"We don't have the resources for two major missing persons cases."

"Don't say that. We can work them simultaneously."

"As best we can, we will. But the priority right now is Ashley van Auden." The phone on Nick's desk buzzed. Quinn answered it, and a few moments later hung up.

"That was Jeanne Price, the assistant clerk from the Clerk and Recorder's Office. Apparently, Nick spent five hours copying maps and property records yesterday afternoon."

"What are we waiting for? Let's go."

Three hours later, Quinn and Miranda sat at the Clerk and Recorder's Office staring at the piles of maps and land records Nick had pulled.

Neither Quinn nor Miranda could make any sense of the thousand pages of information. When Miranda asked Jeanne Price what specific copies she'd made for Nick, she was informed that Nick made all his own copies.

"Do you think he had a lead and pursued it? Got into an accident or some sort of trouble?" Miranda stared at Quinn, worried.

"Nick's too smart to go off without backup," Quinn said. He frowned.

"What?" she asked.

"He was feeling overwhelmed yesterday. Between the press, and the lack of evidence, and the national media coming in — I don't know. I can't see him doing anything on his own, but maybe it was a long shot."

"Long shot. He should have told *somebody* where he was going!" She'd always been ready to run off in any direction, but Nick had repeatedly insisted she alert dispatch every time she went into the field. Finally, it had become a habit. Why hadn't he followed his own established protocol?

She sighed and ran a hand through her

hair. "I don't even know where to start." She stared at the documents in front of her. "Land ownership records going back twenty years . . . maps of the entire county . . . he had to have had some thought, but I can't make the connection."

"I don't know," Quinn began, when his cell phone rang. "Peterson." He listened for several minutes, then said, "Great, we'll meet you there in an hour."

"Who was that?" Miranda asked when he'd pocketed the phone.

"Olivia. She's coming down with the state lab director to talk to your professor. The preliminary results from Quantico came back on the red clay. Your professor was right — it's from the Four Corners states and the analyst is leaning toward Utah. Olivia is hoping he can take a look at the sample and technical data to narrow it down further. Quantico is calling in an expert from the U.S. Geological Survey, but that's going to take another day."

"What about these maps and records?" Miranda stared at the overwhelming stack of paper.

Quinn looked both frustrated and angry. "I don't know what the hell Nick was thinking. We might spend all day on this and still not come up with something. And frankly, without something specific to go on, we can't waste any more time here." He stood. "It's three o'clock and you haven't stopped to eat."

"Neither have you," Miranda countered. She didn't need to be baby-sat, though in the back of her mind she appreciated that Quinn noticed.

"My stomach isn't growling as loudly as yours."

"My stomach does not growl!"

"Wanna bet?"

She almost laughed. "Let's pick something up on the way to campus."

"Fast food?" He wrinkled his nose. "If we must."

"We must," she teased.

It felt so good, so comfortable, to be back just chatting with Quinn. Though the stress of the Butcher investigation and now Nick's disappearance should have made them tense, Miranda realized that they had developed an easy camaraderie. Like they used to have.

She didn't want it to end.

CHAPTER
25

"Liv!" Miranda exclaimed in the courtyard of Traphagen Hall.

Miranda wrapped her arms around Olivia St. Martin, though she kept the hug short. Olivia didn't like hugs and casual touches, something Miranda had never understood but respected. Olivia had always been a class act.

"You look good," Olivia said as she tucked her chin-length bob behind her ear. "Considering you haven't slept much," she added with concern.

Miranda glanced over at Quinn and frowned. "Don't believe everything you hear."

"Quinn didn't have to say anything. I know you." She touched Miranda's arm lightly. "Are you doing okay? I know this is a really bad time for you."

Miranda took a deep breath and nodded.

"I'm okay. Really." She glanced again at Quinn discreetly, but Olivia still noticed.

"You and Quinn patch things up?"

"Not really." She shrugged. "But it's a little better. He's been a rock." Quinn had always been solid. The realization that she'd started leaning on him again unnerved her. He hadn't become her crutch by any stretch, but she found herself more comforted by his presence than angered.

When had that happened?

"How are *you* doing?" Miranda asked.

"I'm okay."

"When's the next parole hearing?"

A cloud passed over Olivia's expression. "Three weeks."

"That soon? It's been less than three years since the last one!"

Olivia had testified several times against the parole of her sister's killer. Wisely, no parole board had released the bastard. But every time she went back to California to face the vicious murderer and tell her story, it drained her. Miranda greatly admired her perseverance and considered her friend a role model.

If Olivia could sit in the same room with the man who raped and murdered her sister, certainly Miranda could face the Butcher when the police arrested him. But the thought of seeing her attacker in person, even behind bars, terrified her.

Quinn had been talking to the state lab director and brought him over. "Miranda, this is Dr. Eric Fields from the State Lab."

"I'm very pleased to meet you, Ms. Moore. I've heard so much about you." Dr. Fields was a small, wiry guy with silver-rimmed glasses. He looked barely old enough to shave.

Miranda took a half step back and glanced down. She didn't like being a celebrity, particularly for the reason she was well known.

Olivia broke the awkward silence. "Dr. Fields has been really great in giving me full access, and he definitely has a clean, well-run lab. We're still analyzing the evidence. I don't know what will be useful in court yet, but we're working on a possible fingerprint."

"We have a partial from a locket of a previous victim," Quinn said.

"Yes, I have that report to work with as well," Olivia said. "I can stay as long as you need me. But I think this soil will give you the best lead."

"Let's talk to the professor," Miranda said, and led the way to his office.

After introductions, Professor Austin looked at the soil and the report. Miranda waited, hardly breathing. Certainly this was it. He'd tell them exactly where the dirt, or clay, came from.

"It's definitely not from Montana," he said with certainty. "And not New Mexico or Arizona. This clay is too fine. Utah is my educated guess. Possibly western Colorado."

Miranda bubbled with excitement. "This is great. We just need to match up one of the men from the files with recent travel to Utah or Colorado. Let's go."

Miranda was both excited and apprehensive. This was it! They had a real lead. Something tangible from her search for the shack where Rebecca had been held captive. Why was she so nervous?

"Before you go," Olivia said. "Dr. Fields and I re-examined the trace evidence from the Croft murders. This same red clay was found on the mattress. A small quantity, but preliminary tests indicate an eighty-seven percent match. I've sent it to Quantico for further comparison, but that's at least something solid to tie in with the Douglas homicide."

"So we're looking for someone who was in Utah or Colorado both recently and three years ago?" Miranda asked.

"Exactly," Quinn said. "We need to get back to the office. If we can narrow the list down quickly, we can start the interviews today."

Professor Austin rummaged through some papers on his desk. He pulled out a map of the United States. It amazed Miranda what he had at his fingertips — and that he could find anything in the mess.

"Let me mark out the region for you." He picked up a red pen and outlined an area that included most of Utah and the north-western portion of Colorado.

"Thank you, Professor," Quinn said, taking the map.

"Glen. Glen's my name."

"Thank you, Glen. This will help immensely." He folded and pocketed the map, then his cell phone rang. "Excuse me," he said, and walked several feet away.

Miranda half listened to Olivia and Dr. Fields talking. She watched as Quinn's face grew hard. He snapped shut his phone and caught her eye.

"Nick's truck has been found," he said, holding back emotion.

"And Nick?" But Miranda already knew the answer.

"He's still missing."

CHAPTER
26

Dr. Eric Fields offered to help with evidence collection at the crime scene, and he and Olivia followed Quinn and Miranda to the highway where Nick's truck had been found. By the time they arrived, a dozen Sheriff's Department vehicles lined the road. Two deputies directed the minimal traffic, and crime scene tape had been posted around Nick's truck.

Quinn doubted Nick was still alive, but he didn't say that to Miranda.

He wondered what Nick had been after. Had he been following up on a hunch? Why had he gone out without backup? Or at least letting someone know where he was headed. Or, had he simply been at the wrong place at the wrong time?

Sam Harris barked orders to his deputies, then spotted Quinn and Miranda as they got out of the Jeep. "I have everything under control," the undersheriff said as he approached.

"I'm sure you do," Quinn acknowledged.

Dr. Fields approached. "Sam, good to see you again." He extended his hand.

"Dr. Fields. I didn't know you were down here." Harris seemed flustered and impressed with the lab director.

"I came down with Dr. St. Martin on another case, and when we heard about Sheriff Thomas's disappearance, I wanted to see if I could help. We're heading back to Helena as soon as we're done here, and I'll expedite any processing of evidence. Do you think this is connected with the Butcher investigation?"

Quinn didn't like the way Fields was playing right into Harris's ego, but then he caught Fields's eye. The doctor gave him a slight smile and Quinn had to give him credit for diplomacy. Quinn expected Fields was older — and wiser — than he appeared.

"We're not jumping to any conclusions right now, Dr. Fields," Harris said. "Sheriff Thomas may have been following a lead in the van Auden disappearance; we're still piecing together his day."

"May I take a look at his truck?"

"Absolutely. I have my crime scene technicians processing it right now. I'm sure they would be pleased to have your guidance." Harris walked Fields over to Nick's truck.

Quinn couldn't help but smile. "I didn't think Fields had it in him to manipulate Harris. He seems so . . . Doogie Hauser."

Olivia laughed. "Eric has a huge list of credentials, including running the Oklahoma City crime lab. He worked closely with our people after the bombing in 1995 and has been very happy to have our help in his lab. I don't always get such a warm reception."

"Harris has been a thorn," Quinn said.

"I told Nick when he first made him undersheriff that it would be a problem," Miranda said. "Harris was his opponent in the election."

"That explains it."

Miranda's eyes clouded with unshed tears as she stared down the road at Nick's truck. "Quinn, Nick's dead, isn't he?"

"We don't know that," Quinn said, hating to see her hurting. He touched her arm. "We don't know much of anything at this point. Think positive."

She looked at him, chewed on her upper lip. "I feel so helpless!"

"You're not. We have two deputies scouring the files right now based on the information Professor Austin gave us. We'll have that list narrowed down to a handful. I have two agents coming in tonight. We'll have answers sooner rather than later. We're getting close, Miranda. We're going to get this guy. I can feel it."

"Before he kills Ashley?"

"God, I hope so."

Twenty minutes later, Dr. Fields motioned for Quinn. They leaned against Fields's car.

"Anything?" Quinn asked.

The lab director tapped his bag. "I'm taking custody of the evidence. The interior was wiped clean."

"No fingerprints?"

"Not Nick's, not anyone's, on the steering wheel, dash, or doors. Harris said that he had a witness, a trucker, who called in the abandoned vehicle."

"Witness?" Quinn fumed. Harris was keeping valuable information from him. Quinn was ready to take over jurisdiction and nail the jerk for obstruction of justice if it continued.

"The witness didn't see anyone in or around the truck. He drove down this road at one thirty this afternoon, turned south on 191 to eat and gas up at a popular truck stop about three miles down. He logged it all in his book. He left the restaurant at three and the sheriff's truck was here. He almost hit it coming around the bend. Called it right in."

"Gives us a time line. Good." Quinn's mind grappled with the information. "Someone dumped Nick's truck. Why? Because he wanted it to be found. There's a million places it could have been left where no one would find it for days, or longer. He did it to divert attention," Quinn answered his own question.

"Sounds right to me," Fields said. "One more thing. Though the car was wiped down, I collected a sample of dirt in the grooves of the brake pedal. At first glance, it looks like the same dark red clay we found in the Douglas murder. It's a very small sample, less than a gram. I can't say for sure it's identical until I run tests, but I think for caution's sake you should assume it's from the same source."

"Meaning, the Butcher has Nick."

Olivia and Dr. Fields left directly from the scene to return to Helena. Quinn and Miranda headed back to the Sheriff's Department and upon their arrival, Deputy Booker called them over.

"We have four possibles," he said, his pale eyes darting back and forth with excitement. "I can't believe out of all those files, we could narrow it down so fast."

"Follow the evidence," Quinn said. "Every detail helps." He took the list from Booker, mindful that Miranda was looking over his shoulder.

"The first guy," Booker said, "is still on campus. Mitch Groggins. He's a cook at the cafeteria. Been there for seventeen years. Forty years old. His mother lives in Green River, Utah."

Quinn nodded, his entire body humming with anticipation. This was it. The killer was on this list. He felt it.

"Have you talked to his mother? Found out if he visited recently?"

Booker shook his head. "We've been busy narrowing down the list, we haven't had time, I'm sorry—"

Quinn put up his hand. "You did the right thing." He made a note in his pad.

"The next guy graduated the year after Penny Thompson went missing. He only had one class with her, an advanced biology class, and he didn't live on campus. David Larsen. He left town after he graduated and got his master's in wildlife biology at the University of Denver. I checked their records and he's on staff there."

Denver — that was in the middle of Colorado. Quinn consulted the map Professor Austin had outlined. Denver was out of the region. Still, a wildlife biologist would probably work outdoors. It warranted follow-up to find out if the guy worked in the field. "How old is he?" Quinn asked as he flipped to the fact sheet in the file Booker had put together.

"Thirty-seven."

"Okay. Next?"

"Bryce Younger. Thirty-five. Freshman at the time of Penny's disappearance. He was in the same dorm as her — North Hedges. MSU has co-ed dorms, you know, guys on one floor, girls on another."

"I know," Quinn said.

"So, he was on the floor directly beneath hers. They knew each other, had one class together. And get this — he's from St. George, Utah. He went back there when he graduated and is in construction. Never married, no kids."

Construction — probably physically fit, capable of subduing a woman.

"Any reason to believe he's come up to Montana recently?"

"His construction company is pretty big, they have projects all over the western U.S. — including building the new science wing at Missoula."

The University of Montana in Missoula was about two hours northwest of Bozeman.

"The last guy is forty-five, a little older than the others. Brad Palmer. He was a teaching assistant in one of Penny's classes and left shortly after her disappearance. They'd been involved. He's this big ex-football type. Apparently, he had a football scholarship and played at Stanford, then busted out his knee. Graduated, coached high school, came up here to get a degree in mechanical engineering. He was interviewed several times about her disappearance, according to the records. Nothing stuck.

"But get this," Booker added. "He lives in Grand Junction, Colorado."

Quinn looked at his map. There it was, Grand Junction. Right over the line on Professor Austin's map.

Miranda listened to Quinn take charge. She had to admit, he did it well.

She stared at the photographs of the four men — any one of them could be the Butcher. Goosebumps rose on her skin.

She sat in the corner and absorbed Quinn's orders more than listened. He'd called the two agents expected this evening and directed them to Colorado. First to Grand Junction to check on Penny's ex-boyfriend, then to Denver to investigate the wildlife biologist.

He called the St. George Police Department, filled them in on the investigation, and asked them to check on Bryce Younger. He sent Booker and Zachary to Missoula to investigate the construction company owner and see if Younger had been around in the last three weeks. He was on the phone, dispatching deputies, and massaging Sam Harris's ego all at once.

But Miranda caught all of this from the periphery. She focused on the University photographs of the four men. In her mind, she imagined each of them shooting Sharon in the back. She couldn't rid her mind of the image of each of them tying her down, raping her. Then feeding her bread and water like she was a wounded bird.

She didn't want to go back, but she was already there. She tried to steel herself for the pain, but it came crashing through, her barriers shattered.

Deep down, she wanted to go home and let Quinn do his job. What did she think she could do here? She worked for the Sheriff's Department, but she wasn't a cop. She searched for people. Sometimes, she found them. But she'd never forget all the women she'd never found, or the ones she'd discovered too late.

But if she hid under her warm comforter,

the Butcher would still be out there. Ashley van Auden would still be strapped to the ground, cold and in pain, certain she was going to die and that no one cared, no one would save her. Nick would still be missing. Was he dead? *Please, no.*

But how could he be alive? Why would the Butcher keep him alive? He wouldn't. He'd kill him and dump his body. They might not find him until after they caught the Butcher.

She'd always wondered whether she'd be able to face the man who attacked her. After all these years, the nightmares, and the sacrifices, perhaps at last she was on the verge of finding out.

"Let's go," Quinn said to Miranda.

She looked up. She hadn't noticed the room had cleared out, or that Quinn was standing in front of her.

"Where?"

"The University. To talk to Mitch Groggins." He glanced at his watch. "I just talked to the cafeteria supervisor. He's there until nine in the evening. We should be able to catch him."

"Me?" She blinked. He didn't actually mean for her to go with him? To be only feet from the man who might be the Butcher?

Quinn stared at her. His face was blank, but his eyes questioned. "Weren't you paying attention for the last ten minutes?"

"I guess — my mind wandered. I don't know how good I'd be to you."

She wanted to go, desperately wanted to face each of the four men and have them speak. Close her eyes and listen to the cadence of his voice. She would know which man was the Butcher because she'd heard his voice in her nightmares.

This could be it — if Mitch Groggins was the Butcher, they'd have him behind bars today. Why was she hesitating?

Quinn sat beside her, took her hands. They were alone; everyone else had gone off on their assignments. Miranda didn't want to feel so inadequate, so scared, but couldn't help it.

"You're shaking," Quinn said quietly.

"What if Groggins is him? I—" She paused. "Maybe you were right all along."

"Excuse me?"

"About me. I'm not cut out to be an FBI agent. I don't know if I can face him and not either scream or scratch his eyes out. I always thought once I knew who the Butcher was, once he was behind bars, I could stand there and spit in his face and tell him he was going to be injected with poison, that he would die and go to hell. And somehow, that would make me feel whole again."

"Miranda, I—"

"But," she interrupted, not wanting to hear excuses or little white lies to make her feel better, "now that we are actually getting close, that I believe for the first time in twelve years that we are going to stop him, I don't know if I can look him in the eye knowing what he did to me." Her voice cracked, and she turned away from Quinn. "You were right to have me booted from the Academy."

Quinn touched her chin, forced her to look at him. She blinked back tears, expecting to see *I told you so* written all over his face. Instead, his jaw clenched and his eyes flashed in anger.

"You can handle anything, Miranda. I never doubted your strength, I never doubted your ability. You would have made a great FBI agent — I just felt at the time that you wanted it for the wrong reasons. That you never would have been content to head down to Florida and work bank robberies, or political corruption in D.C. I thought that you would only have been satisfied as the permanent agent here, in Montana, working *this* investigation.

"I wanted you to take a year to really think about what you needed in your career. You were so positive you could find the Butcher once you had a badge. Your choices were all about *him,* not about *you.* I was so proud of what you'd accomplished at the Academy. You should be proud. Not only were you an exceptional student there, you've been an outstanding asset to the Sheriff's Department here."

"Everything I've done, everything I've become, is because of *him.* I don't know who I am." Miranda tried to turn away, but Quinn didn't let her.

I never stopped loving you.

She didn't deserve Quinn. For ten years she'd blamed him for what happened at the Academy when all she had to do was look into a mirror to stare at the guilty party.

Quinn's eyes swam with emotion. "*I* know who you are, Miranda. And I've never admired anyone more than you."

"I don't—"

"We have to go. You can do this. I'll be there with you. I will *never* let him hurt you again."

She found herself nodding. She didn't know if she believed him, but he had faith in her.

She vowed not to disappoint him. Or herself.

Mitch Groggins wasn't the Butcher.

While he was the general height of her attacker — which Miranda had loosely guessed at between five eleven and six two, along with half the male population over eighteen — he was skinny. He didn't have the same build.

Yet, it had been twelve years since she'd seen his silhouette.

As soon as she heard his voice, the whiny, nasal tone, she knew beyond a doubt he wasn't the Butcher. She didn't know whether to be relieved or scared.

But she'd done it. She'd faced a suspect and hadn't screamed or shot him. She'd been terrified, but she'd faced him and felt stronger for it even though Groggins was innocent.

Quinn grew worried about Miranda as he drove her Jeep back to the Lodge. She didn't have to tell him she was worn out, physically and emotionally. Preparing herself to face Groggins as the Butcher, then realizing it wasn't him, had drained her. He wished he could gather her up and hold her, help her find her strength.

Her courage was there, he knew. He hoped she realized it. Facing Groggins was the first step.

The police in St. George, Utah, called his cell phone when they were halfway to the Lodge. They'd spoken to the construction company owner, Younger, and he was belligerent. But the fact he was in southern Utah at present put him at the bottom of the list, if not completely off it. He claimed he was at his office all day, and the local police were following up on his alibi.

The only way Younger could have made it back to Utah from Montana in the seven hours since Nick's truck had been discovered would be to fly. Quinn called the Bureau and had someone work on flights in and out of Las Vegas, the closest major airport to St. George, as well as the private airports in the area.

He checked in with Colleen Thorne, his on-again, off-again partner, who was already in Grand Junction on her way to see Palmer, Penny Thompson's boyfriend at the time of her disappearance.

"Palmer's now at the top of the list," he said when she picked up her phone. He filled her in on Groggins and Younger. "Proceed with caution."

"Will do, but don't you think if he's the Butcher he won't be home?"

"It's not that far from Grand Junction to Bozeman. Ten hours, maybe. He could return to throw suspicion off. But if he's not there, we'll put an APB out on him for questioning."

"I'll let you know. We're almost to his house. I also spoke to the president at the university in Denver," she said.

"And?"

"He's more than happy to help. He's contacting the head of the wildlife biology department to find out what projects Larsen is assigned to, and we should be able to talk to both the director and Larsen tomorrow morning. It was after hours, so it took a little time to track them down. But I have Larsen's address — he has a small apartment near the university — and an updated photo from his employee ID. Do you want me to send it to you?"

"Now?"

"I have it on my Blackberry."

Quinn smiled and shook his head. "Modern technology. Sure, shoot it through to my e-mail. I'll download it when I get to the Lodge."

He hung up and turned down the Lodge driveway. He glanced at Miranda. She appeared to be sleeping, but he knew she wasn't.

He'd meant every word he said back at the Sheriff's Department, but he knew she didn't believe him. Frankly, he couldn't blame her. She'd had ten years to create worst-case scenarios in her head about why he did what he did. He'd tried to explain then, but he should have continued. He loved her and shouldn't have given up on her, thinking she'd come to her senses on her own.

She'd been scared and worried and angry. Even if she had seen the truth then, she was too stubborn to admit it.

But part of her strength was her tenacity. Her stubborn determination helped her survive; it formed her character and gave her the motivation to continue moving forward against almost insurmountable odds.

He loved that about her.

But she was also insecure. About her own strengths and fears. That the fear would win. How could he convince her that she would persevere? How could he explain that being an FBI agent wouldn't have made her fearless?

Quinn pulled up behind the Lodge and shut off the ignition. "Miranda."

"Yeah?" Her voice was low, quiet.

"You heard my conversation with Colleen."

"Yeah."

"You want to talk about it? Do you have any questions?"

"No questions." She paused, opened her eyes. "I hope it's one of them, Quinn. If it's not, we're right back where we started."

"It's one of them."

"Is that your experience talking?" She gave him a half-smile.

"No, it's my gut instinct. Listen to yours."

"Okay." She reached for her door handle.

"Let me walk you to your cabin," Quinn said.

She nodded and kissed him lightly on the cheek. "Thank you."

Dear God, when would it end?

Long after the sun took the minimal warmth it had offered in the dank, dark cabin and retreated for the night; long after the first howl of a coyote pierced the quiet stillness; long after Ashley had cried herself to sleep, Nick lay awake waiting.

The Butcher would return. And Nick could do nothing to protect Ashley.

He couldn't have imagined how unbearable the night would be.

Each struggle against his ropes pulled them tighter, binding his hands to his feet behind his back. While he was pushed against the wall, Ashley was restrained in the middle of the small room. Finally asleep, finally with some peace after a day of mounting fear.

When his head had cleared somewhat,

he'd encouraged Ashley to try to scoot over to him, see if she could untie his binds. But she was chained to the floor, unable to move. And every time he tried to roll over, his bonds tightened.

Nick tried to assure her they'd find a way out. Tried to convince her that his people, and the FBI, were close to learning the identity of the killer.

But how would they know where to look? Nick didn't know who the Butcher was, only that he'd been hanging around the Parker place. He could have been a friend, an employee, a tenant of Richard Parker's. Or he might be a squatter. Or Richard Parker himself.

Would Quinn follow his trail? Would he see what Nick had seen? Probably not. On his way up to Parker's Nick had thought the whole trip was a wild-goose chase. Being born and bred in southwest Montana had shed light on the parcel and property records through the lens of history and experience more than by following hard evidence.

Having the right instincts didn't make him feel any better. He was going to die. And Ashley would be hurt, hunted, and slaughtered.

Nick had to find a way out.

The night creatures suddenly quieted, as if

a larger, more dangerous predator was on the move. Nick's ears pricked. Someone approached the cabin.

A moment later, the chain on the door shifted, then rattled. Nick felt Ashley startle awake.

"No," she whimpered. "No, not again."

"It's okay," he said, his voice rough.

"No, it's not! It's never going to be okay!"

The cabin was already chillingly cold, but when the door opened the night wind touched his body with an icy finger and he shivered. For the first time, he realized how frigid Ashley must be.

The door closed. The Butcher said nothing.

Nick heard the clinking of something metal, then Ashley screamed in pain.

"Stop! Don't hurt her!"

Nick pleaded with the rapist as he struggled against the ropes. Ashley's cries were continuous, falling off to sobbing, then a sudden scream pierced the cabin walls.

The rapist spoke little, just as Miranda had said. An occasional word — *mine, forever* — with grunts and sounds of exertion.

Tears sprang to Nick's eyes. Of pure hatred. Of anger. Of helplessness. He heard the sick slapping of flesh on flesh as the Butcher raped Ashley and used something metallic to mar her flesh. Her breasts.

He'd seen Miranda's scars. Now he knew how they got there.

How had she survived such brutal torture? How had she grown into the incredible, strong, fearless woman she was? His blinders were gone; he saw that Miranda was more than a victim, more than a survivor.

She was the victor.

Ashley screamed again and sobbed. The Butcher's virtual silence was more disconcerting than had he shouted obscenities. As if being silent was to prove something to himself.

Nick didn't know how long the Butcher stayed to torture Ashley. It was as if he didn't know Nick was there — he ignored every plea, every curse, every accusation. But he finally left, chaining the door behind him. Ashley was silent.

Had he killed her?

No, he wouldn't do that. He needed the hunt. She'd probably passed out. He listened with bated breath until he was confident she was still breathing.

Nick wanted to comfort the girl but didn't know how. What could he say to take away the pain and humiliation of what she'd just endured?

Instead, he mentally prepared for escape.

Maybe the Butcher would find it a challenge to hunt the sheriff. Nick devised psychological manipulations to encourage the Butcher to let him go.

You shoot weak women in the back. Aren't you good enough to hunt down a man?

Women are easy. They cry and stumble and beg for mercy. What's the sport in that? You let me out, you won't be able to catch me. See what you're really made of.

If Nick could taunt the Butcher into pursuing him, it might give Ashley a real chance to escape. He had to convince her to run in the opposite direction.

And not look back.

The Bitch had told him not to use the cabin anymore in case the cop had told someone where he was headed. She thought she was still running the show.

He didn't mind sleeping outdoors, though. He had a forty-below sleeping bag, a space blanket, and hot coffee he'd picked up at a gas station after leaving his girl.

It had been difficult to concentrate on her when the damn cop wouldn't shut up. He'd considered just killing him and getting it over with — he'd kill him eventually, anyway — but the thought of hunting a *cop* excited him. He'd be a tough opponent. He might even try to attack.

But the cop would lose, of course.

I'm at the top of my game.

He'd been thinking for a while about tying up loose ends. The Bitch had told him he couldn't have Miranda Moore. That would change. The Bitch was no longer in charge.

He'd kill the one who got away. She'd been difficult. Haunted him, even now. When he looked at her picture, it brought bad dreams. He couldn't fully remember the nightmare, only that he'd awake soaking in sweat, with an image of her slicing open his heart and eating it while he watched.

She would then morph into his mother.

He found his hands pummeling his sleeping bag. He forced himself to calm down. Don't think about *her.* She was dead. Gone. Good riddance. Why even think of his mother?

It was Miranda. *She* brought back the damn memories. The one who got away.

The Bitch wouldn't let him kill her, but he didn't care anymore. If she said anything about it, he'd slice her throat, too.

Maybe he'd do it anyway.

CHAPTER
27

They rocked on her porch swing drinking a glass of wine, watching the shadows and listening to the sounds of night. It almost — *almost* — felt like before. Before she'd left for Quantico and lost her dream.

But had it really been her dream? Or had she been running away from something?

Miranda had been positive that being proactive, working in law enforcement — becoming an FBI agent specifically — would give her the strength she needed to conquer her demons. That if she had the badge, the courage would follow. And her nightmares would fade.

Weeks after her attack, Miranda feared the Butcher would come after her. Kill her in her sleep. Take her back to the middle of nowhere and hunt her again. She'd wake up, a scream caught in her throat, her feet kicking as if running.

That nightmare faded, but others replaced it. Calling out for the women who'd disappeared. Yelling until her voice was hoarse and her feet were weary. Then falling into a bottomless grave. Tumbling down, down . . . until she woke up in a cold sweat.

It wasn't her physical safety she worried about. It was her state of mind. As long as the Butcher preyed on women, he would control her dreams.

"What if the Butcher isn't Palmer or Larsen?" she asked Quinn.

"Then we broaden the search. Truck drivers, salesmen — maybe we missed someone in the stack of files from the University. We review every interview, every note, reinterview people. Olivia is working the evidence hard; they're prioritizing every test. If there's DNA in a rock, she'll find it."

"But we need a suspect's DNA to compare."

"I know how hard this is on you."

"I feel like I should be out there right now. Looking for Ashley. And Nick."

Her eyes burned and her head ached from staring at the maps and property records, trying to figure out what Nick had seen and where he had gone.

"Honey, I don't want you getting your hopes up about Nick." Quinn's voice cracked; he was as torn up about Nick's disappearance as she was.

"I can't help but think he's alive. Why else would the Butcher plant just his car? If Nick's dead, why not leave his body, too?"

"I don't know. Maybe he feared there was evidence that could be gathered from the body. If there was a struggle, some of the assailant's skin or blood might be found on Nick. Best to dump the body where it can never be found."

"Then why leave the truck by the side of the road?"

"To distract us. Split our resources. If we're focusing on finding Nick, we're not focusing on finding Ashley — and finding Ashley will lead us to the Butcher." He ran a hand through his hair. "But I'm only guessing. Though the Butcher has never before taunted the police, maybe this is his way of saying he's smarter than all of us. 'Look at me, I can kill the sheriff and you can't catch me.'"

Quinn's phone rang and Miranda tensed. News this late was never good.

He squeezed her hand and didn't let go. She squeezed back.

"Peterson."

Miranda was sitting close enough to hear a woman's voice on the other end.

"It's Colleen. Toby and I just left Palmer's place. I'd say there's a next-to-zero probability that he's our guy. He drinks his meals. He gets winded walking from the La-Z-Boy to the refrigerator."

"Shit."

"I have his employer's contact info; Palmer says he hasn't missed a day in weeks. He's pretty bitter about what happened with his girlfriend, doesn't like cops, but I think he's harmless."

"I trust your instincts. Where are you now?"

"We're driving to Denver. About two hours to go. In the morning we're all set to talk to Larsen's department head. She called me directly, says Larsen is in the field but she can send someone to fetch him."

"In the field? Doing what?"

"The guy is an expert in —" she paused "— um, falcons, I think. He tracks them, monitors breeding, that sort of thing. The research facility is based in Craig, but Larsen works near the Dinosaur National Monument."

"Where's that?"

"I know," Miranda interrupted.

"Hold on, Colleen." Quinn turned to her.

"It's in the northwest corner of Colorado. Less than an eight-hour drive to Bozeman.

And fully within the boundaries of Professor Austin's map."

Miranda couldn't sleep. She tossed and turned for an hour.

"This is ridiculous," she muttered to no one as she tossed off her comforter and pulled on her boots.

Quinn had left at midnight after getting a call from Olivia that the preliminary tests confirmed that the soil found in Nick's truck matched the soil found in the shack where Rebecca had been held. In addition, they extracted a good shoe print — size eleven — from the truck's floor mats. Nick wore a size twelve.

Quinn had told her to get some sleep. She needed it, and she wanted it, but her mind was spinning. Every time she closed her eyes, she remembered David Larsen's small photograph from his University file.

It seemed unreal: putting a face to the Butcher. Could it be Larsen? She didn't know. She'd now seen his face, but she couldn't definitively say it was *him*.

She'd almost asked Quinn to spend the night. She wondered if he'd been waiting for her to ask. Now she wished she had.

The anger she'd held on to so very long seemed to have dissipated these last few days. When she had first seen Quinn, she'd been so angry, so shocked, so worried that he would see right through her tough façade. She feared he'd question every decision she made, everything she said, every action.

But when she woke up this morning, she didn't fear what he'd say if he saw she was struggling under the strain of the investigation. Instead, she found herself wanting to see him.

She pulled on her warm coat, pocketed her gun, and left the warmth of her cabin. She paused on the porch, breathing in the cold air, shivering even though she was bundled up. It would be forty-five degrees tonight. Not cold enough to freeze poor Ashley, but cold enough that she'd probably wish she were dead.

Miranda had.

She half ran to the Lodge and let herself in through the employee entrance. She didn't give herself the opportunity to second-guess her decision. She walked right up the stairs to his room and knocked on the door.

Opening the door, Quinn wore gray sweat pants and nothing else. Miranda sucked in her breath at the sight of his chest. She thought she'd forgotten how handsome he was, but she hadn't. She remembered every well-defined muscle on his lean body. There wasn't one extra fat cell.

He was as perfect now as he had been at thirty.

"I couldn't sleep," she said, sounding a tad breathless. Her heart pounded with anticipation. Coming here, she had known what would happen. What she hoped would happen.

She needed him. Quinn would chase away her demons and make her feel warm. Desirable. More a woman, less a victim.

"Miranda—"

She stepped inside and closed the door. Quinn reached out, took her hand, and drew her to him. "I didn't realize how much I've missed you," she said, her voice unusually husky.

"God, how I've missed you, Miranda."

He kissed her.

There was nothing tentative about this kiss. He held her face and sunk into her. She felt like she was coming home.

She'd never stopped loving him. Quinn had been so patient with her, so incredibly supportive. He'd done everything for her, including recommending her for the Academy when he hadn't thought she was ready.

Miranda's feelings of betrayal and fear were washed away in his warm embrace. The heat flared. She wouldn't be satisfied with just a kiss. She wanted more. Everything.

She wanted him back.

Quinn pulled away, looked at her, and frowned. "What's wrong?" he asked.

"Wrong? Nothing."

"These?" He wiped tears from her cheek. She hadn't known they were there. He kissed his damp fingers, then her cheek.

"Miranda, I've been waiting so long for you to come back to me."

She took his hand and kissed his palm, holding it close. "I realized something over the last couple of days. You were right. I wanted to be in the FBI for the wrong reasons. I thought the badge would buy me courage. It would be a shield against the fear I lived with every day."

"Miranda, you have more courage than anyone I've ever met. You never needed a badge to confirm it."

"I understand that now. But I don't know if I have the courage to make it through tomorrow without you. If Larsen really is the Butcher, I don't know how I'll face him."

"You don't have to."

She nodded. "Oh, but I do. I was going to say, I don't know how I'll face him, but I will. I will prove to myself that I *can* do it. But it'll be easier with you at my side."

Quinn pulled her as close to him as possible with her bundles of clothing. "Miranda, I'll be there every step of the way."

"Can I get rid of the jacket?"

Quinn smiled and kissed her forehead as he helped her off with the jacket. Her sweater. Her shirt. She stood in her camisole and jeans. Quinn looked as if he wanted to eat her up. She warmed under his intense perusal.

She leaned up and kissed him.

He held her face in his hands and kissed her again and again, as if trying to make up for all the kisses they'd missed over the years. How had she given up such affection? Each kiss brought back the intimacy they'd once shared, Quinn's patience, his support, and the first time they'd made love.

A moan escaped her lips and he gently pushed her down onto the bed. "You're beautiful, Randy," he whispered, his lips trailing kisses down her neck, then back up again. She shivered, little currents of electricity running up and down her spine.

She reached for him, wanting to pull him down with her, to fully kiss him, but he teased her with the light caresses, his fingers walking down her arm and back up, skimming over her breasts, then back again. A seductive touch that made her want to peel off his sweatpants.

Except she was enjoying every delicious moment. It had been too long, much too long.

She reached out for him, ran her hands up and down his hard back. His dark eyes looked down at her, his strong jaw quivered with suppressed desire. "Miranda, are you sure?"

She nodded, leaned up, and kissed him.

Quinn wanted to make love to her. Now.

The first time they made love more than a decade ago, he knew she hadn't enjoyed it. She had wanted to get it over with, prove something to herself. That she trusted him with her body and heart had been a heady experience, and he'd never pushed her. But as their relationship grew and Miranda became more comfortable in bed with him, their lovemaking turned passionate and full of heat.

Her touches now sparked that same intense desire. And by her body moving to meet his, he was hitting all the right spots.

He took off her jeans and pulled off her sexy little camisole.

The first time he'd seen the scars the Butcher had left on her breasts, he hadn't been able to conceal raw anger. Miranda interpreted it as disgust, and it took him days to make her understand.

She was beautiful, scars and all. He had convinced her of his sincerity and his love, but every time she exposed her breasts she tensed.

He kissed them. Lightly. Lovingly. He didn't spend too much time on her chest, knowing she wasn't completely comfortable. He remembered everything about her. She'd lost weight and her ribs showed. He should have been here to keep her eating right, keep her healthy. But her muscles were tight and hard. She was in better physical shape now than she had been at the Academy, but that didn't surprise him.

He was proud of her, that she'd worked so hard to get where she was. And she thought she lacked bravery? She was the epitome of courage.

Miranda gasped when Quinn's tongue lightly skimmed over her stomach, sending glorious shockwaves tingling up and down her body, heating her from within. His teeth bit her panties and pulled them down so his tongue could tease and tantalize her, getting closer and closer without touching the one area she wanted him to fully explore. With firm hands, he stripped her, staring at her body.

"You're beautiful," he repeated, bending down again to kiss her thigh.

"Make love to me," she said, her voice urgent. She wanted him *now*.

She felt more than heard a chuckle from his lips on her inner thigh as his mouth moved down to her knee, her calf, trailing kisses and warmth.

He kissed her toes and she shivered, slivers of fire beginning to pool in her center. His patience was admirable in many ways, but right now she wanted him inside her. Making love to her.

"Quinn," she gasped.

His lips trailed back up her leg, searing her skin. She was never cold in Quinn's arms. She was hot. Combustible.

She reached down, trying to draw him up to her mouth where she could sink into him, become one with him. Instead, he parted her legs and used his thumbs to rub small circles everywhere but *there*, the one place she needed him.

"Quinn, I'm ready."

She moaned and arched her back.

"I know," he murmured, but did nothing to speed up his foreplay.

It was as if he wanted to get to know her all over again. He'd spent so much time in the past touching, holding, petting every inch of her skin. She'd missed the attention, both the sweet affection and the hot passion. As Quinn explored her body, the memories of everything that had been right between them flooded back. How he had not only accepted her flawed body, but helped her learn to love herself again. He made her comfortable in her own skin.

His mouth drew closer, closer . . . she arched in anticipation. He didn't disappoint. As soon as his mouth clamped down on her mound, she orgasmed. A hot, fast purging that had her gasping for air. His hands stroked her thighs, her back, taking her up, then easing her back.

He kissed her inner thighs, her navel, her stomach, her breasts, all the way to her neck.

She rolled over with him so she straddled him.

"What?" he asked, his wicked grin illuminated by the glow of the desk lamp. But his light manner was betrayed by his hard body trembling beneath her. He wanted her as much as she wanted him.

I need him.

She pushed her needs aside. She didn't know what would happen after tonight. She didn't want to think about the sunrise and the stark light of reality it would bring. She didn't want to think of Quinn leaving again, of going back to being alone. Without him.

Seize the time they had now. Embrace rediscovering a small part of what they'd shared in the past. Pretend nothing had happened in the last ten years to keep them apart.

She kissed him, her hands running over his skin as he had touched her. He held her close, their bodies molding together. She slid down, out of his arms, and pulled off his sweats. *This* was what she wanted. A complete union.

Quinn's patience was drawing to a close. He wanted to make love to Miranda in the worst way. Where sex and love merged. He watched her in the dim light, her long, dark hair falling in front of her face, looking like a wild woman with large, luminous eyes. His satisfaction at having given her pleasure quickly turned to urgency, and he moaned as she reached between his legs and squeezed.

"Wait," he said. He didn't want to lose it too soon. He had wanted to make love to her, hold her. Take it nice and slow. But the way she held him, slow was the furthest thing from his mind.

"I don't think so," she said, slightly mocking.

He made the mistake of looking down and

seeing her bend between his legs and take his hard length into her mouth. Her luscious lips enveloped him, and the combination of watching her and feeling her hot mouth and wet tongue suck him caused his cock to throb, making him ready to explode.

"Miranda."

He pulled her slowly up, until he could kiss her lips. "I want to make love to you," he whispered.

"Yes," she breathed into his ear.

He'd dreamed about this for ten years: holding Miranda, making love to her. It almost seemed a dream. He'd never thought they could regain what they'd lost.

He never wanted to let her go. He didn't want to lose any more time.

He let her control the pace. Just like the first time they made love, he let her decide when and how deep and how fast.

There would be time for more later.

She was so incredibly sexy as she spread herself and slowly, almost painfully, slid onto him. Her hair was a wild tangle of long curls, her lids heavy on her eyes, her mouth parted. So gorgeous. He resisted the urge to speed up their lovemaking, wanting to end it now and keep going forever at the same time.

Miranda gasped as she fully sheathed Quinn within her body. It had been so long since she had made love, but her first orgasm had paved the way.

"Are you okay?" he whispered.

She looked down at him, marveling at the deep affection she saw in his face. He reached up and rubbed her arms.

"Yes," she said. "I've been waiting for you a long time."

Unhurried, she moved on him. Up and down, enjoying every sensation as together, their orgasms built. She felt him tense beneath her as they moved more urgently in unison. The sheer joy of being one with Quinn again brought her to the peak.

"God, I love you," Quinn said, his voice husky with emotion and lust. "Come with me."

His words sent her over the top as much as feeling his body against her. His muscles tightened, his arms pulled her down onto his body and they became one, united in a bond that had been stretched thin over time. But, like a rubber band, had snapped back as soon as they'd seen each other again.

She never wanted him to leave.

Miranda collapsed onto Quinn's chest, feeling more relaxed than after an hour in the hot tub. Every limb was liquid, and she slid into the nook of his arm. He wrapped his arms around her, stroked her, and she soaked in his warmth and strength. Paradise in his embrace.

"I love you, Miranda."

She snuggled against him, her head on his shoulder, and sighed. She loved him, too. She wanted to tell him. She wanted to have everything back the way it was before Quantico. She wished she'd never gone in the first place. Had she stayed in Montana, things would have been so much different. She'd have had the last ten years feeling as loved and protected as she did right now.

Thinking about what might have been was pointless. But maybe they could rebuild. After David Larsen was caught and convicted, maybe they could have something together again.

She wanted to try. But now . . . she was so tired. She yawned.

Quinn knew the moment Miranda fell asleep because her entire body melted against him.

He pulled the comforter around them and stared at her while she slept. She looked at peace, and he was pleased to be able to give her one calm night.

He touched her hair, gently caressed her cheek. He loved her so.

CHAPTER
28

Quinn's cell phone rang and he bolted upright, instantly aware from the quality of light he'd overslept. A quick glance at the digital clock confirmed it: 7:45 A.M.

Next to him, Miranda stirred. Her hair fanned out on the pillow, her long neck kissable, and he wanted nothing more than to make love to her again.

His phone chirped again. Duty called.

"Peterson," he answered.

"It's Colleen. I'm getting a bad feeling about Larsen."

"What happened?"

"The wildlife biology department director, a — um, Sarah Tyne — called the university's off-site research lab in Craig. That's up in northwest Colorado. Wanted to pull Larsen's log sheets. He last checked in on Monday."

"The day after we found Rebecca's body."

"Right. He said he was going back to monitor some peregrine falcons. That's his specialty. So one of the research guys went out there early this morning."

Quinn's stomach flipped. "He wasn't there."

"Nope. In addition to his Denver apartment — which is empty — he lives in a trailer way out in the middle of nowhere, and his field supplies were there, but no Larsen. They tried calling him on the radio — the researchers are required to keep them on at all times when in the field — no answer."

"Did you find out what kind of car or truck he drives? Is it there?" Quinn pulled out his pad and made notes.

"He drives a truck, but I don't have the details. It's not with his trailer."

"I'll check on car registration. Get out there and see what you can find. If he turns up, detain him. I'm going to put an APB out on him. For questioning only — I don't want him getting spooked. And do it quietly — I don't want him panicking and killing Ashley van Auden. He's only had her two days. She's probably still alive."

"Got it."

"If you find him, Colleen, I get first crack at him." Quinn shut his cell phone.

Miranda spoke quietly. "David Larsen. It

386

seems like such a normal name."

He leaned over and kissed her forehead, brushing the hair back with his fingers. He wanted to take away her pain, steal her memories so she'd never again think about David Larsen or the women he had killed. Quinn would have to give Miranda lots of good memories to replace the bad. They'd started last night, but it was only the beginning.

"You okay?" he asked.

"I will be."

She didn't sound like herself, but he didn't press it. He would, later.

He kissed her again and rolled out of bed. "I'm going to the Sheriff's Department. Want me to drop you off at the University?"

"Yeah. I need to check in on my team."

"Don't go anywhere alone. *Anywhere.*"

"I won't." Her voice sounded distant.

"Miranda, we'll find him. He's not going to touch you. And for the first time, I think we can get to him before Ashley dies."

"I think so, too," she said. "And there's nothing I want more, except—" She paused. "Nick. Ashley might be alive, but what about Nick?" She stopped, unable to go on. She slid out of bed and dressed. "I'm going to take a quick shower and I'll meet you in twenty minutes at your car."

Quinn stopped her before she walked out. "He'll pay for killing Nick."

"I know. But it doesn't seem like enough."

At the Sheriff's Department, Quinn went first to Lance Booker. "Booker, I have a favor to ask."

"Anything."

Good kid. No wonder Nick had liked him. "Could you go to the University and stick with Miranda? Anywhere she goes, I want you nearby."

"Did something happen?"

"We have a suspect. David Larsen."

"The wildlife biologist?"

"He's missing, he had opportunity, and we've ruled out the other three men on the short list. My people are doing an in-depth background check on him right now. I'll call you with more information as I get it. But if he feels pressured in any way, he might do something unpredictable. I don't want Miranda in his sights."

"I'll stick to her like bees on honey."

Not *that* close, Quinn thought.

"Booker, keep the info under your hat. Miranda knows — but I don't want the press getting hold of it yet. Not until we have more information."

"Got it." Booker left.

Quinn entered Nick's office and was only partly surprised to see Sam Harris had taken over the desk. He was on the phone and looking at a fax. Quinn recognized the masthead.

Federal Bureau of Investigation. Seattle. *His* office.

He pulled the paper out of the undersheriff's hands. It was the background information on David Larsen.

Truck ... recent model, four-wheel drive. Powerful. Graduated from MSU ... doctorate at Colorado ... wildlife biologist ... very little detail. He knew most of this stuff.

Parents — deceased. Siblings — one sister. One sister? What about her name, residence, status?

Harris slammed down the phone. "What are you doing?"

"This fax was addressed to me."

"It came in to my office."

"It was addressed to me," Quinn repeated, temper rising.

Harris stood, walked around the desk. "Agent Peterson, you didn't tell me you had a suspect. What kind of respect does that show my department?"

Quinn ran a hand through his hair. "You knew we were narrowing down the list. I got the call this morning about David Larsen, not much more than an hour ago."

"If the sheriff were still here, you would have called him first thing."

That was true. Quinn hadn't even thought to call Sam Harris — he was too busy contacting his own superiors for immediate access to resources and information.

"Point taken. I'm sorry."

Harris's jaw worked and his face grew red. "You Feds think you know everything. Fine. Solve this case without me. But you'll be sorry."

Quinn had to have heard wrong. "What's that supposed to mean?"

"Nothing," he snapped, and walked out.

Shit, the last thing Quinn needed was a pissed-off cop. "And you're supposed to be the diplomat," he muttered to himself.

Quinn crossed over to Nick's desk and searched through all the papers to see if Harris had pulled anything else addressed to him off the fax. He didn't see anything. He called the small Helena field office and requested a couple of agents for the next two days. He needed help, and he wasn't afraid to ask for it.

Not when the life of a young woman was at stake.

His eyes rested on a small photo partially hidden under the blotter. He pulled it out.

It was actually a series of four photos, Miranda and Nick, taken in one of those two-dollar photo booths. Miranda smiled the same in each shot, a little self-conscious even though no one but she and Nick was likely to ever see these pictures.

Nick, on the other hand, was more animated. First smiling wide, then making a silly face, and in the third he was making rabbit ears with his fingers over Miranda's head.

In the last picture, he was looking at her, and Quinn could see he had loved her.

All jealousy at Nick's past relationship and friendship with Miranda flew out the window. Raw emotion climbed his throat thinking about his friend who was now probably dead.

One mistake, and Nick had paid with his life. It wasn't fair, and Quinn vowed to make Larsen pay, not only for the women he'd killed and what he'd done to Miranda, but for Nick as well.

He put the pictures in his wallet, planning on giving them to Miranda. Then he went out to talk to the deputies and assign them tasks.

There was a lot of ground to cover and little time.

Miranda had six deputies assigned to Search and Rescue, and she sent one with two volunteers into the area south of Gallatin Gateway. Quinn had come in and briefed everyone about David Larsen, telling them to proceed with caution. *Do not pursue.* They were there to find Ashley and rescue her, not apprehend a suspect.

He stressed that Larsen was only wanted for questioning, but everyone knew what that meant.

They had their first real suspect in twelve years.

Miranda didn't have a lot of hope that her team would find Ashley, but going through the motions helped her push to the back of her mind that she knew the identity of the Butcher. Once everyone was gone and she was alone, she sank into a chair and closed her eyes.

And pictured *him.*

She'd only seen that one photograph of Larsen, but it was too easy to animate it, to put his picture on the faceless man who'd tortured her and shot Sharon in the back.

Run. Run!

She'd never seen David Larsen. She would have remembered his face. But she knew his voice, the low monotone, cruel in its lack of emotion. His words and actions not matching the distant, almost bored tone.

She was certain she'd never seen him because surely his evil heart would be visible.

His hatred for women etched on his face.

But in the photograph, David Larsen appeared neither evil nor hate-filled. His was the face of an ordinary man. Pleasant on the surface. *Normal.*

The Butcher was anything but *normal.*

She remembered a biblical lesson from her father. That evil could masquerade as beauty, that black hearts were sometimes clothed in compassion. Evil didn't have a calling card alerting everyone to its pending visit. Evil came and went with a smile, laughing at the lives destroyed in its wake. The serpent who enticed Eve to sample the forbidden fruit couldn't have been repulsive, or she would have run in terror. No, the serpent must have been a thing of beauty, a thing that called all to trust it. Don't trust what you see with your eyes.

Evil lurks beneath the surface.

"Miranda?"

She jumped out of her seat and reached for her gun at the same time.

It was Deputy Booker.

"Shit, Lance."

"I didn't mean to scare you."

"I wasn't scared." She'd been terrified. Sitting here alone, thinking about the Butcher and David Larsen and Sharon . . . "What can I do for you?"

"Agent Peterson asked me to stick by you today. You know, since they can't find Larsen and all."

Last week, she would have been furious at Quinn's protectiveness. She would have sworn she was capable of defending not only herself, but everyone else, from the Butcher and any other evil that stepped foot in her state.

But while she had been trained in self-defense, taught it to the women at the University, and kept in shape, and knew she could find her way in any part of the county, the thought of facing David Larsen in person paralyzed her.

"Thanks, Lance," she said.

She crossed over to the wall map and stared, gathering up courage to get through this day. If they found Larsen, would he lead them to Ashley? Would he tell them where Nick was? Whether he was dead or alive?

What had Nick been looking for at the Recorder's Office? He'd pulled the property records of every landowner in the region. Including her dad, she'd noticed when she and Quinn were looking through them. Nothing jumped out at her; what had so caught Nick's attention that he would risk his life to investigate it? He must have thought it wasn't dangerous, otherwise he wouldn't have gone in alone.

She missed Nick. She wished she could have told him she was sorry things hadn't worked out between them. She'd never wanted to hurt him; he'd been so good to her. He'd given her space and let her do her job and supported her in everything she did. The problem was she hadn't loved Nick the way he loved her.

The way she loved Quinn.

She warmed, remembering last night and how he had touched her. Gently. Slowly. He hadn't forgotten where she liked to be touched. He hadn't forgotten her sensitivity about her breasts, her preferring to be on top, all her little idiosyncrasies that had been forged by one madman and one week of terror.

With Quinn, she relaxed and gave herself, willingly, happily. They were partners when they made love.

It had been on the tip of her tongue to tell him she loved him. She had wanted to. But the words wouldn't come. Some part of her held back and she didn't know why.

Quinn said he knew her. How could he know her so well when she was scrambling to discover herself? So she had held back and said nothing, even when his words rang true and she wanted to ask him to never leave.

Maybe, ultimately, that was her greatest fear: that he would leave her again. She wasn't the easiest person to get along with, she knew that, and maybe sometimes she deliberately became difficult so people wouldn't get too close. It was easier to keep people at arm's length than to let yourself be vulnerable.

People died violent deaths. Her mother's painful bout with cancer. Sharon's murder. And now, probably, Nick. All gone.

What would she do if anything happened to Quinn?

Quinn called his office in Seattle and spoke with Bonnie Blair, a pro in background research. If there was anything to find on David Larsen, Bonnie'd find it.

"Hi, Bonnie. I got your report. Not much there. Do you think you can work a little of your magic and come up with something else?"

There was a long pause. "What more do you want?"

She sounded ticked off.

"Well, to start I'd be interested in his parents' names, his sister, where he was born —"

Bonnie interrupted him. "That was all there. I sent sixteen pages."

"Sixteen? I got one." Sam Harris. He must have taken them. But why?

Had there been something in the faxed pages Harris had wanted to hide? Or someone he wanted to protect?

"I'm sorry, Bonnie. Would you mind faxing it again? I'm sitting right by the fax machine."

"For you, yes. But don't think I'm not going to expect some chocolate on my desk when you get back."

"You got it."

He opened the door and motioned for the desk sergeant to come to Nick's office. "Sergeant, please contact Sam Harris and tell him to return to the station *immediately.*"

The sergeant raised an eyebrow, but didn't say anything as he went back to the main desk and picked up the phone.

Quinn was back in Nick's office when the first page came through. It was the one he'd already seen.

Fifteen followed. As they emerged from the fax, Quinn saw the life of a serial killer in the making.

Born and raised in Portland, Oregon. Father, Kyle Larsen, deserted the family when David was three and apparently had no further contact with the family. He was killed in a drug deal gone bad nine years later.

Abusive mother . . . David had been removed from the home twice by Child Protective Services as a minor, but each time he'd been returned. Bonnie noted that they would have to petition the courts for the files.

Two sealed juvenile crimes. Again, they'd have to petition for the files.

One arrest for rape when he was eighteen. Interesting. He'd been a freshman at Lewis and Clark College in Oregon. He'd been arrested for rape, but the victim recanted her statement. He stuck with his alibi — that he was at his sister's house all night, which his sister supported. Had the victim been so traumatized she didn't want to go through the justice system?

One point caught Quinn's eye: the victim's breasts had been permanently scarred with a knife.

It made perfect sense. Fatherless home, abusive mother — probably sexually abusive. He'd need to see the CPS records to be sure. Grows up in a female-dominated environment. Mother molests him. Breasts are both sexual and maternal. He damages the breasts of his victims as he wished he could do to his mother.

His older sister became his guardian when he was fourteen after the death of their mother. Cause of death was simply listed as "accidental." His sister had been his alibi for the rape charges. Either she was protecting him or terrified of him. Or both.

Sister, sister . . . Quinn flipped through the pages.

Delilah Larsen.

Delilah. Where had he heard that name recently? Richard Parker. His wife was Delilah. The name was so unusual, it had to be her. Delilah *Parker* certainly hadn't seemed like a victim to Quinn, but he knew appearances could be deceiving, and he'd only met her that one time. He would have appraised her as meticulous, organized, and intelligent.

But even the most distinguished woman could be abused and manipulated by a person she loved or feared. Quinn would have to proceed with caution with the Parkers.

If Delilah Parker didn't suspect that her brother was dangerous, she could be in denial and attempt to warn him. Quinn had seen it happen in several cases where a close relative, friend, or lover didn't believe someone they trusted could kill.

On the other hand, if she did know what David Larsen did to those women, a whole other dynamic was going on. She obviously hadn't gone to the police with any suspicions. She could be abused and manipulated by him, essentially brainwashed into protecting him. Or, she could be complicit in his activities.

Delilah Parker needed to be watched closely.

Quinn read the remainder of the report and found the confirmation he needed:

After the rape charges were dropped, David Larsen transferred to MSU and lived with his sister, who took a job as a secretary in the Board of Supervisor's office.

Richard Parker had been a supervisor during the time she worked there.

Sam Harris had taken the report to give Parker a heads-up about his brother-in-law. Parker was an influential judge — but what was Harris thinking? Jeopardizing the entire investigation in order to save someone's political ass?

Unless he thought he could ascertain the whereabouts of David Larsen from his sister and try to bring him in alone.

The fool!

Quinn jumped up. He called to the desk sergeant, "Have you reached Harris?"

"No, sir."

"Keep trying. Who's available to go out on a call with me?"

"We're pretty thin here, sir." The sergeant looked at his sheet. "I can call in Jorgenson. He's on traffic duty."

"Do it."

Ryan Parker was playing video games in the living room after lunch when a sheriff's car pulled into the driveway. His mother walked in. "Ryan, please clean up and go to your room. We have company."

He shut down his game even though he'd almost defeated Darth Maul.

"It's just Sam," his father said from his desk in front of the large windows.

"Richard" was all his mother said, but she gave him *the look*. The one that said, *don't argue with me*. Ryan knew it well.

Ryan put his video game away, closed the cabinets, and went upstairs. He opened and closed his bedroom door, because his mother listened for things like that. But instead of staying in his room, he tiptoed back to the top of the stairs where he could listen without being seen.

The boy learned a lot that way.

"I wish I were here under more pleasant circumstances," Sam Harris said.

"Is it about the girl who was kidnapped?" his father asked.

"There's no easy way to say this, which is

why I asked my deputy to stay in the car. I felt you needed the opportunity to consider the situation first, without gossip and detractors using the information to damage your career, Judge."

"What are you trying to say?"

Ryan knew that annoyed tone. His father didn't like people who "kissed butt," as he called it. It meant that they tried to be your friend because of what you did, not who you were. Since his father was a judge, an important position, he said a lot of people tried to kiss his butt, but he didn't respect them.

"I'll get right to the point," Sam said. "The FBI is on its way to interview your brother-in-law, David Larsen. He is now considered a suspect in the Butcher investigation."

"Davy? I don't believe it," his father said.

Uncle Davy? *The Butcher?* Ryan slumped against the wall. That would mean he killed that college girl Ryan had found last week, the girl who wouldn't leave Ryan alone in his dreams, eyes staring at him like a dead doe.

Not Uncle Davy. He took Ryan fishing at the end of every summer. Mom went with them to their cabin by Big Sky Lake, but she didn't like to fish. Uncle Davy knew everything about the birds, trees, animals. He'd taught Ryan how to figure out which berries were edible and which would kill you.

Uncle Davy listened to him, really listened. Ryan couldn't talk to anyone else about his parents, especially about his mother. Ryan didn't think she really liked him. Oh, she probably loved him — all mothers did — but all the things she did for him, from baking cookies to washing his clothes to meeting with his teacher, seemed like things she just had to do. Like she had a "How to Be a Mom" checklist.

His uncle understood. "Delilah doesn't really like anyone," he told Ryan once. And when Uncle Davy said it, he'd realized it was true.

Ryan missed part of the conversation downstairs and he strained to hear. His mother had said something, her voice so low he couldn't make it out.

"I'm really sorry, Mrs. Parker. I know this comes as a shock to you, which is why I wanted to let you know before the press gets wind of it. I'm keeping it under wraps as long as possible, but you know these federal cops. They're a bunch of media hounds, just aching to get their picture in the paper. And if they hurt good folks such as yourselves, they don't care one iota."

"I'll have my attorney be in touch. Consider Davy as having counsel, Sam."

"I understand."

The deputy left, and at first Ryan didn't hear anything except mumbled voices.

"Did you know?" His father's voice was raised. His dad *never* raised his voice to his mother.

"No!" his mother said. "Davy had nothing to do with what happened to those girls."

"Shit, Delilah, this is bad."

"You know how the FBI is. They're always trying to railroad someone."

"You don't really believe that."

"Davy has nothing to do with this."

"I wish I believed you. I need to contact my attorneys."

Ryan retreated down the back stairs and walked out the kitchen door, careful to ease it closed. He ran to the barn and didn't realize he was crying until his vision blurred.

Why would the police think Uncle Davy had killed that girl if he hadn't?

He'd seen Uncle Davy last night, camping in the back meadow. That wasn't unusual; his uncle liked sleeping outdoors. He came up all the time and camped or stayed at the cabin. But Ryan usually knew beforehand when Uncle Davy was visiting.

His mother hadn't said anything about him coming last night. Maybe she didn't know.

Ryan quietly saddled Ranger and walked him out of the barn until he was out of sight of his house, then he mounted the horse.

He didn't know what he was going to do. He wanted to warn Uncle Davy, tell him the police had it all wrong.

But what if they didn't?

The camp was a mile from the house. Uncle Davy had camped there before, so Ryan knew exactly where it was. But as he approached, he saw no one.

He spotted gear neatly packed and stowed in the rotted-out trunk of a ponderosa pine. He frowned. Why hadn't his uncle come up to the house for breakfast this morning like he usually did when he camped? Where was he now?

Boot prints headed down toward the canyon that formed the western border of the Parker Ranch. Ryan wasn't supposed to go down there, but he'd done it many times. There was a really cool boulder field at the bottom. He, Sean, and Timmy went there whenever they thought their moms wouldn't find out. But steep slopes and sudden drop-offs made it dangerous, especially for Ranger.

Still, he knew the area. He'd be careful.

He was about to dismount when the sound of movement stopped him. Someone was walking up the steep slope.

"Uncle Davy?"

His uncle came into sight at the same time he reached for the rifle slung across his back.

That's when Ryan noticed the belt buckle Uncle Davy wore. Why did it look strange?

Then he knew. Uncle Davy had always worn the bird buckle. Just like the one Ryan had found in the woods near the dead girl. Only now, Uncle Davy's bird belt buckle was gone.

CHAPTER
29

Quinn called Miranda while driving from Bozeman to the Parker Ranch. He tapped the steering wheel, eager to get there, hating that it seemed to take forever. There was a lot of ground under the "Big Sky."

He told her about David Larsen's family connections. She didn't say anything for a long minute. "Are you sure?" she finally asked.

"Yes."

"And they didn't know?" Her voice caught.

"He didn't live with them; it's very likely that they didn't know about his activities. But—" He paused. How much should he tell her?

"But what?"

He had to trust her with the truth. It would all come out sooner or later.

"Larsen was arrested for rape when he was

407

eighteen. The charges were dropped when the victim refused to testify. His sister, Delilah, was his alibi."

"And you think he was guilty."

He took a deep breath. "Yes, I do." Then he told her why. "The girl had her breasts cut."

"And his sister *lied* for him?"

"We don't know what happened then. She could have been threatened by him, manipulated. Maybe she lied because she thought he was innocent but didn't have a good alibi. We can't know until we talk to her. That's where I'm going right now."

"I can't believe that a woman would protect a rapist. She'd have to be sick, just like him."

"Are you still at the University?"

"No. Booker drove me to the Lodge an hour ago. I was going stir-crazy. We're going to take a section south of here. I need to do something."

"You can communicate with all the search teams, correct?"

"We have a dedicated radio band."

"Good. If I get anything from the Parkers about where Larsen might be keeping Ashley, we'll change course and send everyone into a new area. Hang at the Lodge for a while longer, okay?"

She paused. "You don't want me to go out?"

"Not because I think you can't handle it, Miranda, but because I need to be able to contact you."

"You're right. I'm sorry."

"Keep the Parker connection quiet for a while. I think Sam Harris might have already spilled the beans, but I'm going to give it a shot."

"Harris! What did he do?"

Quinn told her about the fax. "He's not answering calls from dispatch and I've told every cop if they see him to arrest him or I'll have their badge. Harris is obstructing justice and I'm not going to let him get away with it."

Miranda wasn't surprised Harris had gone off on his own. He'd always been a loose cannon. She wished Nick had had a better second-in-command.

She filled Booker in on the details as they walked from the dining hall to her cabin. She was too antsy to sit still. She hoped Quinn would call soon.

She heard the hooves of a horse galloping on the path, heading right for her. She turned and saw a kid on a very tired horse.

Ryan Parker.

"Whoa!" Booker said.

Ryan slowed down and slid off the horse. He was panting almost as hard as the poor animal.

"What's wrong?" Miranda asked. The vast Parker holdings almost surrounded the Moore property, but the ranch itself was several miles south. "Did you come all the way up here from your house?"

"My, my uncle."

Ryan's uncle was David Larsen.

"What about him?" She was surprised her voice sounded normal.

"I knew, I knew," Ryan repeated. "When I saw his belt buckle."

"Slow down." Miranda reached into her backpack and pulled out a bottle of water, handing it to the boy. "Drink this."

He did, coughed some out, then drank more. He sat on a small boulder that lined the path and poured the rest of the water over his head. Miranda sat next to him.

"What happened, Ryan?"

"I heard. Sam Harris told my parents that Uncle Davy was the Butcher. But I didn't believe it. I mean, he's my friend."

Miranda's heart went out to the poor kid. His world was crashing around him just like hers had.

"I saw Uncle Davy last night. Camping in

the south meadow. He does that sometimes. Or at the cabin."

"Cabin?"

"We have a cabin right at Big Sky Lake. We go fishing and stuff. Uncle Davy stays there."

"Do you know where it is?"

"Of course." He rattled off an address.

"Maybe he's there," Miranda said to Booker. "We need to call Quinn."

Ryan shook his head vigorously. "No. No, he's not. I saw him. And the buckle."

"What buckle?"

"I thought it looked familiar. The bird. But I didn't remember. Then I saw him coming up from the canyon, and I just *knew*. I looked at his belt, and it wasn't there. He had a horse or something, not the bird he always wore." Ryan pulled a broken belt buckle from his pocket. "Just like this one."

Miranda was confused. "You took this from him? Why?"

Ryan looked down at his hands, turned the piece of metal over and over. "I didn't take it. I found it near the body of that girl who was killed. The next day I went back and watched you all."

His voice was rough with tears and he backhanded his face to wipe them away. "I'm sorry. I didn't know. I didn't mean to take it, I just found it. I wanted to tell my dad, but I thought he'd be mad that I went back there. So I hid it in my room.

"But after I saw my uncle today and realized the buckle was his, I ran home to get it." Ryan sniffed. "He was acting so strange. He wasn't happy to see me. He had his rifle. And a knife. I think he killed her."

Miranda's stomach lurched in her chest. "Where is he now?" she asked.

"I don't know. I told him I was just riding and saw his gear and had to get back home. My mom and dad were fighting, so I came here because it was the closest."

"You did good, Ryan." She stood. "Can you take us to where you saw your uncle?"

Ryan nodded. "You can drive most of the way there."

"Good." She pulled out her cell phone and dialed Quinn's number.

Quinn answered, but his voice was cut off.

"Dammit!" She tried again, and this time got his voice mail. "Quinn, call me. I have Ryan Parker with me and he knows where Larsen is." She looked at Ryan. "Where?"

"The south meadow. About a mile behind my house. There's a path."

"South meadow behind the Parker house. I'm going there now. Meet me there, Quinn." She slapped her phone shut. "Ryan,

I know where that is. I don't want you coming. It's too dangerous."

"But—"

"No. Stay here. I'm going to take you to Gray so you can take care of your horse." She stared at him. "Anything else?"

He nodded. "Uncle Davy came up from the canyon on the far side of the meadow. At the very bottom there's a boulder field and creek."

"I've been down there."

"I don't know why he'd go down there." Miranda did.

Sitting in Parker's living room, Quinn Peterson explained to Richard Parker his theory about David Larsen.

"But why do you need to talk to Delilah? We see Davy at holidays and for the occasional fishing trip, but Delilah never talks about her brother. They had a difficult childhood and they aren't that close."

"Did Delilah ever tell you her brother was arrested for rape?"

Richard looked stunned. "No."

"Sixteen years ago in Oregon. The charges were dropped when the victim refused to testify, and Larsen had an alibi: his sister."

"So Davy must have had nothing to do with it."

"The woman's breasts were cut."

Quinn watched the realization hit Richard then. "But — Delilah? Protecting him? I — I just don't see it. My wife isn't an affectionate person, Mr. Peterson. She's hard to get close to. I don't see her lying for anyone, even her brother."

"What about to protect herself?"

"Excuse me?" Parker's tone bordered between angry and confused.

While driving to the Parker Ranch, Quinn had talked to Hans Vigo, the FBI profiler. Vigo's gut feeling was that Delilah Parker not only had protected her brother when he was accused of rape in Oregon, but also was aware of his crimes in Montana.

"He hunts in his sister's hometown, while he lives hours away," Quinn told Parker, repeating what Vigo had told him. "Either he does it to torment her, a threat to keep her mouth shut, or he does it because this is his home. If your wife doesn't know for sure, she's definitely suspected from the beginning."

Parker buried his head in his hands. "My son — I let my son go fishing with that bastard. I let him eat at my table and sleep in my house! I gave him a cabin to stay in, paid for his education, took care of him like a brother." He pounded a fist on the coffee table hard enough to cause several knick-knacks to jump.

Quinn zeroed in on an important point. "Judge, you gave him a cabin?"

"Thirty minutes south of here. Almost to Yellowstone."

"I need to see it. Now. Can you take me there?"

"Absolutely. Anything to help."

Quinn's cell phone rang. "Peterson," he said.

"He . . . anda."

"Miranda? You're breaking up." Then the phone went dead.

"It's the house," Parker said. "You can go outside and get reception."

"Where's your wife now?"

"She left after Sam Harris came by. She was very upset by this whole thing with Davy."

"Sam Harris was here?"

Quinn listened to what Harris had told Parker. "I'm sorry, Judge, but I need to bring her in. Either she has information we need about where her brother is, or we need to protect her. I can't let her walk the streets. Not until I have her brother in custody."

He stepped out of the house and dialed dispatch to issue a detain order for Delilah Parker and find out if Sam Harris had called in. He hadn't. Dammit. He told the dispatcher to tell all on-duty cops that Harris was oficially removed from the Butcher investigation and wanted for obstructing justice. Quinn couldn't allow Harris to further screw up their search for Larson.

Richard Parker followed him out. "Ready?" Quinn asked the judge.

"I'll take you there." They climbed into the police-issue SUV that Deputy Jorgensen drove. Parker gave him directions.

"Tell me exactly where. I'm going to call in a team to meet us." Quinn needed everyone he could get.

Ten minutes later he'd finished his calls, including one to his boss to fill him in on the status. When he slammed shut his cell phone, his voice mail beeped. He dialed in and listened.

"Turn around," he told Parker, his voice strained.

"What? Why?"

"We're going back to your house. The fastest you can get us there, Jorgensen.

"Your son saw David Larsen there less than an hour ago."

CHAPTER
30

Davy Larsen watched from an upstairs window as Miranda Moore and a cop walked around the outside of the house. Then they left.

But they didn't go back down the drive. Instead, they headed toward the meadow.

Ryan, his own flesh and blood, had ratted him out.

How could the kid do that? Hadn't he loved him like a big brother? Ryan had the perfect life, the life Davy never had. But that was okay. It wasn't like Davy was jealous or anything. No.

Why did he go to *her?* To tell Miranda where to find him?

No good. He couldn't let them get his girl. Ashley was his, and he wasn't done with her yet.

The Bitch was leaving, and that was fine with him. He didn't need her.

She'd never understood. She'd stood there and watched, excited and agitated, never interfering with him when he had the stage. But she gloated and made cryptic comments.

"Do you feel better now, Davy?" she'd say afterward, as if talking to a child.

He wanted to shoot the smug look off her face, that self-satisfied grin. As if she knew something he didn't. She'd stolen even this from him, his women. When she watched, she claimed part of them, as if she were the director and he were a mere puppet.

Well, he intended to cut the strings of the puppeteer. He had finally agreed to meet her in Missoula tonight, and they'd drive from there to wherever. He'd had to agree. If he'd told her what he was going to do, she wouldn't have left him.

No, tonight was the hunt. Tonight he would be free. He would take his prize and then just keep going. He could live for months off the land this summer. He'd walk all the way to California if he had to.

She would never find him. He would be free at last.

And his hunts, his women, would finally be his own.

He left the house quietly and went the long way to the meadow. He had another path to get down to his girl.

First things first. Follow Miranda Moore. He would take great pleasure in slitting her throat. He had wanted to kill her when she had first escaped, but The Bitch said no. Like she was pleased one got away. She had laughed at him, taunted him, and he longed to take her neck into his hands and break it, like the neck of a chicken. *Crack*. Toss her by the side of the road and let the cougars chomp on her, the bugs crawl in and out of her mouth. It would serve her right.

But of course he didn't. Not then. He'd always believed that without her, he would be nothing. Without her, he would have perished years ago. She'd saved him more times than he could count. He'd been grateful. He'd loved her.

He hated her now. And this hate trampled all over any love he'd ever had for her.

He started down the slope toward the gulch below, planning his kills. First, Miranda Moore and the cops. Then, his girl.

And then, his fucking sister.

Two gunshots echoed from the canyon below. *His girl.* They were stealing his girl.

The bitch would pay!

He trekked faster down the mountain. The hunt was on.

"We can't wait for Quinn," Miranda told Booker.

They'd gone directly to the south meadow in her Jeep. When she didn't see Quinn, they drove up to the house.

No one answered.

She tried Quinn again, got voice mail again. Damn him, didn't he have call waiting?

Miranda took a deep breath. The mountains wreaked havoc with cell phones. She had call waiting and half the time calls went directly to voice mail because the towers got mixed signals. It didn't help that the weather was turning; the bright, sunny morning had disappeared, leaving a gray pallor over the entire mountain. The serious storm was supposed to hold out for late tonight. She hoped it would.

Quinn would be here soon. She knew he would. But could she wait? Between the weather and their not knowing the whereabouts of David Larsen, Ashley's fate was in question.

Miranda sensed she was close. She had to try. If Ashley died today down in the canyon locals called Boulder Gulch, and Miranda had waited to search, she'd never forgive herself.

Besides, Lance Booker was with her. He was a good cop, strong too. It was two against one. And Larsen didn't know the police were on to him. The element of surprise would be an added benefit.

"Ashley's down there. I know it," she told him. "If he feels the pressure of the police on him, he could kill her and disappear. Right now. We have to get to her first. We can't wait for Quinn or my team." She'd called everyone off their searches and told them to meet at this location and proceed with caution.

"You're right," Booker relented.

She slowly let out her breath. She wasn't sure what she would have done if Booker hadn't agreed to go down to Boulder Gulch with her. But if they were going to track Larsen's steps, they needed to do it while it was still light.

She pulled out her topo map and folded it so she had Boulder Gulch and the surrounding area clearly visible. She pocketed it, looked along the ridge of the slope. She saw the disturbance in the leaves and dirt from where Larsen had come up the slope and greeted Ryan.

"Here." She motioned for Booker, her heart pounding so loud she worried the deputy would hear her fear.

Could she do this? Knowing she might

come face-to-face with her attacker?

How could she not? If she waited even ten more minutes, Larsen might get to Ashley first and kill her.

What if Ashley was already dead? But Miranda felt she was still alive. It was too soon to hunt her. Larsen was cocky. He liked to keep them long enough to break them. To weaken them, so they didn't have a chance to survive his hunt.

He hadn't broken Miranda. He hadn't killed her. She'd gotten away, and now she would take away his prize. Ashley.

She called her team leader, Charlie. "Booker and I are going after Ashley."

She followed Larsen's path. He'd zigzagged his way up the slope to keep from falling. Some places were dangerous: if she started to slide down, she wouldn't be able to stop until she hit a tree.

Boulder Gulch was a narrow, two-thousand-acre canyon that cut through the mountain with a seasonal creek. It had incredible rock formations. She'd come here with Professor Austin's geology class. The trip had been treacherous, even though they had followed an easier path, on the canyon's far eastern slope. But now they'd have had to drive nearly an hour around the mountain to get to it.

Coming down this side was the fastest way to the bottom.

They'd been virtually scaling down the mountain without ropes for fifteen minutes. Booker and she didn't talk because they couldn't. In the back of her mind, Miranda knew Ashley would be in no condition to come back up this way. They'd have to go the long way out of the gulch. That meant miles of relatively flat river rock, hours of walking.

Or running.

She could see the bottom of the gulch. "Booker." She gestured down the slope. "We need to find another way down."

"This is how he came up," Booker said.

"But he was coming uphill. He could use his momentum to pull himself up, grabbing trees for support. It's nearly three hundred feet down. And the last fifty feet are boulders. It's too dangerous." She'd had too many of her team members injured over the years trying to get up and down the sometimes sheer face of the mountainside.

Booker didn't look happy. "We could be far away before we find a better place."

"It looks a little better over there. Then we'll backtrack when we get to the bottom. But we need to hurry. We don't know when he'll be back."

She turned, walking parallel to the canyon

bottom. The wet dirt beneath the thick layer of pine needles made the stretch difficult. The air was cooler down here, and it didn't help that the day had become overcast. Almost on cue, a fat raindrop hit her face.

"Watch out. The moisture is going to make the needles slippery," she told Booker.

"Miranda, I've lived here my entire life. I know the mountains."

"Sorry," she mumbled.

He flashed her a smile. "Let's go down here." He pointed to a slope that didn't look much safer than the area they'd passed up. Lots of pine needles, a few fallen trees, the occasional protruding boulder. And a sharp angle downward.

"You sure?" She looked in the direction they were walking. There didn't seem a better place within sight.

"Absolutely. See how it slopes at the bottom? It's just the next fifty feet that'll be difficult."

"All right." She wasn't as confident, but another drop of water hit her face. She feared time was running out.

Booker started down first. She followed in his footholds, keeping her body nearly flush with the mountainside to maintain her balance.

She saw Booker slide as the ground gave

way beneath him, layer upon layer of loose dirt and leaves unable to support his weight. The week of drying from the rains had left the ground moist, but loose.

"Lance!" she called. He struggled to control his descent, but he slid faster and faster, then started to roll.

He hit the bottom. Half covered with debris, he didn't move.

Miranda scrambled down the mountain as fast as she dared. It was easier with all the loose dirt gone.

"Lance, are you okay?"

He rolled over, but when she got to the bottom of the gulch, winded, she saw he was in pain.

"What happened?"

"I think I cracked a rib. It might be broken."

Her heart beat so hard she thought it would burst through her rib cage. They were at the bottom of the gulch. Alone. And the Butcher would be coming back sometime tonight.

She had to get Booker out of here, but there was no way he could make it up the mountain. And it was more than a five-mile trek down the gulch to the other side — they might be able to make it, if they stopped frequently.

But what about Ashley? How could Miranda leave her when she was so close? When the Butcher was going to come back?

"Go find her," he said as if reading her mind. "I'll be fine."

"I'm not leaving you. That's one of my rules — when your partner falls, you stay until help arrives."

"These are extraordinary circumstances." He sat up, wincing. "I'll go with you far enough to find a place to hide."

Miranda helped him up, grimacing at the pain on his face. "You'll be okay, Lance. But if you have trouble breathing, you can't move. If your rib is broken, sudden movement could puncture a lung."

"It just keeps getting better and better."

They backtracked along the boulders until they found Larsen's trail again. But with the rocks it was difficult to see where he'd come from before heading up the mountain.

"Look around, Lance. Any sign where he went?" The few raindrops had turned into a misty drizzle. It felt good now, but soon it would make visibility poor.

"There," Booker said, pointing across the creek toward the rich, thick growth that bordered that side of the gulch.

Sure enough, a small sapling had been trampled.

It could have been done by a bear or a mountain lion. But it was the closest they had come to a trail, and they took it. As they went deeper into the woods, it was obvious by the soil prints that a two-legged predator had come this way.

"You okay to go on?"

"I'm fine for now."

Still, they went slower than she would have liked. She took out her radio and called her location in to Charlie. Charlie was on Miranda's team and had ten years more experience than she did. Though filled with static, it was good to hear his voice. Charlie's team was ten minutes from the Parker Ranch.

That meant it would take them at least an hour to get to the bottom of the Gulch.

"Charlie, I'm out."

"Roger that, take—"

"Wait."

Then she saw it: the shack.

"Miranda?"

"It's here. I think I found Ashley. I'm checking."

"Proceed with caution."

She swallowed. "I am. Out."

The dilapidated wood structure sagged with age and Montana's cold, wet winters. The tin roof was rusted in spots, but unlike

Rebecca's prison, this one had at least one window.

Every pore of her body screamed, "Be careful!" He could be here. David Larsen, the Butcher.

"Miranda," Booker whispered. He stood right behind her. He looked pale and was sweating profusely.

"You have to sit down," she said quietly.

"I can't. What if he's there?"

"Be backup."

They drew their guns. She was surprised her hands weren't shaking, although every hair on her body seemed to be tingling.

Holding her gun with both hands, she cautiously approached the structure. Booker motioned for her to go one way and he'd take the other. She pointed to the window. He nodded, and she squatted beneath it, trying to keep her breathing under control. She was almost gasping, her fear bubbling to the surface.

Not now. Please, not now. Ashley's life depended on her. If she failed . . .

No. She couldn't, wouldn't fail.

Slowly, she peered into the room. As her eyes adjusted to the near dark of the cabin, she saw a naked woman tied on a filthy mattress in the middle of the floor. Her blonde hair looked dark from dirt and blood.

Sharon.

The pain, the anger, the humiliation came flooding back, overwhelmed her, and she sank to her knees. Oh, God, why? Why did you create such a monster?

It wasn't Sharon, it was Ashley. And Ashley needed her.

What if she was already dead?

Miranda took a deep breath and stood, looking through the window again. As she watched, she saw the rise and fall of the woman's chest. She was alive. Maybe there was a God after all.

Then Miranda realized Ashley wasn't alone.

Miranda was ready to shoot the man through the window. He was lying next to Ashley as if basking in the afterglow of sex. She'd shoot him and cut off his balls and stuff them down his throat. Hate and rage filled her and she lifted her gun.

She paused when she saw a glint of metal. She tried to see the man's face, but couldn't. He was restrained, tied with rope, his hands and feet bound behind his back.

The body was familiar. Dark hair. Beige shirt.

Nick.

He was alive!

CHAPTER
31

Miranda rushed around the side of the shack. Damn, the door was chained.

She pounded on the door. "Nick! Nick it's Miranda! I'm going to shoot off this lock and get you out of there."

She heard a faint voice but couldn't make out what he said. Ashley cried out, a cross between pain and joy.

"Booker! Where are you?" Miranda glanced from side to side, but didn't see him.

"Here." His voice came from the other side of the cabin, faint. She feared his injuries were worse than he'd let on.

"Nick's inside the shack with Ashley. I'm going to get them out. Larsen is nowhere in sight, but keep a lookout."

Silence.

"Lance? Are you okay?"

"I'll be fine. I just need a minute."

Dammit, now she had two seriously injured cops and a civilian. First things first: free Nick and Ashley. Then she could figure out a way to get them all out of here.

She aimed her gun at the lock. It took two bullets to bust it, then she kicked open the door.

The stench of blood, violent sex, and human waste filled her senses, sickening and familiar. She gagged and turned her head. She and Sharon had lived in such filth.

She froze. She wanted to go in, make sure Nick was okay. But her feet felt filled with lead, embedded in cement, and the harder she tried to make them move, the heavier they became.

Her body trembled. Just the thought of crossing the threshold of the shrinking space numbed her. Slowly, her peripheral vision closed in.

No. Not now. Please.

She fell to her knees. *I can do this. I can go in. Save them.*

No I can't. I'm weak. He defeated me. He'll come back and finish the job. He took Sharon and I ran. I couldn't save her. Now I can't even save myself.

"Miranda?"

Nick's voice. Gruff and raw.

"Miranda!" Still raw, but commanding.

"Nick. I—" She took a deep breath. She

was going to hyperventilate if she wasn't careful.

"I need you. Ashley needs you. Get in here. He's going to return."

After all these years, the Butcher would defeat her. He made her claustrophobic. He gave her fear.

"I. Can't."

"You can, Miranda. I know you. I trust you. Take a deep breath." He sputtered and coughed, struggling to get the words out. "You can do it," he said, ending on a gasp of air.

She could, couldn't she? She could overcome her fear. She had to. For Nick. For everything he'd done for her, for his support and encouragement and friendship. She hadn't come this far to fail.

And she loved him. She could see it so clearly now, the difference between Nick and Quinn. She loved them both. She hadn't realized that before. But she could love two men. One as her lover. The other as her brother.

Breathe in. Breathe out. In. Out.

She took another deep breath and forced herself to enter the shrinking room. The walls started to cave in around her, each step drawing them closer. Her chest tightened. She had no air. No air.

Not now. No, not now.

Shaking, she reached for the ropes that bound Nick. Her fingers struggled with the elaborate knots. The walls reached out, grabbing for her.

"Miranda." His voice was raw.

"I'm getting you out of here." Her voice sounded weak and her body trembled. She focused on the knots. If she simply worked on them she could forget the shrinking walls, the foul stench, the memories of violence. She had to. For Nick. For Ashley.

For herself.

"Forget me. Get Ashley out of here. Send someone back for me."

"I can't. Nick, the Butcher is David Larsen. Delilah Parker's brother. The police can't find him, but he was seen near here. I can't leave you, he'll be back tonight." Or sooner.

"I don't think I can make it," Nick said, his voice strained.

"I'll never leave you." She swallowed her fear, the shame that she would fail, and worked the knots so she wouldn't think about how much smaller the room had become since she'd entered. "We thought you were dead."

"I made a mistake."

"You can tell me all about it later," she said.

Dammit, the knots were too complicated and tight! Her knife. Why hadn't she thought of it first? Her mind was going. The room was stifling. Sweat poured from her face, her body saturated in her own panic.

If she didn't pull herself together, Ashley and Nick would die. And if she didn't find a way out of this, she and Lance Booker would join them.

But there was safety in numbers. Four against one, even if three of the four were in less than prime condition.

She pulled out her knife and carefully cut through the ropes so she wouldn't injure Nick. A minute later he was free. She then went to work on Ashley.

The girl was sobbing. "He's going to kill us."

"No. No, I'm not going to let him." Miranda pulled off the tight blindfold that bound Ashley's eyes. The girl tried to open her eyes, but failed. "Don't force it. Give yourself a minute."

"No! He's going to come! He's going to get me!"

"I escaped him once; we'll escape him again." She wished she were as confident as she sounded. "And then he *will* pay for what he did to you."

And to me, she added silently.

Ashley was so petite Miranda was able to pick her up. "No! No!" she screamed.

"I need to get you out of here, Ashley. You need to stretch your muscles."

Miranda carried her from the shack and put her down outside the door.

The sobbing girl was covered in dried blood and bruises. It was like looking in a mirror from twelve years ago. Miranda swallowed uneasily, tears springing to her eyes. The girl shielded her breasts with her arms, but Miranda didn't need to see the damage. She looked down and found her own hands on her breasts. She dropped them as if her breasts burned.

She wanted to tell Ashley to be quiet, he would hear — but she had no idea how close or far David Larsen was from the shack. If he planned to come back tonight — or now.

Instead, she took off her backpack, unzipped it, and extracted her extra sweater. She pulled it over the girl's head. Then she handed her a water bottle. "Drink it slow," she told her.

Ashley took it, sobbing, huddled inside the too-big sweater.

Miranda pulled out two pairs of thick socks and knelt next to Ashley. "You need to cover your feet to retain warmth."

"Don't touch me!"

"Okay." She held out the socks. Like a skittish animal, Ashley tentatively reached out, then grabbed them fast and pulled them close to her. "Put them on. Both pairs."

She looked for Booker, didn't see him. "Lance!" she called, not too loudly.

"Here," she heard faintly. The voice came from around the side. He hadn't moved since Miranda had gone inside. She carried Ashley to where Booker leaned against the shack wall. She put the girl down.

Miranda turned to Lance. "Why didn't you tell me you were this bad off?" She pulled up his shirt. Already she saw his chest was bruised and swollen. She gently touched his ribs and he bit back a cry, his face twisting in pain.

"At least one is broken."

His breathing was labored, and Miranda worried he'd punctured a lung.

"Nick, we can't leave him here."

"Is he okay?" Booker asked.

Miranda looked over her shoulder and frowned. She'd thought Nick had followed her out of the cabin.

"I don't know." She turned to Lance. "Radio in our location and ask for an ETA on reinforcements. Tell them we need a full mountain rescue. I'm going to bring out Nick."

She went back to the entrance. "Nick?"

He still lay on the floor. She hadn't realized he was so badly hurt. She took a deep breath, hesitated only a moment, then plunged back into the airless cabin.

She knelt next to him. "Nick, get up."

"I can't. My head. I can't see anything."

"I'm going to get you out of here, but you're going to have to help. Can you walk?"

"Probably some."

It took several minutes, precious time, to bring Nick from the shack. She sat him down next to Booker.

His head was covered in dried blood. He felt hot to the touch. Too hot. His eyes were unfocused. He had a severe concussion, and most likely a raging infection.

There was no way he'd walk out of this canyon.

He needed a hospital.

"Miranda, go. Take Ashley and get out of here before he comes back."

"I can't just leave you here. He'll kill you." But she couldn't see another solution.

"I'm giving you a direct order, Miranda."

"Don't pull rank on me!" She rested her head in her hands and took a deep breath.

"Dammit, Nick, I thought you were dead and it tore me up. Don't do this to me. Don't even think of doing anything stupid."

He closed his eyes and sighed. "I'm not going to make it on foot, Miranda."

She touched his head where an ugly, bloody gash had dried. "Nick — you have a fever. You need a doctor."

"Well, call one when you get to town."

"Lance, who did you reach? What's their ETA?"

"I talked to Charlie. Forty to forty-five minutes."

What could she do? Carry two grown men miles over rocky, open terrain? What about Ashley?

David Larsen might be five minutes away. They couldn't sit here and wait for a rescue. He'd pick them off one by one. And she wasn't about to leave anyone. By the time she returned with help, it might be too late.

She glanced at the girl, still hunched over, hugging her knees, rocking back and forth. The dark green sweater Miranda had given her — for warmth and camouflage — stretched over her body.

Her face was bruised, her hair filthy and matted. She smelled of her own waste. The cuts and bruises on her body were now concealed, but Miranda had seen them and knew Ashley was in pain, emotionally and physically. Miranda had been there. But over time the wounds had faded, all of them.

She found strength in Ashley. The girl needed her. They couldn't sit here and wait for help. Not when they didn't know where Larsen was.

She bit her lip and looked around. The shack was at the far end of the canyon. Seventy feet behind them it narrowed. There would be no easy way to get out. In front of them the canyon widened, stretching to hundreds of feet wide in places, narrowing to as little as thirty feet in others. But she knew exactly where the gulch led. Right here, there were few places to hide. Definitely no place for four adults.

And Miranda couldn't possibly leave the injured men and Ashley while she searched for a better hiding spot until help arrived. Yet there was no way Nick and Lance would be able to walk far.

She turned back to Nick. "Here." She handed him her extra gun.

"I won't take your gun."

"I have another, Nick. I'm not leaving if you don't take it." She took his hand and wrapped it around the grip. He held it tight.

She slipped her map into a plastic cover to prevent the drizzle from soaking it and showed Booker her route. "I'm heading east through the gulch. It curves south here. It doesn't end for miles, close to Big Sky, but I know a shortcut at the bend that will get us to—" she pointed "—here." She looked from Lance to Nick. "I'm going to stick to the canyon as much as possible, but to hide our path we might have to trek up one of the slopes. I have my radio, but I'm setting it to sixty-four. Okay? That's all-silent, no chatter. The best thing you can do is keep yourselves alive."

Miranda looked around and pointed fifty feet up the slope. "Lance, see those boulders up there?"

He followed her finger. "Yes."

"Can you get Nick up there?

"I think so."

"You have to. You're both sitting ducks out here. Get up there and hide. Radio Charlie and tell him the plan. If you see Larsen, call my frequency and tell me how much time I have." She adjusted her radio. "If he sees you . . . shoot to kill."

It wasn't the best plan, but they were running out of time.

She squeezed Nick's hand. "Okay?"

"Okay."

She glanced at her watch, rubbing mist from its face: 4:35. It had been only fifteen minutes since she'd first seen the cabin. It seemed much longer.

They had three hours until sundown.

They wouldn't make it out before then, even if they ran the whole way.

"Ashley, we have to go."

"No, no. I can't. Let me stay with them."

"He's going to be looking for you." In addition, there was barely enough room up slope behind the boulder to hide two men.

Miranda had faced her fear in the cabin and won. If she could conquer her claustrophobia, she could certainly lead Ashley to safety. But only if the girl would cooperate.

"Let's go," she said.

"I can't," Ashley wailed, tears running down her cheeks.

"Yes, you can. Don't let him win."

Nick said, "You're stronger than you think, Ashley."

Something in his tone made Miranda look at him. Though his eyes were closed, she saw on his face that he was worried. And more. A quiet understanding. He knew. He'd lain next to Ashley and witnessed her rape. Miranda hated that he'd been through that.

But for the first time in her life, she didn't dwell on what happened all those years ago. She'd escaped the Butcher then, and she would elude him now.

"We need to go," she said. "Lance, don't forget to call Charlie as soon as you're hidden up slope."

"I will."

Ashley whimpered, her body heaving with dry sobs. But she seemed resigned to going with Miranda as she slowly got to her feet, her arms still wrapped tightly around herself.

Miranda turned one last time to Nick as she strapped on her backpack. "I expect to see you alive when I get to the end of this canyon."

CHAPTER
32

Quinn searched the Parker residence with Deputy Jorgensen while two other cops searched the grounds.

"Clear," Quinn called.

Richard Parker looked ghostly, his face drawn, when Quinn stepped back out on the porch. "He could have killed Ryan. He could have killed Delilah."

"Ryan's safe," Quinn reminded him. "I sent a deputy over to the Moore place to watch over him. Every available cop is looking for Delilah and David."

"She didn't know. She couldn't have known."

Parker had been repeating this mantra in the car until Quinn was ready to slug him.

"Agent Peterson!"

One of Nick's deputies came running up. "We were checking out the south meadow like you said and heard faint gunshots down in the gulch."

"Where?"

"It was hard to tell with the echo, but it was from the bottom most certainly. It's obvious that several people have walked down the slope; there's recently disturbed dirt and plants." The deputy wiped a hand over his face. The drizzle had been steadily increasing, but it wasn't fully raining yet.

A series of four-wheel-drive trucks came down the driveway. Quinn recognized the driver of the first truck, Charlie. Quinn didn't wait for him to get out, but met him next to the gravel area by the barn.

"I just talked to Lance Booker," Charlie said. "They found the girl. And get this: Nick's with her."

Quinn slammed his fist on the hood of Charlie's truck. What was Miranda thinking going down into that canyon alone? He didn't care that she had a deputy with her; she wasn't a cop, she wasn't a federal agent. Why?

It hit him: She thought she could save Ashley. He would have done the same.

"Let's head down to the meadow. I'll catch a ride with you — we'll need the four-wheel-drive if this rain gets any heavier."

"It will," Charlie said grimly.

The drive was short and bumpy. As soon as the truck stopped, Charlie's radio buzzed.

"GCSR, GCSR, anyone there?" GCSR was the acronym for Gallatin County Search and Rescue. Miranda's unit.

Charlie answered. "Roger, Charlie Daniels here."

"Charlie, it's Lance Booker. I'm calling to give you coordinates. Can you take them?"

Charlie pulled a pencil and pad from the visor. "Give them to me."

Booker gave the coordinates. When he was done, Quinn took the radio. "Booker, it's Agent Peterson. Put Miranda on."

"I can't, sir."

"Why the hell not?"

"There was no place here to conceal all four of us and she took Ashley farther down the gulch."

"Explain."

Quinn closed his eyes when he got off the radio with Lance Booker. Damn, damn! Miranda had no other choice — she hadn't had many options. But to have her running with an injured, scared woman . . .

"Let's get going. Booker says it'll take forty-five minutes to get down to the gulch."

"I'll cut that time in half. Ever rappel down a mountain?"

Davy stared at the open door. Red rage exploded in his chest, filling every blood vessel with potent hatred.

That *bitch* stole his girl.

Where did they go?

She was a smart bitch; she wouldn't go up the gulch. It only grew steeper, narrower. A trap. She hadn't fallen for his traps before. Down Boulder Gulch would land them out near Big Sky. Hard going over the rocks, and they'd have to cross several creeks. With the rain last week they were running high. Waist deep at least. It would slow them down.

She wouldn't be able to take his girl up the mountainside. Too steep. He'd picked this location because of the trap to the west. He wanted to corner the girl. See the hot fear in her eyes when she realized there was no way out. Would she run toward him? Or cower against a mountain she'd never be able to climb?

Instead, the bitch must have taken her down the boulders, taking the sport out of it. What was the fun of shooting them in open space? He'd done that before.

He wanted something new.

The bitch would pay for what she'd done. He should have killed Miranda Moore twelve years ago.

He would have her begging for mercy before he cut out her heart.

★ ★ ★

Miranda winced at the buzz of her radio. She had it turned low, but it still made noise.

"Moore here," she said, mindful of the echo. The rain was coming down steadily, helping to mask the noise, but if the Butcher was on her tail she had to take every precaution. They were keeping close to the north slope so they weren't completely out in the open, but the rain made the ground slick. She had on hiking boots yet still fell once; she'd had to pick Ashley up more times than she could count.

They were not moving fast enough for her liking.

"It's Booker. The Butcher came and left, ninety seconds ago at a quick pace. He was not happy."

Booker's voice came through fuzzy.

"Roger."

"I tried for a clean shot, but I couldn't get one."

"Better to stay hidden. If you missed the first shot, he would have known where you were. How's Nick doing?"

"He's going in and out of consciousness. I was talking to him, keeping him awake, until I spotted Larsen and had to keep quiet. He faded then."

Damn. Nick needed medical attention soon.

"I talked to Peterson," Booker continued. "They're on their way down."

Good. At least she had reinforcements.

"I'm turning off my radio," she said. "I don't want any noise. Out."

She glanced at Ashley. The girl didn't know the meaning of the word quiet. Every time she slipped she let out a yelp, then started crying again about how she was going to die.

Miranda couldn't blame her. Ashley was scared to death. She knew what had happened to all the other victims of the Butcher. She'd had a lot of evil things happen to her during the last two days.

But Miranda needed to explain the facts of life — and death — to Ashley van Auden.

She turned off her radio and pocketed it. Ashley stepped on a sharp rock and fell to her knees. "Ow!" She sobbed into the dirt.

Miranda picked Ashley up off the ground, her muscles straining. Though Ashley was several inches shorter and ten pounds lighter than Miranda, she was drenched. Miranda felt sluggish with the weight of the water and backpack.

The rain had cleansed Ashley's body, washing away the blood and body odor, leaving her smelling like the wet wool sweater and fear — the fear rolling off her was palpable.

Or was that Miranda's own terror?

She carried the girl to a thick ponderosa and propped her against the base.

"Listen to me, Ashley," she said in her sternest voice.

"He's going to kill us," Ashley interrupted. "You know it. You know he's coming after us. I heard. I heard on your radio. That cop said. He's coming to kill us. We're going to d-d-die—"

Miranda grabbed Ashley's arms and gave her a firm shake. "Shut. Up." She didn't want to lose her temper, but her heart was racing. They didn't have time. Larsen would be eating up the ground three, four times faster than they were. Even with their twenty-minute lead — shit, they might have ten minutes. If they kept moving.

If they ran.

No. No more running. It would end here and now.

Rain pounding down, she observed her surroundings. She could use the terrain to her advantage.

They were in a wide part of the canyon. The boulders seemed to pile in the center, with a shallow creek running both north and south of the rocks. Though the south slope was steeper, there were more fallen trees here. Better places to hide.

"Ashley!"

"Why are you being so mean to me? You don't understand." Her swollen lips pouted and tears rolled from her eyes. "You don't know anything. Let me go!"

Miranda didn't release her hold. "Do you know who I am?"

"Mir-anda." Ashley's voice trembled.

"I am *Miranda Moore*. I escaped this bastard once. I'm not going to let him kill me — or you — now."

Miranda was surprised her voice sounded so strong. Inside, she was a mess. She had no idea what would happen when she saw Larsen. She didn't know if she would freeze or panic or scream in rage.

But she did know there was no way they could outrun him. And this time, she had a weapon, she had physical strength, and more important, she had the element of surprise.

She would not be a victim again.

Ashley blinked, oblivious to the rain running in rivulets down her face. She was shivering, but didn't seem to notice.

Her voice was small, like a child's. "Promise?"

"So help me God, he will have to kill me

before I let him touch you. But you have to do exactly what I say. *Exactly.*"

Ashley slowly nodded. "Okay."

Ten minutes. She had ten minutes to see if her plan would work.

Or Quinn would find her dead.

CHAPTER
33

Quinn helped Charlie rig mountain-climbing gear to the trucks at the top of the mountain. They would rappel straight down, cutting off a huge chunk of time getting to the bottom. They had only two ropes long enough, so Quinn and Charlie would go first, followed by additional teams of two.

"Ten minutes, tops," Charlie said.

They were about to start down the slope when Charlie's radio buzzed. "Charlie here."

"It's Deputy Booker. Larsen was just at the shack and went off in the same direction as Miranda. I warned her. She's radio-silent now."

Damn. Quinn wanted to talk to her, find out exactly where she was. Find out how she was holding up. Tell her to watch her back. Assure Miranda of her strength and perseverance.

Most of all, he wanted to hear her voice.

"Sheriff Thomas is bad off," Booker said. "He needs a doctor."

"We'll send the medic down next," Charlie said. "Twenty minutes."

"Roger that."

Charlie turned to Quinn. "Let's do it."

Quinn was in good shape, but rappelling down a mountain used muscles he never knew existed. By the time they got to the bottom, he was winded.

But he couldn't stop. His eyes scanned the gulch. Where was Miranda?

Where was Larsen?

Charlie radioed Booker, who said he and Nick were about three hundred yards west.

"Okay, Booker. Hang on. The medical team is on their way."

Charlie turned to Quinn and pointed to the ground. "Look."

The rain was falling faster by the minute and Quinn could barely see his feet clearly. Then he saw what Charlie did.

Deep impressions in the leaves leading to the boulder outcrop. "This way," Quinn said.

Miranda sensed the hunter before she saw him.

She didn't know exactly *how* she realized they weren't alone in this part of the woods, but suddenly the wet air felt electric, the gray sheets of rain sharpened, and her ears picked up every sound. The rain pounding on the boulders in the rising creek below. The faint creak of the trees swaying in the storm.

Her own sharp breath.

She had attempted to cover their tracks, but it was virtually impossible with the limited time she had to set her plan in motion. She hoped Ashley stayed quiet. That was all she had to do. Hide and be quiet.

Twelve years ago, Miranda had harbored a deep resentment of Sharon as they ran from the Butcher. Every time Sharon cried out, Miranda cringed, fearing her friend was leading the Butcher right to them. That he would catch them and they would die.

And Sharon had.

Times had changed. Though Miranda winced every time Ashley whimpered, she understood. How could she hate her for her fear?

That same fear crawled up Miranda's spine, step by step, eating away at her resolve.

She should have kept moving. Eventually, Larsen would have caught up to them. But maybe not. She should have stayed with Nick. If she had looked harder, maybe she could have found another place to hide.

Gone back into the shack and waited for him to walk in.

She had to stop second-guessing herself. Her fear was rising because *he* was getting closer.

Dammit, where was he? He should have been here by now.

He wouldn't stroll down the middle of the canyon. He'd follow their tracks, keeping close to the trees so he would have an element of surprise. Miranda had planted false tracks on the north side of the canyon, opposite of where she was hiding.

She expected him in camouflage to blend in with the environment. Every muscle rigid, she waited and watched.

There.

A movement to her left. Faint. Directly in front of Ashley's hiding spot. She looked and saw nothing. Maybe it was the rain playing tricks with her peripheral vision.

The sunlight had all but disappeared under the gray skies; visibility was minimal. The trap was a bad idea. She'd never be able to see him.

But maybe this was okay. He would pass by, and she and Ashley could sit tight until Quinn came.

Yes. That would work.

To her far left she sensed movement.

Dammit, Ashley! Get down. Stay down. Hadn't she listened to her? *Don't move. Stay low. Don't even look.*

Straight in front of her, forty feet away, she saw him. He stood perfectly still. She'd marked a trail going another two hundred feet past her hiding space, before she had backtracked — why had he stopped there?

Did he hear something?

Smell something?

Had he seen Ashley move in the rotting tree where Miranda had tried to hide her?

Dammit, what did he know?

She was panicking. He couldn't know where she was hiding. Or Ashley.

Please stay down, Ashley. Please be quiet.

Larsen was listening. He stood so still that if Miranda hadn't known he was there, she would have questioned her sanity. But she *had* seen a glimpse of him, and if she focused she could make out his silhouette.

Run. Run!

No, she would not run. She would stay right here, behind the low boulder. She was flat on her stomach, watching him from above. Watching, with her gun sights on the Butcher. He was too far for a certain hit. And she couldn't afford to miss. One miss, and he would bolt and come at them again. With the knowledge of where they were.

Walk on by, Larsen. Walk on by.

Her plan was to backtrack once Larsen passed them. In the ten minutes she'd had to plan, she determined the best trap would be to not get caught. Let him pass them, then backtrack as fast as possible to Nick. At some point before they reached him, they'd run into Quinn and the others.

Her number-one responsibility was to protect Ashley, not to catch the Butcher. But even through her fear, she wanted to stop him. Now. Give him no other opportunity to hurt another woman.

But getting Ashley safely out of the mountains was her job, and one she took very seriously.

Walk on by. Come on, come on! What are you waiting for?

He stood there, unmoving. Why?

She sensed more than saw Ashley's panic.

Everything seemed to happen in slow motion — Ashley jerked forward, out of the log. Back again.

Larsen turned his body and stared at the log. He raised his rifle.

Ashley screamed and scrambled out of the dead tree. Miranda aimed her gun at Larsen. He dropped to his knee and turned his rifle toward Ashley.

Miranda fired once, twice, three times.

Larsen fell flat to the ground. Had she hit him?

Ashley screamed again and Larsen used his forearms to crawl along the ground. He swung his rifle around and fired at Ashley.

"Ashley, get down!" Miranda yelled as she fired three more rounds at Larsen. But he was already rolling away from her and then he disappeared behind a boulder.

Shit! Where had he gone?

Ashley stumbled to Miranda's hiding spot. "I'm sorry, I'm sorry, I thought he'd seen me, I had to run. I'm sorry."

"Shh. Stop."

"I'm sorry."

"Be quiet," Miranda commanded. She had to think. She stared at the boulder forty feet in front of her. Visibility was so poor, she couldn't see beyond. Was he cowering on the other side? Had he crawled away? Would he try to get them from the right? The left? The rear?

He had to know where they were. But Miranda didn't dare move.

She would wait him out. She had no choice.

CHAPTER
34

One minute ticked off.

Miranda didn't move. She barely trusted herself to breathe. The only sound she heard other than the steady beat of the rain was Ashley shivering.

Her eyes swept the landscape. Back and forth. Looking for movement, something that told her where he'd gone.

Nothing.

Another minute ticked off.

Fear coated her mouth, a foul taste that made her want to spit. But she didn't dare open her mouth. Her chest tightened as her eyes darted back and forth, back and forth.

She felt like prey frozen by primal terror. Unable to move, unable to save herself. She was going to die out here after all, like a lamb led to the slaughter. Helpless.

No. You will not die without a fight.

"Ashley." She whispered right in the girl's

ear. "I'm going to crawl down to the creek."

"No!"

"Shhh." Damn, damn! What was with this girl? Didn't she understand that the prey had to be quiet? Above all, quiet.

Miranda was losing it. *Get a grip.*

"I'm going to—"

She heard the sharp report of a rifle at the same time a chunk of the boulder she hid behind exploded next to her face. She stifled a scream, but Ashley didn't.

"No!" Miranda yelled as Ashley jumped up and ran down the slope.

Whap-whap!

Ashley stumbled and rolled down the hill.

He killed her. Dear God, no!

Miranda started crawling down the slope on her belly, making herself a smaller target, then saw Ashley move.

She wasn't dead. Falling had saved her life.

Out of the corner of her eye she saw movement. She turned and aimed her gun downhill. He was partly shielded by rocks, so he was lying low, too.

His rifle was raised.

Ashley was on her feet, running away.

Miranda fired a shot to distract Larsen. Her bullet hit the ground right in front of him, but he didn't flinch.

He was going to shoot Ashley in the back. Just like Sharon.

She jumped up. "David Larsen!" she yelled at the top of her lungs.

That got his attention. He turned the rifle on her at the same time he moved away from the shield of the rocks.

They fired at the same time.

Miranda rolled to the left, the bullet coming so close to her head she felt its warmth against her cheek.

Larsen grunted. Had she hit him? Where?

She didn't dare look and scrambled toward the relative safety of a pine.

She couldn't see him.

Another minute ticked off. She ejected the empty clip from her gun, slammed in a full clip, and chambered a round.

She could no longer see Ashley, which meant neither could he. Unless he'd gone after her.

She had to distract him.

"I know who you are!" she shouted. "Everyone knows who you are, David."

She heard the distinct sound of him reloading. Much, much closer than she thought. He wasn't talking.

He'd never talked much.

"The FBI is all over this mountain. I've been talking to them in on the radio. They know exactly where you are. You'll never get out of this canyon."

She felt his breath on her neck. An icy shiver ran from the base of her skull down her spine. She hadn't even heard him approach.

He chuckled faintly. "Run."

She pivoted sharply to the left and swung her right leg high up, startling him into dropping the rifle.

He grunted and attempted to grab the stock. She kicked him in the gut, using her momentum to push him to the ground and roll away from him. Her wrist hit a rock and she lost her grip on her gun.

He grabbed her leg as she scrambled for her gun, but it was just beyond her reach.

He yanked her toward him, trying to climb on top of her. Not to rape her, but to kill her. He grunted as he grabbed her waist and pulled himself over her body.

No! Not again. Never again.

She used the slope and gravity to roll left, forcing him off her. He hit her in the right kidney and she cried out.

But she felt the barrel of his rifle at her fingertips.

She swung it and the stock hit him in the head as he loomed above her. He collapsed to the ground, shaken. Scrambling up, she aimed the rifle at him. "How do you like being the hunted?"

Her breath came in sharp gasps, adrenaline pouring through her. His life was in her hands. One shot to the head and it was over. She aimed. Pressed the trigger.

Click.

She looked down. She hadn't chambered the round.

He didn't hesitate and grabbed the end of the rifle. She fought for it, but he yanked it from her hands. Then he slipped, losing his grip on the gun, and it slid down the slope out of reach.

She saw the glimmer of a knife in his belt. This was it. She'd never be able to defeat him in hand-to-hand combat. He was skinny, but tall and much stronger than he looked.

He glared at her, his crystal blue eyes cold with hate. Then he smiled slyly.

"You will die today."

He jumped on her.

Quinn heard gunshots. They were so close, but what if it was too late?

He ran as fast as he could, stumbling over rocks and splashing through the rising creek.

He heard a startled cry. Miranda. He couldn't see her, but she wasn't far off. He added speed, desperate to call her name but not wanting to alert Larsen.

He burst into a clearing, stopping just in time to avoid sliding down a boulder. Right below him, Larsen had Miranda pinned to the ground. In Larsen's hand was a knife.

Quinn reached for his gun.

Her heart raced, adrenaline pumped through her veins. It was as if her eyesight had become sharper, her hearing better.

Larsen's body pinned her down, his left arm pressed hard across her throat. The knife in his right hand shimmered, rainwater dripping from the blade onto her face.

Her greatest fear was she would be paralyzed. That she'd never be able to defend herself when her life was on the line. That the years of self-defense classes she took, the ones she taught, the exercise, the determination, was all for naught.

That he would win in the end.

This is it. The day I die.

No. NO!

She reached up with her left hand and gouged his eyes as deeply as she could. He roared in pain and leaned away from her, raising his right arm high above his head, the sharp blade of the double-edged hunting knife coming down, down.

She arched her back and used his precarious balance to throw him off.

She didn't wait to see how he landed. She jumped up, but he grabbed her foot and pulled her down again. She was on her stomach, the worst possible position. A hot burn seared the back of her calf. Warmth oozed out of her body, molding her jeans to her leg.

He'd stabbed her.

Miranda heard someone shout and the Butcher paused, his weight easing off her.

It was just enough.

Using her arms, she pushed herself up and back-kicked him with her damaged leg. Pain radiated through her body and she wobbled with vertigo. She shook it off.

Larsen stumbled, fell, and dropped the knife. They lunged for it at the same time.

Miranda felt her hand clasp warm, sticky metal. Sticky with her blood.

She stared at him and their eyes locked.

Larsen's soulless eyes told her everything she needed to know about him.

He killed because he could. It was the hunt that thrilled him.

The hunt was over.

He lunged for the knife. Without hesitating she shoved the blade into David Larsen's chest. His blood spilled over her hands and he reached for her. She cringed, but didn't let go of the knife.

His mouth worked, but only gasps came out. He was trying to say something.

It sounded like *Theron.*

She didn't understand the reference to the Greek god, if that's what it was.

She watched him die, looking at his face clearly for the first time.

He didn't look evil.

This man had raped her. Brutalized her body and scarred her breasts. This man had killed her best friend in cold blood, and at least six other women. He'd terrorized the women of southwest Montana for twelve years, making them scared to be alone. To drive alone. Or even in pairs.

Even though he was dying, no one would ever forget his reign of terror.

But he didn't look like a monster. He looked like a scared kid. Blood dribbled from his mouth and his eyes looked skyward.

"Ther-on."

She released the knife and staggered backward. He crumbled in front of her, his hands clutching the knife that still protruded from his chest.

She sank to the ground, her leg aching, her heart racing, her mind numb.

She had killed someone. Not just anyone. The Butcher.

Tears flowed down her face and she breathed as if she'd been without oxygen for hours. She stared at David Larsen, at his blood seeping into the ground. At his eyes glazing over.

She watched him die.

"My God, Miranda."

"Quinn?" Her voice sounded odd, distant. She had trouble gaining her focus. Shock as the adrenaline wore off.

Arms wrapped around her. Strong arms, pulling her close. "Miranda, I thought—" He didn't finish his sentence.

She turned into his warm chest, breathed in his comforting scent, and never wanted him to leave. She clutched at him as if she were drowning, her sobs buried in his body. And he held her. Just held her.

His deep, quiet reassurance soothed her. "It's over, sweetheart. It's finally over."

CHAPTER
35

By the time Quinn brought Miranda back to the Lodge, it was well after midnight. Miranda was unusually quiet. He wasn't surprised: she'd gone through a second horrendous experience in the woods.

It had taken nearly two hours for the medics to transport Nick, Lance, and Ashley from the canyon to the Parker Ranch, where ambulances waited. A medic bandaged Miranda's leg while she sat in a temporary shelter. She was fixed to a board and brought slowly up the mountain after the others.

Miranda had wanted to go straight home, but Quinn drove her to the hospital to get stitches. He wasn't about to let her out of his sight, and held her hand the entire visit.

Though David Larsen was dead, all Quinn could think about was how he'd almost lost Miranda again.

Bill and Gray were waiting in the bar. Bill rushed to his daughter as soon as she limped in with Quinn's help. "Randy," he said, his voice thick with emotion.

"I'm okay."

She was more than okay. She was a survivor. Quinn had always known it, and she had proven her courage in the face of evil.

He hoped she believed in herself now. No self-doubts, no what-ifs. She had grown into the woman he knew she could become.

"Sit," Gray said, pulling out a couple chairs.

They sank into them, and Bill poured them both doubles of his best Scotch. "Oh, wait, you can't drink on pain medication," he said, holding back her glass.

"Give it to me, Dad," Miranda said, holding out her hand. "I didn't take the pills. You know how I hate taking drugs."

He handed her the glass and sat down at her side. "It's over. You're safe."

Quinn didn't trust himself to say anything. He hadn't gotten over the shock of seeing Larsen's knife puncture Miranda's leg.

Most people hadn't had a serial killer touch their lives. Twice.

Quinn filled Bill in on the abbreviated version of what happened.

"I can't believe Delilah Parker's brother —

poor Ryan, to find out like that," Bill said, shaking his head.

Miranda spoke up for the first time. "Ryan is brave. I don't know why Larsen didn't kill him. He must have sensed Ryan knew."

"From what I know about serial killers," Quinn said, "they have their own set of morals."

Bill guffawed. "Morals!"

Quinn explained. "Perhaps 'rules' is a better word. Some killers won't touch animals, for example. Larsen was a wildlife biologist, and according to everyone my partner talked to in Denver, he loved the birds he cared for. He even named them."

"Theron," Miranda murmured.

Quinn turned to her. Sudden, hot emotions threatened to overwhelm him as he thought again about how close she'd come to dying. "Excuse me? Did you say *Theron?*"

She nodded. "When he died, he said, 'Theron.' I didn't understand what it meant."

"Could be one of his birds." Quinn turned back to Bill while squeezing Miranda's hand. "Larsen might have felt a kinship with his nephew. They went fishing together. Ryan felt his uncle was a good listener. Larsen probably couldn't conceive of killing him, but he also probably didn't believe Ryan would turn him in."

"But why didn't he just leave? Disappear?"

"He had to finish what he started."

"I gave Richard a suite of rooms," Bill said. "He and Ryan are staying here a few days. Richard's worried about Delilah. He thinks Larsen killed her."

"It's possible," Quinn said, though he couldn't figure out the time line on that scenario. Richard and Delilah had been at the house together when Sam Harris visited. Richard said she left shortly thereafter, very upset. Ryan met up with Larsen at about the same time Delilah left the ranch.

There was an hour of Larsen's time unaccounted for, the time it took for Ryan to ride his horse to the Lodge.

From evidence at the Parker Ranch, Larsen had gone into the house at some point, but Quinn didn't know when.

Had Delilah Parker returned during the short time Quinn and Judge Parker had left? Had she and Larsen had a confrontation? There was no evidence of violence in the house. They hadn't made a complete search of the property because of the rescue in the canyon. Tomorrow a full team would be out there, as well as at the Parker cabin outside of Big Sky where Nick had stumbled upon Larsen's hideout.

Or maybe Delilah was scared that he would go after her and went into hiding. She'd return, then, tomorrow, when she learned he was dead.

Or maybe she fled because she felt guilty. That she knew what he was doing and hadn't stopped him.

Quinn didn't know, but he didn't like loose ends, and Delilah Parker's role in her brother's life was one big mess.

Nick was still unconscious. He had a serious head wound and an infection they had yet to get under control. Quinn hoped to God he made it.

It looked like JoBeth Anderson would pull through. And Ashley's parents had already arrived from San Diego. She would be released from the hospital in a day or two, and had already decided to go back to California.

"What happened with Sam Harris?" Miranda asked, stifling a yawn.

Quinn tensed. "He eventually came back to headquarters and the dispatcher told him he'd been relieved of duty. He left the station, apparently furious. I'll deal with him tomorrow."

Frankly, he didn't know what he would do about Harris. He'd jeopardized the entire investigation and Quinn would like nothing more than to make an example of him, but he should probably leave the situation in Nick's hands once he was fully recovered. He'd write up a formal report for the Sheriff once they tied up the loose ends in this investigation.

Like, where was Delilah Parker? Was she dead — or alive?

Miranda yawned, and Bill told Quinn to take her back to her cabin. "Take care of her, Peterson," he said. Quinn didn't miss the double meaning.

Bill hugged his daughter. "I love you, Randy," he whispered in her ear, tears making his voice raw.

"Love you too, Daddy."

Miranda disliked being fussed over, and Quinn was going overboard. He kept making sure she was comfortable in bed, her leg elevated, her pain medication and a water bottle on her nightstand, even though she insisted she wasn't going to take the pills. He started a fire in the wood-burning stove to ward off the chill that descended once the sun had set, and offered her food, another drink, water. He told her it was late, and she needed to get her sleep.

All in all, though, it was kind of sweet.

"Quinn, sit." She patted the bed beside her.

"I don't want to hurt your leg."

"You won't. Please." She reached out for his hand, and he took it.

Quinn sat, and Miranda saw the fatigue in his rich chocolate eyes. Fatigue and worry and relief.

And love.

Tears sprang to her eyes, but not of pain or sadness.

For the first time since the Butcher had changed the course of her life, she felt truly, wonderfully alive.

She wanted to share it all with Quinn.

His hand reached out and caressed her cheek. She leaned into it and sighed, closing her eyes.

"I love you, Miranda."

Her eyes opened. She saw him searching for her response. She had been unable to say it before. Not because she hadn't felt deeply for him, but because she had been afraid. She couldn't bear losing him a second time, and she didn't know how she'd be able to work through her resentment and feelings of betrayal.

But the fear was gone, along with her confusion. The past was just that — gone.

"I love you too." Her voice cracked. "Quinn, I was such a fool. I'd been so hurt all those years ago I never understood what you'd done and why. I don't know if you were right, but it doesn't matter anymore. My stubborn pride got in the way. I thought you doubted *me,* and that hurt more than anything."

"I'm so sorry I hurt you." Tears glistened in his eyes. "But I never doubted you. I hope you believe me."

"I believe you. I hurt you too. I said cruel things that I regret." She paused. It was so hard to open her heart, even to Quinn, whose love for her radiated on his face.

She took a deep breath and asked for what she wanted, what she needed: him.

"Can we get back what we had?"

He leaned forward and kissed her lightly.

"Randy, we can't go back. We're not the same people. But—" he kissed her again "—we can move forward."

Hope blossomed in her heart. But she had to hear him say it. Exactly. "What do you mean? What do you want?"

"I need you. I want you. My life has been empty without you in it. I never fell in love with anyone but you. You've always been in my heart. I should have come back earlier, but I ended up being as stubborn as you." He shook his head and tucked her hair behind her ear.

"I thought for sure, after time, you'd call

me," he said. "Maybe yell at me, but in the end you'd tell me you loved me and ask when was I coming to visit."

"Well, I think it's pretty well established that we are two very stubborn people."

He squeezed her hand and held it close to his chest. "Randy, you are incredible. You beat back your demons by sheer will. Every time I watched you, I feared you wouldn't find your inner strength, that you would let your doubts win. I could only tell you so many times that you were brave and courageous. You had to prove it to yourself."

He kissed her. Soft, warm, sweet. "And you did."

"I feared I'd never be able to face the monster who took so much from me."

Her hand trailed to her covered breasts. Tears sprang to her eyes. She would always be marked, always bear the evidence of a killer on her body.

"Sweetheart, I don't see the scars. I see you. I know they're there, just like you do, but they are all on the outside. The scars inside have faded. And I'll do everything in my power to make sure they never return."

Her tears spilled over and Quinn wiped them away.

He kissed her, his lips light on hers. She leaned in, wanting more than a feather of a caress. She wanted him, completely and fully. And forever.

He leaned away as if afraid of hurting her.

"Don't," she said, pulling him back.

Their lips were inches apart, his eyes locking hers in an intangible embrace. Her breath caught.

"Marry me, Miranda. I love you, and I'm not going to let you walk away this time."

She nodded, her heart beating fast and sure. "Oh, yes. If you can put up with me." She tried to laugh, but it was almost a sob. "I can be a little — obsessive about things." She tried to make light of it, but it was true. When she cared about something, she focused. Hard.

"Only about the things that matter," Quinn said. "And *we* matter."

"Yes, we do."

CHAPTER
36

Quinn met Special Agent Colleen Thorne and her current partner, Toby Wilkes, early the next morning, outside Richard Parker's fishing cabin near Big Sky. The small A-frame had a wraparound deck and view of the lake below.

Though the rain had stopped sometime during the night, the air was heavy and wet, and a gray mist hung low to the ground.

Two deputies had been stationed outside the cabin all night after securing it, and two more had arrived right before Quinn. Introductions were made and Quinn's phone rang. It was Deputy Zachary, calling in that he was relieving the cops outside Miranda's lodge. He hung up, and Colleen raised an eyebrow.

"You have a patrol watching the Lodge? Why?"

"Actually, I have more than a patrol. I

have one car outside, a deputy in the Lodge, and another outside Miranda's cabin."

"You told me Larsen was dead."

Quinn shifted uncomfortably. Colleen was a facts-and-logic agent, and a damn good one. His concerns were based on feelings. "It's Delilah Parker. She might be harmless, but . . ." His voice trailed off. How could he explain the odd sense he had that she knew all along what her brother was up to? "She was his alibi for the rape in Oregon. Until I know why, I'm treating her as a threat."

"Caution in this case is probably warranted. Ready?" She nodded toward the door.

Quinn broke the seal on the door while Wilkes investigated the grounds.

"How's Miranda?" Colleen asked.

"Remarkably resilient."

"Back together?"

He smiled. "The only question is how fast we can make it to the altar."

Colleen grinned. "I'm glad."

The cabin had a dark, cold, empty feeling. The main door opened into a large multi-purpose room: living area to the left, kitchen and dining to the right. The kitchen door led to the back deck, and two other doors led to a bathroom and large storage room filled with canned food and fishing gear.

The downstairs was bare and utilitarian: sturdy pine furniture with dark coverings; a large round table with six chairs; a corner stove that would easily heat the small cabin.

There was nothing personal downstairs, nothing to suggest anyone had been living here except for a lone coffee mug in the sink. Quinn made a note and bagged it for evidence.

A spiral staircase led to a loft. Though the deputies had already secured the house, Quinn cautiously went upstairs.

At first glance, the room appeared unused. The bed was made, the solitary dresser devoid of personal effects. No clothing littered the floor, and the hamper in the corner was empty.

A window overlooked a small meadow and the slope of a pine-studded mountain. It could have been romantic as a lover's hideaway.

Under the window was a desk. Simple, with one long, narrow drawer. A wooden chair had been pulled up to the writing area.

With gloved hands, Quinn opened the drawer. Considering the house seemed vacant, he didn't expect to find anything.

Inside were pens, loose paper, paper clips,

and the like. A box, the kind that stationery came in, sat in the middle of the clutter.

Quinn's chest tightened as his instincts hummed. Carefully, he extracted the box and placed it on the desk.

"What's that?" Colleen asked, looking around his shoulder.

He didn't answer and took off the lid.

It was a journal of sorts. The leather cover was worn and faded from repeated handling. He carefully lifted it from the box.

Several business cards fell onto the desk top. No, not business cards.

Driver's licenses.

Heart pounding, he picked one up, turned it around, and stared at the motor vehicle photograph of Penny Thompson.

Bile rose in his throat as he counted twenty-two driver's licenses and identification cards. Twenty-two victims over fifteen years. Sharon Lewis. Elaine Croft. Rebecca Douglas. His hands trembled as he held Miranda's youthful license.

He opened the journal.

Penny lied to me. She told me she wasn't dating the jock. But I saw them. Their lips locked together. I knew what he wanted to do to Penny. He wanted to fuck her. He wanted her breasts. . . .

With increasing horror, Quinn flipped through the pages.

The Bitch let her go. I had no choice but to kill Penny. Didn't Dee understand that Penny would have stayed if only I had more time with her? More time to convince her how much I loved her? That I could take care of her?

Dee? *Delilah?*

Quinn skipped the account of Miranda and Sharon's abduction and the documentation of the rapes. He couldn't read it now. Quinn should have turned the case over to Colleen right then; he was far too personally involved. But he didn't. Larsen was dead.

Dee wouldn't let me kill her.

She said the Moore bitch was too strong for me. That she'd won and I had to accept my losses.

I hate Dee. She pretends to love me but she hates me. Just like Mama. Always like Mama. Oozing kindness with their mouths while their hands and their breasts torment me.

The hairs on the back of Quinn's neck rose when he saw an entry a few pages later.

I almost killed the Moore bitch. She was alone. Walking. In that field she always goes to near her house. I had her in my sights. I could have taken what was stolen from me.

But she won fair and square. Dee said I couldn't have my trophy.

I hate them. I hate her. Hate her hate her hate her hate her!

But Dee's right. I don't deserve my prey this time. I wasn't fast enough. I failed. I won't fail the next time.

I already found the next one. She's beautiful. She'll lie, too. They all lie.

I hate her. Hate her hate her hate her . . .

The handwriting deteriorated over the rest of the page as his pen dug into the paper, tearing it in two places. Quinn didn't know if Larsen hated Delilah or Miranda, or both. He turned the page and found a new entry dated a week later. Ironically, the same week Miranda had left for Quantico. The handwriting was again neat and orderly.

I have one in the old Carson shack. I didn't think it would hold up, but Dee said it was fine for our game . . .

Quinn slammed the book shut, handing it to Colleen before he did something stu-

483

pid like shred it.

"Put an APB out for Delilah Parker. She should be considered armed and dangerous."

It was all Miranda Moore's fault.

Delilah wept for Davy. Her little brother was dead. She'd cried out when she heard the news as she hid in the Vought family vacation house. They wouldn't be arriving from their home in California until their kids were out of school next month.

She could stay here until Friday, when the caretaker came to air out the place and dust, but she feared the police would investigate all known vacation houses in the area.

Delilah assumed the police knew everything. She would not go to prison. Locked in a cage like an animal. No. She was not an animal. She had done the best she could. Didn't anyone understand? She had done her best!

The news on television was vague, just that the Bozeman Butcher had been identified as David Larsen and that he was pronounced dead on arrival at Deaconess Hospital.

Her gut churned. She was supposed to protect Davy, make sure he was never hurt, never caught.

She hated him.

Pain pounded her head. She didn't hate her brother. No, he needed her. She only hated the attention he'd had when they were growing up.

Growing up, Davy had been shy and quiet. Until they went to college, Davy wasn't even taller than her, scrawny as a malnourished kid. But he seemed to blossom when their mother died in a car accident. He grew six inches and started working out and turning into a man.

Delilah didn't like it. Not one bit. Davy was *hers*. Hers to control. Hers to manipulate. Hers to tell what to do and what not to do. He had always listened to her. Always. He had always done what she told him to. And she protected him as best she could. Well, maybe not *the best*. Like, how could she stop her mother from touching him?

Once, when she was fourteen, she hid in the closet. She watched through the slats as her mother touched Davy's privates. Davy seemed to *like* it. His penis grew hard and he spurted sperm all over their mother's breasts.

She knew it was wrong, what her mother had Davy do. But who would she tell? Who would believe her? And Delilah had her own problems, anyway. Like how to put a snake in Mary Sue Mitchell's locker and not get caught.

A poisonous snake. After all, Mary Sue had held hands with Matt Drake in the all-school assembly last week. Did that bitch think she wouldn't notice?

Davy had always had Mama's special attention, anyway. Delilah had been the unwanted daughter. Sometimes she preferred the freedom that came with being unwanted; the rest of the time she alternated between hating Davy and their mother.

But she did step in front of their mother's heavy hand many times, taking the brunt of the beating so Davy wouldn't have to. If she didn't love her brother, would she have taken the beatings for him?

But he wasn't normal. She figured that out at an early age. How could he be normal when his own mother raped him?

You raped him, too.

No! I loved him. He loved me. He always came back, didn't he? He always said he needed me.

You hurt him.

No! Nothing I did marked him. He understood — pain and pleasure. It was her. *Miranda Moore. She killed him. She*

486

stabbed him. His blood is on her hands.
Kill her.

After sixteen years of marriage, Delilah was surprised she felt nothing but irritation for her husband. He hadn't loved her. She had done everything for him, kept his house, raised his brat, cooked and cleaned and attended to his stupid functions. She had been the perfect wife.

And he looked at her as if she were a stranger.

The only other thing that bothered her, really bothered her, was Ryan. As if she would hurt her own child! She was not her mother. She painstakingly avoided ever touching Ryan so she wouldn't be tempted. Not that she was tempted.

She was not her mother.

She hadn't wanted a child — most definitely not a son. But when she learned she was pregnant — what good was birth control if it didn't work? — she just *knew* the baby would be a girl.

A girl to raise the way a daughter should be raised. To be lavished with attention, dressed in beautiful clothes, taken to fancy restaurants, given a big debutante coming-out party.

She laughed bitterly.

What she had was a boy. Another Davy.

But she was a good mother, dammit! She did everything for him, too. Baked fucking cookies. Cleaned his fucking room. Went to every fucking teacher's conference and play and soccer game.

What more did he want? Her blood? Would that satisfy him? Would it satisfy any of them?

She took a deep, calming breath. It wouldn't do to lose control. Her control had kept her from doing stupid things.

Like the night she almost suffocated Ryan in his crib. At the last minute, she pulled back the pillow from his face. Richard would have known, have her thrown into prison.

Or the time she threatened to tell the police about the girl in Portland. She almost didn't give Davy an alibi. The stupid, stupid idiot! He was throwing away everything for some rich-bitch slut from the Delta-something sorority.

But in the end she gave him the alibi and was very convincing. Because without Davy, her life would fall apart. She needed him just like he needed her.

Together they were stronger.

Now he was dead.

It was all Miranda Moore's fault. The bitch would pay.

CHAPTER
37

Miranda woke up late, the sun streaming through her picture windows. Below in the valley a gray fog had settled, but it would soon burn off.

The day promised to be beautiful.

She rolled over expecting to find Quinn beside her. Instead, she found a note.

Miranda —

I didn't want to disturb you. I'm meeting Colleen down at Big Sky to do a quick walk-through of the cabin. I should be back by lunchtime, or I'll call if I'm delayed.

I called the hospital. Nick is the same, which is more or less good news. JoBeth Anderson is awake and alert. Ashley was asking for you. She's going to be okay, thanks to you.

Stay at the Lodge. I have four deputies assigned there. Until I know what's up with

Delilah Parker, I'd rather play it safe.

I love you.

Q.

P.S. Stay off your leg. If you have to shower, make it quick.

She smiled. Just last week, she would have thought police protection was overkill. But today, she allowed Quinn his paranoia.

Her smile turned into a worried frown. She couldn't imagine what Delilah Parker was going through right now, finding out her own brother was the Butcher, a rapist. Miranda was certain Quinn's fears were unfounded; how could a woman participate, even just by remaining silent, in the rape and torture of another woman?

It was sick. Almost as sick as what David Larsen had done.

, She slowly maneuvered herself out of bed. Cautiously, she stood. Her injured leg was stiff and sore, but she could walk without crutches if she went slowly. Moving around was the best medicine. In fact, the leg didn't hurt any worse than the huge bruise on her shoulder from hitting the boulder.

She needed a shower. She'd had one at the hospital, but the water was tepid.

She turned on the water and waited for it to get hot. She wished Quinn were here. She took off her pajamas and looked at herself in the mirror.

Her breasts had been scarred with nineteen slashes, all about an inch long. She had counted them. Over and over. Her nipples had little sensation, her nerves having sustained permanent damage. She closed her eyes, always feeling revolted at the sight of her disfigurement. The scars on her wrists and ankles from being chained and the long one on her inner thigh didn't disturb her half as much as her damaged breasts.

Then she forced herself to look again, to stare at herself until the mirror clouded with steam and she could no longer see her reflection.

The scars were part of her now. She had to stop feeling sorry for herself. Quinn had never been as repelled by them as she was. Angry, yes. She'd seen the flash of anger in his eyes.

Anger didn't bother her; pity did.

No more of what-might-have-been! She was growing more comfortable in her skin each day. The Butcher was gone; Miranda had to bury her self-pity and anger with him. She had a full life ahead of her, with Quinn.

And he loved her just the way she was.

She stepped into the hot shower and thought about what life would be like married to Quinn. Fun. Challenging. Exciting. Frustrating. She was stubborn; so was he. But making up was half the fun of arguing, right?

It had taken them years to find their way back to each other, and Miranda didn't want to waste a single minute. As soon as possible, she wanted to get on with their wedding. When Quinn returned to Seattle, she would go with him. Certainly she could find a job in search and rescue in Washington state. Seattle had rivers and waterways and the Cascade Mountains. Miranda had experience in all kinds of terrain.

And for the first time in more than a decade, she thought about having a child.

With Quinn.

She shut off the water and reached for the towel that hung on the hook outside the shower. She didn't feel it. Odd. She thought for sure she'd put one there. Must have fallen to the floor. Opening the door fully, she stepped out.

And faced a nine-millimeter semiautomatic.

She looked up into the cold, wild eyes of Delilah Parker, who appeared nothing like the society matron Miranda had known.

"Washing my brother's blood off your hands?"

When there was no answer at Miranda's, Quinn used the radio to check in with the deputies stationed at the Lodge.

"I've had an APB put out on Delilah Parker," he said. "She should be considered armed and dangerous. There is strong evidence that she assisted her brother David Larsen in abducting his victims."

"Good God," he heard one of the deputies say.

"Check in. Name and location."

"Jorgensen, main entrance outside and perimeter check every twenty."

"Zachary, main entrance inside and interior check."

"Ressler, trails, barns, parking — all clear."

Silence.

Jorgensen spoke. "Walters, check in."

Silence.

Quinn's heart rose into his throat. "Ressler, you and Jorgensen get down to Miranda's cabin, stat! Zachary, check on Richard Parker and his son immediately. Call all guests and employees into the dining hall and keep them there until you get the all clear. I'm calling in reinforcements. ETA is ten minutes."

He slammed down the radio. "Goddammit!" Why had he left her? He thought she'd be safe. Four cops protecting the Lodge. Few criminals blatantly took out a cop. They waited for a hole, where they couldn't be seen.

But Walters was down. Delilah Parker had gotten to Miranda.

Quinn accelerated the truck, taking turns fast and dangerous.

He and Miranda had finally found their way back to each other. He wasn't about to lose her now.

CHAPTER
38

"If you so much as squeak, I'll kill you. Slowly. And then I will kill your lover."

Miranda believed Delilah's threat. She didn't want to die. Not now, after she'd finally put her demons to rest. She couldn't bear thinking of Quinn finding her dead body.

Delilah Parker was a sick woman.

Her hands bound behind her back, goosebumps rose on Miranda's damp skin. She wore a thin cotton robe and nothing else.

Shaking and barefoot, Miranda stumbled down the path, her leg aching. She had no idea where Delilah was taking her, but she wasn't dead yet. She would find an opportunity to escape.

"Why are you doing this?" Miranda asked.

"Because I want to," Delilah said like a recalcitrant child. "Now keep moving."

Keep her talking. Miranda remembered

that from her criminal psychology classes.

"Why did you help your brother kidnap women? You're a woman. Certainly you would have sympathy."

Delilah shrugged. "It was interesting."

Interesting? She thought raping and shooting women in the back was *interesting!*

"You just handed us over to your brother and walked away? Knowing what he was going to do?"

"Keep your voice down," Delilah hissed.

Miranda couldn't believe what she was hearing. She pushed on, though she kept her voice low, mindful of the gun in her back.

"How could you do that? Just walk away?"

"I didn't walk away. I'm not a coward. Not like Davy."

Miranda stumbled at her words. Delilah prodded her up. "Keep moving."

"My leg."

"Who gives a fuck about your leg? Davy's dead."

Miranda bit her tongue, tears springing to her eyes. "You knew? You *saw?*"

"I wanted to watch. To see what it took to break someone. Davy insisted that if he found the right girl she would want to stay with him forever. I told him he was a fool. I was right."

How could Delilah ignore the endless

screams? She watched her brother rape and torture women and it was *interesting?* To see what it took to break a human being? Miranda's stomach twisted and bile rose to the back of her throat. She forced herself to swallow, the burning sensation making her grimace.

Delilah was as twisted as her brother!

She continued. "You know, it's not my fault. Davy took that first girl without telling me. Can you believe that? He just kidnapped her and raped her. He thought that if she knew how much he *loved* her," Delilah said, eyes rolling, "she'd stay with him."

"Penny," Miranda said, almost to herself.

"He wasn't supposed to touch another woman without my permission. But I knew, like a wife knows her husband is cheating, I knew he had another woman. I followed him. And there she was, tied on the stinking floor of some abandoned cabin. I watched Davy through the window. Begging her to say she loved him, blah, blah, blah.

"Davy left an hour later and I let her go. I told her how to get down from the mountain. She begged me to take her with me. Like I wanted to help her? I sent her further into the canyon and caught up with Davy before he got to his truck." She laughed, a surprisingly light and airy sound considering her words.

"I told him he had to kill her. She would turn him in to the police if he didn't." She shook her head. "I waited for him. It didn't take long."

She pushed Miranda forward. Miranda stumbled over a tree root and fell to her knees. Her stitches pulled and a thin trickle of blood slid down her leg. Delilah kicked her. "Get up!"

Miranda pushed herself up with her calves, legs spread for balance, her anger rising. She was terrified of what Delilah was capable of doing. She showed a complete and total indifference to the pain and suffering of others.

"You're sick, Delilah. You. Getting a thrill out of watching your brother rape women."

Miranda braced for an attack that didn't come. Delilah remained silent, and Miranda realized then where they were headed. Her field. Her special meadow where she went to think, to relax, to celebrate life.

Had Delilah watched her sit in the middle of the wide, open space? Followed her? Stalked her? What about her sick brother? Had he?

At the far edge of the clearing, Delilah pushed Miranda down. She stumbled and couldn't avoid her face hitting the ground. Tears sprang to her eyes, more from indignation and fear than pain.

Delilah looked delicate, but she was strong. She pushed Miranda up against a tree and sat her down, the rocks and sharp pine needles stabbing her butt and legs, but Miranda resisted the urge to cry out. She wouldn't give the bitch the satisfaction. Delilah untied Miranda's hands.

This was her opportunity.

Miranda swung her arms together toward Delilah. Anticipating the move, Delilah used the grip of her gun against the side of Miranda's head. Miranda fell to the ground, her breath coming harsh and deep. She ground her teeth against the pain and nausea. Delilah pushed her up against the tree, binding her hands around it. Delilah pulled hard on her arms and Miranda cried out.

"What are you doing?" Miranda managed to ask.

"Waiting."

"For what?"

"For your lover to show himself."

"You'll never get away with this." That sounded so stupid! Worse, she feared Delilah was desperate enough to do anything.

Miranda ran scenarios through her head. She could scream, but Delilah would simply render her unconscious. She could kick out, hope to loosen the gun from her grip, but tied to the tree Miranda had no opportunity to seize the gun. The best chance she had was to warn Quinn when he came close enough. Warn him that it was a trap. She could only hope he would figure it out before it was too late.

"I watched you and that cop," Delilah continued. "Screwing each other last night."

She was there? She'd been so close and they hadn't known. Miranda felt tainted that her most intimate moment with Quinn, their reunion, had been observed by such a twisted, sick individual.

"When I was little I never understood what was so wonderful about sex. It seemed so messy. Sweating bodies and all that. I used to watch my mother, after my daddy left us. Watch her with men. Watch her with Davy."

Miranda's ears perked up. Her mother had molested her own son? The whole family was deranged. A faint spark of pity shot through Miranda's soul, but she suppressed it. *We all have choices. They chose to be evil.*

Delilah said nothing for a long moment. Then, "I used to hate Davy. Mama loved him more. Cuddled him. Hugged him. I was the unwanted daughter. Daddy had loved me, but he left and never came back. Never, not even once. Just walked out the door." She took a deep breath and shook the child-like tone from her voice. "But Mama loved Davy more and took him to her bed. Did everything for him. And I hated him. Of course, once I realized she was fucking him I sort of felt sorry for the kid. He'd lie there and cry. So pathetic. Why didn't he fight back? Why didn't he just leave?" She shook her head.

"I didn't let him kill you," Delilah told her.

Miranda stifled a response. Now was not the time to challenge Delilah.

"After you got away, he wanted to kill you, but you fought back. I admired that. And look how you repaid me. I gave you your *life* and you killed my brother!" She hit Miranda in the face and her head slammed into the tree. Miranda literally saw stars and shouted in pain.

"You sick bitch!"

"None of that," Delilah said. She pulled a handkerchief from her pocket and stuffed it in Miranda's mouth, then tied a length of rope around her face to keep the gag in place.

Miranda was now helpless to warn Quinn. Her stomach lurched. Please, please stay away.

I can't bear to watch you die.

Officer Dick Walters was dead. Shot in the back of the head. And Miranda was missing.

Quinn turned from the cop's faceless body on Miranda's small porch and gave orders to the half-dozen sheriff's deputies already there. More were on their way, plus additional FBI agents, but time was of the essence. Quinn couldn't wait for more help.

Delilah hadn't even attempted to cover her tracks. She expected them to follow. Wanted them to follow.

What was her goal? She had Miranda, presumably alive — there was no blood inside the cabin — but why keep her alive?

Delilah wanted someone or something, and taking a hostage would give her leverage.

Quinn hated hostage negotiations. The intense stress of being responsible for the lives of innocent people had destroyed some of the best agents he had worked with. But it was worse when the hostage was someone you knew.

Or someone you loved.

"Proceed with caution," he told the deputies, directing two to the right, two to the left, and two with him directly up the trail Delilah had taken.

They hastened, staying as close to the tree

line as possible in case of an ambush. They didn't go far, not even two hundred yards, before the trail opened into a meadow, camouflaged by a thick growth of trees.

Quinn couldn't miss her. Miranda's white robe practically glowed in the green and brown of the tree-lined meadow, like a beacon advertising her location. She sat up against a tree. He pulled out his field binoculars and stared.

She was tied to the tree and gagged. Her hair was wet and she wore only a thin robe. But the cold was the least of her problems.

Quinn couldn't see Delilah anywhere. He smelled a trap.

He ached to run to Miranda, but took a step back. It would do neither of them any good if he was gunned down.

He spoke quietly into the radio. "It feels like a trap. Do not, I repeat, do not walk into the clearing."

He turned to Jorgensen. "Bullhorn."

The cop handed it to him.

Quinn took a deep breath. This was it.

"Delilah Parker," he said into the bullhorn, his voice loud and tinny-sounding.

"Delilah, I'm Special Agent Quincy Peterson of the Federal Bureau of Investigation. You might remember me. You graciously served me lemonade and banana bread when I first came to town."

Quinn said the first thing that came to his mind, but it felt right. He motioned to the other men to take either side and stay out of sight. He nodded to Jorgensen, who turned and headed back to the Lodge. Plan B was a last resort.

Quinn feared it was their only option.

Delilah Parker was all about control and image. Quinn remembered what Nick told him about her need to be the hostess, how you never turned down a drink or meal from Mrs. Parker.

He needed to appeal to that side of her.

Not the side that watched her brother rape nearly two dozen women.

"Delilah? Can you come out so we can talk?"

"No! He's doing it wrong!"

Delilah was angry and Miranda glanced from her to Quinn nearly a football field away.

Delilah had been hiding behind a hollowed-out, rotting tree. Her goal was to shoot Quinn when he came for Miranda. So Miranda could watch him die.

But Quinn wasn't playing her game, and now Delilah was angry. She pounded the ground and pouted.

Quinn's voice came over the speaker. "Delilah, this is between you and me now. No one else. You tell me what you want, and I'll figure out how we can get it for you. Okay?"

"No!" Delilah jumped up and strode over to Miranda, the tip of the gun touching her head. Miranda couldn't stop shaking. She'd seen Dick Walters's body. Delilah would kill her, too.

And she would kill Quinn if she had an opportunity.

"Put the gun down so we can talk," Quinn said. He was walking around the short side of the meadow. Seeming to be moving farther away, but Miranda knew what he was doing. Trying to get closer. Trying to distract Delilah from everything else going on. Miranda saw only one cop among the trees. There had to be more.

"No, no, no!" Delilah kicked the ground. "Don't you see?" she shouted. "Don't you get it? She has to die. But it doesn't mean anything unless she sees you die, too. She killed Davy. She needs to suffer for taking him. Don't you see that?"

"Delilah, I understand what you're going through," Quinn said. "Grief is a powerful emotion."

"You know nothing about grief."

"Try me."

"No. You're buying time. What are you doing? Getting a SWAT team to run in here and shoot me? Well, I'll tell you, your girlfriend'll die too."

Delilah's hand was steady, but she sweated profusely. Her eyes kept darting back and forth, like a rodent's. Miranda waited for an opportunity to do something, but she had no idea what. She watched Quinn for a signal, but he wasn't looking at her. His eyes were on Delilah.

He moved closer.

"Delilah, you don't mean that. You made some wrong choices, but you didn't kill any of those girls, right?"

"Who cares? No one cared when I told them what my mother did to Davy. They didn't believe me."

"I believe you, Delilah."

"I'm not stupid, Special Agent Peterson," she shouted. "I know what you're doing. You're trying to get me to break down in remorse and say I'm sorry. Well I'm not sorry. The only thing I'm sorry about is I didn't let Davy kill this bitch—" she kicked Miranda in the side "—when she got away."

Miranda started to close her eyes, ready for the pain of a bullet, when she saw Quinn motion with his hand. It was sign language. They were required to learn it at the Academy.

Get low.

From the opposite side of the field, a voice shouted, "Mom! Don't!"

Delilah turned and the gun moved away from Miranda's head. Miranda leaned down as far as she could.

"Ryan? You would betray me too?" Delilah turned the gun toward her son.

Then the noise.

Whap! Whap whap whap whap whap!

Delilah's body was thrown backward into the tree as the bullets hit her. She fell into Miranda's lap, her eyes looking right into Miranda's.

"Peace," she gurgled.

Her body jerked and she died. Miranda stared at Delilah Parker's dead body.

Quinn knelt at her side and pushed Delilah's body off her, then pulled out the gag. He untied her as he tried to hold her at the same time.

Quinn got her hands undone. She grabbed on to him, holding him tightly to her, silent tears running down her face. He picked her up, carrying her farther into the trees, away from death.

He kissed her, held her close. "I'm sorry

we had to bring in Ryan, but — I only did it as a last resort."

"I know."

"Now, Miranda, it's really over."

CHAPTER
39

Two weeks later.

The first day of June boasted clear blue skies and unseasonably warm weather. Miranda's dress was a simple crepe — backless with spaghetti straps, a draped bodice, and gently flared floor-length skirt. Elegant and classic without seeming out of place for the informal affair. She was pleased she'd made the effort to pin up her mass of curls and actually put on more make-up than a touch of mascara. The look of appreciation and pride on Quinn's face was obvious. She felt like a giddy teenager beaming over her first love.

Quinn *was* her first love. First and last.

She smiled at herself in the mirror. A real, genuine smile. She suspected she bounced when she walked, a definite change for her. But when your world suddenly opened up and the weight of fear lifted from your heart, you simply felt lighter all around.

A knock on her cabin door disrupted her moment of solitude. Quinn had left before she dressed — yeah, she knew the groom and bride weren't supposed to see each other, but that was a stupid rule she was only too happy to break.

"Come in," she called from her bedroom. "Couldn't stay away for even ten minutes?"

"Try ten years."

Miranda dropped her makeup brush and rushed from the bedroom.

"Rowan!" She hugged her friend tightly to her. "I can't believe you're here."

Along with Olivia, Rowan Smith had been her roommate at the FBI Academy ten years ago. She left the Bureau when she sold her first crime novel. Rowan had recently survived her own living nightmare when a brutal killer re-created her fictional murders and sent her sick mementos of his crimes.

Now that the ordeal was behind her, she looked as happy as Miranda felt.

"Quinn called," Rowan said, her eyes twinkling. "Did you think I'd miss you and that stubborn fool finally tying the knot?"

"I knew it would happen." Olivia stepped into view. Miranda reached for her hand and squeezed it.

"I thought you'd gone back to Virginia."

"I did. I just returned to Montana last night." She smiled. "You look happy."

"I am." She glanced around. "Rowan, did you bring the guy Quinn told me about? John?"

"He's talking with Quinn and your dad up at the Lodge. We were sent to change and fetch you." Rowan looked at peace, like a huge weight had been lifted off her shoulders. Miranda knew exactly how she felt. Yet Rowan walked like she was still in pain, and eased herself into a chair, her face deliberately blank.

"What's wrong? Quinn said you were fine."

Rowan waved off her concern. "I *am* fine," she said. "It's just been a long day and my body isn't rebounding as fast as it did in the past. When that bank robber shot me eight years ago, it only took me two weeks to feel like myself." She laughed. "I'm getting old."

"Hey, I resent that," Liv said, crossing her arms. "I'm five years older than you."

"And you look five years younger," Rowan countered.

Miranda noticed two garment bags from a Bozeman dress shop and wrinkled her nose. She loved her simple white wedding dress, but had no intention of wearing anything other than jeans after the reception. "What are those?"

"We're your co–maids of honor," Liv explained with a wide smile.

"I can't believe it."

Rowan shrugged. "I didn't think Quinn had a romantic streak, but it was all his idea."

Rowan slowly rose from the chair. "We'd better get changed, Liv."

Miranda was about to follow them into her bedroom when her cabin door opened and the love of her life stood on the threshold.

She smiled and said, "Isn't there some sort of rule that you're not supposed to see the bride before the wedding?"

Quinn crossed the room and pulled her into his arms. "You look beautiful. I don't think I've ever seen you in a dress."

"Don't get used to it."

She kissed him and his hands trailed down her neck to her shoulder, making her shiver with anticipation.

"I love you, Miranda."

"I know," she teased, then realized he wasn't smiling. "What's wrong?"

"I almost lost you. It's not something I'm going to forget anytime soon."

"I'm okay."

"Are you? Really? Because I'm not." He ran a hand through his hair, fidgeting.

"I am really okay. For the first time since the attack, I feel free. I faced David Larsen and didn't panic, didn't run. I did the best I could with what I had."

"You sure did. But I'm also thinking about what happened ten years ago."

"I told you, the past is the past." Why did he keep bringing it up? What did he hope to accomplish?

"What happened then kept us apart."

"It's more my fault than yours." She truly believed that. "I could have returned. And maybe under different circumstances, I would have." She paused, trying to figure out how to explain her feelings, ideas that had just started forming over the last two weeks since David Larsen and Delilah Parker died.

"I'll never understand fate. Why Sharon died. But I do believe there was a reason I didn't go back to Quantico. At the time, it was easy to blame you and the shrink and my own fears. But looking back on my decision not to return to the Academy, I realize it was the right choice. Maybe I didn't think it through like that, but in hindsight if I wasn't here, maybe Ashley and Nick wouldn't have been found until it was too late.

"I can't discount my contribution to this investigation, just like I know if you hadn't returned to help things might have ended a lot differently. So I think everything happened the way it did because it was supposed to. And I'm not going to regret my choices, even if I made them for the wrong reasons."

Quinn wrapped his arms around her waist and kissed her. Long, slow, warm. This was exactly where she was supposed to be.

"And you're okay about having to postpone the honeymoon?"

"Oh, please." For some reason, Quinn felt bad that they couldn't go on their honeymoon until September. He'd taken the last two weeks off to put together the wedding. "We had the honeymoon before the wedding," she said and laughed.

He grinned. "We sure did."

"I love you, Quincy Peterson. And now you're stuck with me, warts and all."

"What warts?" He smiled and kissed her ear, sucking on her lobe.

"Stop that or we'll be late for our own wedding."

"So?" he murmured. "They can't have a wedding without the bride and groom."

She laughed. She'd laughed more during the last two weeks than she had in the previous ten years. She looked forward to many years of joy with the man she loved.

The ceremony was peaceful and small, just their closest friends at the Lodge. Quinn's parents had flown in for the day, joining Miranda's father, Gray, Nick, a couple of the deputies, and her Search and Rescue team.

"Good afternoon, Mrs. Peterson."

Quinn smiled as he kissed her lightly.

She arched her eyebrows. "Mrs. Peterson? I thought I'd keep my maiden name."

"Whatever you want, Ms. Moore."

She laughed and threw her arms around him. "I think Mrs. Peterson sounds perfect."

He spun her around and she laughed again. When was the last time she'd felt so free?

Out of the corner of her eye she saw Nick approach. She squeezed Quinn's shoulder, and he released her.

"Nick, I'm so glad you came. How are you doing?"

He nodded without emotion. Her heart twisted for her friend. His eyesight still hadn't fully returned and glasses didn't completely correct his problem. The infection had run its course, leaving him thin and hollow-looking. Though he didn't talk about it,

Miranda knew the decision he made to go down to Richard Parker's cabin alone haunted him.

She hugged Nick tightly. He'd been a solid friend when she'd needed one. "It's finally over, Nick. We got him."

"It was my life for years." He looked at her pointedly. "Your life, too." He glanced at Quinn. "I'm glad you've been able to get beyond it. Really I am."

"If you want to talk about anything, call me. You know I'd do anything for you."

"I know, but you're moving to Seattle."

"They have phones in Seattle."

"True." He smiled wanly. "I'll be fine."

Miranda nodded, though she still worried about Nick. He hadn't bounced back as quickly as she'd thought he would, and had been talking about not running for reelection. She hoped he would change his mind, especially since he'd decided not to remove Sam Harris from his position as undersherriff.

"Take care of her," Nick said to Quinn with a look that meant business.

"I will." Quinn wrapped his left arm around Miranda and squeezed while extending his right to Nick. They shook hands and Nick left.

"I'm worried about him," Miranda said,

pulling her eyes from Nick's retreating back and looking into Quinn's chocolate-brown depths.

"I know. He'll be okay. He just needs to do a little soul-searching." Quinn kissed his wife. "You know I love you."

She smiled and nodded. "I love you too."

"Do you think we can sneak back to your place?" He whispered in her ear. Shivers ran through her body as he lightly kissed her neck.

"Ummm. Don't tempt me."

"Why not?" He kissed her ear.

"Your mother is watching."

"So?"

"Quinn!"

He laughed and hugged her. "One hour, max. Then I'm taking you to bed."

"I don't know if I can wait an hour." There was nothing more she wanted to do than take Quinn to bed. Now.

He smiled. "I think we can sneak off in ten minutes."

"I'm holding you to that."

And she did.